ALSO BY FRANCES KAZAN

Good Night, Little Sister

Halide's Gift

Halide's Gift

A NOVEL

Frances Kazan

Random House New York

Library of Congress Cataloging-in-Publication Data
Kazan, Frances.
Halide's gift / Frances Kazan.
p.   cm.
ISBN 0-375-50511-3 (acid-free paper)
1. Turkey—History—1878–1909—Fiction.   2. Mothers and daughters—Fiction.
3. Istanbul (Turkey)—Fiction.   4. Women—Turkey—Fiction.   5. Spiritualists—Fiction.
6. Sisters—Fiction.   I. Title.
PS3561.A933   H3   2001
813'.54—dc21   00-068409

Random House website address: www.atrandom.com
Printed in the United States of America on acid-free paper
2   4   6   8   9   7   5   3
First Edition

Book design by Jeanette Olender

For Elia, with love and gratitude

The past resembles the future as
water resembles water.

Ibn Khaldun

This is a work of fiction loosely based on the early life of Halide Edib Adivar and her immediate family. Halide was born into a prominent Ottoman family in Beshiktash, on the outskirts of Constantinople, in the closing years of the nineteenth century. She was the first Turkish student to graduate from the American Girls College in Constantinople. I have changed many details of her life and the lives of her family and friends so that, although based on a true story, this is a work of fiction. The task of exploring the interior life of any character can only occur through speculation, projection, and inference. In this case, I have embroidered some of the details of Halide's life and the lives of those close to her. Therefore this novel should not be read as a historical account of the life of Halide Edib; it is intended as an homage to this remarkable woman and a record of the extraordinary times she lived through.

Part One

Chapter One

O n the upper floor of the harem the blinds were drawn against the afternoon sun and the cavernous rooms were silent. The dim stillness was as dense as winter fog. Since the end of Bairam the dancing and singing had ceased, and the small salon beyond the main reception rooms, usually used for the evening entertainment, had been converted into a sickroom for the Pasha's daughter, Selima. Her grieving husband, Edib Bey, had bought a great canopied bed from an Italian merchant in Galata to ease her pain and afford her more comfort. Its lumbering presence upset the women of the harem, and when Selima's condition deteriorated, it was rumored that the bed was cursed.

A wind blew across the Bosphorus, rushed up the hill toward the mansion, and rattled the shades. Huddled in a corner near the window, seven-year-old Halide started, surprised by the sudden sound. She had been there since noon, watching for a sign that her mother might wake. She had important news to tell her, something that would make her mother very proud. But Selima did not stir.

Halide had been born in this room, as had her mother and grandfather before her. In happier times her grandmother, Fatma Hanim Efendi, had impressed upon her the importance of continuity, for her family were direct descendants of Eyoub, the standard-bearer of the Prophet, whose remains were preserved in the most sacred mosque in the city. During the period of reform,

when the Sultans turned toward Europe and change began to un-
ravel the fabric of the old order, her grandmother was married to
Ali Pasha, her first cousin, because it was understood among the
family elders that lineage and tradition had to be maintained.

Someone had placed incense on the windowsill and thin strands
of smoke curled through the room. Halide struggled to stifle a
sneeze, fearful of alerting the adults. Halide's father had brought
in Dr. Hermann von Schlesser, a German physician with offices in
Pera near the embassy. With unfeeling authority that had scandal-
ized her grandmother, the doctor had banned the women from
the sickroom. Ignoring the boundaries that ruled harem life, he
came and went with the assurance of a family elder. Furthermore,
he discarded the remedies prescribed by Peyker the seer and
brought in bottles of pills labeled in German, a language that no
one, not even Edib Bey, was able to read. Only Arzu, the chief
housekeeper, was allowed to enter when he was not there, for
in her silent and resentful way she had impressed him with her
competence.

Since she had fallen into this strange and endless sleep, it
seemed to Halide that her mother had grown smaller. The outline
of her body was barely visible beneath the covers. Overcome by a
desire to touch her, Halide slipped off the divan and walked across
the carpet until the top of the mattress was almost level with her
eyes. Standing on tiptoe, she studied the sleeping woman. Selima's
face, turned slightly to one side, was as immobile as a mask.
Halide's lively, laughing mother had disappeared, and in her place
lay this stranger whose features she scarcely recognized. Her skin
had a translucent glow that seemed to come from within; *"guzel
veremli"* the women called it, the disease that brought an ethereal
beauty to its victims.

Halide leaned forward and put her lips close to her mother's ear,
pleading with her to wake so they could play once more in the rose

garden and feed the stray cats that lived near the well. Selima's eyelids fluttered, and for a moment it seemed to Halide that her pleas had been heard. Then the sound of voices issued from the corridor, the handle clicked, and the door creaked open. Halide scrambled under the bed just as her father, Edib Bey Efendi, and Arzu walked into the room.

Edib had hurried from his quarters at Yildiz Palace directly to the harem. In his haste he had forgotten to change out of his court dress, a long black coat cut close to the body and fastened high at the neck with gold buttons. He walked stiffly, with his fists clenched at his side; the atmosphere of the harem made him ill at ease. Arzu followed him over to the bed. A thin, olive-skinned woman in her late sixties, Arzu had presided over the harem for more than forty years, ever since Fatma Hanim had come to the mansion as a young bride. Her pragmatism balanced the vague and mystical temperament of her mistress.

"She is at peace now, sir," Arzu sighed.

"Thank goodness Dr. von Schlesser was able to arrive here in time. I was afraid we'd lost her," Edib murmured.

"We prayed for deliverance, sir. God must have heard our prayers." Poor man, Arzu thought, the strain had added years to his face. Already the hair above his forehead was thinning and a deep crease fractured the center of his brow.

"Tell me exactly what happened." Edib grasped Arzu's wrist and led her to the head of the bed.

"I was sleeping on the divan, sir, right over there near the window, when the dawn light woke me." Arzu shifted uneasily. "I looked up to see her covered in blood and tossing from side to side. Her mother was trying to stem the flow with a sheet."

"What was Fatma Hanim doing here?"

"Madam must have entered during the night while I was sleeping."

"Von Schlesser's instructions are clear," Edib said slowly. "Selima must have absolute quiet."

"If you don't mind my saying so, sir, I never heard anything so stupid. The sick need their loved ones around them. It's inhuman to let them suffer alone."

"Selima will never recover if the doctor's orders aren't obeyed," Edib cried out impatiently. "Why, even my Lord Sultan does exactly as he asks."

Arzu shook her head. What was the world coming to when the Sultan, God's representative on earth, listened to the wisdom of infidels?

"Why didn't anyone give her the medicine? It's beside the bed."

"We cannot read the labels, sir."

"It's simple enough." He gestured helplessly. "One lozenge night and morning and a spoonful of the yellow liquid." Perhaps Arzu wasn't as reliable as he thought; the doctor's orders had been repeated to her in Turkish at least three times.

"My old mistress is uneasy about these cures."

"Must I stay here every night and make sure . . ." Edib's eye wandered to the window. "What's that?"

"Incense," Arzu murmured. She leaned across the bed, suddenly intently occupied by smoothing the covers.

"What's it doing there? Remove it at once, before we're asphyxiated."

"Right away, sir," Arzu said briskly, hoping he would not ask more questions. They had smuggled Peyker the seer into the harem as soon as the doctor's evening visit was over and, sensing the presence of evil, Peyker had taken action, warning everyone to be alert while dark spirits were about.

"I would appreciate it if you would not allow this to happen again." Edib was certain Arzu knew who was behind this, but he had long since abandoned any hope of eliciting a straight answer from the women of the harem. "The world has moved on, Arzu; we must accept the inevitable and be prepared to change for our own good."

"As you say, sir." Move on indeed, she muttered to herself. Once the knowledge of the infidels invades our lives, the only place we are going is straight to hell.

EDIB WAITED until the sound of Arzu's footsteps had died away before he eased himself onto the bed beside his wife, taking care not to disturb her. It was terrifying how fragile she had become. This illness had run in the family; she had told him many times she was doomed to get it. At first he had dismissed her predictions as nothing more than superstition, but as the illness took hold his fears had increased. In vain he had tried to persuade her to stay with him at Yildiz, where the German doctor could treat her uninterrupted, but she had refused, preferring to stay close to her parents and the harem she had grown up in. Edib edged closer to her body, as if hypnotized. When he was close enough to feel her breath coming in faint gasps, the familiar smell of her skin moved him to tears.

He caressed her cheek and ran his hand down her neck. The tips of his fingers caught on a metal shard concealed by the coverlet. Curious, he folded back the edge of the bedspread. Nestled in the curve of Selima's throat lay a locket set with emeralds. He drew his breath; the necklace was magnificent. Was it a family heirloom? he wondered. If so, why had he never seen it before? He put his hand around his wife's neck and unfastened the chain. Dr. von Schlesser was expected later that day, and it was sure to interfere with his examination.

Edib walked to the window holding the locket at arm's length, and opened one of the shades. Light flooded into the room. He eased onto the cushioned windowseat and swung the locket to and fro. It was a jewel fit for a Sultan. Soon curiosity overcame him. Where had it come from, and who had placed it there? He found a small clasp cleverly concealed under an egg-shaped emerald and eased it apart with his thumbnail. The locket fell open in the palm of his hand. Inside was a dried rose held by a delicate grill of gold threads, and a miniature of a young man. He drew back with a start: he recognized the man at once as Ali Shamil, albeit younger and plumper than the man he knew. Startled, he snapped the locket shut.

Edib wrapped his arms around his torso and rocked to and fro, his body shuddering with pain. To Halide, concealed beneath the bed, the sound of his sobbing seemed to go on for hours. She longed to sit in his lap and embrace him, the way they had when Mother was well, but those days were gone, and Halide had a feeling her kisses would not soothe him now.

Gradually Edib's crying ceased and he wiped his face with a kerchief. He didn't want one of the women bustling in and finding him in this condition. His grief was private, not a matter for harem speculation. Wrapping his fingers around the locket, he thrust it into his jacket and strode out of the room. The door slammed behind him with such force that Halide felt certain the noise would bring servants rushing to the room. But nothing happened. Silence descended once more on the salon.

As soon as she felt safe, Halide crawled out from under the bed. Her heart was pounding so hard she felt short of breath. She drew level with her mother and stood still, watching her with a mixture of awe and concern. Selima's body, partially exposed now, had grown paler.

Taking care to be gentle, the child closed her fingers around her mother's palm. Selima let out a sigh, a strange despairing sound that seemed to come from the back of her throat. In that instant, Halide knew her mother was dead.

She stood still for a long time holding her mother's hand, watching the color drain from her face. Dusk gathered beyond the window, casting long shadows across the room. Outside, in the pine grove, the cicadas began their mournful chorus. I am alone with her for the last time, Halide thought. The moment of death was both more quiet and less frightening than she had imagined. Halide studied her mother's face, desperate to retain every detail. I won't cry, she told herself, I won't give way until I have her image fixed so firmly in my mind it will last forever. At last Halide placed her mother's limp hand on the sheet and, without a backward glance, made her way toward the door.

THE DISTINCTIVE cry of mourning rose from the harem and seeped through the walls of the men's quarters, like the wailing of the wind in a storm. Edib closed his eyes and tried to picture the women preparing Selima's body for burial. First they would bathe her in rose water; then they would wrap every limb in calico, in readiness for her final journey to the cemetery. There was a time when he had ridiculed the belief that the corpse felt pain after death, but now he found comfort in knowing that her body was being treated with care. On her deathbed he had scarcely recognized her, but her mother assured him that when they were finished it would be his own sweet wife he saw once more. When Dr. von Schlesser came to certify her death, Edib had denied him entry to the harem. It was over; there was nothing more for the doctor to do. He surrendered her willingly to the care of the women who loved her.

An attendant brought in a glass of coffee and placed it on the small octagonal table beside him. Soon afterward a second man entered, pulled the heavy curtains, lit the oil lamp in the corner of the small salon, and withdrew with a bow. Edib did not move. He sat on the edge of the divan staring at the floor, his elbows resting on his knees, chin cupped in his hands. It was hard to believe it was finally over. If only he hadn't found that cursed pendant, he would have stayed with her until the end.

He thrust his hand into his pocket. It was still there, like a lodestone dragging him down, blurring his grief with jealousy and anger. Yet Ali Shamil was his friend—that was the irony. These ambivalent feelings confused him, for he thought of himself as a dependable man, and ambivalence was, in his mind, the outcome of imperfect reasoning. In men he regarded it a character flaw. Women of course were different; with few exceptions they were governed by unruly emotions.

"Sir, may I come in?"

Edib looked up to find Riza, his protégé, watching him from the doorway. "I'm not good company, dear boy."

"The commandant gave me the news, I came as soon as I could."

"It happened this afternoon. I'd been at her bedside not ten minutes before. She was sleeping peacefully."

"A quiet death is a blessing."

"Yes, I suppose. . . . I can't bear to think of her dying alone."

Riza sat down on the floor and put his hand on Edib's arm. "My leave from the academy lasts until dusk tomorrow. Is there anything I can do?"

"Talk to me," Edib said, "lest I go mad with grief."

There was no one in the world Edib felt more at ease with than Riza. Intelligent and resolute, he was everything Edib would have wished for in a son. Born in Mostar to a Christian family, Riza had been orphaned at an early age during the Balkan wars. He had been abducted and brought at the age of seven to Constantinople to be trained in the service of the Sultan. While he was serving in the men's quarters of Osman Pasha, a secretary at Yildiz, he'd come to the attention of Edib, who'd brought him to the Beshiktash mansion, where he was treated like a member of the family.

"If only I had been more insistent, I might have saved her."

"Don't torment yourself," Riza said with feeling. "Your wife was a delicate woman."

"I should have brought von Schlesser in as soon as she became ill."

"You tried, but no one listened; even the old Pasha resisted."

"I should have been firmer. I'm her husband—I was. It's all past now."

"Selima Hanim was in poor health from the day I met her. You said yourself she was never the same after Halide's birth. Even if the Pasha and his wife had listened to you, I doubt von Schlesser could have saved her."

"Regardless, I behaved like a coward! I didn't fight. I gave in to the weight of tradition. I shall be haunted by this knowledge for the rest of my life." Edib aimed a kick at the brass tabletop, sending it across the room. His coffee glass shattered into a dozen pieces. Appalled by his outburst, he buried his head in his hands.

"Sir, you are deeply distressed. Let me send for a sleeping draft." Riza held his arm out to prevent his friend from doing any more damage. Edib sagged against him, as if about to collapse.

"What will sleep do but bring a rush of nightmarish memories?" he sighed.

"You need all your strength for the day ahead."

"I hope you will accompany me to the mosque. If you are not seen at the funeral, people will talk, and who knows who will be listening."

"So long as I am here," Riza said stiffly, "I will not leave your side."

"Your hatred of religion worries me, Riza. If you want to advance in the military, you must overcome it. Think of it as a useful means of ordering society. A way to unify the Empire."

"Trust me, I am very discreet. Besides, I have found that I am not the only cadet who feels this way."

"You must take care, my son. These are dangerous times. The Sultan does not tolerate disloyalty."

"Shall I send for Halide so that she can kiss you good night?" Already Riza regretted having said too much.

"Ah, my dear daughter. Have you noticed how she's growing to be the image of her mother? At least I have the comfort of knowing that Selima will live on through our child."

"Halide has inherited her mother's looks and your mind," Riza said carefully.

"Halide is an exceptional girl," Edib concurred.

Riza motioned toward the divan. "Lie down and get some rest. I'll summon the serving man to fetch the child from the harem."

"Leave Halide where she is," Edib murmured, closing his eyes. "I don't want her to see me looking like this. From now on I will have to be the strength in her life."

Chapter Two

It was early afternoon when they reached the mosque, and the courtyard was deserted except for a small boy playing by the fountain where the men made their ablutions. Despite her immense size, the Pasha's wife moved with light steps. She held her back straight, refusing to be bowed by the grief that consumed her. That afternoon her traditional mourning robe was covered by a dark cloak and a heavy veil hid her face. In her youth Fatma Hanim had been a beauty, and even in old age her green eyes and flawless skin drew admiring comments, but grief had added lines to her cheeks and cut deep furrows across her brow.

Halide clung to her prayer beads, refusing to surrender them to Arzu while she removed her shoes. The beads had belonged to her mother, and she feared that the act of relinquishing them might divide her from her mother's spirit. Less than twenty-four hours had elapsed since Selima's death, and in all that time Halide had been unable to cry.

Although women were not usually allowed in the mosque between prayers, the elderly guardian made an exception for the Pasha's wife. He lifted the heavy felt curtain to let them pass and offered a murmured condolence. News of their loss had spread rapidly through the *mahalle*. Everyone agreed the Pasha and his wife did not deserve such a tragic loss.

Inside, the air smelled musty and the temperature cooled. Overhead, dozens of small oil lamps suspended from the ceiling by invisible chains flickered like fireflies. Thin slivers of daylight entered through the stained-glass windows, throwing beams of color across the gray air. Halide looked up and caught her breath: particles of dust whirled in the light like celestial dancers, and the vast empty space beneath the domed roof vibrated with movement. She remained by the door while her grandmother and Arzu, still fingering their prayer beads, ambled slowly across the carpeted floor and settled themselves in the women's section beside a fluted pillar.

At this hour the mosque was almost empty. Here and there solitary figures prostrated themselves in prayer. Halide thought she recognized the grocer from the corner store but was too shy to acknowledge him. A white-robed Imam leaned against a wall covered with sayings of the Prophet, a group of students at his feet, reading a passage from the Koran. Although she did not understand Arabic, Halide stopped to listen. All at once, an enchanting voice issued from the back of the mosque. The students paid no attention and the Imam continued to read. Only Halide turned around to see who was singing.

In the balcony, behind the carved screens, Halide could just see the outline of a young girl dressed in white, with flowers entwined in her dark hair. Her hands were clasped in front of her and she was swaying back and forth to the rhythm of her song, the Mevlud, the traditional Turkish hymn ascribed to Mohammed's mother as she waited for the birth of the Prophet. Staring closely, Halide saw that the girl's eyes were closed and that her face, turned upward toward the dome, had a look of rapture. Halide was mesmerized. The heavy sadness that weighted her heart lifted, and her body was filled with an airy lightness. Then, for no apparent reason, the girl stopped, pulled her veil across her face, and disappeared from sight.

The sound of the singer's voice rang in Halide's ears long after her departure. She was destined to hear the Mevlud chanted many times in her life, but none of the subsequent renditions were as beautiful or as poignant as the song of the young girl in white that morning at the mosque.

Light from the windows began to fade from white to gray and Halide decided it was time to rejoin Granny. The old lady remained stooped in prayer, but Arzu stooped to kiss Halide's forehead as she slipped into place between them.

"What took you so long, child? I was getting worried."

"I stopped to listen to that girl singing the Mevlud," Halide said, leaning against Arzu's side.

"What *are* you talking about? Girls aren't allowed to chant in the mosque."

"There was a girl about my age," she explained, "in the women's section upstairs. She sang like an angel—you must have heard her."

Arzu's gaze shifted upward. "I can't see anyone."

"She was standing behind the screens, dressed in a white—"

"You are right, child, she sang like an angel." Her grandmother touched her arm and gave Arzu a meaningful look. Arzu stared down at the carpeted floor, her lips moving in a silent prayer.

"Who is she, Granny? Why haven't I seen her before?"

The old lady watched her silently through half-closed eyes. Halide wondered what she was thinking.

Soon the muezzin cried out from the minaret: it was the hour for evening prayer. Halide had been so preoccupied she had failed to notice that the mosque had filled with men who now stood in quiet rows, their faces turned toward Mecca. When she looked around, it appeared that the entire population of their neighborhood had gathered. There was a movement near the door. Heads turned and the crowd parted to make way for a procession led by her father and grandfather. In their midst she saw six men she recognized from the men's quarters carrying a stretcher on their shoulders. Atop, shrouded in white muslin and strewn with flowers, lay her mother. The procession straggled into the courtyard, where the coffin was placed on a table. Halide watched in disbelief. No, it was impossible! At any moment she was certain her mother would reappear and draw her close to her side to stop her shivering in the chill air of winter.

The prayers, as was the custom, were brief. After offering thanks for Selima's life the Imam turned to the congregation and asked if they had known her to be a good person. In unison the men replied yes. Turning his attention to Edib, the Imam asked him to surrender his earthly rights to his wife. Overcome with emotion, Edib could do no more than nod. The Imam hesitated. Realizing that something more was expected, Riza stepped forward, and in a clear voice renounced Edib's claim to Selima and acknowledged that her soul had returned to God. Edib squeezed Riza's shoulder in gratitude. With care the men lifted the bier onto their shoulders and carried it out of the courtyard to a waiting carriage. Selima was to be buried in Rumeli Hisari, in a family plot overlooking the Bosphorus.

THE MOURNERS had long since dispersed to their homes and the night watchman had extinguished the lamps in the *mahalle,* but for Fatma Hanim and Arzu sleep was impossible. They sat together in the seat at the bay window that overlooked the garden, waiting for the night to pass. Outside it was pitch-dark. A crescent moon dipped toward the horizon, and in the thin silver light they caught sight of a large owl flying over the well.

"My mother used to say those birds were nothing more than peris in disguise." The old lady managed a wry smile. Her eyes, once famous for their luminosity, were rimmed with red from weeping.

"Peris are very crafty, ma'am; one can never be sure what disguise they might assume. I don't know what it was the scullery girl saw lurking at the bottom of the well last week, but peris favor deep dank places, and we must be on guard, ma'am."

"I am familiar with the ways of peris, Arzu, and I'm telling you there was nothing there—the girl was being hysterical. It was a difficult time, what with the doctor coming and going and Selima sinking into her final sleep."

At the mention of Selima's name grief gathered them into its clutches, and they fell into silence.

"But now we know the gift has passed on to Halide," Granny said at length, twisting her prayer beads through her fingers.

"On this day of all days," Arzu murmured.

"It is the will of God."

"I couldn't believe my ears when Halide told me she had heard a girl singing in the mosque, of all places! I felt quite faint."

"That's where we always sat, behind the carved screens in the upper section."

"Year in, year out."

"Selima sang so beautifully when she was a child. Remember when the Imam of the mosque of Eyoub wanted her to become a Koran chanter?"

"You were right to refuse; she wouldn't have lasted five minutes with those old men telling her what to do." Arzu gave the old lady a weak smile.

"And she had no patience for learning Arabic."

"She preferred to sing the Mevlud, it was her favorite."

"She always knew what she wanted." Granny closed her eyes. The years fell away and the image of her daughter rose before her. Selima was seven once more, standing in their home, with her hands clasped in front of her and her head raised in song while the family sat spellbound.

"When will you tell Halide what she saw, ma'am? After her grief subsides?"

"I'm not sure it's wise to explain anything yet. She's so devoted to her father, and I don't want to upset Edib, with these modern ideas of his . . ." Granny's voice trailed off. The question had troubled her all night.

"But surely, ma'am, if Halide goes on seeing spirits she will think she is losing her mind."

"Children are very accepting. I will stay close to her, and with my guidance she will learn to take her gift for granted. After all, the boundaries between the tangible and the intangible world are fluid. Fortunately Halide is a serious child, so my task won't be too difficult."

Arzu frowned. The Pasha Hanim's plan made no sense to her, but if that was her wish it must be respected.

"Edib Bey is not like my dear husband," Granny continued. "He is a modern man, and he would never understand the significance of Halide's powers. If he came to hear about them he might unwittingly try to destroy them."

"He mixes too much with infidels," Arzu said hotly. "It was much better when we all lived separately, each to his own life."

"I fear these foreigners have affected him," Granny sighed. Throughout Selima's illness it had become clear to her that Edib's professions of faith were illusory. He practiced the rituals, but he had lost his belief.

"Alas, ma'am, that is a failing of many people these days."

"Still, he is a good man," Granny said decisively. "He loved my daughter and I think he always will."

The old lady turned her head away and stared out the window. A line of blue-gray light had appeared on the horizon, heralding the start of the second day without her child. She slipped the prayer beads through her fingers and murmured a saying of the Prophet under her breath. She imagined the sun rising over the tomb of her father and her father's father in the cemetery at Eyoub, climbing into the sky above the graves of her husband's forebears in Karaca Ahmet, across the water in Scutari, and warming the fresh earth covering the body of Selima in the graveyard at Rumeli Hisari. The beads passed rapidly through her fingers, around and around, until the first light of dawn caught the amber glass.

Chapter Three

Gripping the handrail, Halide descended the main staircase. She was wearing the navy serge dress her father had ordered for her from his tailor in Pera, with long sleeves and a knee-length skirt. Her legs were encased in dark woolen stockings that scratched her skin, and her new leather boots squeaked when she walked. When she'd first seen the outfit, she'd wanted to cry. Other children of her class and upbringing were allowed to wear bright satins and ruffled velvets, but Edib believed elaborate clothes encouraged vanity. He had read the work of Edmond Demolins, and subscribed to his theories on Anglo-Saxon superiority. The strength of the British Empire was due, in part, to the disciplined manner in which they raised their children. Over her grand-mother's objections, Edib had placed Halide on a diet of fresh vegetables and bread dipped in milk. Sweets were forbidden, and meat was restricted to once a week.

When Halide reached the bottom stair a broad expanse of hall fanned out in front of her, and here the inhabitants of the harem were gathered for late-morning prayers. Their number fluctuated according to the time of year. During the religious festivals, when relatives came from the provinces, the mansion was often filled to overflowing, but now there were only two elderly cousins in residence, frail birdlike women from Isparta who smelled of rose oil. Halide gave them a wide berth because they were always grasping her in a tight embrace and the feel of their bony arms reminded her of skeletons. The kitchen maids winked at her, and the sturdy Anatolian cleaners nodded respectfully. Even the sour-faced cook, who was still wearing her apron and clogs, smiled when she passed by.

With every eye on her, Halide blushed. She regretted having lingered so long in Teyze's library. Adding to her embarrassment were the audible gasps that came from a group of elegant women clustered at the back of the hall, cooling themselves with ostrich-feather fans. Dressed in lace-trimmed gowns weighted down with embroidery and artificial flowers, they stood out from the rest of the harem like peacocks in a flock of pigeons. They were former slaves from the Imperial harem, women of indeterminate age who had failed to make prestigious marriages. Since Fatma Hanim could no longer afford to buy her own slaves on the black market, she had invited these women to the Beshiktash mansion to entertain the household with music and conversation during the long evenings of winter. Sometimes they stayed for months at a time.

It was a pity to dress a retiring girl like Halide in dark colors, Granny reflected as she watched her grandchild move unsteadily through the hall, swinging her arms in an unfeminine way that would have to be discouraged once the mourning period was past.

"Sit down," Granny murmured, patting the empty seat beside her.

"I'm sorry I'm late. I was reading one of the books Teyze left for me and I forgot about the time."

"Reading?"

"Teyze said I had to practice while she was away or I'd forget everything she has taught me."

"I'd quite forgotten she was teaching you to read," Granny said vaguely. Since Selima's death, everything had faded to the edge of her thoughts.

"Just the easy books with pictures. Teyze brought them with her from Yildiz Palace."

"Teyze is a wonder."

"I miss her. I wish she'd come back soon."

Distracted by quiet laughter rippling among the kitchen girls, the old lady did not reply.

A man's face pressed against the stained-glass window beside the front door. Taking a closer look Granny recognized the distorted features of Emin, Edib Bey's manservant. Outraged by his intrusion, she sent Arzu to see what it was he wanted. A few minutes later the housekeeper returned and reported that Edib Bey had been summoned to the palace and expected to be away for at least ten days. He had asked to see Halide before leaving.

"I DIDN'T MEAN to disturb you at your prayers." Edib reached for his daughter's hand and led her across the harem courtyard. They walked through the kitchen garden and along the path to the men's quarters, passing between patches of bare earth waiting to be planted with eggplants, zucchini, runner beans, and cabbages.

"Emin gave us all a shock—the kitchen girls thought he was a peri!" Halide was almost out of breath. Her father took long purposeful strides, and she had to skip to keep up with him.

"I'm sorry about Emin's behavior. I'll write to your grandmother and apologize as soon as I return to the office."

"She's lost her glasses again and can't read anything. But if you use simple words, I'll try to read it to her."

"That's very thoughtful of you, Halide, but you still have a long way to go before you can read formal script." Her concern for her grandmother touched him, but he did not like to hear her making exaggerated claims.

"But I can read, Father," she insisted, gripping his hand. "I know all my letters, and as long as you leave the vowels in I will be able to get through it."

"When did you learn this?" he asked with concern.

"Just before Mother went into her long sleep." This was the news she had longed to tell her mother, but by the time she had managed to slip unseen into the sickroom, it was too late.

"Why wasn't I informed?" Edib stopped in his tracks and looked down at his daughter.

"Teyze and I wanted to tell you, but you were busy," Halide said with a mixture of embarrassment and pride.

Edib gripped her hand and walked on.

"I'm slow," she continued, "and long words are difficult for me, but I can manage simple sentences."

"Never mind, that's a remarkable achievement for a child of your age."

Halide skipped on down the path, blushing with pride. Edib looked after her and frowned. If she was reading at seven, this confirmed his suspicions that she possessed an unusual intelligence. He hadn't begun to master elementary Ottoman until he was ten, maybe twelve years old. The path veered to the right and dwindled into a flight of moss-covered steps, still slippery after the morning rain. They left the garden behind and were soon within sight of the men's quarters, whose smooth lawn was bordered with lavender and terra-cotta pots planted with flowers. Halide dashed onto the grass and, spreading her arms wide, twirled around and around like a dervish.

"Look at me, Father! Teyze showed me how to do it without getting dizzy."

"Teyze taught you that?" He had noticed that her name was on Halide's lips a lot recently.

"She said it's good for me."

Edib wondered where and how Teyze had acquired this knowledge. To spin like a dervish required intense discipline and focus, and the practices of the dervish sects were looked upon with suspicion at the palace. Sultan Abdulhamid II, through his overlapping web of spies, kept a close watch on their activities.

"It's not hard, Father. Why don't you come and try?"

Edib shook his head and laughed. "I must leave for the palace within the hour," he said. "And the Sultan won't like it if I return with dirty boots."

"You're leaving so soon?" She stopped and dropped her hands to her side.

"Yes, the Sultan summoned me back this morning."

"Will you be gone long?"

"Several days, perhaps a week."

"I will miss you," Halide said.

"I'll miss you too, Halide. Remember, if you need me for any reason, just tell Arzu and she will dispatch a messenger to the palace."

"You mustn't worry; I have Granny and Grandfather."

"But they are old and in deep mourning."

"I wish they weren't so sad."

"It's normal after such a . . . such a tragic loss." He thought her remark strange, but let it pass. After all, she was still a child.

"Can I tell you a secret?" Halide confided, prancing around her father with excitement.

Closing his eyes, Edib nodded.

"You mustn't tell Granny, or Grandfather, I don't want to upset them . . ."

"I promise faithfully not to tell anyone," he said with a smile.

"Well," she said quietly, confident her news would help him, "Mother is still here. I've seen her many times. Sometimes she comes in the day, but mostly at night in my dreams."

Edib recoiled. Dr. von Schlesser had warned him that young children had difficulty understanding death, but he had not expected to hear his daughter voice her delusions so clearly and calmly.

"You're imagining things, Halide. The dead cannot return."

"No, Father, you don't understand. I know Mama died, but she didn't leave us."

"Halide, my dearest girl, your mother is lying in her grave at Rumeli Hisari. She's gone."

"But not completely, not from me or from this house."

"I dream about your mother every night, but I know my dreams are not real," Edib said.

"Yes, they are, Father. We leave our bodies when we sleep, we go into another world that is as real as this one."

"Who told you this?"

"Granny."

"When people are old they become confused." He almost choked on his words.

"Was Mama confused too?"

"Of course not, she was young."

"She used to see people from her dreams in this life. She told me so."

Beads of perspiration trickled down Edib's forehead. When he dabbed them with his kerchief his brow felt hot and damp.

"Are you ill?" Halide said, distressed that her secret had failed to lighten her father's mood.

"I think I'm catching a cold. Let's go inside and get some tea."

For the first time in his life, Edib was afraid. If he did not act decisively, his daughter would be drawn back into the web of ignorance that condemned women to perpetual servility. He turned toward the mansion and walked across the terrace where Selima used to sit and watch the sunrise on warm summer mornings before their daughter was born. He had had his chance then and lost it. He wasn't going to make that mistake again.

Chapter Four

While Edib was away, Teyze returned to the harem at Beshik-tash. She had been on an extended visit to Bursa, the ancient capital of the Ottomans, close to the mountains beyond the sea of Marmara. In Bursa she had stayed in the mansion of her friend Zeynep Hanim Efendi, the widow of a wealthy silk merchant. Zeynep, like Teyze, was a devoted scholar of Jalaloddin Rumi, the medieval mystic and poet. Together they had studied the ancient texts, discussing nuance and meaning and daring, privately, to question the prevailing interpretations of the Koran in the light of Rumi's poetry. Teyze was by nature melancholy; despite her education she felt that a true understanding of life would always lie just beyond her reach.

Teyze was Circassian by birth and still spoke with the trilling birdlike accent peculiar to the Caucasus. When she was very young she had been purchased from her parents by traders who'd recognized that her pale beauty would command a high price in Constantinople, where there was a flourishing slave trade among well-to-do Ottoman women. Circassian slaves were in great demand as brides for princes and wealthy landowners; they were symbols of status and enhanced the prestige of their owners.

She was bought by a childless couple who treated her like the daughter they'd never had. Along with instruction in music and dance, they gave her a classical education, and by the time she was sixteen she was able to read Arabic, Persian, and Ottoman, a rare accomplishment for a woman. To augment her dowry they gave her jewels and gold coins, which she concealed in the false bottom of her blanket trunk. The sudden and unexpected death of her owners in a cholera epidemic ended her hopes of making a prestigious marriage. The Sultan, in desperate need of funds, seized their estate, and Teyze was given to Gulistan, the Sultan's sister, in payment for a debt. For over a decade she lived in the Imperial harem, waiting and hoping for an offer of marriage. She kept her dowry hidden; even the Imperial eunuchs who supervised the harem were unaware of its existence.

Time passed and her beauty began to fade, and had it not been for the intervention of Fatma Hanim Efendi, Teyze might have stayed in the palace until the day she died. When she moved to Beshiktash she was able to come and go as she pleased, and in the somewhat dull routine of the traditional harem she found a measure of peace. She was given a suite of rooms on the third floor and furnished them in fashionable European style, with satin upholstered chairs, gilded tables, and brocade curtains bordered with tassels. When Selima fell ill and the old lady became preoccupied with looking after her daughter, Teyze decided to take Halide under her wing.

"NO, NO, not like that! Grasp the fork in your left hand and put it in the meat to hold it before you cut it." Three days after her return from Bursa, Teyze and Halide were eating their evening meal seated at her dining table, the only one in the harem.

"Why can't I use my hands and pull it apart like I usually do?" Halide protested.

"Because that is not the way the Europeans eat, and I am trying to teach you new customs. Now watch how I do it; it's not difficult."

"What's wrong with sitting on the floor and eating with our fingers?"

Teyze frowned as she tried to think of an answer.

"I've seen you eating that way many times," Halide persisted.

"When I am dining with your grandmother I observe her tradition, but in my own rooms I prefer to live as I did in the palace," she said cautiously.

"Does the Sultan have his meals sitting at a table like this?"

"I never saw the Sultan or any other man; we were kept secluded. But the princess told me that his quarters are very modern, very *à la franca,* as they say."

"I thought you used to watch the men through the carved screens."

"Sometimes we observed the Imperial processions," Teyze said, giving a shy smile. "But we never dared to spy upon the Sultan himself."

"Did you see my father?"

"Once or twice when he first came to the palace, but that was long ago, before you were born."

"Did you like it at Yildiz?" Halide never tired of hearing Teyze's stories about the Imperial Palace.

"Very much at first, but alas, nothing good lasts forever."

"Then why did you leave?"

"Princess Gulistan grew tired of me."

"Why?" Halide thrust her fork into the meat and pinned it against the plate.

"I'm not sure. She was a very unpredictable woman."

Once Halide had overheard her grandmother telling a guest that the princess had been jealous of Teyze's intelligence, because it threatened her preeminence in the eyes of the other women.

"I'm never going to eat all this with a knife and fork," Halide said, laying her utensils against the side of the plate.

"You must eat something, child."

"I'm not hungry."

"Think how proud your father will be when you show him your French table manners."

"He knows I can read, so he's already pleased with me."

"You told him?" Teyze asked sharply, trying to contain her disappointment.

"He wanted to write to Granny. She had lost her glasses again, you were away, and there was no one else who could read it to her, so I asked him to write in simple words . . ."

"That was sweet of you." Teyze had imagined the two of them surprising Edib with the news of Halide's achievement. Closing her eyes, she could almost hear him complimenting her, in that low cultivated voice she found so compelling. He might even have taken her hand and squeezed it in gratitude; she was, after all, almost a member of the family. But now it was not to be. The vision faded—she would be forced to put it, like so many other dreams, behind her.

⚜

"I AM HONORED by your visit," Edib said, facing his in-laws across his small reception room. Edib continued to maintain a house near the main entrance to Yildiz Palace. He had lived there before his marriage and kept it up more from habit than necessity.

"The honor is ours, my son— Forgive me, I mean Edib Pasha." The old man faltered. He had almost forgotten that Edib had been granted the rank of Pasha by special dispensation of the Sultan. Etiquette was, for the old Pasha, a matter of great seriousness.

"Sir, you are like a father to me, and you must always call me your son." Edib bowed. It was hard for him to look at Ali Pasha, for grief had altered him almost beyond recognition.

"Your promotion is a well-deserved honor, my son."

"It does not mean much to me now," Edib said despondently.

"Come now, you are a young man and you have a great future ahead of you."

There was a time, not so long ago, when I shared your optimism, Edib thought to himself. The Sultan, once an enlightened, forward-thinking man, had changed. His judgment had become clouded by paranoia. Edib was worried but said nothing to his in-laws; these days the walls had ears.

"I invited you both here to discuss Halide's education. She is able to read Ottoman, an extraordinary achievement for a child of seven."

"She's a clever girl," said the old Pasha. He leaned forward and patted the head of his grandchild, who was sitting cross-legged on the floor at his feet.

"I would never forgive myself if I allowed Halide's intellect to go to waste," Edib continued.

"But the matter is taken care of. I believe she is already enrolled at our local school." The old Pasha smiled and turned his heavy-lidded eyes toward Fatma Hanim Efendi, who nodded. She rarely joined in the conversation when the men were speaking.

"I don't think Miss Theo's classes are—how shall I put it?" Edib glanced at his daughter. He knew she felt bored and out of place among the rowdy local children. "I don't think they are sufficiently advanced for someone of Halide's intelligence."

"The children of our household have always gone to the local school, and Halide seems content," the old Pasha said mildly.

Edib took a deep breath. He had anticipated this response and had his answer prepared.

"If I hadn't had an Ottoman patron who brought me to Istanbul and paid for my classical education, I shudder to think where I would be today," he began. The old man nodded vaguely; he had forgotten the details of Edib's early life.

"I want my daughter to have the same privileges I had."

"That is understandable," the old man said.

"To that end, I have made arrangements for Halide to be tutored at home by some of the finest scholars in the city. She will learn Arabic and Persian; the lessons will begin next week."

Halide, who had been listening with mounting excitement, suddenly stood up and caught hold of her father's arm. "But I want Teyze to be my teacher," she said.

Edib drew back a little. He wasn't used to having his decisions questioned. In his department at the palace his word was law. "Teyze Hanim will continue to teach you Ottoman," he said.

"But she can read Arabic and Persian, so why can't she tutor me?"

"The arrangements have been made and cannot be changed," Edib said decisively. He did not want to hurt Halide's feelings by voicing his doubts about Teyze's intelligence. She was, as he recalled, rather beautiful, but he had never heard her say anything of interest.

Halide bit her lip and remained silent.

"I hope these lessons will be conducted in the men's quarters. I like to see her every day—it reminds me of the past," the old Pasha said wistfully.

"That shouldn't be a problem until she reaches an age when such behavior would no longer be appropriate."

"And then it will be time to think of a betrothal," Granny interjected.

"Possibly." Edib smiled. He had a plan fermenting, but first he had to find out more about this American girls school he had heard about.

A servant appeared at the door carrying a silver coffee warmer, cigarettes, a pitcher of lemonade, and four small cups. Halide helped herself to a glass of lemonade and wandered through the

French doors and onto the terrace while the adults sipped their coffee and continued their conversation.

"I hear poor Murad is in failing health. How long are they going to keep him locked up in Ciragan Palace?" the old Pasha said once she had left the room.

"Until the Sultan sees fit to release him." Edib sighed. "A deposed ruler is a constant threat to stability."

"It's been fifteen, sixteen years since the poor soul last saw the world beyond the palace. Why does my Lord Sultan still feel so threatened?"

"Murad was declared mad and therefore unfit to rule."

"High-strung perhaps, but not mad. What utter nonsense!" The Pasha spoke with unusual vehemence. Edib put his fingers to his lips.

The circumstances of Murad's deposition and arrest were clouded in mystery. It had been rumored that the former Sultan was an unbalanced alcoholic for whom affairs of state were too great a responsibility, but that was far from the whole story. The grand vizier, Midhat Pasha, had been eager to enact a constitution and had supported the succession of Abdulhamid, who had promised to continue progressive government reforms. Within three years of his coming to power, however, Sultan Abdulhamid had annulled the constitution, dismissed the government, and sent Midhat Pasha into exile in Syria. At the time Turkey had been at war with Russia, and Edib believed the Sultan had acted in the best interests of the state.

"It is Murad's daughters I feel sorry for," said Granny, speaking up for once. "The poor things are confined to a life of spinsterhood and childlessness."

"A man is one with his family," Edib said sharply, not wishing to prolong this conversation. His comment was followed by an awkward silence.

"Speaking of family," he resumed at last, "I have news of Ali Shamil."

"Ali Shamil?" the old Pasha asked quizzically. "Our Ali Shamil?"

"He has been placed under house arrest and will soon be exiled," Edib said, offering no further elaboration.

"What for?" The old Pasha tightened his grip on his stick.

"It's rumored that he killed the chief astrologer in a fit of rage."

"Has he gone completely mad?"

"When was this?" Granny pushed herself up on her elbows and craned forward inquisitively.

"Not long ago, three or four weeks."

"Just after Selima died," whispered the old man.

"I suppose it was," replied Edib. He had never thought to connect the two events. "I told him about her death. I had to—he came to my office in the palace with one of his brothers and a nephew."

The Pasha fixed his watery gaze on Halide, who was standing on the terrace with her back to them. "But how did he learn of her illness? I thought all contact had ceased?"

"Word gets around. Very little stays secret in this neighborhood." Granny bowed her head and Edib noticed that her hands were shaking.

"What will happen to the child?" the old Pasha asked.

"I'm doing my best to take care of the matter, but I have to move cautiously."

"We are grateful to you, my son, very grateful." Edib caught the look of trust in the old man's eyes. Their faith in him was so transparent it put him to shame.

Through the open window their conversation reached Halide in snatches. She had heard the name Ali Shamil Pasha before, but could not remember where or when. She had come outside because she thought she had seen her mother under the trees at the end of the garden, but on closer inspection the figure turned out to be a statue of a girl in Greek robes, like the stone figures in the public gardens at Pera. Teyze had told her that all the fashionable homes in the city possessed one.

Chapter Five

In the early 1800s, Ali Pasha's grandfather had built a large wooden mansion on one of the hills above Beshiktash. In those days Beshiktash was nothing more than a sleepy fishing village noted for its ancient baths and an elaborate kiosk Selim III had constructed for his mother. When Abdulhamid moved his court to the forested hills of Yildiz Park, just five minutes from the quay, Beshiktash began to change. Rows of modern homes sprung up across the hills, and pastoral land vanished beneath new mansions and their luxuriant gardens. Lanes were widened to accommodate the increased traffic, and the road to the city, once no more than a muddy track, was paved and planted with rows of plane trees.

These days Granny rarely left the picturesque environs of the mansion. There was something so reassuring about the familiar beauty of her world that she saw no reason to venture beyond its boundaries. Yet the meeting at Edib's had disturbed her, and after several sleepless nights she decided it was time to consult Peyker the seer, whose wisdom and advice she valued above all others. Ten days later she set off with Halide in the family carriage and, with some trepidation, began the two-hour journey to Peyker's home in the old city in Fatih, near the great mosque.

It was early in the morning when they began their outing and the road was empty save for the occasional oxcart lumbering to market, weighed down with produce. It did not take them long to reach the new waterfront palace of Ciragan, concealed behind imposing clifflike walls. Halide entertained herself by counting the sentries posted along the side of the road. As they approached the great wrought-iron gates of Dolmabahçe Palace, now abandoned and silent, they swerved to avoid a troop of cavalry officers galloping at great speed from the Imperial stables. The coachman cursed under his breath, too afraid to express his frustration more openly. High on the hills of Pera they caught sight of the newly built German embassy gazing out across the Bosphorus toward Scutari and the hills of Anatolia. As they approached the Galata Bridge the streets narrowed, crowds pressed against the carriage, and the air filled with the sound of ship's horns, gulls, and the cries of *simit* sellers.

By the time they crossed the Golden Horn, Granny was asleep, lulled by the sway of the carriage. She had no desire to see the old city, for the Stamboul of her youth was gone. Buildings had become run-down, the streets were littered with rubbish, and the old inhabitants had been displaced by rougher working people. Things were no different on the other side of the Galata Bridge. Foreigners with their strange ways and ungodly religion monopolized the districts of Pera and Galata. Nowadays an Ottoman Turk could feel like a stranger in his own city. She often asked herself why God had brought these people to their land.

Edib's plan to educate Halide like a boy had given her many sleepless nights. The child's chances of making a good marriage would be ruined. Men needed to feel superior; they did not want a wife who would challenge them. What good would come of an education if the girl could neither dance for her husband nor run a household? In her consternation Granny had even approached her husband, Ali Pasha, with whom she rarely discussed such things, but his answer had been the one she had anticipated: God's will would take care of Halide's future; to interfere would be to challenge fate.

Halide pressed her face against the window. She had never seen neighborhoods like this before. Her previous visits to the old city had been restricted to the Great Bazaar and the Suleimaniye Mosque, where the family celebrated Bairam. By now they had left the busy waterfront and were winding their way through narrow streets of wooden houses, their somber facades relieved here and there by boxes of scarlet geraniums. A thin stream of water coursed along a dip in the cobblestones where the drain was supposed to be. The houses gave way to cramped stores, huddled close as if some giant hand had pressed them together with great force. Suddenly the road veered downhill and dust rose under their wheels as the carriage gathered speed. They raced through a square shaded by a circle of plane trees where a boy waved as they whirled by. Finally they came to a halt.

A fire had destroyed the houses across from Peyker's and the once tidy row of homes had been reduced to a pile of rubble. As Halide climbed out of the carriage, the lingering odor of burned timber and smoke made her sneeze. She ran after her grandmother, who was hobbling down the path on the coachman's arm, oblivious to the brambles catching on the hem of her cloak.

Peyker's house was a two-story affair with a pointed roof and carved fretwork along the gutter. A cascading fig tree obscured the windows. Its branches fell over the door, bending the lintel with their weight. A young woman was waiting for them just inside the doorway, and when she caught sight of them she waved her arms and made strangled gurgling sounds.

"Why is she making those strange noises?" Halide whispered.

"Hudai is a deaf-mute," Granny replied matter-of-factly.

"Is she Peyker's daughter?"

"No, she's a gypsy child, but they thought she was cursed and brought her to Peyker, who treats her as if she were her own."

They entered a tiny hall that smelled of incense. The sweet aroma clung to the frayed fabrics covering the walls and hanging in loose folds across the doorways. The worn planks creaked underfoot as they walked. Hudai caught Granny by the elbow and waved her arms excitedly.

"She wants us to wait in there," Granny said, lowering her head to pass through a doorway so small Halide's curls brushed the top of the frame. The darkened room was lit by a dozen large candles secured in old-fashioned copper holders. The smell of incense seemed to fog the air.

Granny lowered herself onto a divan and arranged the loose cushions so that her back was supported. Halide stayed close; she felt safe pressed against the comforting bulk of her grandmother's body. The strange atmosphere in the house made her uneasy. Hudai brought a tray of tea and placed it on the floor next to their feet.

"I hear gypsies live off the blood of bats," Halide whispered once Hudai had left the room.

"Who has been telling you such nonsense?" Granny snapped.

"The kitchen girls. They say the gypsies live in hovels carved out of the city walls and no one dares to venture near them after dark."

"Ignorant people invent stories to justify their fears." A woman's voice startled Halide, and she turned to see Peyker standing beside them. The low ceiling made her seem tall. Her dark hair, turning to gray at the temples, flowed over her shoulders in a careless torrent. Beneath her red robe her shoulders were hunched and her body thin to the point of emaciation. Her eyes, unexpectedly blue, surveyed Halide with frank curiosity. As she extended her hand for the customary kiss, Halide noticed that Peyker's knuckles were covered with hennaed triangles. Her nails were dyed to a deep shade of chestnut.

"So you are Selima's child. I see it in your eyes." Peyker curled her fingers under Halide's chin and tilted her face upward.

"My granddaughter is the image of her mother in every way," Granny said, finishing her tea and placing the cup deliberately on the copper tray.

At Peyker's prompting, Granny sent Halide outside to play in the garden. At first Halide was reluctant, unwilling to be left alone with the gypsy child roaming nearby.

🍀

PEYKER SAT cross-legged on a floor cushion close to Granny and spread her hands over her knees.

"So tell me, my friend: why is your face filled with anxiety and your voice cracking with pain? I know the loss of your child weighs heavy on you, but there is something else."

Granny began to relate the details of her discussion with Edib. Just talking about it wearied her. She leaned back against the cushions and sighed. "So Halide will be tutored in Arabic and Persian, just like a boy," she concluded, "and her head will be filled with useless knowledge."

"Arabic is the language of the Holy Koran," Peyker said, looking at her intently.

"I know Edib—this won't end with Arabic. Don't you remember how hard he tried to convince Selima to learn English? Fortunately she had the sense to know that learning the language of infidels would interfere with her faith." Tears welled up in Granny's eyes, and she dabbed them with a kerchief.

Peyker reached over and grasped her hand. "What about Ali Pasha, didn't he object?"

"When has my dear husband ever protested anything? He

calmly accepts the complications of life as the will of God and moves on accordingly."

"That's the Bektashi dervishes for you," Peyker said with a smile.

"I have great admiration for the faith of the brotherhood, but I'm the one who's left to worry about the family and make the important decisions." Granny crumpled her kerchief into a ball and stuffed it into the folds of her shawl. "I don't understand what Edib wants for Halide. How will she find a husband? Prospective suitors will be frightened away if she is too clever."

"Edib is a good man; he acts with the best intent for his daughter."

Through the dusty window Granny caught a glimpse of her granddaughter skipping in the long grass.

"Halide's destiny will be different from that of any other Turkish girl who has gone before her," Peyker said, following her gaze.

"Are you trying to tell me she is fated never to be married?"

"I can't answer that." Peyker closed her eyes and was silent for a moment. "She will be tutored by nonbelievers, by Christians."

"You are making me nervous." Granny shifted to the edge of the divan.

"When it comes to matters concerning the infidels, our spirits cannot predict what will happen. The future is blurred; it's hard to see through these mists." Peyker waved her arms as if pushing aside a curtain. "Wait. They are telling me that you must be vigilant. Guide Halide's spirit, pay attention to the growth of her soul."

"What should I do?"

"The time has come to tell her about the gift she has inherited. Her father's plans for her future make it imperative that she understand her obligation."

"What should I say?"

"Repeat what your mother told you."

"I can scarcely remember," Granny moaned. "It was so long ago."

"You are the link to the past, my friend. Have faith and the chain will never be broken."

"I will talk to her as soon as we get home," Granny promised. "But it won't be easy—there is so much that can't be said."

"Remember that she is guarded by the spirit of her mother, who remains close by. But wait, they are saying something about the other child . . ."

The old lady gasped and put her hand to her mouth. "She is coming to live with us. Edib told me; the authorities are upset with her father again."

"This is Selima's doing. She wants the girls to be together."

"She has a strange way of going about it," Granny said, allowing herself a wry smile.

"The chief astrologer was dangerous. Had he lived, he would have pressed for the arrest of Edib Pasha, on account of his liberal views." Peyker's mouth tightened, and her body became rigid. She lifted her chin and moved her head from side to side, as if searching the air for confirmation.

"Edib is an honest man," whispered Granny, who appeared not to have understood her.

"COME, CHILD, sit down, I have a story to tell you." Granny patted the cushion beside her. She was sitting in her favorite window seat, on the second floor. Night had long since fallen and the garden was shrouded in darkness.

"It's late, Granny. Aren't you tired?"

"No, I feel I could sit here all night and watch the stars." Granny pulled her shawl tight around her shoulders. Never fond of the chatter and din of daily life, she savored time for reflection.

"I'm ready for sleep." Halide scrambled up beside her grandmother and, smothering a yawn, lay her head against her arm. For several minutes they rested together in silence while the old lady considered how to begin.

"When your mother was your age, about eight or nine," she said at length, "she used to stand over there, near the door, and chant passages from the Koran. Did I ever tell you she was a gifted singer?"

"No," Halide murmured.

"Her favorite song was the Mevlud." Granny sighed.

"The Mevlud?" Halide pushed herself upright and looked into her grandmother's watery eyes, but they stared past her, as if absorbed in memories of another time.

"Your mother had the voice of an angel," she said at last. "Even the nightingales sounded like foghorns by comparison."

"Like the girl I saw on the day of her funeral?"

"That was no mortal child. It was the spirit of your mother."

Halide looked up at her grandmother in disbelief.

"She returned to comfort you. Life is eternal, Halide; she wanted you to know that."

"Did you see her too?"

"No." The old lady paused, wondering how best to explain this. "It was you she wanted to reach, not me; at my age I don't need reassurance about death."

"The girl was so real. I saw her as clearly as I see you—she wasn't make-believe."

"I know," Granny said quietly. "This is our family gift. It passes from mother to daughter, from generation to generation.

When my own mother died she returned many times until my sister and I knew we need not cry anymore."

"But why?" Halide struggled to make sense of what her grandmother was telling her.

"Why?" echoed Granny. This was unexpected; she had always accepted her ability to hear spirits and never thought to wonder at the purpose. "What do you mean?"

"Why do they come back? And why to us?"

"I've never questioned the will of God," Granny replied. "Remember, Halide, we are descended from the standard-bearer Eyoub; through him our family has an ancient connection to the Prophet himself."

Halide leaned against her grandmother's arm. "Will I see her again?" she asked at length. "I've seen her in my dreams but never"—she hesitated—"never when I was awake."

"You are young yet; I don't know what form your gift will take," Granny said quietly.

"If I see her again," Halide said, "I will ask her if she loved me."

"What an extraordinary thing to say!" Granny exclaimed. "She loved you dearly, but she was ill from the day you were born."

"If she loved me, why did she leave?"

"She left us all," Granny said, shaken by Halide's response. She drew Halide close, kissed her forehead, and offered a silent prayer for the preservation of Halide's gift.

Chapter Six

Although her tutors came every morning, during the long hours between noon and nightfall Halide and Teyze spent every moment together. Gradually a routine evolved. While the sun was high they rested in the shade of the acacia walk, or the cool cypress alleys beyond the men's quarters. Toward the end of the afternoon they walked to the graveyard near Yildiz. If the weather was warm they went down the shaded lane into the village, and crossed the main square in the direction of the quay. Seated on a bench outside the ticket office, they watched the water traffic churning across the straits, and fed the gulls, who circled and shrieked overhead. When the water was calm they hired a caïque to take them to Arnavutkoy, sometimes even venturing as far as Bebek. Before darkness set in they returned to the mansion for evening prayers and the late meal. At night they slept side by side on old-fashioned beds.

Word of their growing attachment had reached Edib Pasha, who was, on the whole, pleased that his daughter had a companion during the period of mourning. The little he knew of Teyze pleased him. She was well educated and close to his mother-in-law, and her days in the Imperial harem would have instilled in her a sense of propriety rooted in tradition. Quite why this mattered to him he did not know, for in every other way he wanted his daughter to become a modern, educated woman.

One afternoon in late June a storm threatened to break over the city. Halide and Teyze retreated to the small salon Teyze had converted into a library. Of all the rooms in the harem, this was Halide's favorite. A musty smell of leather and wax hovered over

the book-lined walls. There were rows of ancient volumes, some
fastened with locks fashioned by the silversmiths of Kayseri. On
the lower shelves were piles of yellowing manuscripts Halide
longed to read.

The sky had grown so dark that Teyze had to light the candles
in the chandelier. Without a word she returned to her novel, which
had been delivered that morning by her book merchant in the Sahaflar Carsisi.

"Teyze, I'm sorry to interrupt you," Halide began.

"Mmm." Teyze did not look up.

"Who is Ali Shamil Pasha?"

"Now, where did you hear that name?"

"Father was talking about him with Granny and Grandpa."

"Then you must ask him."

The wind picked up and light from the chandelier swayed to
and fro across the room. Disappointed, Halide reached for a book
of adventure stories and opened it flat on the table. Reading excited her. From the words and pictures another world emerged,
stirring in her an urgent desire to know more of life beyond the
harem.

Suddenly the storm broke and rain pelted on the roof. Lightning seared the sky with jagged cracks of silver. Halide leapt to her
feet.

"Are you frightened?" Teyze asked, looking up from her book.

"The lightning is so beautiful—it makes me feel as if my entire
body wants to explode."

"Why don't we watch the storm up close . . ." Teyze started
across the room, but Halide pulled her back with a sharp tug on her
skirt.

"*No,* don't leave me alone, stay right by my side, please,
Teyze."

"I was only going to the window."

"I don't want to see it. I like being safe inside while the storm rages." Halide grasped Teyze's arm and held it in a tight grip. Rain pounded on the roof. Teyze glanced up, half expecting its force to shatter the glass, but it held firm.

"My entire body is tingling—can't you feel it?"

The wind roared and thunder rumbled. Loose tiles cascaded down the roof. Suddenly there was a crash, followed by a rush of cool air. The candlelight vanished in a chime of crystal, and the room was plunged into darkness. Teyze groped for Halide's hand and held it tight.

"Don't be frightened."

"The chandelier must have fallen," Halide whispered. In the dark her senses realigned themselves. The sounds of the night seemed louder, smells took on a sharper edge. The shape of the room gradually emerged from the flat darkness, assuming a shadowy depth. Teyze's perfume seemed more pungent; the sandalwood incense lingered. Then Halide discerned another, more ominous odor.

"Something is burning! I can't tell where it's coming from." Instinctively, their fingers tightened and they drew close together.

"We must find the door. Hold my hand tightly, stay close." Teyze groped her way across the room and felt for the doorknob. When she tried to turn it, she couldn't get it to budge. Her hands shook, her arms felt like jelly. She took a short breath. Smoke was beginning to tickle the back of her throat.

"Let me try," Halide said. She felt inwardly still in the face of Teyze's mounting panic. Moving with deliberate ease, Halide forced the bolt to release. She pushed against the door with her shoulder, until its weight finally gave way under force.

"You go for help," urged Teyze. "I'll stay here."

"I can't leave you alone."

"Do as I say, don't waste time arguing. I must go back to retrieve my books."

Something in Teyze's voice urged Halide to obey, and she raced
down the corridor to the stairs. Alone now, Teyze realized she had
to act quickly. It did not take her long to locate the source of the
smoke. She spotted an amber glow near the wainscot under the
window. The dense wool weave of the carpet appeared to be burning slowly. How long, she wondered, before the glow ignited into
flames? Placing her hands over her mouth and eyes, she edged
along the wall until she reached the bookshelves. Holding her
breath, she began to pull books down two at a time. The effort ex-
hausted her, and when she tried to carry the heavy volumes to the
door they tumbled from her arms. The gloom was disorienting.
Smoke stung her eyes and seeped into her pores. Breathing became
difficult. Coughing, she felt the darkness slipping over her like a
cloud across the moon.

EDIB PASHA was the first to reach the room. He carried an oil
lamp and a heavy walking stick. Behind him, three grooms filed in,
bearing buckets of water. By now the smoke was dense, filling the
room with acrid fumes.

When he saw the outline of Teyze's body crumpled on the
floor, Edib rushed to her side. Slipping one arm under her shoulders, the other under her knees, he carried her into the hallway.
Her hand fell from his grip and dangled limply, and her head rolled
against his chest. Edib had not been this close to a woman since his
wife had died. He placed her gently on the floor in the hallway,
eager to discharge his task. He drew back and looked at her smoke-
blotched face with compassion. Without warning, Selima's image
came into his mind.

The fire was soon extinguished and one of the grooms wrenched the screen from the window and pushed open the shutters. The men whooped with pleasure as cool air flooded in, dispersing the smoke. The sound of voices roused Teyze, who stared at Edib with puzzled amazement.

"Stay still, madam, or you might injure yourself." At the sound of his voice, Teyze became visibly uncomfortable. She made a futile attempt to push herself up onto her elbows. The exertion made her head spin, and she fell back with a groan.

"My books, I must rescue my books," she whispered.

"Lie down," he said. "Nothing has been damaged."

"They are irreplaceable," she said, still struggling to breathe freely.

"Nothing will be touched, you have my word of honor." Edib's assurance calmed Teyze, and she allowed herself to close her eyes once more. As he watched her, something shifted inside him. He found the intimacy of their encounter unsettling.

❧

AT GRANNY'S insistence, Teyze was placed in the bed where Selima had died. Great care was taken with preparing the room: she knew how fastidious Teyze was when it came to her surroundings. The damask spread was replaced by a scarlet shawl, embroidered with dragons. Pillows were covered in freshly laundered linens, and a pot of sweet basil was placed on the table beside the bed. After months of darkness, the shutters were flung open and fresh air and sunlight flooded the room once more. Light lifted the spirit, Granny believed. Yet there were moments when she saw her daughter's frail form superimposed like a specter over the living, breathing Teyze. Despite her faith in God's will, the pain sometimes became unbearable. To escape its clutches, Granny busied herself with the duties of nurse and cook.

"Come sit with me, you look tired." Teyze was propped up in bed sipping sage tea, a restorative proven by time and tradition.

"I've made you some of my pistachio baklava; the pastry is so fine I can see through it." In the past, Granny was renowned for her sweet-making skills. At Bairam, the annual festival following the month-long fast of Ramazan, the poor families of the *mahalle* used to line up in the street to wait for their traditional gift of preserved quince and sour cherries stewed with honey. For the family she made jars of colored sugar syrups and Noah's dessert, in honor of her husband. These skills were learned from her father, who had been the chief sweet maker of Sultan Abdulmecid, the Dweller of Heaven.

"Let one of the kitchen girls fetch it—I hate to see you going up and down stairs on my account."

"If I don't pay attention to your recovery myself, mistakes will be made and Edib will have that infidel doctor here."

"Why . . ." Teyze checked herself. "My health should not be of concern to Edib Pasha. He has affairs of the court to worry about."

"That's what I told him," Granny said testily, "but he has been here every day asking after you."

"He was always a considerate man. When he first came to Yildiz, even the princess remarked favorably on his character. She predicted that his rise would be fast."

"We were lucky to find such a good son-in-law. Sometimes I forget how long you have known him."

"He was just a young man, but so alert, so intelligent."

"I remember when he started calling here. It seems like yesterday." Granny's voice trailed off. The memory of Edib standing in the lane beyond the gate, waiting for Selima to appear at an upper window, came back to her as sharply as if it were yesterday. How she had pitied him then, so low in rank yet so vehement in his pursuit! Despite their shared concern that Selima was marrying beneath her, she and Ali Pasha had accepted his offer with gratitude. Their daughter was, after all, lucky to have found a loyal and loving husband, considering everything she had been through.

"It's strange how life comes around," Teyze mused. "Who would have thought that one day his child would be like a daughter to me."

"She is devoted to you, it is true."

"I enjoy her company. She is so brilliant, so eager to learn."

Granny sighed. "I worry about her. She's such a serious child, and she keeps everything bottled up inside. It's not natural."

"If you will forgive my offering an opinion on family matters, Fatma Hanim, I think the tutoring schedule her father has set for her is taking her mind off her loss."

"That's what Ali Pasha says. But Halide should be learning to dance and sing like a nightingale, not cluttering her mind with Arabic and Persian as if she were a boy." Granny checked herself, not wanting to hurt Teyze's feelings.

"Halide is only seven," Teyze said with a smile.

"I was betrothed at ten. The alliance was agreed upon by both families when I was born."

"When the time comes, I'm sure Edib Pasha will find a suitable suitor."

"Excuse me, ma'am." Arzu approached her mistress carrying a letter on a silver tray. "This was delivered to the harem by messenger. It is addressed to Fikriye Hanim."

"It's from the palace," Granny said, looking at the official seal of Yildiz stamped on the envelope.

"Who would be writing to me after all these years?" Teyze murmured. "My pupils are grown men by now, and the princess, well, she wouldn't deign to contact me even if her life depended on it." Feeling apprehensive, Teyze cracked the seal and unrolled the single sheet of vellum. The letter was beautifully written in black ink, obviously the work of a skillful scribe. As her eye traveled down the page her confusion mounted, and by the time she had finished her hands were shaking. Stunned, she sank back into the comfort of the pillows.

"Is it bad news? You've turned pale."

"I have received a proposal of marriage," Teyze said quietly.

"Praise be to God for such an unexpected blessing." Granny was so astonished she sank down on the bed without the aid of her stick. "May I ask who it is?"

"A good man, of rank."

"I will go to Eyoub's tomb this very night and pray for your happiness."

"Save your prayers, dear friend; it is you who needs the comfort in this time of mourning." Teyze patted the back of Granny's hand.

"Does this suitor know you will be able to provide your own dowry? I hope he is not a fortune hunter."

"There is no danger of that."

"You must be very careful. I'll ask Edib to handle the negotiations—he understands legal matters." The old lady was so stunned by this unexpected turn of events that she could only think of practical matters.

"Pray don't mention this to him just yet," Teyze said, her pulse quickening.

"I'm so happy for you," Granny babbled on. "A woman needs marriage to anchor her to the world."

Teyze nodded and turned the letter over in her hand. For a proposal, it was disappointingly sparse. Although he gave a glowing assessment of her intellectual skills, there was not one word of affection, nothing to indicate that her carefully concealed feelings were returned. It was obvious that her closeness to Halide meant a lot to him, but of their potential love match, Edib said nothing.

Chapter Seven

Halide sat cross-legged on the wall, in a place where she had a clear view along both banks of the Bosphorus. Caïques dotted the blue waters, skimming like mosquitoes between the shores of Asia and Europe. Behind her the mansion rambled over the hillside, casting long straight shadows across the grass. Every window in the harem was shuttered and the stone terraces were deserted. Farther down the hill doves clustered on the tiled roof of the men's quarters, cooing and warbling in the bright sunlight.

Halide liked to play by herself, away from the attention of the adults who hovered over her, voicing concern for her well-being. Left alone she felt free to let her mind wander to the world she inhabited in Teyze's books, an imaginary landscape peopled by romantic heroes and adventurers, a world without limits. It was also, she imagined, the world where her mother lived on, released from the constraints of time.

Two days earlier, Halide had seen Selima again, sitting on the stone bench in the rose garden, humming a lullaby. The echo of the melody lingered, leaving Halide with a dreadful sense of emptiness. She had not seen her mother leave the garden; her eyes had filled with tears, and in the moment it had taken to wipe them away, Selima had vanished.

The French doors of the men's quarters were thrown open and Halide's father walked out onto the terrace, deep in conversation with a younger man. Behind them was a girl Halide had never seen before. These days Edib came and went like a shadow, never saying when he might return. Sometimes Halide had the impression he wanted to avoid her.

The two men leaned against the low stone wall separating the terrace from the garden, shielding their eyes against the bright sunlight. As soon as their backs were turned the girl darted into the house, and the younger man immediately rushed off in pursuit. Who were these visitors?, Halide wondered. Since her mother's death six months before, there had been so many people streaming in and out of the house that she had started to feel like a stranger in her own home.

When Edib caught sight of Halide running up the path toward him, he felt dismayed. He still had not yet planned how he would explain the newcomer's presence to her. He was not a man who left things to chance, and he hated to lie for any reason. Maybe it was better to say nothing, he thought, watching his daughter draw closer.

"Father, what a wonderful surprise!" Halide said, racing toward him.

"Come and give me a hug, dear girl." He caught her under her shoulders and lifted her high above his head.

"Have you come home to stay for a while?" she asked hopefully, waving her arms in the air.

"Unfortunately, I have to return to the palace before the last call to prayer," he said, setting her back on the ground. The wind had blown her curls awry, and he tried to smooth them into place. She hung her head to hide her disappointment.

"Why are you out here all alone? I thought you and Teyze spent the afternoon together?" Twenty days had passed since Edib had made his proposal, and he had not received a response. He was beginning to wonder if he had acted too hastily.

"Since the fire she has been in bed," Halide said.

"Has she seen a doctor?"

"I don't know." Halide drew back and pretended to watch the insect-sized caïques as they scudded to and fro across the Bosphorus. She did not want to tell him that, at Granny's invitation, Peyker the seer was taking care of Teyze.

"Fortunately we managed to contain the fire," Edib said. "I can't bear to think what might have happened to you."

"It was God's will," Halide murmured.

"I dare say it was," Edib sighed, drawing a cigarette case from his pocket. From the far end of the men's quarters he heard the sound of a girl laughing. What was Mahmoure up to now, he wondered.

"Sit down and tell me how your lessons are going." Edib held out his arm and motioned in the direction of four wrought-iron chairs arranged in a semicircle around a low table. The furniture, recently arrived from England, had caused considerable comment in the household.

"I like to learn new things," Halide said cautiously.

"But?"

"The Imam who teaches me Arabic smells strange," she whispered, longing to tell him that she missed Teyze, who made every aspect of learning exciting.

"Don't sit too close to him then," Edib said, at a loss as to what to think of this remark. Halide didn't have a chance to respond. From within the men's quarters came the sound of a girl screaming. Who would dare make such a noise when her grandfather was sleeping? Moments later a young girl came hurtling through the French doors, followed by a heavy-set youth. When they caught sight of Edib they stopped, and the young man bowed.

"Forgive us, sir. My cousin shames my family with her behavior." He was out of breath and spoke in short gasps.

"Why don't you leave me alone? You'll never catch me, you're so fat!"

"Calm down at once, Mahmoure." Edib clenched his fists in frustration. His mother-in-law had warned him that the girl could be difficult.

"I wanted to swing in the trees, but he stopped me," she complained mischievously.

"I was charged by your father to look after you."

"Enough," Edib said, stepping between them. Halide stared at Mahmoure with a mixture of awe and envy. She was wearing a cream silk dress with scalloped flounces, layered petticoats, and a wide red ribbon around her waist. It was the kind of dress Halide would have given anything to own.

"I want you to meet my daughter, Halide." Extending his hand toward her, Edib motioned for Halide to move closer. She shook hands uncomfortably with the newcomers, feeling self-conscious in her dowdy English clothes. Except for their dark coloring, the two strangers bore little resemblance to each other. He was in his late teens, handsome in a heavy way, his hair slicked back from his forehead. The girl was slightly taller than Halide. Her body bristled with contained energy, like a cat about to pounce on its victim. Her round face was framed with short curly hair, and her vibrant eyes had a mischievous light in them.

"Hasan, I asked for some sherbet for all of us but the manservant seems to have forgotten. Go inside and find out why there is a delay."

"At once, sir."

As soon as her cousin was out of sight, Mahmoure bounced over to Edib and gazed up at him with a pleading smile.

"You'll let me climb trees, won't you, Edib Pasha? My father always let me do as I please, not like that fool Hasan." She thrust her chin in the direction of the house. "He thinks he has to throw his weight about to be a man."

"Hasan was responsible for your safety." There was something so disarming about this child. Edib could not help but smile. However irresponsible she was, it was hard to resist her.

"Well, I'm here and I'm safe, so he can leave me alone. Can I run in the gardens? My father said there was lots of space here for me to play in." She let go of his hand and rushed to the edge of the terrace. Halide edged up to her father and caught hold of his arm.

"Father?" she whispered. "What is she doing here?"

"Mahmoure has come to live with us for a while."

"For how long?"

"I don't know. Her family has to leave the city indefinitely, and her father made me her guardian."

"Have Granny and Grandfather met her yet?"

"Yes, they have." Something in the tone of his voice stopped her from asking any more questions.

"My father said I was to call you sister," Mahmoure said. She was sitting on top of the wall, drumming her heels against the stone. "But obviously I am older, so you must call me *abla*."

"How old are you?" Halide asked suspiciously.

Mahmoure looked puzzled. "About twelve I think, or maybe eleven. But I'm taller than you, so obviously I'm older, aren't I, sir?"

"You are twelve," Edib said. When he was sitting in his office in Yildiz Palace, this introduction had seemed to be a simple matter, but now. . . .

At that moment Hasan emerged from the men's quarters, followed by two servants. Mahmoure removed her shoes and tossed them under a rosebush, seized Halide's hand, and pulled her across the lawn.

Edib stood with his back to the house, watching the girls skip to and fro. There was so much of her mother in Mahmoure, in her bubbling laughter and the carefree way she tossed her head when she spoke. Edib reached into his pocket for a cigarette and his fingers brushed against the hard rim of the locket, which he carried with him as a cautionary reminder. He was an important man now. When he had met Selima he had been young. He had let his heart run away with him. Now he vowed to himself never to allow such a thing to happen again.

Chapter Eight

Teyze waited in the main salon. She had been there for more than an hour, trying halfheartedly to read a French novel. The thought of seeing Edib made her apprehensive. His proposal had taken her by surprise, and she wondered if he would be disappointed when he saw her again. Although once a beauty, Teyze was acutely aware that she was no longer young, and her childbearing years were coming to an end. Arzu scurried in, carrying the silver coffee salver. The air was sultry, and a faint rumble of thunder could be heard in the distance.

"I hope he arrives before the storm breaks," Teyze said with a sigh, fiddling absentmindedly with her hair. It was hard to remain composed in this sweltering heat.

"If I may say so, you look beautiful, ma'am." Arzu set the salver close to Granny, who was sitting in one of the window seats watching the purple wisteria waving in the wind.

"He is blessed to have had such luck twice in his life," the old lady said.

Teyze blushed with pleasure. She had taken great care with her appearance. In the morning she had gone to the baths with her servant, where the attendants had pummeled and scrubbed her until her skin shone like polished marble and the smell of jasmine seeped from every pore. Selecting the right dress had proved difficult; she wanted to look her best without appearing conspicuous. In the end she had settled on a gray silk gown trimmed with lace, clasped at the waist with a mesh belt of finely wrought silver. On her feet were a pair of matching high-heeled slippers, too delicate to be worn anywhere other than indoors. She had finished her toilette by twining a string of artificial flowers through her hair.

"You have always been like a daughter to me, Teyze, and this betrothal will seal that bond."

"My dear Fatma Hanim Efendi, I am so happy to hear you say that. My great fear was that if I accepted Edib our friendship might suffer." For as long as she had lived at the Beshiktash mansion, Teyze had addressed the mistress of the house formally. To do otherwise would have been a serious breach of etiquette.

"I am not going to lose you; that would have pained me. As it is, Halide has gained a mother, and I don't have to worry should anything happen to me."

"I hope she'll feel the same way."

"Of course she will. She is very attached to you."

"I still think we should tell her."

"*No*, no, what with the arrival of Mahmoure and the upheaval that has caused, news of your marriage will only confuse her."

"I would have liked her to be present at the ceremony."

"Trust me, Teyze, I know what is best. Besides, you won't be having many guests—a simple wedding is most appropriate. Selima has only been in her grave for seven months, and out of respect for her memory I think Edib would prefer . . ." Granny's voice faded. Once she had recovered from the shock of discovering the identity of Teyze's suitor, it had not taken her long to appreciate the practical aspects of this union.

"When I have given him my formal acceptance I will ask for a quiet wedding." Teyze spoke with some sadness in her voice. There was nothing she would have liked more than a large ceremony filled with music and celebration, but as with so many things in her life, fate had directed otherwise.

"I will reassure him that my husband and I give you both our full blessing."

"I am sorry to hear the Pasha feels unwell today," Teyze murmured, wondering why Edib needed reassuring.

"Ali Pasha is getting old; the hot weather upsets him."

"These storms make breathing uncomfortable. What a strange summer this has been." With a flick of her wrist, Teyze opened her white ostrich-feather fan.

"Ah, that fan is beautiful. I have always admired it."

"The princess gave it to me. I believe it was a gift from the Italian ambassador."

"The princess, of course—I should have guessed," Granny laughed. "I wonder what she'll say when she hears you are married to Edib Pasha."

"What a relief not to have to care!"

"Princess Gulistan will be impressed. Edib is a rising star in the bureaucracy at Yildiz Palace and a handsome man besides." Granny looked squarely at Teyze.

"Even if she hears about my marriage, I doubt the princess will care. She has probably forgotten who I am."

"Nonsense! You were a threat to her preeminence. She was jealous of your beauty—that is why she refused every offer of marriage you received. I think she acted out of sheer spite."

Sultan Abdulhamid had numerous half siblings, offspring of the concubines and wives of his father, Sultan Abdulmecid, but the princess was his only full sister. She had mixed feelings about her brother's repressive regime, which unraveled the reforms their father had instituted.

"You should be grateful to her," Granny continued. "When she asked you to tutor the young princes she saved you from the boredom and depression that afflict most of the women in the Imperial harem."

"My skills were useful to her. Her sons needed an education so that they might have the advantage, when the time came, to find a successor to the Sultanate."

"I'm sure you're right," Granny chuckled, "but it saved you nonetheless."

"I tried to teach some of the younger women to read, to help them pass the time, but the chief eunuch put a stop to that."

"Ach, those poor things, sitting around all day with nothing to do except wait for the Sultan to notice them." Granny shook her head. Under the watchful eye of the white eunuch, the inhabitants of the harem were guarded day and night. They rarely left the confines of Yildiz and had little idea about life beyond the palace walls.

"They number at least five hundred—even the Sultan doesn't have that much time and energy." Teyze giggled like a young girl.

A servant from the men's quarters came to announce that Edib was changing his clothes and would join them in a few minutes. At the mention of his name, Teyze's heart beat faster. She was about to accept a proposal of marriage from a man she had loved from a distance for longer than she dared to admit. It was the crowning achievement of her life, the realization of everything she had been trained for. Why was it, then, that now that the moment was here she felt let down?

Chapter Nine

Halide and Mahmoure had reached the top of the hill. To their left, running along the base of a hollow, was the great wall that enclosed Yildiz. From the high ground where they stood, they could look into the palace grounds. Autumn had come late this year, and the trees were still full; a few gray buildings were partially visible through the brown-and-gold foliage. The treetops dipped into a valley, then rose like a great wave toward the crest of the next hill. Directly below them they saw the sloping roof of a greenhouse glittering in the noon sun and beyond it, between a break in the trees, an open space where horses were tethered on long reins held in the ground by pegs. Other than the horses, there was no sign of life.

"So that's where the great tyrant lives. Where is his palace?" Mahmoure whispered.

" 'Tyrant'—what does that mean? "

"I'm not sure," Mahmoure said slowly. "My father always called him that."

"Do you have any idea where we're going?" Halide sat down on a raised tuft of grass and started to remove her boots. She had never ventured so far from the house before and her feet were aching from the walk.

"I'm trying to find a way into Yildiz, but there doesn't seem to be a gate anywhere."

"We can't go into there—it's forbidden," Halide said quietly.

"So what? Don't you want to see for yourself where the Sultan lives? "

"If you'd told me that's what you wanted to do, we could have asked Father. He works there."

"Really?" Mahmoure's eyes opened wide in amazement.

"He is first secretary to the Sultan," Halide said proudly. "He has an office at the palace."

"Fancy that. I thought he was a cavalry officer like my father."

"I thought you told me he was a prince," Halide said suspiciously. Mahmoure talked about her father all the time, but her description of him changed constantly. When Halide had tried to ask her father about him, he'd coughed awkwardly and changed the subject.

"He was a prince once upon a time, before I was born. Then he became a cavalry officer like the rest of his family." She paused before adding, "He has over a hundred brothers. I have so many cousins we've lost count of them all."

Halide ignored this remark, assuming it was another of Mahmoure's exaggerations.

"You must miss your father. If my father had to go away, I don't know what I'd do."

Suddenly Mahmoure flung herself on the ground and buried her head between her knees. Her shoulders shook and, to her horror, Halide realized she was crying. For the past two months Halide had tagged along behind Mahmoure with an admiration bordering on awe. They had explored the lanes and byways of Beshiktash, places she had never been before, and it had never occurred to her that her fearless friend could be so easily hurt.

"Don't cry—I didn't mean to upset you." She leaned over and touched Mahmoure on the shoulder. "It was stupid of me to say such a thing."

"His wives were jealous of my mother because she was his favorite; she died giving birth to me, so they hated me too."

"You're safe with us until he returns."

"Do you think he will ever come back?" Mahmoure raised her head and tried to wipe her tears away with her hand.

"With God's will anything is possible." Halide bent forward and dabbed at Mahmoure's tear-streaked face with the hem of her pinafore.

"How can you believe that stuff? My father says we are masters of our own fate." Mahmoure scrambled to her feet and brushed the dirt off her dress. "Now you and I are going to find a way into the palace."

"But we can't!"

"Who's going to stop us? There is no one about—I bet they're all asleep. Come on, Halide! We'll only go as far as those horses."

Halide followed Mahmoure down the hill to the wall separating their estate from the palace. Under the force of Mahmoure's influence, she felt compelled to act in ways she would never have dared, and since Teyze's unexpected departure no one paid much attention to her behavior. Soon after Mahmoure had arrived, Teyze had packed her trunks and left for a short trip. Where she was going and why she did not say. At first Halide felt betrayed, but before long she was climbing trees with Mahmoure and creating imaginary castles in the rose garden. Once the two girls even went so far as the quay in Beshiktash by themselves, where they were found by an indignant harbormaster as they flicked stones across the water. Except for the mornings when Halide was tutored, they spent all their time together.

"*Look!* There's a break in the wall where they've tried to build around the trunk of that big tree."

"It's very small," Halide said, hoping to hold her friend back.

"We can squeeze through—come on." Mahmoure's feet sank into the ground as she ran through the soft grass, passing parallel to the base of the wall, where poppies grew in great profusion. "If I turn sideways I can just make it."

Mahmoure slipped her leg through the gap between the wall and the trunk of the tree. Then, maneuvering to avoid the rough edges of the stone, she managed to inch her way through the narrow space without scraping herself. She landed with a thud on the other side and put her arm through the space to help Halide.

"Come on, don't be afraid! There's no one around."

"How will we get out again?" By now Halide's heart was pounding so loudly her ears were ringing.

"Same way we came in—now hurry!"

Being the smaller of the two, Halide was through the wall in a flash. She found herself in a wooded area, carpeted with dead leaves and bracken. Overhead a canopy of leaves cut out the sunlight. Mahmoure was already some distance ahead of her, skipping along the path as if she didn't have a care in the world. No sooner had Halide started after her than they heard the sound of dogs barking.

"WE ARE THE daughters of Edib Pasha, first secretary to Sultan Abdulhamid himself. If you do not believe me, send someone to his offices. He will confirm the truth and you will be in serious trouble." Mahmoure glared straight ahead of her to avoid the eye of their captor, a fresh-faced soldier scarcely older than she was. They stood facing each other on the path, while the dogs strained excitedly at their leashes. At first Mahmoure had wanted to run away, but Halide had held her back. She was used to animals and knew it was safer to stay still so as not to excite the hounds.

"What are you doing here?" The soldier eyed them steadily. He spoke slowly, with a heavy Anatolian accent.

"We were looking for the stables and lost our way," Halide said without thinking. "My father had ordered his barouche to be prepared to take us home." She was conscious of Mahmoure watching her with astonishment.

"Why isn't your father with you?"

"Edib Pasha is a busy man," Halide said quickly. "He has the affairs of the Sultan to take care of."

The young soldier furrowed his brow and let his grip on the dogs relax. Sensing they were no longer needed, the dogs lay down on the ground, their heads extended between their paws. Halide smiled. She loved dogs, and these two looked suddenly deceptively docile.

"You two follow me," the soldier said gruffly, after having given her statement a little thought.

"Where are you taking us?" Halide asked.

"To the stables. Didn't you say that is where you were going?"

"Is it far?"

"Nope, just beyond that clearing."

When the soldier turned around, Halide and Mahmoure exchanged a look of relief: he had believed their story. They walked in single file through the trees, following the path. The dogs made snuffling noises as they lurched along, nose to the ground, pulling at their leashes with such force the young soldier had difficulty holding them back. It wasn't until the rear wall of the stables loomed into view that Halide became frightened. Once it was discovered that there was no carriage, and no orders from her father, what would she do?

"I don't see no carriage," the soldier said, striding into the stable yard.

"Are you sure we've come to the right place?" Halide looked around at the empty stalls. There wasn't a sign of life anywhere.

"This is the only stables around here. There's more on the other side of the palace, but you wasn't going that way." For the first time he sounded doubtful.

"I don't understand. My father was very clear with his command. Perhaps the carriage is around the back." Halide wondered how long she could keep this up.

"Stay here and don't move. I'm going to take a look." Giving them a threatening glare, he started to walk around the yard, poking his head around the doors of the empty buildings. The girls waited in a corner under the shade. By now the fall sun was high, and the heat reflected from the cobblestones warmed their faces.

"Shall we make a run for it?" whispered Mahmoure.

"No, it'll give us away at once."

"What happens when he finds out there's no carriage?"

"I'll think of something."

"Quiet there!" The soldier shouted at them with such authority that Halide was afraid a spark of suspicion had struck his dull mind. There was a clatter of hooves, and before they had a chance to react a horse and rider cantered through the gate, reining to a halt barely inches away from where they stood.

"Whoa there! Get out of the way, girls, you shouldn't be standing so close to the. . . . My God, Halide! What on earth are you doing here?"

It was hard to tell who was more astonished, Halide or Riza, Edib's protégé, who was staring down at them from his saddle, the sun glistening on his gold epaulets. Riza was in full military dress, complete with high boots and scarlet jacket. As he dismounted, his sword clanked against his spurs.

"That soldier brought us here. He thinks we're trespassers," Halide explained. Hearing the commotion, their captor had started back across the yard. He stopped in his tracks as Riza whirled around and pointed his whip at him accusingly.

"Tether those dogs at once. They should not be in the stables, they'll frighten the horses."

The young soldier snapped to attention, saluted with his free hand, and led the dogs away without a word.

"Well, that's got rid of him." Turning back around, Riza surveyed the girls with puzzled amusement.

"So, Halide, you didn't answer my question."

"Well, er, we went for a walk and got lost." Under the scrutiny of those clear blue eyes, she found it hard to respond coherently.

"You're a long way from the harem, and I know for a fact your father didn't invite you here today. So what are you doing at Yildiz?" It wasn't like Halide to be evasive, and he wondered what the two of them had been up to.

"We came in through a hole in the wall, it's all my doing," Mahmoure said, stepping forward and putting her hands on her hips. "I brought her here to have an adventure." Mahmoure stared at Riza defiantly. She had never seen such a good-looking man before.

"Well now, who are you?" Riza asked with a smile, restraining himself from laughing at such impudence.

"My name is Mahmoure. I have come to live at Beshiktash at the behest of Edib Pasha, who is a friend of my father's."

"Yes, I remember now. Edib told me the circumstances." He stroked his chin and frowned. "If my memory serves me, your father ran afoul of the Sultan. It's dangerous for you to be here. I hate to think what might have happened if one of his enemies had recognized you. Fortunately for you it's Friday and everyone is at Yildiz mosque marching in the *selamlik* parade. It's the only time the Sultan ever leaves the palace."

"Friday prayers, of course! That's why the place is deserted." Halide wondered why an enemy of the Sultan would be a friend of her own dear father's. And how could it be that the Sultan left the palace only for Friday prayers? He was a man who cared about the lives of ordinary people, or so she had heard Father say. Surely he would go and see them himself.

"The parade will be over soon and this place will be crawling with guards. Get on my horse and we'll leave by the side gate. The sentry there knows me."

Mahmoure gathered up her skirts and mounted alongside Riza with such agility that it was obvious she was accustomed to being in the saddle. But there was no time for questions. Halide held her hand out to Mahmoure and hopped up behind her. Within minutes they clattered out the yard and down the drive toward the Beshik-tash gate. Mahmoure sat bolt upright and stared at the back of Riza's neck, where a few strands of fair hair escaped from beneath his fez.

Part Two

Chapter One

"Look at that hat, Halide!" squealed Mahmoure. "The pink one with feathers and ribbons. How does she keep it on in the street?"

"It's secured by hat pins this long." Halide held her hands up in front of her. "Teyze has some, I've seen them with my own eyes."

"There are so many feathers she looks like she has a pink swan on her head."

"Hush, she might hear you." Halide looked down uncomfortably as Mahmoure, undeterred, continued to stare.

"None of these people speak Turkish, not even the waiters," Mahmoure whispered conspiratorially. "They can't possibly understand us."

They were sitting in the Tea Salon on the Grande Rue de Pera, celebrating Riza's graduation from Harbiye Military School with an elaborate tea. The salon was a bustling, hectic meeting place furnished with velvet banquettes and marble-topped tables imported from Paris. It was the girls' first exposure to the fashionable world of Pera, the European district of Constantinople, and, to Riza's amusement, they could not stop staring around them.

"How do they get along without being able to speak Turkish?"

"They live in their own world here. They never come into contact with ordinary Turkish people," Riza said.

"That's peculiar. Why, even the Armenian Christians speak Turkish." Halide stole a glance at the people sitting next to them.

"If I told that group they were ugly as sin they would never know it!" Mahmoure turned abruptly back to Halide, and as she spun around her veil caught on an upholstery button and ripped. "Oh, not again," she moaned.

"Don't move, I'll undo it." Riza slid across the banquette and began to extricate the light fabric with his fingertips.

"I hate wearing this stupid thing. I'll never get used to it!"

They were interrupted by the appearance of a waiter in a black tailcoat, who coughed politely and stood stiffly beside them. Riza sat upright, embarrassed at being discovered lying on his side. He fired off their order in rapid French, as if to compensate for his compromising position. Halide was impressed. With his fair looks and fluent French, Riza fit so easily into this milieu; she felt by comparison like an awkward outsider.

"I ordered the Sacher torte," Riza said when the waiter had gone. "I'm told it's tastier than the real thing in Vienna."

"What's that?" the girls asked in unison.

"Wait and see, it's delicious."

When the cake appeared, embellished with spirals of cream, sugared cherries, and slivered almonds coated with silver, the girls shrieked with excitement. Sweets still held the fascination of the forbidden for Halide. She cut into the slice placed in front of her and lifted it to her lips. The taste was like nothing she had known before.

As they ate in silent pleasure, a woman entered the salon. Her face was pale and angular, and her bright lips were accentuated by a black beauty spot nestled in the curve between her nose and cheek. She waited by the partition and stared about her with the assurance of a woman who knows she will attract attention, lifting a gloved hand to her chin and tapping it impatiently. The headwaiter hurried over, followed by the maître d'hôtel. The woman was shown to a table at the front of the room, where she arranged herself on the banquette so that her tiered dress flowed around her in a semicircle.

"Look at all the men going over to talk to her." Mahmoure said, watching the rush of activity. "What good fortune that so many of her relatives are here at the same time."

"Why are they making such a fuss, is she a princess?"

"Goodness, they're even kissing her hand in public!"

"They are not her relatives, they are merely friends," Riza said, fixing his eyes on the tabletop. "This is the way things are done in Pera."

"Why is that?" Mahmoure asked mischievously, lifting the edge of her veil.

"The people here are not of our tradition. There's no prohibition in Europe on women's dress or public deportment. You'd better put your veil down," he said gently. "You're setting a bad example for Halide."

The look Mahmoure gave him caught Riza by surprise. Sometimes her rebellious nature gave way to a sadness that was almost unfathomable to him. "I can't imagine living this way for the rest of my life," she whispered.

Riza put his hand over hers and held it there for a moment. "Change is a slow process," he said warmly. "But change will come—don't lose heart."

Riza spoke with a firm sincerity that impressed Halide. He wasn't loud and boastful, like the other cadets she had seen around Beshiktash. He was like her father; it was no accident they held each other in such high regard.

A crowd of European men in top hats and greatcoats had gathered near the door to the street. They were, for the most part, diplomats and international traders. Life in Pera was a far cry from the old city of Stamboul, whose narrow cobbled streets echoed with the cry of the muezzin. The boulevards of Pera were light and broad, bordered with shops, theaters, and cafés, more akin to the streets of Paris than the Levant. Tramcars rumbled up and down and filled the air with the unfamiliar smell of the machine. For more than six hundred years, since the Genoese first came to Galata, the two worlds had faced each other across the watery divide of the Golden Horn.

Pressed against the glass partition separating the reception area from the main café was a narrow-faced man whose curling mustache and wary manner marked him as a Turk. He pushed his way to the front of the line, clutching his fez, and stared around the tearoom. When he saw Riza he began to weave his way between the tables, heading in their direction.

"Is this a friend of yours?" Mahmoure asked, looking up from her plate. Riza glanced behind him.

"What in God's name . . ."

"I saw you through the window, old fellow. Any news in my absence?" The stranger was beside them now. He wore a high-necked frock coat like the palace bureaucrats, and white spats over polished boots.

"I'm chaperoning the daughters of Edib Pasha," Riza said, standing up and nodding at the girls. The stranger took a step back and appeared to notice them for the first time. His eyes behind his spectacles grew wide with concern.

"Forgive me, I didn't realize."

"Another time, perhaps." The two men looked at each other and, without a word, the stranger turned and walked away. When he reached the desk near the door he exchanged a few words with the maître d'hôtel, who clapped him on the shoulder and laughed. It wasn't until he had left the café that Riza relaxed.

"Who was that?" Mahmoure asked eagerly.

"Someone I haven't seen for a long time."

"Why not?"

"He's been away." Riza sank back into his seat, momentarily lost in thought.

"Why didn't you ask him to join us?"

"It would not have been correct," he mumbled.

"Since when did you care about such conventions?" Mahmoure teased.

Riza seemed not to hear her over the din and chatter of the café. He pushed his cake around his plate but did not eat so much as a crumb. Chattering lightly, Mahmoure and Halide went on eating their Sacher torte in the European way, with silver forks.

AS THEY left the café the clouds to the west were tinged with purple, the first signs of dusk settling over the city. A watchman carrying a lamp on the end of a long pole lit up the gaslights along the Grande Rue. Lights flickered on in cafés and stores, casting a dull yellow haze across the sidewalk. Walking arm in arm, Halide and Mahmoure shivered in the chilly air. Riza strode ahead of them, his cloak pulled tight around him.

"How would you like to live there?" said Mahmoure, pointing up to a white stone building embellished with intricate wrought-iron balconies and columns.

"I prefer our *konak*," Halide said, without elaborating.

"But imagine what it must be like not have to wear a veil, and to come and go as you please."

Halide frowned, and said nothing.

"Imagine the fun we could have shopping in these fine stores." Mahmoure nudged her excitedly. "Then dressing up and visiting the cafés, even going to the theater."

"I'd miss the gardens and boating on the Bosphorus," Halide said, uncertain of what a theater was.

Despite the late hour, the street was crowded, and all around them Halide heard many languages being spoken. There was none of the hushed silence of the Turkish quarter; here even the women were talking loudly.

"Where are we going?" Mahmoure asked, tugging at Riza's cloak.

"I have to drop a note off at a friend's house," he said. "Then we'll take a carriage home."

"Is it far?" she moaned, slowing to a dawdle.

"Just around the next corner."

"Must you do it now?" Not waiting for an answer, Mahmoure sat down on the steps of a nearby house and refused to walk any farther.

"Come now, it's just around the next corner," Riza pleaded.

"I won't. I'm cold and I want to go home."

Riza paused and then walked over to her. He took her by the shoulders and shook her gently, forcing her to turn toward him.

"Listen, Mahmoure," he pleaded. "I have to get there tonight. If you have any feelings for me, you'll do as I ask. My life may depend on it."

Standing a little way off, Halide knew he had not meant her to hear this. She looked down at her feet to hide her concern. The urgency of Riza's appeal was not lost on Mahmoure, who got up and begrudgingly walked on under the gathering canopy of darkness.

Just before the Swedish embassy, Riza turned down a narrow flight of steps. Darkened buildings loomed over them, and above the echo of their footsteps they could hear strains of plaintive music. The stairs opened into a small plaza where, under the light of a single gas lamp, an organ-grinder and his monkey were performing for a small crowd.

"You girls wait here," Riza said. "Pretend to watch the show."

"Where are you going?" asked Mahmoure.

"My friend lives over there. I won't be long."

"Are you all right?" She caught him by the hand.

"Don't ask questions I can't answer," he said sharply. He caressed her cheek with the tips of his fingers, turned abruptly, and ran off.

Halide and Mahmoure stood in the shadow of the corner building, a simple stone house of modest proportions. The plaintive strain of the organ-grinder's song made them melancholy, the excitement of the afternoon long since dispelled. As the music grew louder the monkey waved its arms in the air. Above its wizened face a fez wobbled perilously in time with the music.

Chapter Two

The harem occupied two adjacent wings of the great wooden mansion at Beshiktash, built around an open courtyard where trellises and vines covered the enclosing walls. Windows were shuttered in summer and winter, and opened wide during spring and fall to allow the gentle winds from the Bosphorus to cool the interior. The main entrance was approached from the driveway through a pair of paneled double doors polished to the hue of chestnut. Beyond these doors was the central hall, two stories high, and here and there other doors led to more formal reception rooms, some rarely used except on religious holidays.

At the far end of the great hall, twin staircases swept up to the second floor, where the schoolroom and private apartments were located. Corridors off the landing led to a warren of smaller rooms rarely seen by visitors. In keeping with the simple style of the Ottomans, the rooms were sparsely furnished with divans, low copper tables, and wooden chests. Apart from restoring linens and curtains, Fatma Hanim Efendi had made few changes since she had moved into the harem forty years before. Life continued in the women's quarters much as it had for generations.

The only sound in the hall was the ticking of the grandfather clock Edib had presented to the harem in a vain attempt to persuade Fatma Hanim to use European time. Twelve o'clock, according to Islamic time, always came at sunset and was therefore, by European calculations, at a different time every day. This created confusion between the communities, particularly when it came to catching ferries. Granny looked up at the indecipherable lines etched on the brass face of the clock and shrugged.

Thin sunlight filtered through the stained-glass window above the front door. The cold weather gave a somber aspect to the house. Granny felt a pang of longing for spring, then promptly scolded herself for her lapse in spirit. There was nothing to be gained by being despondent.

"Are you all right, ma'am?"

"I'm fine, Arzu, don't fuss. Is there any sign of our visitors?"

"Not yet. I sent one of the maids to the top of the street to look out for them."

"It's hard to believe that Mahmoure has reached a marriageable age," Granny said wistfully.

"Time spins by us, ma'am. Over one year has passed since she took the veil."

Granny shook her head. "And how that child chafes at wearing it."

"She is her father all over again, ma'am."

"Yes, she is, God help us." Granny was silent for a moment. "So, is everything ready?"

"There is coffee in the silver carrier, ma'am. I lit the warmers myself. As soon as they arrive I'll send for cigarettes. Fusun Hanim likes those French ones Teyze smokes. Why don't you go and rest in the day salon? I'll announce the guests when they arrive."

Taking her hand, Arzu guided the old lady through the double doors into a cozy room with velvet-covered divans. Now that winter had settled in, the room was heated by a stove of massive proportions. Edib had installed it when Selima had first fallen ill. Its outer surface was covered in Iznik tiles, each hand-painted with interwoven vines and flowers of turquoise, blue, and orange. Granny felt comforted by the familiar simplicity of her surroundings. The visit of the *görücü* revived disturbing memories of another time, and another visit, when her daughter had come of age.

"Why do they need to look her over?" she mused aloud to Arzu, who had brought her some tea. "I have a candidate in mind: Kemal Pasha's grandson."

"A rather solemn boy, if I recall, ma'am."

"But from an eminently suitable family."

"Oh indeed, ma'am, none better. The *görücü*'s visit is just a formality. The ladies would be upset if they thought this household was breaking with tradition."

"You're right, Arzu; we must observe the formalities." Granny slipped her shawl off her shoulders. The room was warm; she had to admit that the stove was an improvement.

"The dress Edib Pasha bought for Mahmoure is laid out upstairs, but we haven't been able to find her," Arzu said cautiously.

Granny clicked her tongue. "That child will be the end of me. Why can't she be more like Halide?"

The clock in the hall struck noon. Arzu counted the chimes

under her breath. "Ten, eleven, twelve: that means it is noon and Halide's lesson with the Imam has almost finished."

Granny looked at Arzu with a mixture of surprise and concern. "You understand that infernal instrument?"

"Halide taught me. No point in having a clock if one doesn't know how to tell the time," Arzu said, pursing her lips.

"But we Ottomans have done without clocks for generations."

"Nowadays all the best households have them, ma'am. Ferid Bey's cook told me that their *selamlik* has a clock that plays military marches."

"How extraordinary."

"Now if you'll excuse me, I'll go and find Halide. She's sure to know where Mahmoure is hiding."

Granny stared after Arzu long after she had left the room. Strange whirring sounds emanated from the interior of the grandfather clock and the spindly metal hand moved with a click. Granny closed her eyes. This desire to measure eternity was beyond her comprehension. Time on earth was short enough; one hardly needed to be constantly reminded.

HALIDE STROLLED along the acacia walk, swinging her arms and scuffing the soles of her boots on the stones. She was certain she would find Mahmoure in the old woodshed at the far end of the well enclosure. With uncharacteristic domesticity, Mahmoure had lined the damp outbuilding with discarded horse blankets and covered the windows with felt to keep out the cold. It was, she had told Halide in confidence, a place where she and Riza could meet undisturbed. She had not elaborated, and Halide had been too shy to question her further. Mahmoure thrived on secrecy; balancing the open and hidden facets of her life gave her a sense of control.

Down by the rose garden Halide mounted a set of steps. She

soon found herself at the lower gate leading to the well. Contained on three sides by a high wall, the well enclosure was large enough to hold three ancient fig trees and a copse of pines. In the center was a patch of grass, traversed by a path trodden by generations of water carriers. As Halide closed the latch behind her, one of the garden cats raced over her feet, scattering dirt in its wake. Startled, Halide watched while it slipped into the narrow opening at the foot of one of the fig trees and vanished. Tiptoeing over to the tree, she got down on her hands and knees and put her ear against the damp wood. Sure enough, a faint mewling issued from inside. She decided to return later with food smuggled from the kitchen. On numerous occasions this love of animals had gotten her into trouble with the cooks.

Dead leaves drifted from the trees and fell into the dank greenish depths of the well. Halide watched them disappear. The harem was rife with rumors concerning the peris who lurked in the still water at the bottom of the well. Granny claimed to have heard them moaning just as the sun went down. Halide didn't want to believe that these unworldly spirits skulked about the grounds. Peris, it was said, disguised themselves as mortals, playing tricks on the households where they settled. Good or evil, their intent was to waylay unwary humans and create havoc. Granny had warned her to take care, and to keep away from the well enclosure, especially after dark.

Halide heard a scuffling noise behind her, in the pine grove. Her heart beat faster and she didn't dare turn around.

"Halide, Halide, over here!"

"Mahmoure?"

She half turned and saw Mahmoure emerging from the trees, looking decidedly disheveled. Dead needles clung to her hair, and her dress was splotched with mud. Ash fell from the cigarette clutched in her hand.

"What's the matter?" Mahmoure asked accusingly. "You look as if you've seen a ghost."

"This place is frightening."

"That's why I hide here. No one will look for me near the well—they're all afraid of the peris. You're not . . ." Mahmoure moved closer until her face almost touched Halide's. She sucked her cigarette defiantly and blew smoke rings in the air. "You're not frightened, are you? That stuff about the peris is nonsense."

"Granny's looking for you," Halide said quickly, unwilling to admit she was terrified.

"I know, I know."

"You'd better go in before you get in more trouble." Was it her imagination or had Mahmoure been crying?

"I'm in enough trouble as it is. It can't get any worse." Mahmoure tossed down the stub and ground it into the soil with her heel.

"Why? What's going on? I saw trays of sweetmeats laid out in the kitchen, and Arzu is going around in circles cleaning everything in sight."

"The *görücü* and her entourage are coming to look me over."

"The matchmaker? Surely not, there must be a mistake!"

"Granny wants me to put on a dress, comb my hair, and act demurely so that these women I don't know can tell all and sundry that I'm available for marriage. Well, I won't do it. I refuse." Mahmoure kicked the ground with the toe of her boot.

"It must be a mistake. Maybe Father can sort it out. No, wait, Father's at the palace. Maybe Teyze can do something." Bewildered, Halide started in the direction of the harem, but Mahmoure pulled her back.

"Don't go—no one must know where I'm hiding."

"But you can't stay out here. Sooner or later they'll find you."

"You're the only one I can trust, Halide. Please help me."

"What can I do?"

"*Mahmoure, where are you?*" Suddenly they heard Riza's voice coming from the direction of the men's quarters.

"It's him, I've got to get away," hissed Mahmoure, clutching Halide's arm so tight her grip burned her skin.

"But why? I thought Riza really liked you."

"We are, that is, we were. . . . I don't know what happened. When we heard the *görücü* was coming he promised to talk to your father about our betrothal, and then, without any warning, he became like a stranger." Mahmoure stumbled over her words, on the verge of tears.

"You're too young to get married," Halide said. Since the day of Mahmoure's abrupt appearance almost eighteen months earlier she had come to think of her as the sister she'd had never had. She was a playmate and companion, a child like herself. Marriage belonged to the adult world, barely visible on the distant horizon.

"I'm old enough to wear a veil, therefore I'm old enough to marry."

"But you're only fourteen! Who gets married at that age?"

"They cover us up so that we can't be seen by other men, which means we must be desirable. If I've become desirable, I can be married."

"Desirable?" Halide sensed they were straying toward matters she did not understand.

"Riza wants to marry me. Or so he said, until he went to see Edib Pasha."

Before Halide had a chance to respond they heard Riza's voice again, this time close by.

"I'm going. If I stay here any longer I'm doomed." Mahmoure spun around and started off toward the gate. Without giving the matter a second thought, Halide hurried after her.

Mahmoure vaulted over the wall and ran along the path toward the garden adjacent to the men's quarters. The two of them dashed down the hill through the apple orchard until they reached the wall dividing their grounds from the outskirts of Beshiktash. At last Mahmoure stopped. Behind them, Riza's voice was nothing but a faint echo.

"Don't come any farther, Halide. It will mean trouble."

"Where are you going?"

"Promise not to tell?"

"Only if you're not in danger." Halide shivered. Dusk had begun to close in around them and there was something about this time of day that made her uneasy.

"It's a secret, a matter of life and death."

"I swear on my heart I won't tell a soul."

"My father has returned and I'm going to our old house to see him."

Halide leaned back against the wall and looked at Mahmoure, her eyes wide with astonishment. "I don't believe you," she said in a hushed tone. "You told me he was in exile."

"He's come back. I overheard your father telling Ali Pasha."

"How would my father know?"

"They're friends, my father told me. Now I'm off. Take care, Halide, and don't try to follow me."

"Mahmoure, wait—" Panic rose in Halide's throat at the thought of being left alone again, but Mahmoure paid no attention. She was streaking down the hill toward the road, exhilarated by the prospect of seeing home.

Chapter Three

"Oh, the shame of it!" Granny twisted her prayer beads through her fingers. The *görücü*'s visit was still fresh in her mind. The smell of cigarettes lingered in the salon, a fateful reminder of the dreadful afternoon.

"She has ruined her prospects of making a successful alliance," said Teyze, looking at Edib out of the corner of her eye.

"It will be the talk of the neighborhood," Granny sighed. People would say this latest calamity was inevitable, that Mahmoure was cursed with the same reckless nature as her parents. She could not escape from fate.

"It's a good thing you have already found an appropriate suitor, Fatma Hanim Efendi, or I dread to think what the future would hold for her."

"The financial arrangements will be completed next week, God willing."

"Ladies, ladies, please, we're missing the point." Edib clicked his tongue impatiently. He did not approve of the *görücü*. Marital alliances were the business of the family, not inquisitive women like Fusun Hanim. Parting the curtains with his finger, he peered through the glass into the darkened garden. "Do you think she is still out there?"

"She hasn't returned to the harem; we've searched every room," said Teyze.

"Then where is she? I can't stay here all night." Edib's breathing was labored. He felt as if a thousand fists were pressing on his chest. There was urgent business to be dealt with at the palace: papers lay piled on his desk awaiting his attention, and first thing in the morning he was meeting with the grand vizier about strengthening ties with the Arab world, particularly the Hashemites from the Hejaz, a clan he had never trusted.

Edib wondered if this move to befriend former enemies of the regime was a deliberate step, on the part of the Sultan, to separate the Ottomans from Europe. Recently the Sultan had been influenced by the ideas of an Egyptian cleric, Jamal al-din al-Afghani, a man of great intellectual stature who, in fiery speeches and articles, appealed for the unification of the Islamic world. Afghani had defended the faith against attacks from French intellectuals, and sought to raise the moral and intellectual stature of Islam in the eyes of the West. Edib admired his mind but abhorred his anti-Western politics. There was talk of Afghani coming to live at Yildiz, and Edib had been given the task of providing accommodations for him. Why, he wondered, would the Sultan need such a man as a permanent guest?

"Ali Pasha ordered a search of the garden. The men found nothing except a pile of blankets in the old woodshed. Obviously that is where she was hiding," Granny said, laying her beads in her lap.

"What a mess," Edib muttered under his breath. Noticing how upset he was, Teyze took a glass of tea from the tray and brought it to him. The look he gave her as he accepted the glass told her that he was concerned. She had come to know his moods in the fifteen months since they were married. Edib was an even-tempered man who tended to be rather pessimistic, especially when he was tired. Fatigue also made him irritable, and she could see he was becoming impatient.

"Halide must know where she has gone," Teyze said quietly. "I saw them both running through the garden just before dusk."

"Then call her here at once." Edib struggled to keep his voice steady. He had been informed that Ali Shamil had returned to the city, ostensibly to reclaim a dozen of his finest Arab horses left behind in his hasty departure. The animals had been cared for by fellow Kurdish officers from the Sultan's cavalry while Ali Shamil had been in Antalya setting up his new home. Edib had the uneasy feeling that his last letter to the Kurdish chief about his daughter's infatuation for Riza might have had something to do with the timing of this return.

❦

"WHERE ARE we going?" Halide asked.

"To Yenikapi, near the Mevlevi lodge. That's where her father used to live." Teyze held on tight to her prayer beads and mouthed a silent plea for their safety.

"Where is that?"

"It's beyond Fatih, on the hills overlooking the sea."

"A long way away," said Halide, whose sense of distance became vague beyond the familiar boundaries of Beshiktash.

"We'll be there soon." Teyze watched the blurred outline of the city unfold through the mud-spattered window of their carriage. She sank back into her seat and allowed herself at last to relax. Through the flimsy floorboards she could hear the creaking of the springs as they jolted over the cobbled streets of old Stamboul. At this hour the city was almost deserted; only packs of wild dogs roamed at will through the narrow alleyways.

"Have we crossed the Galata Bridge yet?"

"It's far behind us." Teyze pressed her thumbs hard against her prayer beads. If they were stopped, difficult questions would be asked. The Sultan's network of spies was far-reaching and dangerous; informers had infiltrated every walk of life, setting neighbor against neighbor, creating fear and suspicion. Teyze had debated the possible dangers with Edib, and in the end her logic had prevailed. Edib would risk ruin if he were found near the home of Ali

Shamil Pasha. Old Ali Pasha, despite his vehement protests, was too frail and sick to travel. Teyze was quick to volunteer. It made sense to go with Halide because a woman with a child would arouse less suspicion. Besides, Teyze reasoned, Halide's presence might help once she reached the home of Ali Shamil.

"I didn't think Father would agree to let me come," Halide said, excited to be out so late and in the city.

"You're the only one who could persuade Mahmoure to return. If we find her, that is." Teyze was certain that Mahmoure was too headstrong and stubborn to listen to her.

"I hope she's safe," Halide said quickly.

They rode on in silence, listening to the carriage wheels clattering over the stones, occasionally gripping the velvet handles near the door to balance the violent movement.

"Do you know her father?"

"Only by reputation. His name is Ali Shamil Pasha; he is the leader of the Bedirkhans, a great Kurdish family."

"I heard Father talking about him with Granny and Grandpa."

"That's possible," Teyze said warily.

"He's done something wrong, but I don't remember what it was. Is that why he had to go away?"

"You'll have to ask your father, Halide. I cannot answer these questions."

"He'll never tell me," Halide said despondently, and turned to peer out the window. When Teyze had told her about her marriage to Edib, Halide had been shocked and confused. She'd wondered why he hadn't told her first and how he could do such a thing so soon after her mother's death. Halide loved both of them and wanted desperately to please her father, so she'd kept her feelings hidden. But Teyze had guessed that she was hurt and had done everything she could to alleviate her pain.

For a man who believed in an open, honest approach to political negotiations and deplored the intrigues of court life, Edib's secrecy concerning family matters was puzzling. Teyze had urged him to be straightforward with Halide about Mahmoure, but he'd ignored her suggestions. The unanswered questions left both girls feeling confused, and Teyze believed this had led directly to the present difficulties.

A light mist crept inland from the Sea of Marmara and drifted over the cobblestones. When the carriage came to a halt, Halide found herself in a narrow alley. The driver directed them to an unassuming door set close to the street, where they waited for some time in silence. Teyze was about to turn back when an unveiled woman ushered them into an open courtyard with pillared arches and elaborately tiled mosaics.

Trays of tea and sweetmeats had been laid out on silver platters in a chamber off the courtyard. Women soon appeared with bowls of steaming water perfumed with rose oil. Teyze and Halide dried their hands with towels as soft as silk.

No sooner had they settled into the divans than their welcome was interrupted by the appearance of three soldiers, chests crisscrossed with belts of bullets. Their complexions were darker than Halide had ever seen, and their bushy brows were almost hidden by their scarlet turbans. The men held their rifles close and arranged themselves at an equal distance beside the pillars. Teyze felt her heart race. The Kurds were, by reputation, a fierce and unpredictable people, answerable only to their own laws. She played nervously with the folds of her veil, leaving her tea untouched, and scrutinized her surroundings. The mosaics and carved pillars in the room, identical to those in the courtyard, were of the finest quality. For a man with such a reputation for fierceness, Ali Shamil seemed to possess a refined sensibility.

Halide slid onto the floor and helped herself to the tempting array of stuffed apricots, honeyed pastries, and sweet cherries. She was munching away contentedly when she heard the echo of footsteps coming across the courtyard. The guards hoisted their rifles to their shoulders and snapped to attention.

An energetic stranger swept into the room, his weathered face wreathed in a smile. He was taller than the guards, but had the same coloring and bristling mustache. Over his angular torso he wore a simple white caftan and a waistcoat embroidered with threads of pure gold. A scarlet turban was jammed on his head at a curious angle, as if thrown on in a hurry.

"Welcome to my home, Fikriye Hanim Efendi. I trust that you are refreshed after your journey." He faced them squarely, his hands planted on his hips. Halide was intrigued.

"I am exceedingly grateful to you for receiving us at this unusual hour," Teyze murmured. The man stood with his back to the light; behind the protective covering of her veil, Teyze's view of him was blurred.

"My household is at your disposal; I do not seek gratitude."

"I trust the messenger reached you," Teyze said. His perfunctory tone annoyed her: he wasn't addressing a servant.

"The boy came before sundown. I have attended to the matter: the streets are being searched." Drawing himself to his full height, he proffered an extravagant bow to Halide. "I haven't seen you since you were a baby, Halide Hanim. What a beautiful girl you have become."

Flattered by his attention, Halide tilted her head to one side and smiled.

"Aaaah, you have her look about you. That sweet smile I remember so well."

"It is often remarked how Halide has grown to be the image of her mother," Teyze rejoined quickly.

"If her spirit is that of her mother, she is blessed. Isn't that so, my child?"

"I hold her in my heart, sir," Halide said. "So in that way her spirit is indeed part of me."

"You have a philosophical perspective for one so young," Ali Shamil said with a smile.

"My father has engaged tutors for me so that I can learn the philosophies of both East and West."

Ali Shamil started. "My esteemed friend can always be trusted to know what is best for the women of his harem," he said at last. "It is rewarding to see a child, male or female, absorbing their lessons. It assures the continuity of proven wisdom."

"And opens the door to new paths," Teyze said curtly.

"How do you know my father?" Halide had warmed to him at once. Men who radiated assurance had that effect on her.

"Fate threw us together in the holy city of Mecca during the great cholera epidemic. I succumbed to illness and he nursed me without a thought for his own safety. Without his devotion, I would not be here today."

"That was very brave," Halide said wistfully. There was so much about her father's past she didn't know.

"I owe him a great debt," Ali Shamil said with a frown.

Halide's inquiry trailed off. She was distracted by the sound of crying that seemed to come from within the walls. Then a voice, faint but clear, began to sing the haunting cadences of the Mevlud.

"Alas, destiny has led us along separate paths. Are you ill, child? Your face is suddenly pale." He walked around the table and pressed his hand to her cheek.

"Don't you hear it?" she asked, turning to Teyze. "She's come back." Halide began to sway unsteadily.

"This has been a long day," Ali Shamil said decisively. "You must both rest." He clapped his hands, and at once the guards snapped to attention. Teyze shifted closer to Halide, eager to protect her.

"Why has my mother returned now?" Halide said as the voice grew fainter and the haunting melody died away.

"What is the child talking about?" Ali Shamil looked at Teyze expectantly.

"She hears these things from time to time," Teyze said.

"My first wife . . ." he began, then checked himself. "Come, I will summon a servant to take you to the harem, where you must spend the night. I will send word to Beshiktash."

"We didn't mean to intrude—" Teyze started to protest when Halide suddenly slumped sideways and fell across her lap.

"Halide needs a rest. I will take her myself." Ali Shamil gathered the child's limp body in his arms and carried her across the courtyard. The guards followed, and Teyze found herself alone. Somewhere in the recesses of the house was a fountain, and though she strained to catch the sound of singing, she heard only the rhythmic lap of water over stone.

❧

HALIDE WOKE with a start, wondering where she was. Then the memory of the previous day's events returned in a rush. First the dim recollection of someone carrying her through a maze of passageways, and then the echo of voices murmuring in her mind, crying and calling her name. They were silent now, but throughout the night they had haunted her dreams. She sat bolt upright, her heart pounding with fear. The voice of her mother was quieted, and Halide asked herself why she had come back so unexpectedly. Was she looking for something? Were the voices warning her of imminent danger? She did not know. Although her grandmother had told her to pay attention to the voices, their message was indistinct, and Halide sensed she had not yet grasped the full impact of her gift.

Outside it was still dark but pinpoints of light penetrated a grilled window set high in the wall. Nearby Halide heard the even breathing of someone lost to sleep. Turning her head, she saw the outline of a body. It wasn't Teyze, who was delicate and small-boned. Who was it? She lay still, unable to sleep. Unlike Beshiktash, here there were many sounds disturbing the night: the howling of street dogs, a low thud of waves breaking against the seawall, the cry of the night watchman. Nearer at hand she could hear voices raised in laughter: human voices this time and cheerful company by the sound of it.

Halide slid off her bed and shivered as her feet touched the stone floor. Holding her breath so as not to disturb the sleeping stranger, she tiptoed across the room. The door swung open at a touch, and she found herself in a gallery running alongside an open courtyard. The garden was filled with skeletal trees and shrubs outlined by the silvery-gray moonlight. The night air was cold, and Halide sneezed. Fearing discovery, she slipped back into the shadows. The laughter ceased and night pressed in. Keeping a watchful eye on the garden, she crept over the flagstones without any idea where she was going. Suddenly the sound of a man's voice startled her. Without realizing it, she had strayed into the men's quarters.

"It is madness to roam in the streets after dark. If Abdul hadn't found you, I shudder to think what might have happened."

"No one would dare to harm a blood relative of Ali Shamil Pasha."

Halide stood stock-still. The second voice was Mahmoure's.

"Your reckless behavior has caused great distress to Edib Pasha and his family."

Halide drew back into the protective shadow of the wall.

"They wanted to pledge me to a stranger. The grandson of an Imam, someone I've never met in my life."

"I have given my consent to the betrothal. Who are you to question these arrangements?"

Through the wall Halide heard the sound of sobbing.

"Compose yourself. Your tears will not move me."

"But I care for someone else."

"I know all about him; Edib sent word to me in exile."

"Riza is Edib Pasha's friend. I don't understand what you have against him. He'll be a good son to you—"

"He is a penniless orphan, an army officer who repaid his sponsor's generosity by seducing his charge. Your association has brought shame on our family."

"But I was as much to blame as him."

"That's enough." Ali Shamil cut her short. He was not interested in excuses.

"Why won't you listen?"

"Your husband-to-be is the grandson of the Imam of Suleimaniye. You are fortunate to make such a match."

"I don't care if he is the Sultan himself," Mahmoure cried. "I won't marry him!"

"How dare you speak to me that way. You forget yourself."

"Why are you turning against me? I was sure you, of all people, would help us. I don't have to obey Ali Pasha, only you—you are my father!" Mahmoure was shouting hysterically.

"Enough! You will do as they ask. They are your grandparents." Halide pressed closer to the wall, unable to believe what she was hearing.

"You're joking, tell me you are joking," Mahmoure cried.

"Ali Pasha and Fatma Hanim are your mother's parents."

"You're just saying this to make me agree to this betrothal."

"Selima and I parted when you were an infant. I agreed to her parents' demands for a divorce on condition that you would live under my roof."

"You told me my mother was dead."

"I lied to protect myself from questions you were sure to ask. I loved your mother. To survive I had to erase her name from my memory." Ali Shamil's voice grew fainter, and Halide had to strain to hear every word.

"So they are my family," Mahmoure said, stunned. "My blood relatives."

"Get down on your knees and praise God for your good fortune."

"Then let me stay with them—don't make me marry a stranger!"

"It is my duty to see you are settled."

"I don't want to be married to a stranger."

"You will do as you are told so that I may return to Antalya with some measure of peace in my heart."

There was a scuffling sound on the other side of the wall and Halide could not tell what was happening. Gradually Ali Shamil's voice faded and Halide heard a door slam. She turned away and crept into the garden, where she sat cross-legged on one of the marble benches and stared at the fountain.

So Mahmoure was her sister after all. She'd always had the sense they were bound together by ties deeper and more profound than simple friendship. But now they were going to take her away. The prospect of being alone again was more than she could bear. Sobbing quietly she returned to her room and lay awake all night, until the sky turned gold, then blue, and another bright winter morning dawned. It was only later, on the way home to Beshiktash, that Halide thought she understood why she had heard her mother's voice again.

Chapter Four

Teyze's currency rose after that night, for she had risked her life and defied the secret police to bring Mahmoure home, but the escapade disturbed the tranquillity of life at Beshiktash for some time. Dangerous memories were dredged up and rehashed in a swirl of gossip. Those servants who were old enough claimed to remember the events as if they had happened yesterday. The younger ones listened with amazement. Ali Shamil Pasha was a name known only by reputation. They marveled to learn he had once lived under this same roof for two turbulent years while married to the Pasha's daughter. What a strange match it had been! Of course it had ended in disaster, when one of Ali Shamil's brothers accidentally shot Shayeste Hanim, an old and valued servant, during one of their boisterous rampages. The bullet holes could still be seen in the hallway ceiling near the stairs.

The Pasha and his wife, their powers of recollection dimmed by old age, saw things in a rosier light. Fate had returned their grandchild for the second time; surely Selima was watching over them. Confirming this sense of deliverance was a letter written personally by Ali Shamil in the flourishing Arabic script he had learned as a child. It was addressed to the old Pasha. Just as they were getting into the carriage to return to Beshiktash, one of the guards had pressed it into Teyze's hand and sworn her to secrecy; no one, not even Edib, must know of its existence. His master's life depended on it.

Someone had to tell Mahmoure that the plans for the betrothal were still in effect. While Edib was wondering how to do this, Ali

Pasha hobbled into the room. Edib hurried over and took his arm. Lately the Pasha had become so thin his hands looked like gnarled twigs. Edib wondered what had brought his father-in-law downstairs, for usually the old man rested in the afternoon. Without saying a word they walked to the long windows overlooking the *selamlik* garden. The terrace was littered with shattered pots and spilled soil.

"It's beautiful here, even when the land is bare. We are blessed to live in such a city," the old Pasha whispered in a cracked voice.

"Fortunate indeed," concurred Edib.

"See how the ice bends the boughs of the old fig tree," he murmured, moving his hand slowly across the window.

"It is a miracle that tree has survived."

"It is God's will, my son. When the spring comes round again the warm air will melt the ice and He will cause the tree, and everything else we see, to bloom again."

The Pasha sighed. Faith in God had guided him for his whole life. Even the greatest hardships could be tolerated with a clear understanding of God's compassion. The old man took pride in having lived an honorable life, serving first as chief coffeemaker in the court of Sultan Abdulaziz and, later, in the offices of the grand vizier. Like his father and his father's father, who had perished in the purge of the Janissaries over half a century before, his ties to his fellow Bektashi dervishes ran deep. The continuation of the order was vital in these unsettled times.

"I'm going to install another heater in the *selamlik*. If this winter is as bad as the last, I'm worried . . ."

"Worried about what?"

"I don't want you to suffer from the cold," Edib said. Shoving his hands into his pockets, Edib started to pace restlessly up and down the narrow space between the divan and the window.

"You seem distraught, dear boy. Is something troubling you?"

"This business with Riza is very upsetting."

"I thought he had left the city."

"Yesterday at dawn. He received a commission with a cavalry unit in Bursa and had to join them immediately." Edib shook his head. "Can you believe that he feigned surprise when I questioned him about Mahmoure's disappearance? He did not say a word to me about their attachment."

"Perhaps he thought it more honorable to say nothing."

"I feel betrayed. Mahmoure was entrusted to my care and I failed to protect her."

"I don't think Riza is entirely to blame. They are both young, and Mahmoure has an impetuous streak in her."

"Riza did not behave with honor."

"Ah, Edib, where these matters are concerned it is hard to maintain a code of conduct."

"Fortunately, word of her affection for my former protégé has not reached her fiancé's family. They have agreed to announce the betrothal next week, and the wedding is planned for early spring." Edib sounded abashed. "I don't like duplicity, but in this case I feel it is in the best interests of everyone concerned. Mahmoure won't do such a thing again, I am certain."

"What makes you so sure?"

"Ali Shamil gave me his word in a letter. She would not dare dishonor her family name."

The Pasha regarded him through half-closed eyes. Sometimes Edib's naive faith was baffling. When he had heard that Edib had nursed Ali Shamil through the cholera epidemic in Mecca, he had asked his son-in-law why he had risked his life for a man of such quixotic and unpredictable temperament, a man who might have slain him on the spot had he known Edib was married to Selima.

"Ali Shamil is a man of honor," Edib had replied at the time. "I trusted him." And that was all he'd ever said.

"I saw no reason to bring up the subject of Riza to Ahmet's family. Was I wrong?" Edib said, breaking into the Pasha's thoughts.

"No, no, no, you did right. Why stir calm waters? It's just that I'm not convinced that Ahmet is the right choice."

"The boy's grandmother is a cousin to Fatma Hanim Efendi."

"Second cousin," said the old man, laying ambiguous emphasis on the word "second."

"He is the grandson of the chief Imam of Suleimaniye. They are a family of position and means."

"My dear wife is a practical woman. She would never promise her granddaughter to a penniless man. I'm sure the spirits concur with her on that point," the Pasha added with a smile.

"He is devout, hardworking, and quite agreeable looking."

"You're right; take no notice of my meanderings. The sooner you tell her, the better."

Outside, the sky had turned an ominous shade of gray. It was going to be a hard winter, he felt it in his bones.

"The emotions of young women are unpredictable. I have no desire to upset Mahmoure any more than is necessary, but she must understand that the marriage will be for her own good."

"Women see these things differently. If I were in your position I would have consulted my dear wife. What does your wife advise?"

"My wife?" Edib looked momentarily puzzled. "Oh, you mean Teyze. She thinks it is a good idea, although she has reservations about Mahmoure's age. These days fourteen is unusually young."

"Her mother was only fifteen when—"

"I know, I know," Edib said hastily.

"Sometimes youth is necessary for producing children."

"That is true," Edib sighed. The old man had unwittingly struck at the heart of one of his problems. How had he allowed his life to become so complicated?

"Has Ali Shamil been told?"

"Of course. I would not dream of acting without his approval."

"He didn't have any candidates of his own lined up then?" chuckled the old man.

"Oh no," said Edib. "He may be in exile for a long time, and he wants to see his daughter safely settled. Her unruly behavior displeased him."

"Did it?" mused Ali Pasha. "How curious, coming from the most unruly man I have ever known."

"Age has tempered his wild spirit."

"Yet he stands accused of murder."

"There were no witnesses, only the testimony of a known secret agent. The Bedirkhans have been a thorn in the side of the Sultan for many years."

Many years before, Bedirkhan Pasha, Ali Shamil's father, had been brought to Istanbul after an uprising in Kurdistan that had almost toppled the Ottoman regime. In exchange for their vast lands in Kurdistan, the government had given him and his ninety sons homes in the city, good salaries, and commissions in the cavalry. From that time on the Kurds were frequently employed as troubleshooters, and it was in this capacity that Ali Shamil had been sent to Mecca by Abdulhamid to help depose the mutinous Serif Abdullah. Edib admired the Bedirkhan family. Like the hooded falcons used by the Arabs to hunt down prey in the desert, they were proud and fearless. Since their fateful encounter in Mecca, Edib had loved Ali Shamil like a brother, and the news of his banishment had troubled him deeply.

"Whatever happened, it was God's will. Even Ali Shamil cannot escape his destiny," the old man added with a smile.

Just then he noticed Mahmoure and Halide crossing the hallway, followed by Teyze. Both girls had come to resemble their mother in unexpected ways. With Mahmoure, the likeness was more subtle. She walked with the same light gait, swinging her arms and moving her head in rhythm with her body. She had a defiant, optimistic spirit about her, while little Halide, physically the image of Selima, trotted behind obediently, her curls bobbing on her shoulders.

When she caught sight of her husband, Teyze hurried over, arms outstretched to embrace him. "You look tired, my dear," she said.

"I have a meeting with von Bieberstein later, and you know what that means." Edib gave her a quick smile and turned away; he did not like these outward displays of emotion.

"Oh dear." Teyze drew back with concern. Since the visit of Kaiser Wilhelm the previous year, she knew her husband had been worried about the growing influence of the Germans. Edib favored an alliance with the English, but the Sultan feared the British and their designs on Ottoman territory. His fears were fanned by the German ambassador, Baron Marschall von Bieberstein, and Edib felt obliged to move with caution when dealing with him.

Edib believed that the Sultan was too easily swayed by the trappings of German power and money. The Ottomans, who did not understand commerce, were already in debt to the West. Borrowing more money from Germany to build up the army would only set them on a dangerous trajectory. The Empire was crumbling, and centralized power, once the ballast of the regime, had weakened. Nationalist uprisings had brought chaos to the Balkans, and now it was spreading to the Arab provinces. Locked up in his palace with his visions of restoring the Islamic Empire to its former glory, the Sultan appeared to be oblivious to the forces gathering in the outside world. His reforms improved the lot of the ordinary man, but the better-educated populace would one day revolt against his draconian rule—of this Edib was certain. The only hope for the future lay with liberal-minded men like himself. Edib's principles obliged him to remain at court no matter how difficult circumstances became. Beneath the layers of religious mania, the Sultan was, Edib had to believe, a progressive man.

When they were first married, Edib had shared his concerns about the Sultan with Teyze. Since their marriage they had grown closer, although Edib seemed afraid of stepping across a certain boundary of intimacy. Teyze was saddened by this. She had hoped for an intimate, more passionate marriage. She did her best to conceal her true feelings and was at all times composed and even tempered, but as the months passed her brilliant disguise began to weigh on her. Love was an unruly emotion, but she was unafraid; the dizzying void it promised was at once exciting and enticing. Given the chance, she would have broken out of her shell and loved him with all her heart.

Edib continued to be polite but distant. Eight months into their marriage their lovemaking had ceased. Alone in the harem Teyze often wondered how she had failed her husband. When she broached the subject, he brushed her concerns aside. Their placid relations suited his vision of the perfect marriage; he was an organized man who disliked uncertainty. The loss of Selima had turned his world upside down and he dared not risk such suffering again. His only comfort had been their daughter, Halide. He would be eternally grateful to Teyze for helping him with her upbringing and education.

Chapter Five

High on a hill beyond the men's bathhouse was a little-used building that had once served as the formal reception rooms for the men's quarters, back in the days when the house was surrounded by open country and the Sultan lived closer to the city. Halide remembered a time when an elderly cousin of her grandmother's had paid an extended visit with her retinue of slaves and servants; the building had been refurbished to house the overflow, much to the chagrin of Arzu, who had to oversee the cleaning. Halide had dawdled behind her grandmother on her final inspection tour, following her through a succession of gilded doors into what she remembered as spacious and gloomy rooms.

Since her return, Mahmoure had been transferred to a suite in the wing where, under the guidance of a capable Anatolian, she was being taught to run her own household. It was rumored that Ali Shamil himself had written to the old couple asking that his daughter be kept under lock and key until she was safely married. The wedding was planned for the end of April, nearly three months away. Mahmoure and her husband were going to live in Suleimaniye, where a suitable house had been found and furnished by her future in-laws. As the day of the wedding approached, night after night Halide cried herself to sleep. No sooner had she discovered her sister than fate had conspired to snatch her away again.

Ten weeks had passed since Mahmoure had returned from her father's house, but the sisters saw each other only at mealtimes, surrounded by the din and chatter of the harem. On those occasions Mahmoure was morose and withdrawn and rarely spoke except to ask for water. Halide held her secret close, waiting for an opportunity that never came. If she could only be alone with Mahmoure, she thought, even for a few minutes, then they could talk as sisters bound by the blood of their mother. But as the winter rolled on she started to lose hope. During the afternoons when she was supposed to be studying English verbs she passed the time devising a plan to get into the old building without being seen.

Her chance came one wintry afternoon in February, when Teyze was confined to her room with a chest ailment. Her grandmother, along with Arzu and a group of slaves, had left early that morning to visit Mahmoure's future in-laws in the old city. By the time Halide's lessons were over the main rooms in the harem were deserted. Wrapping herself against the cold, Halide crept out by way of the kitchen. She was lucky: the gardeners had been called to a neighbor's to help rebuild a fallen wall. She slipped through the garden unobserved and crept around the side of the bathhouse. Directly ahead was an open yard bounded by a low wall. She had expected to find it deserted, but instead she came across a boy she had never seen before sprawled on the ground playing with a kitten.

He did not come from the village: his waistcoat and breeches were made of leather, richly embroidered with gold thread. Halide drew closer. The boy looked up, sensing that someone was nearby. His face was in the shadows, and she could only see his curly hair, cut close to his head, which stuck out in tufts around his ears. When he caught sight of her watching him, he waved. Halide's apprehension mounted. Who was he? And what was he doing here? He waved again, this time more insistently.

"Come see my kitten," he called out.

"Who are you?" Halide edged away from the bathhouse wall, wondering if she should run back to the harem.

"You mustn't be afraid. The old woman's gone to a funeral in Beshiktash."

The voice was familiar and Halide moved closer, narrowing her eyes against the light. She stopped dead in her tracks and then raced forward. Now there wasn't a doubt in her mind: the "boy" was Mahmoure!

They moved inside to a faded reception room, a melancholy setting for their reunion. There was no furniture, so they sat cross-legged on the floor, while the kitten wrestled with a ball of twine.

"You're very convincing. From a distance I mistook you for a boy." Halide's voice echoed off the bare walls.

"My father used to say I have a boy's spirit, but things got mixed up in the womb and I was born in the wrong skin."

"Where did you get those clothes?"

"I brought them back from Yenikapi. They belonged to my father. They're beautiful, aren't they?" Mahmoure ran her hand over the soft leather. She could smell her father's dried sweat in the folds of the shirt, and if she closed her eyes she could see him standing before her.

"I cut my hair off with the poultry shears. I did it this morning after my keeper left."

"You had such pretty curls," Halide said wistfully.

"I don't want my husband to desire me. When he takes my veil off on our wedding night I want his stomach to churn with disgust."

Halide nodded mutely. The marriage night was an encounter fraught with tension and excitement, a test of wills and a source of untold heartache. This much she had learned from harem gossip.

"The thought of a stranger touching me makes me sick."

"I hear he's a nice man."

"Good or bad, it makes no difference. There is only one man I want to marry, and they've sent him away." She bit her bottom lip, fighting back tears. Crying would not bring him back.

"A cavalry commission is a great honor."

"I don't believe he wanted to go to Bursa. He talked about going to Damascus to join the other revolutionaries from the military school. They are working to restore the constitution." Mahmoure paused. "Riza told me that the Turks had their own constitution once upon a time, but Abdulhamid did away with it."

"I didn't come here to talk to you about Riza," Halide said. At any moment one of the servants might return and find them here.

"What else is there to talk about?" Mahmoure snapped. "My future in-laws?" The kitten fell on his back with a yelp of pain, his paws caught up in the twine.

"I wanted to talk about our mother." Halide paused, waiting for Mahmoure to react, but she said nothing and watched the kitten squirming with a half smile.

"Remember that night I came to Yenikapi?" Halide persisted. "I overheard you talking to your father. I was shocked—I didn't know my mother had been married before."

Mahmoure picked up the kitten, unwound the string, and set it free. "I was pretty surprised at first," she said evenly. "But then it all started to make sense."

"Why didn't they tell us? Even when you came to live here in Beshiktash, no one said anything. Why?"

"Who can tell with adults." Mahmoure shrugged.

"There must be a reason."

"They eloped; it caused a great scandal."

"Our mother eloped?" Halide flushed with astonishment.

"When she was fifteen."

"I can't believe it."

"Their marriage was a love match," Mahmoure sighed. "But

my father's unruly ways drove your grandparents to distraction and they demanded a divorce. Selima was a dutiful daughter; in the end, she obeyed her parents."

Halide gasped. "Who told you this?"

"My father. To this day he has never forgiven himself. He loved her more than he loved any of his other wives. I'm afraid for him, Halide. He looked so desolate, and when we parted he wept. I've never seen my father cry."

Halide grabbed her sister's hand. "I don't want to lose you. I promise I will go to Grandfather and plead with him. You shouldn't have to marry a man you don't care for."

Mahmoure gave her a weak smile. "You're supposed to be the clever one, Halide. Haven't you learned that life is not so simple?"

Chapter Six

At the end of February the snow fell steadily for two days, enveloping the mosques and markets in a blanket of white. Clusters of icicles hung from the houses, and snow blocked the roads. The great house at Beshiktash was marooned in a sea of white. An arctic wind descended from the north, freezing the waters of the Bosphorus and covering the Golden Horn with a canopy of ice. Soon the harsh conditions began to take their toll across the city. Corpses awaiting burial accumulated at the mortuaries, because the frozen earth was too hard to pierce.

With her tutors stranded in their homes, Halide passed the time reading and daydreaming. She liked to sit in the bay window of the upstairs reception room, where the glass was patterned with faint traces of frozen snowflakes. The sky was leaden, and a lone bird circled above the yard. A swirl of snow, borne up by a squall, pirouetted through the garden and an avalanche of loose snow fell off the branches of the pine trees, tumbling noiselessly to the ground. Halide watched transfixed, until the last flake vanished in the dark air. Suddenly she heard her grandmother calling for her. Obediently she went in search of Granny, assuming she would find her in the men's quarters with Great-uncle Mehmet and his elderly retainer, both of whom had recently arrived from Erzurum.

Over the course of the winter the old Pasha had become increasingly frail. The gravity of his condition had not dawned on Halide until early February, when she'd plucked up the courage to talk to him about Mahmoure. Since he had become so delicate Halide was permitted to enter the men's quarters at will. She found him sitting alone in an upper room staring vacantly into space. When she tried to bring up the subject of Mahmoure's marriage, he seemed not to have heard her. Reaching out his hand, he patted her head and called her by her mother's name. Granny hurried in and led her away. Turning to look at him, Halide felt a pang of longing for the energetic man he had once been.

Once more the specter of illness hovered over the household, plunging everyone into a state of uncertainty. Peyker ordered the old Pasha confined to the men's quarters. With Edib stranded at the palace, there was no question of summoning the German doctor.

The moment Ali Pasha became ill Granny had sent word to Mehmet Pasha, his favorite brother, who, spurred by the seriousness of the situation, made the arduous journey from the plains of eastern Anatolia in five days. This feat of endurance fascinated the harem women, who openly longed for such strong and virile, albeit younger, men in their own lives. Mehmet Pasha was rumored to be over seventy, and this miracle was ascribed to a steady diet of sheep's-milk yogurt. He was small and strong, with fierce eyes and a shock of white hair.

"I'm coming as quickly as I can," Halide cried, running along the corridor that linked the harem with the men's quarters.

"Halide, hurry up!"

"Where are you, upstairs or downstairs?" Out of breath, she stopped at the foot of the main staircase and peered through the sweeping banisters toward the upper landing. No response. It was quiet all around; even the clocks had been silenced.

"Granny, I'm here!"

"I'm with your grandfather." The voice seemed to come from all around. Checking over her shoulder to make sure Granny wasn't in the hall, Halide began the upward climb.

"In the upper salon?" she said with one foot on the stairs.

"What's all this commotion?" Mehmet Pasha emerged from one of the side rooms, rubbing his eyes as if he had just woken up. When he saw his great-niece his manner softened. "Halide, what are you doing here?"

"Granny was calling for me. There, don't you hear her?"

"I don't hear anything. It's quiet, as it should be, child. Your poor grandfather is sleeping." Thinking that perhaps the old man was hard of hearing, Halide took his hand and led him to the center of the hall. He stopped and removed his woolen nightcap before turning his attention to his great-niece.

"Well?"

"Halide, where are you?" Granny's tone was becoming exasperated.

"I must go to her at once, she is getting angry." Halide sounded so convincing and looked so woebegone Mehmet Pasha took pity on her.

"Let's go to see for ourselves, shall we? Follow me. Your grandfather is in one of the back rooms." He started up the stairs two steps at a time, his sleeping robe billowing out behind him.

When they reached the door of the room, it was locked. The key suspended from a cord hung on the handle.

"Granny must be locked in—that's why she was calling for me." No wonder she sounded so faint, Halide thought. This explained why she hadn't been able to find her.

"Hush, we must be very quiet." Her uncle put his finger to his lips. With a deft twist he turned the key in the lock and pushed the door open. He poked his head in the room and was about to enter when something stopped him. With the palm of his hand he gently pushed Halide back into the corridor.

"Stay here, don't move. I want to check that he's warm enough."

Although he tried to sound firm, Halide thought she detected a note of anxiety in Great-uncle Mehmet's voice. She leaned against the wall. The hallway had a musty smell, and she put her hand over her mouth to stop herself from sneezing. She was surprised when her grandmother failed to emerge. Had Great-uncle Mehmet forgotten to tell her that she was outside? Minutes passed, and Halide began to grow anxious.

"Take my hand, Halide, and come with me." The old man hastened out of the room, his robes flapping like embroidered wings. Without waiting for a reply he grasped her hand and pulled her along behind him.

Through the half-open door Halide caught a glimpse of her grandfather stretched out on a divan, his head supported by a small pillow. He lay quite still, and there was no sign of Granny. She knew at once that her grandfather was dead; the voices had come back to tell her.

If this was her gift it was a mixed blessing, she decided, for there was nothing she could have done to prevent her grandfather from leaving this world. Like the night at Ali Shamil's, the voices had merely warned her of impending drama. There had to be more, some other way her gift could become uniquely hers, but what it was she did not know.

THE SNOW finally melted in early March and the temperature rose. Boats could pass once more up and down the Bosphorus. As the thaw continued, the streets filled with crowds released from their cold captivity. The ground softened, and the body of Ali Pasha was taken to the Karaca Ahmet cemetery on the hills above Scutari, where he was buried in the dervish enclosure, beside the tombs of his fellow Bektashis. The grave was marked by a simple stone inscribed with a line from the Koran declaring that God is eternal. When the ceremony was over, Halide leaned her head against the stone and whispered a prayer for the family. Mehmet Pasha stayed on to comfort his relatives and to talk about the past. Memories weighed heavily on the household, and the specter of death refused to be dispelled.

At the end of April, Mahmoure was married to Ahmet, the grandson of the Chief Imam of Suleimaniye. The wedding, held in the mansion at Beshiktash, was a muted affair, as the family was still in mourning. The women of the harem had circled Mahmoure's eyes with kohl and decorated her hands with henna because, it was said, the Prophet thought it pleasing for women to be painted in this way. She wore a white silk robe made in Pera by a French seamstress. A veil of heavy muslin covered her face until the moment at the end of the ceremony when she lifted it at the request of her new husband. Halide thought her sister looked beautiful, but Granny bemoaned the loss of her shiny curls.

The groom brought the ring in a wooden box inlaid with

mother-of-pearl, which he cradled in his arms as if it were made of porcelain. When he first glimpsed Mahmoure, standing alone under an arch decorated with flowers and red ribbons, he stopped and looked around, apparently wondering what to do next. The Imam stepped forward and gently propelled his grandson toward his bride. At his approach Mahmoure hung her head and refused to acknowledge him. Edib, who was watching from the terrace, felt a pang of concern. Throughout the ceremony Mahmoure kept her head down and clasped her hands to avoid touching her new husband. This unusual tranquillity was mistaken for a sign of happiness; only Halide knew how her sister was suffering.

"Beyond running away, I've no choice other than to go through with this marriage," Mahmoure had confided to her early that morning as they'd sat in the harem garden watching the sun rise over the Bosphorus.

"I tried to dissuade them, but no one, not even Father, would listen."

"I haven't heard a word from Riza. It's as if he disappeared off the face of the earth. Something's happened, Halide, that we don't know about." Mahmoure tossed the stub of her cigarette onto the ground, then quickly lit another.

"You don't think he's . . ."

"Dead, no, I would have seen it in my dreams."

Halide turned in amazement to look at her sister. "You have dreams too?" she whispered.

"Now what do you mean? Everyone dreams, even animals."

"But my dreams are special, they're strange. Sometimes I see what is going to happen to me and to those I love. And sometimes I see those who have left us when they come back to visit. I can hear them, but they can't hear me. I don't always know what they want, and when they call me I can't hear what they're saying."

"Father had an Arab wife from Medina who used to tell me to

pay attention to my dreams. She said it was God's way of talking to us. I'd laugh and then she'd curse me in Arabic," said Mahmoure with a wry smile, "and call me an infidel."

"Granny told me our dreams are precious, a gift we have inherited from our mother, and her mother before that."

Mahmoure shook her head. "You forget I never knew her."

"You are her child just the same—we are both descended from Eyoub."

"So what?"

"We have been given special powers because our family has an ancient connection to the Prophet."

Mahmoure rolled her eyes. "I can't believe I'm hearing this from you: you sound like that nutcase Granny brings here to cure the sick."

"You mean Peyker?"

"That's the one. She claims that she speaks to the spirits. You'll be telling me next you can do that too."

"But our mother—"

"Our mother is dead, my father is exiled, and I'm here alone and condemned to a future with a man I've met twice. How can you expect me to rejoice in my dreams when my life is the stuff of nightmares?"

"I've heard that your bridegroom is a nice man," Halide said, reaching out awkwardly to touch her sister. "I'll miss you. Will you come back and visit me?"

Mahmoure lit another cigarette and did not reply. Halide looked away. The sun was rising over the Asian shore and the morning fog had started to lift. Faint sounds of laughter emerged from the harem; Mahmoure's wedding day had begun.

Part Three

Chapter One

The death of Ali Pasha marked the end of an era in the mansion at Beshiktash. After forty years of married life, Fatma Hanim moved the entire household to a mansion in Scutari, an ancient Turkish neighborhood on the Asian shore, and leased Beshiktash to Reshat Bey, Mehmet Pasha's eldest son. Leaving the only home she had known since her teens was not as hard as she had imagined. Over the years the cadence of the *mahalle* had been transformed by an influx of new neighbors, high-ranking soldiers and bureaucrats who affected foreign manners and spoke French in the street. One night the voice of her grandmother came to her in a dream and advised her to follow her husband. Fatma Hanim sensed that her courtly, gentle world, ordered by the rhythms of Islam, could not survive long in the new hubbub of modernity.

For centuries the conscious ordering of the Ottoman universe had been circumscribed by the word of God revealed to His Prophet, Mohammed. "Be," He had said, and it was. The enduring and seemingly unshakable domain spread from the borderlands of Persia to the walls of Vienna. Law derived from the Koran bound the Muslim community; the fast of Ramazan was observed at the same time, and the pilgrimage, the Hajj, brought thousands of pilgrims to Mecca. They traveled from every corner of the Empire, confident that their journey was safe under the auspices of the Caliphate.

Then, around the dawn of the nineteenth century, military defeat came swiftly and surely at the hands of the Europeans. Defeat seared the Ottoman soul and shook the people out of their lethargy. Two strong-willed Sultans, Selim III and Mahmud II, cousins who had shared palace imprisonment at the hands of the reactionary old guard, set about acquiring the scientific knowledge needed to build military superiority without disturbing the essential nature of their Islamic realm. Members of the intelligentsia were sent to Europe and marveled at what they found. As the new century progressed, Mahmud II set about destroying the old institutions and pushing forward with modernization and political reform.

To this end, new military and government colleges were established to train the Ottoman elite, and professors were brought in from Europe to teach Western science. Gradually a new educated class emerged, who saw themselves through the lens of Western science and communicated this knowledge in the language of the infidel. These fresh perspectives challenged the proven wisdom of the learned men of the Empire, for whom science and religion were synonymous, expressed simply as *"ilm,"* the knowledge of God's universe.

New perspectives bred dissatisfaction, and trouble festered in the universities. Around the time of Ali Pasha's death, students at the Imperial Medical School formed a secret society for the sole purpose of overthrowing Sultan Abdulhamid. They called themselves the Committee for Union and Progress, the CUP. Participation was anonymous, and members were known to one another only by numbers. Hitherto the only organized opposition had existed beyond the boundaries of the Empire, in cities such as Paris and Geneva, where exiled dissidents, known as the Young Turks, congregated to continue their fight against the "great tyrant." The formation of the CUP marked the inception of the first organized opposition in Constantinople. The movement flourished and quickly spread to other government schools, including the Harbiye Military School, where Riza had been a student.

Human nature being what it is, these secret cells did not remain secret for long, and in the early years of the last decade of the nineteenth century rumors swept the city. In coffee shops and markets, in the Great Bazaar, on ferries crisscrossing the Bosphorus and in the courtyards of the great mosques, men whispered tales of conspiracy and revolution. Eventually word of the growing opposition reached the halls of Yildiz Palace, and Abdulhamid's vast spy network was put on alert. The offices of the secret police were flooded with reports. Arrests were made and dissident leaders summarily exiled without trial. But the opposition did not go away, and by 1896 the CUP membership included prominent men from the ulema, the dervish sects, and the bureaucracy. Then Kazim Pasha, commandant of the first division in Constantinople, was won over to the cause, and everything changed.

With the support of the first division, a coup d'état was planned for the month of August 1896, the same month that Armenian revolutionaries took over the Ottoman Bank and the slaughter of innocents began. The CUP knew nothing of the Armenian nationalist plans and had no sympathy for their ideals, though they were concerned about international ill will fostered by earlier attacks on the Armenian community. August was chosen because the CUP leadership, nervous at the prospect of detection and retribution, felt the need to act sooner rather than later. But a lone conspirator, carelessly drunk in Tokatliyan's restaurant, revealed the secret plan to an agent of the Sultan, and all was lost. Opposition leaders were taken from their homes and, along with their families, later exiled to distant corners of the Empire. The CUP collapsed and never again regained its former importance, although college students put together a new central committee.

Infuriated, threatened, and bitter, Abdulhamid turned his attention to Europe, where the Young Turks continued to publish revolutionary pamphlets and journals. Foremost among these was *Mechveret,* a magazine that reached the major cities of the Empire through the mails. Failing to convince the European governments to help him suppress his enemies, the Sultan dispatched one of his most trusted agents, Ahmet Jelaleddin Pasha, to Paris. His task was to persuade the exiled revolutionaries to return to Constantinople, with extravagant promises of forgiveness, reform, change, and freedom. Incredibly, many of the Young Turk leaders succumbed to the Sultan's offers, lured home by false hopes that vanished as soon as they set foot in the capital. Through lies and manipulation Abdulhamid had effectively ruined the Young Turk opposition.

At this point it may be necessary to say a little more about Sultan Abdulhamid. He was described by those who knew him as a shrewd, intelligent man who managed to hold on to power for more than thirty years. Contemporary observers tended to agree that the Sultan was at once reformer and tyrant, benevolent and wicked, a charismatic leader and a paranoid coward. To some, like the faithful Edib, he was an enlightened ruler led astray by religious fanatics who encouraged his dreams of ruling a renewed Islamic empire. To others he was a despotic tyrant concerned only for his personal security. The Sultan did not have the advantages of the education he brought to many of his subjects. Schooled in the harem and the infamous "cage," where princes of the house of Osman were confined until the time came for their succession, Abdulhamid ruled by instinct, his perceptions colored by the fate of his predecessors.

During his reign, the lives of the ordinary people improved, particularly in the capital, where a purification system provided the populace with clean water, roads were paved, and public education was expanded. Yet at the same time the Sultan's paranoia manifested itself in increased censorship, mass surveillance, and deportations.

By the time the coup d'état was exposed, almost twenty years had passed since the Sultan had closed parliament and dissolved the constitution. His hold on power seemed absolute. But even the most obdurate supporter could not deny that the borders of the Empire were shrinking, as nationalism festered in the Balkan provinces and along its eastern and southern fringes. Greece had declared independence more than sixty years earlier, followed by Serbia and Montenegro. Now a powerful Bulgarian state had emerged, threatening the borders of Macedonia and Albania. Constantinople became flooded with Muslim refugees fleeing the encroaching tides of nationalism.

At the other end of the Empire, in the heart of the Arabian desert, followers of Ibn Hanbal, decrying the decadence of the regime, were clamoring for a return to the pure Islam of the Koran. Under the leadership of Ibn Saud they challenged the right of the Ottoman Caliphate to protect the faith of Mohammed, and for a time took over the holy cities of Mecca and Medina. When the British occupied Egypt in 1882, they turned their attention to the Arabian Peninsula and made friendly overtures toward the disaffected sheiks. With the help of the Germans, Abdulhamid shored up his hold by building a railroad to Baghdad and the Persian Gulf; he later added an extension to carry pilgrims between Damascus and Mecca. The once steady and unshakable realm of Osman was under siege, and Abdulhamid, like a spider caught in its web, held tight to the fracturing threads.

Dispirited by the turmoil within the Empire and the perceived threat to his life, Abdulhamid turned inward until his private world was confined to Yildiz Park. Power had shifted from the Sublime Porte, the official seat of government, to the offices in the Buyuk Mabeyn, the chalet-style building adjacent to the main palace. The Yildiz complex had been turned into a small city as an abundance of new buildings went up, each designed in the most up-to-date style. The Sultan indulged his taste for luxury, with doors decorated in mother-of-pearl and wall lamps and cutlery fashioned from solid gold.

In recent years the Sultan's appearance had deteriorated; his teeth had yellowed, he dyed his beard, and his sunken cheeks made him look cadaverous. His physical decline seemed to mirror and reflect the disintegration of the city; although outwardly as beautiful as ever, Constantinople was riven by intrigue and dissent.

The poets looked on with consternation. Using words destined to haunt the city for decades, Tevfik Fikret called Constantinople a senile whore "shrouded in fog," no longer the bright sun warming the world. In the changing political atmosphere, writers shifted their focus. They no longer wrote of nightingales and roses and of the lovers reflected in still water. Now it was the intellectual life of Europe that held their attention. To avoid the censor, they wrote in a style that was deliberately abstruse, laden with Arabic and Persian phrases so that only the highly educated could comprehend this subtle but revolutionary message.

Despite the fact that his knowledge of European languages was scant, when Edib was promoted to first secretary he was placed in charge of liaising with the European embassies on behalf of Sultan Abdulhamid. This position lasted six months. Then, without explanation, he was abruptly moved to the treasury, for which he was ill prepared. Over the next five years, while retaining the title of first secretary, Edib zigzagged between ministries, never staying more than six months in one post. This erratic behavior neither surprised nor upset him, because everyone at his level was subject to the same treatment. The Ottoman bureaucracy was too large for the Sultan and his trusted advisers to control and supervise. Fearful of even his own administration, Abdulhamid conducted this game of musical chairs with all his high-ranking officials to prevent any one of them from accumulating too much power.

Due to a bureaucratic oversight, in the closing months of 1896 Edib found himself back in the same position he had held some seven years before. He was reappointed as chief liaison between the Sultan and important foreign embassies, a task that tested his diplomatic skills, because the French, Germans, Russians, and British all mistrusted one another. To add to his difficulties, Ottoman foreign policy was inconsistent. Edib was answerable to the grand vizier, but, like every other bureaucratic appointment, the grand vizier was always changing. Edib was left to navigate the diplomatic waters alone.

Negotiations were made more complicated by the constant use of translators. Not one of the foreign diplomats spoke Turkish, and Edib was frustrated by his own inability to speak a European language. He did not like to sit by helplessly while his conversations passed through a stranger, usually a graduate from the school of translation. Their power was disproportionate to their rank, and it troubled him to think that important diplomatic discussions could be made or broken by a subtle change of emphasis, or an untimely turn of phrase.

Edib worked closely with the first secretary at the British embassy. Edward Siddons was a tall, fair-haired man whose self-confidence and impeccable manners had impressed him. Not one word of direct conversation had ever passed between them. Had they been able to communicate, Edib was certain a close friendship would have developed, and he regretted the loss. Besides the simple joy of associating with such a fine man, there were many things he longed to know about the English approach to diplomacy and their view of the world, questions that could not be asked through a translator for fear of word getting back to the Sultan.

Edib knew it was too late for him to learn another language, so he made sure that Halide began an intensive study of English with a tutor recommended by Siddons. In time he would introduce French and German into her curriculum, but for now English was his priority. With extraordinary foresight, Edib believed English would one day be the politically dominant language of the Western world. When news of Halide's English lessons reached Yildiz, the Sultan was displeased. Edib was placed under surveillance and his every move was reported to the Sultan through the offices of Fehim Pasha, the head of the secret police.

THE FAMILY'S new home in Scutari was situated on the crest of a hill known as Sultan Tepe, the Hill of the Sultan, which overlooked the conjunction of the Bosphorus and the Sea of Marmara. In many ways the old wooden mansion was identical in spirit to the one they had left behind. Its empty rooms echoed with memories of a way of life that was passing. Before the family moved in, the mansion had stood empty for months, since few people could afford to live in large homes anymore. Granny felt at ease amid the crumbling stairwells and dusty corridors, where she sensed that the spirits of the old world lingered undisturbed.

The house had been built at the turn of the century by a grand vizier at the court of Selim III, to accommodate his four wives and their children. The harem and *selamlik* were housed in separate wings, connected by a two-story structure that contained the formal salons. From each window along the west wing, where the women lived, there was a view across the water to the minarets of the old city. The facade of the harem fronted an orchard of gnarled apple trees. The east wing, home of the men's quarters, faced the Marmara Sea.

When the *konak* was built, the main entrance consisted of nothing more than a pair of doors facing a courtyard adjacent to the stables. The previous owner, an Armenian banker, had added a larger entrance surmounted by a rococo arch. His intent had been to imitate Dolmabahçe Palace, but the simple lines of the mansion did not lend themselves to the drama of his ambitious designs. Four years after Edib's family moved in, the great earthquake of 1895 hit the Asian shore, and much of Scutari was reduced to rubble. Bazaars, mosques, bathhouses, and homes disappeared, and for days afterward people slept in the streets while the ground rumbled beneath them. At Sultan Tepe a wall between the *selamlik* and the stables collapsed, but no one was injured, and the house itself remained intact. Only the incongruous entrance collapsed in a pile of dust, a sign Granny attributed to the will of God.

For months afterward the ground shook and the harem women whispered among themselves that it was a sign from God warning the Turkish people to be vigilant. Why else had the European side remained unscathed? The infidels, with their strange manners and ungodly ways, were taking over their city and undermining the faith of their ancestors. There was a lesson to be learned from these events, and the older women cautioned the younger girls to observe the daily prayers and the word of the Holy Koran.

Two days before the earthquake, Fatma Hanim Efendi had seen the spirit of her mother wandering in the orchard. No messages had come to her, and she had assumed that the unexpected visit was connected somehow to the changes going on in her mind. Since the death of Ali Pasha, discerning the meaning of her visions had become increasingly difficult. Her inner and outer worlds had merged and it had become almost impossible to discriminate between the two. God was ever present, along with the spirits of her husband and her watchful ancestors, but the signs and the warnings were no longer apparent. When the disaster was over, Granny was left feeling profoundly uneasy.

Fatma Hanim had always been able to speak to the spirits. When she was younger she had used her gift to counsel the women of the harem and their neighbors in the *mahalle*. She was known throughout Beshiktash for her balanced wisdom. She saw the past and future in images that raced through her mind at unexpected moments. Like her mother and grandmother and great-grandmother before her, she treasured her ability and nurtured it with absolute faith in God. The daily ritual of prayer was an invisible wall that guarded her soul so her gift might flourish. But with the coming of old age her perceptions altered, as if seen through a kaleidoscope blending and shifting on a single plane.

Scutari was a quiet town where life moved slowly. The women of the harem adapted to their new surroundings, and their ordered routine continued more or less as before. There was only one change. Sultan Tepe was close to the Karaca Ahmet cemetery, and from the day she arrived in Scutari Granny began to visit her husband's grave, lingering alongside the tombs of his fellow dervishes. Convinced that the spirits of the dead never abandoned the living, she sought their guidance on everything. Death was part of life; of this she was certain.

As long as Halide remained a faithful Muslim, Granny was convinced she would retain her ability to hear the spirits. But Edib's plans for Halide were of great concern to her: the Western education he seemed so keen to give to his daughter threatened to eclipse the gift that had passed from generation to generation in the family. Granny felt she had a duty to protect it, and she had never been weak-willed when it came to getting her way.

WHEN SHE TURNED thirteen Halide was no longer permitted to wander at will in the men's quarters. She was given her own apartment on the second floor of the harem, furnished in the European style according to explicit instructions from Edib Pasha. The greater part of her day was taken up with studies, conducted in a light and spacious room overlooking the orchard. Sukri Efendi, a learned Imam attached to the Mirihma Mosque in Scutari, was engaged to perfect her Arabic, and a scholar from the nearby military academy came to teach her English. But her favorite tutor was Riza Tewfik, a gentle, erudite man who made the journey from the European quarter five times a week to tutor her in French, Turkish, and Persian literature.

Although Teyze had been reading Rumi's poetry to her for many years, it was Riza Tewfik who helped Halide understand the subtle connections between the worldly and the mystical, the religious and the profane, inherent in the language of the Persian poets. Night after night she read poetry until the candles burned low and her eyes ached. No poet was too complicated or arcane for her eager mind: Sanai, Attar, Pir Sultan Abdal, Jalaloddin Rumi, she read them all. The poets spoke of the mysterious oscillation between two levels of being, the transparent veil between the seen and unseen. Halide grasped their meaning as if by instinct, and wondered if the poems were drawn from the same source as her gift.

Poetry opened doors in her mind and led her along passages she might never have entered alone. How, she wondered, did the poets know God directly? Their images were drawn from everyday life; they wrote what they knew. As she read and reread the texts, layers of meaning were revealed just as the petals of a bud open to the flowering rose. With a flash of insight she wondered if the voices she heard, like the voices of the poets, came from within herself and not from some mysterious place in the unseen world Granny talked about.

Since the time of her grandfather's death the voices had come less frequently. Her grandmother had advised her to pay attention to what they said, but she heard nothing more than faint sobbing and strains of the Mevlud. It was her mother—of this she was certain. Selima came to her at times when she could feel the weight of her own sadness, when she missed Mahmoure or wondered why her father's visits to Sultan Tepe had become so infrequent. No sooner had the voice faded than her sadness would vanish, just as the hollow feeling had vanished after she had heard the Mevlud on the day of her mother's funeral.

Riza Tewfik was a scholar, not a Sufi master; there was a certain level in Persian mystical poetry beyond which he could not go. He voiced his concerns to Edib. Halide was becoming wrapped up in the deeper meaning of the poems at the expense of appreciating their beauty and literary value. Edib became very upset; her concerns harkened back to the mystical preoccupations of Selima. It happened that at that time Edib had been debating whether or not to enroll his daughter in the American Girls College. Over the years he had made several visits to the school. He had been impressed by their serious approach to study and their liberal curriculum, which included comparative religion and the new science of psychology. Most important for Edib, the American college was the only school in the city where lessons were taught in English. More than anything Edib wanted his daughter to be fluent in the language he had longed to master. For this he was prepared to risk the disapproval of the Sultan.

The school was housed in a mansion less than ten minutes by carriage from Sultan Tepe. From their first conversation the director, Dr. Mary Mills Patrick, had made it clear that she was eager to enroll their first Turkish student. The conversation with Riza Tewfik precipitated a decision: Halide would be sent away to school, even though the Sultan had banned his subjects from attending Christian institutions. There was no one Edib loved more than his daughter; he could not allow her remarkable intelligence to go to waste.

TEYZE CONTINUED to live in the women's quarters at Sultan Tepe. Both she and Edib Pasha felt that this arrangement would be better for Halide, who needed the continuity after the death of her mother and grandfather and the departure of Mahmoure, who had moved, with her husband, to the Suleimaniye quarter in the old city. Teyze's apartment was on the second floor, linked to the *selamlik* by a corridor and entered through double doors inlaid with ebony. As soon as she'd set eyes on the beautiful rooms, Teyze had claimed them as her own. During the day sunlight poured in through a line of tall windows that looked out across the Marmara Sea; at night moonlight trembled on the surface of the water, reflections shimmered on her ceiling and walls, and the words of the poets came back to haunt her.

> *I see my moon right here on earth*
> *What would I do with all the skies?*

Although Teyze no longer tutored Halide, she was still her constant companion. Together they explored the back lanes of Scutari and went to a small mosque that stood at the edge of the Bosphorus, where the sound of lapping water mingled with the murmured prayers. Three times a week the two of them went with Granny to the Karaca Ahmet cemetery to pray at the tombs of the dervish saints. Edib knew nothing of these outings and, after giving the matter careful thought, Teyze decided not to tell him. He would not understand, and she did not want him to become vexed with the old lady, for whom these visits were the center of her existence. The strain of keeping the secret gradually put a wedge between them.

Edib built a library for Teyze, complete with reading lamps, tables, and leather chairs. At first Teyze was content to spend long days in Sultan Tepe. The peaceful atmosphere of the old Turkish quarter calmed her, and she was happy enough with her books. Edib came every week, after the parade for Friday prayers was finished. He stayed with her in her suite, and for a few months after the move they were happy together.

Edib did not like to speak openly about affairs of state, but it was clear that all was not well at the palace. After the plot to overthrow the Sultan had been revealed, he had surrounded himself with bodyguards and withdrawn further into the protective circle of clerics. Though the Young Turks had been successfully disbanded, the atmosphere at Yildiz remained tense, as everyone fell under suspicion. No one knew whom to trust anymore as colleagues were set against one another and the secret police permeated every aspect of court life.

Continuing trouble with independent Greece now centered on the island of Crete, where the struggle for suzerainty had been going on for almost thirty years. Thousands of Muslims had perished at the hands of the Greek army and many more had fled to Constantinople, exacerbating the refugee problem. Russia and Britain were pressuring the Sultan to agree to an armistice. Their interference infuriated Abdulhamid, who turned his venom on bureaucrats like Edib known to favor an alliance with the English.

The strain on Edib began to show. When he returned to Sultan Tepe he was tired and tense. Desperate to regain his peace of mind, he shut himself away in his room and avoided spending the night with Teyze. Poor Teyze, who had no idea what was going on at court, blamed herself for his indifference. He had once thought her beautiful, but the passing years had traced lines across her face, and her body had become thin and brittle from bearing the strain of his absence. On the rare occasions when he turned to her, the atmosphere between them was fraught with tension.

To make matters worse, Edib was racked with guilt for spending so much time away from Halide. The subject of her education was never far from his mind, and he was always eager to hear about her progress. Teyze, who had once been so involved with his daughter's intellectual development, interpreted his concerns as an insult to their marriage. When he tried to discuss Halide's intellectual development she became silent and stifled her anger at this implied indifference to her own intellectual concerns.

There was another, pressing concern that nagged at Edib, a concern he was too proud to share. His financial situation was perilous. The economy was in disarray and the wages of palace bureaucrats had not been paid for months. He could barely afford to contribute to the upkeep of Sultan Tepe, and most of the costs were maintained by Granny. Although he knew his wife possessed a small fortune in gold and jewels, Edib could not bring himself to ask for help.

Teyze became prone to bouts of melancholy. She spent hours lying on her divan, gazing at the ceiling and saying nothing. Sometimes she did not leave her suite for days on end, refusing food and drinking only mint tea with honey. Now that she was older Halide was sensitive to these changes, and she worried that things between her father and Teyze were not as they should be.

Chapter Two

In early May a stranger walked up the drive to the Scutari mansion, taking long, purposeful strides. Halide watched him from her window. It was unusual for visitors to appear in this manner: gentlemen rarely walked; only peasants and the serving class moved about the city by foot. The visitor was tall and thin, his storklike appearance exacerbated by the fastidious angle of his fez. Despite the warm weather he was formally attired in a dark European suit.

Halide drew back from the window as he approached the mansion and continued to watch him from inside her room. His face was narrow; a wispy beard covered a pointed chin and his thin lips were half concealed by a bedraggled mustache. Yet his forehead was wide and his straight brows neatly brushed. His most striking feature were his deep-set eyes, which had a fixed, distant look about them.

A few yards from the main door of the men's quarters the man stopped and looked around, as if expecting to find someone behind him. He removed his fez and ran his long fingers through his hair; it was a graceful gesture, slow to the point of being drawn out. Then, hunching his shoulders, he moved forward. Moments later a bell rang, echoing through the silent house.

Halide had returned to her studies when a servant came to her door with a note from her father, asking her to join him in the salon. These days Edib Pasha's visits to Scutari were few and far between, so when he was there Halide tried to please him. She changed into a red taffeta dress. Her father was still particular about what she wore, and all her clothes continued to be made by his tailor in Pera. She tugged a comb through her hair, pinched her cheeks to produce a hint of color, and pulled on a pair of matching red boots she had never dared wear before. Since her grandmother allowed her only one small mirror, she had no idea if the overall effect was pleasing. At the last minute she decided against putting on a veil, because her father disapproved. Wearing the veil was, he thought, a sign of regressive thinking.

"COME IN, HALIDE." Her father beckoned to her. "That color becomes you." Giving him a shy smile, she walked over and kissed her father's hand. The stranger remained at the far end of the room, staring out the window.

"I didn't expect you and dressed in a hurry." She smoothed her skirt with the palm of her hand.

"I never know my schedule, you should know that by now." Edib slipped his arm around her waist and propelled her across the room. "Now come, my dear, I want you to meet a friend of mine, Salih Zeki Bey."

The newcomer snapped to attention and bowed. "Your father has been telling me all about you, mademoiselle."

"I hope he hasn't been boasting again," Halide murmured, looking down at the floor. This was the first time she had been presented to a man outside the family since she had started to wear the veil. Without its protection, she felt suddenly naked.

"He was certainly complimentary. But it seems you deserve it; your father tells me you are learning English, Arabic, and Persian." He had a gentle voice and spoke slowly, as if weighing every word.

"I can also read and write in Ottoman Turkish."

"Quite remarkable for someone of your age." He had been about to say "a girl" but had thought better of it.

"Zeki Bey has recently returned from Paris at the personal request of Sultan Abdulhamid himself."

"The Sultan? Why did he ask you to come back?" Halide raised her eyes and looked at him quickly.

"I was offered a post at the naval academy. The Sultan was good enough to offer a high salary and limited responsibilities, leaving me time for my research."

"Zeki Bey is one of our most distinguished scholars and mathematicians," Edib explained.

"Was Paris as beautiful as people say?" Halide asked, gathering confidence.

"Architecturally it is perfect; wherever the eye travels there is an exquisite facade perfectly proportioned, but . . ."

"But . . . ?"

"After a while this perfection becomes predictable. I found myself longing for the confusion and uneven quality of this city of ours."

"So you can't be fond of Pera," Halide said with a smile. "All the new buildings are designed to look exactly like Paris."

Zeki Bey laughed. His eyes rested on her for a minute, causing her to blush. "Pera is an anomaly, a freakish imitation that defies logic. I prefer the old Ottoman simplicity of the architect Sinan."

"Oh, so do I!" Halide cried. "I think the mosque of Suleimaniye is the most beautiful building in the world. Not that I have seen that much, of course."

"Suleimaniye is magnificent, particularily the dome." This girl was a contradiction, he mused, at one moment shy, the next outspoken and bold.

"I am glad you are in agreement with our guest," said Edib, taken aback by his daughter's manner.

"Halide and I will be in agreement on many things," Zeki Bey said with a flourish. He drained his glass and turned to put it on the mantle.

"Nevertheless, I dream of going to Paris one day," Halide persisted, watching him now more closely. In profile, his curved nose and high, flat forehead reminded her of her beloved grandfather.

"Perhaps when you are older we will have the opportunity to travel there," her father said, eager to move on.

"Paris is a city of uncertain moral standards," their guest said dryly. "You are better advised to wait until your daughter is of an age when she can see beyond its superficial sheen."

"You know better than I," Edib replied, and a silence briefly fell over the room.

"So, your father tells me you are leaving soon for the American Girls College," Salih Zeki resumed at last. "To my mind an interesting choice. What are your feelings on the subject?"

"Father wants me to become fluent in English." Halide clasped her hands in front of her and looked down at the floor.

"Ah, the language of the future," Salih Zeki said with a smile.

"Zeki Bey doesn't agree with me," Edib said. "He thinks German will one day dominate the globe."

"German, English, French, who knows. Anyway, it won't be Ottoman Turkish. Whatever language you learn, Halide, you will benefit." The visitor took off his spectacles and wiped them with his handkerchief.

"Halide will be their first Turkish student."

"I must say, Edib, I admire your courage."

"Courage has nothing to do with it," Edib said sharply. "There was no other choice. I don't want to see Halide's brilliant mind go to waste." The clock in the hall struck five. Edib took out his pocket watch and checked the time. "It's getting late—which ferry are you catching back to Galata?"

"I was told the boats run on Islamic time, so I will just go to the dock and wait."

Edib rolled his eyes. "This system is ludicrous. Old habits die hard."

"The last ferry leaves after the night prayers," Halide heard herself saying. "It isn't even dark yet, so you have hours, Zeki Bey."

The stranger nodded with a slight bow.

"You can take an afternoon nap on the ferry," Edib chuckled, just as a second clock in the library across the hall chimed the hour.

Halide settled on the sofa and helped herself to one of the sandwiches on the tea tray, an English tradition her father had instituted. The men walked over to the window and stood together.

"So, what do you think?" Edib whispered.

"She is diligent and serious; she will make an excellent student."

"Would you agree to tutor her in mathematics?"

"It will be my pleasure." Zeki Bey rested his elbows on the window sash and moved back to survey Halide from across the room.

"Thank you, my friend." Edib clasped Zeki Bey's shoulder. "It is the only subject in which she will be behind the other girls."

"I can come once a week, on Sundays, for two to three hours."

"Perfect, perfect. She will catch up in no time."

"The precise demands of mathematics will help balance the tendencies you mentioned earlier," Zeki Bey said in a low voice.

"Once she is away from the harem, I hope this way of thinking will disappear."

"Her mind is young and flexible; I don't see why it cannot be influenced."

"All the more reason for her to leave the harem. Now let me tell Halide the good news—she will be honored to have you as a tutor."

"The honor is all mine." Salih Zeki kept his back to the sofa while Edib rejoined his daughter. Was he doing the right thing? He had not expected to be so moved by the young girl's quiet beauty and restraint. For a man in his position, such feelings were dangerous and would have to be disciplined.

⚜

THAT NIGHT Edib lay awake thinking over the events of the day. The meeting had been a success; now that Salih Zeki Bey was guiding her, he felt assured that Halide was on her way to fulfilling her destiny. Zeki Bey's concise, logical mind would shape her intellect and help her master the discipline of logical thinking. Politically, he felt, there were difficult times ahead, but with her gift of intelligence Halide was going to escape the limitations of her class and upbringing.

Edib rarely slept through the night anymore. Problems crowded into his mind every time he closed his eyes. The previous summer, Armenian nationalists had seized the Ottoman Bank and murdered two guards. In retribution, innocent Armenians had been hunted down and killed in the streets and in their homes by mobs armed with sticks and knives. The government of the Sultan had done nothing to stop the bloodshed. The Western embassies had protested, but their letters had been ignored. Although Edib was able to save the Armenians in the household at Sultan Tepe, he mourned the lives lost in the slaughter, and was appalled by the official silence.

Edib wondered where this was going. What would become of the Ottoman Sultanate, an institution in place for more than five hundred years? In his heart he still believed in its validity, the brilliant balance between politics and religion. If only the Sultan had the wisdom to adapt without feeling threatened! But Abdulhamid hid behind the towering walls of Yildiz Palace, and fanned his fears with networks of spies.

Chapter Three

It seemed to Granny that the days passed more quickly after Edib Pasha's stunning announcement that Halide would leave the harem to live at the American school. In the midst of the confusion that ensued, she turned for practical help to Arzu, who compiled a list of things that had to be done in the four weeks before Halide was due to leave. Halide's English clothes, of which Granny strongly disapproved, were washed and repaired by the housemaids. Arzu, a skilled seamstress, made Halide two new nightgowns and a woolen cloak lined with shell-colored silk. Sheets, towels, and toiletries of the finest quality were packed in steamer trunks ready to be sent on ahead so that they would be waiting when Halide arrived. The cook made several batches of pistachio baklava, enough to feed the entire school, and packed them in a basket lined with cotton, along with several bottles of Granny's fruit syrup.

Three weeks after Salih Zeki's visit, Halide was awakened in the early hours of the morning by the muezzin's first call to prayer. She sat up in bed racked by sadness; she had dreamed about her mother. The dream had lasted a long time but only a fragment came back to her, an image of her mother wandering alone through the streets of a ruined city, searching for a house she could not find. Although her face was covered by a white veil, Halide knew she was weeping. The dream was so vivid that her heart was pounding when she awoke. She wondered if it was connected in some way with her visit to her sister.

Halide and Granny had made it a habit to spend every Saturday with Mahmoure and her family at their home in Suleimaniye. Their visit that morning would be the last for many months, because Halide was due to join the summer session at the American school at the end of June, less than a month away.

Mahmoure never came to Scutari. She made the excuse that the boat trip across the straits was too arduous for her children. There were three of them now, two girls aged five and three, solemn and round like their father, Ahmet, and a boisterous baby with sparkling eyes named Ali Shamil. But her distance from Sultan Tepe masked a deeper malaise. Soon after her first daughter was born, it was obvious to everyone that Mahmoure was not suited to motherhood. She became depressed and paid little attention to the child. As the other children came along her listlessness increased, and there were times when Halide found it hard to remember how lively and daring Mahmoure had once been. The Imam and his wife, who lived close by, made Mahmoure's state of mind worse by hinting that their son had had his pick of prospective brides, many of whom were still available.

Halide rolled up her bed, stowed it in the blanket trunk, and went downstairs. The call of the muezzin continued, and she could hear the women of the harem hurrying to prayer in the main salon. She knew she ought to join them, but she felt that just this once she needed to be alone, without people fussing around and treating her as if she were going into exile. Still, the heavy sadness persisted, and she could not shake off the memory of the dream.

The sun was well on its journey when Halide, Granny, and Arzu reached the quay and boarded the ferry. The straits were calm, so the three of them sat on deck, watching the gulls swoop and scream about the mast. As they rounded the corner of Seraglio Point, Halide thrilled at the sight of the great mosques emerging from the mist, their minarets shining in the early-morning sunlight. The Golden Horn stretched before them, covered by a mass of masts and bobbing hulls. In the distance the purple hills above Eyoub seemed to melt into the sky. If she traveled the world, Halide was certain, she would never find a more beautiful city.

Even at this early hour the quay swarmed with people. They quit the ferry at Eminonu, then found a carriage to take them to Suleimaniye. Mahmoure's family lived in one of the wooden houses in the shadow of the great mosque. Under the supervision of her husband's mother, Mahmoure had furnished their home in the Ottoman style. There were no modern amenities, not even a European bed, although Mahmoure had longed to own one. Their only servants were three local girls who came each day to help with the children and an elderly Kurd who tended their crowded vegetable garden.

There was a great deal of confusion as the children came in, carrying in their arms the latest batch of kittens born to the kitchen cat. Mahmoure, wearing her cloak and carrying a string of turquoise prayer beads, looked in to see what the noise was all about. Instead of joining the group as she usually did, she remained in the doorway, looking absently over the heads of her children.

"I'm just slipping out to go to the mosque," she said. "I didn't attend Friday prayers, which gives my in-laws another excuse to be angry with me." Mahmoure drew Halide into the passageway so that Granny could not hear their conversation.

"But you knew we were coming this morning," Halide said.

"I couldn't help it, I'm sorry. I have to go, for Ahmet's sake."

"Can't I come too? I hate to waste a minute of our visit."

"I'll be back soon."

"But we might not see each other for months," pleaded Halide, wounded by her reluctance.

"We can't talk in the mosque."

"We've been traveling for hours just to see you, Mahmoure. Please let me come with you."

Mahmoure hesitated, then held out her arms. "You're right," she said, "forgive me."

❀

ONCE THEY were outside in the daylight Halide noticed that her sister's eyes were ringed with kohl. Mahmoure had drawn a light veil across the lower half of her face, leaving her eyes exposed, and Halide thought the effect strangely disturbing. The two sisters cut across the garden and slipped through a gate in the wall that opened into the courtyard of the mosque. Hordes of bedraggled men and women were waiting to be fed in the shade of the giant plane trees. A shriek of anger occasionally rang out as someone tried to cut into the line. These were the refugees from Crete and Macedonia her father had spoken of with such concern. More disturbing to Halide were the many children, sitting in quiet groups, too weak and hungry to move.

Mahmoure walked on with her head held high, moving so fast Halide had to run to keep up with her. Soon they found themselves in the main courtyard, alongside the women's entrance. At this hour, just before the second prayers, the steps leading up to the door swarmed with veiled figures. Mahmoure continued across the courtyard toward the gardens.

"We're going the wrong way," Halide said, hurrying behind her sister.

"I'm going to the grave of Ahmet's grandfather."

"Whatever for?"

"Listen, Halide." Mahmoure wheeled around to face her. "I didn't ask you to come."

"I don't understand," Halide said with concern.

"We have to hurry . . ." Mahmoure's voice was drowned out by the cry of the Imam resounding from one of the minarets directly above them.

Crowds clogged the men's entrance and no one paid attention to them as they passed the line of fountains where latecomers performed their ablutions. When they finally reached the cemetery, they found it deserted; even the guardian of Suleiman's mausoleum was nowhere to be found. Mahmoure made her way past the royal tombs to the farthest corner of the cemetery, where more graves were concealed behind the high walls of the memorial for Suleiman's wife Roxelana. She sat down on a clump of grass and burst into tears.

"What is it? What's wrong?" Halide put out her hand and touched her sister's shoulder.

"My father is very ill."

"Oh God, I'm sorry." Halide lowered her head.

"I haven't slept for days."

"But how did you find out? I thought he was in exile."

"The family sent a messenger—he came last week."

"To the house?"

"No, no, he followed me to the market one day. Scared the life out of me." Mahmoure looked up and gave her a weak smile.

"Is that why we're here, to meet this messenger again?"

"He risked his life returning to the city."

"Are you certain this isn't a trick played by your father's enemies?"

"It's all true, Halide, trust me."

At that moment a stranger emerged from Roxelana's tomb. He looked about until he caught sight of the two women huddled by the graves. To all outward appearances he was a workingman, his skin burnt by the sun. He wore loose trousers and a leather waistcoat, but his bearing conveyed authority. He had fine features half concealed under a bushy beard, and when he stopped no more than an arm's length away, Halide noticed that his eyes were a startling shade of blue.

"Who's this?" he demanded. Halide knew the voice, but she could not remember where or when she had heard it.

"Don't be afraid—it's Halide Hanim under that veil," Mahmoure said, wiping away her tears. To Halide's horror, the stranger reached forward and grasped her shoulders. With a cry, she shook herself free and pulled back.

"Don't you recognize me?" he laughed.

"Stop fooling around, Riza. Tell me about my father—we don't have much time."

"Riza, is that you? What are you doing here? How do you know Ali Shamil is . . ." The questions flew through Halide's mind at dizzying speed. None of this made sense!

"It's a long story," he said, pushing the hair out of his face.

"How is Father? I can't eat or sleep for worrying." Mahmoure caught him playfully by the leg and held on fast, pressing her cheek against his calf. He knelt down and gently cupped her up-turned face in his hands.

"A coded message came today from Antalya saying that Ali Shamil is growing weaker. We can only wait and see."

"I can't hang around here while my father is dying. You must take me to him at once."

"It is far too dangerous, Mahmoure. Besides, how can we ride to Antalya without horses and a place to rest?"

"There is an old friend of my father's who lives near Kadikoy." Mahmoure was composed now, and determined. "He will give us fast horses without asking questions."

"You're a married woman. You can't leave your family, even for your father's sake."

"Yes, I can. I care for him more than anything in the world."

Mahmoure tore at the ground with her fingernails, ripping clumps of grass from the soil and tossing them at the graves. Riza put his arms around her and held her fast so that she could not move. Mahmoure slumped forward against his chest and began to sob uncontrollably. Halide did her best to comfort her sister, but she was inconsolable. The tears continued to stream down her cheeks as if all the disappointment and unhappiness of her life was flowing from her and finding refuge in this man's arms.

Chapter Four

As the day of her departure approached, Halide wandered around the harem as if in a trance, fearful of leaving the only home she had ever known, yet excited by the prospect of going away to school. How would she manage, she wondered, without Teyze, and where would she find time to write home in a day that was scheduled with lessons from dawn to dusk?

"I think you should take these prayer beads. They belonged to your mother," Teyze said, walking into Halide's room with a strand of turquoise beads. The floor was covered with piles of clothes, and an open trunk stood in the center of the room.

"What did you say, Teyze?"

"Come, come, child, what's the matter with you these days? These beads, do you want them? Your grandmother gave them to me to bring up here."

"Of course, anything . . ." Halide's voice trailed off. She had forgotten what she was going to say.

"Are you worried about going away?"

"No, it's not that. I mean, yes, of course I'm a little apprehensive. It's just that there is so much to do I hardly know where to start." Halide looked around at the piles all around her. She felt distracted and restless.

"You don't have to do anything except keep up with your studies for your father's sake. He has made a great sacrifice so that you might attend this school." Teyze's voice was sharp. Her own sadness and disappointment were encroaching on everything she touched. Not wanting to upset Halide, she hid her feelings under a brisk exterior.

"I just don't seem to be able to focus," Halide said plaintively.

"Once you've left here you'll find it easier to concentrate."

"I hope so."

"Now make yourself useful and help me pack." Teyze knelt beside the trunk and reached for the closest pile of clothing.

"Teyze . . ." Halide began. There was something else troubling her, but she didn't know if she could trust Teyze where Mahmoure was concerned.

"Yes?"

"Do you know if Father has had any news of Riza recently?"

"Riza? What a strange question. I haven't thought about him for years. I don't think your father has ever mentioned him. It's strange, isn't it—they were so close and then poof, he just disappeared from our lives. Why do you ask?"

"I thought I saw him again the other day in the old city, but I might have been wrong. It must be six or seven years since I last saw him."

"At least seven—we were still living at Beshiktash. I remember because soon after Riza went to Bursa his cavalry unit was relocated to the Dolmabahçe barracks, and naturally I asked your father if Riza would be returning to live with us. He flew into a rage and told me never to mention his name again. It was the first and last time I ever heard him raise his voice."

"How very odd," said Halide. It had been obvious from his unkempt appearance that Riza was no longer in the cavalry, but how, she wondered, was he connected to Ali Shamil?

IN THE LAST week of June, just as Halide was preparing to set off to school, trouble stirred within the Armenian community and the threat of bloodshed loomed over the city once again. The grand vizier ordered all senior bureaucrats to remain at the palace, and Edib was unable to accompany Halide to the American school. Granny insisted on going in his place. She had never heard of a young girl leaving home alone like this before marriage. Halide's departure set a precedent that was, to her mind, both troubling and dangerous.

With the help of Arzu she donned traditional court dress to remind Halide of her place in the world. As a descendent of Eyoub, standard-bearer to the Prophet, she was a member of the true aristocracy, the nobility of the faithful. Under her cloak she wore traditional loose trousers and a silk tunic, and her waistcoat and jacket were embroidered with gold thread. Unfortunately, the weight of the metal slowed her pace and made getting into the carriage difficult.

Halide carried nothing more with her that morning than a small bag and a leather-bound notebook given to her by Salih Zeki. Most of her belongings had been sent ahead in leather trunks. As the carriage lurched down the drive she wondered where her tutor was at that moment: teaching at the university or meeting with his brightest students? She was determined that one day she too would be one of the favored few who studied with him at the university.

"How will I address her, I wonder," Granny said, interrupting her daydreams. "Should I call her Hanim Efendi or Madam?"

"Of whom are you speaking, Granny?"

Granny paid no attention to Halide's question. "I don't think I've ever met an American before. I remember Germans, French, Greek, English, Italian, even Russians, but no, never an American."

"They're just like anyone else."

"What language do they speak in America? If she does not speak Turkish I can still recall a few greetings in Greek, maybe German." She furrowed her brow. "I should have thought of this before. How foolish of me."

"They speak English," Halide said loudly. The old lady looked at her as if hearing her for the first time.

"Why don't they have a language of their own?"

"I don't know," Halide replied, disconcerted by this question.

"In that case, you'll have to talk to her for me."

"To whom?"

"To your chief *hanim*, of course. I sent a messenger ahead of us to announce our arrival."

"Granny, why did you do that? I'm just a student, one of the youngest."

"It would be an unforgivable lapse in etiquette if the daughter and mother-in-law of Edib Pasha were to arrive without being received properly."

"Maybe they do things differently from us."

"Does that mean you will be taught a new code of behavior?" The old lady pulled her cloak across her chest, as if protecting herself.

"I will have to conform to their way of doing things," Halide said cautiously.

"You must never forget your manners, child." Halide nodded

mutely. "And promise me faithfully that whatever they teach you, you will guard your soul. It is a light in you, radiant, like the sun. If it is ever extinguished it will be a tragedy, for you will no longer know who you are."

"Granny, please don't fret," Halide said, leaning across the carriage and taking her hand. "I've promised you a dozen times I will never surrender my beliefs."

"Everyone at this school is Christian. You will be the only Muslim, so you must remember to pray five times a day for protection."

"I will do my best."

"You have a responsibility, Halide. To me, to your mother, and to all our forebears. It is not to be taken lightly." Having said this, Granny settled back in her seat and closed her eyes.

Halide felt the dense air in the carriage closing in on her. These days voices came less often and she rarely saw her mother in her dreams anymore. She had reached the age of fifteen without knowing the true purpose and meaning of her gift. Now that she was about to start at the American school she sensed everything was about to change forever.

The groom announced that they were approaching the gates of the school. Pushing aside the shade, Halide looked out the window and saw they were passing along a drive lined with cypress trees. They rounded a sharp bend and came to a halt in front of an old wooden mansion. An overhanging balcony, crowded with white wicker furniture, ran the length of the facade and wisteria straggled over the red tiled roof. At first glance, the whole place appeared deserted.

Halide leapt out and walked around to the other side of the carriage, where her grandmother, helped by the groom, descended the rickety steps. The old lady stared around her uncomfortably.

Halide took her bag from the front seat and started toward the house. Just then, the tall figure of a woman appeared in the doorway. Her hair was swept up into a chignon held in place with tortoiseshell combs and above a crisp collar her round features were intent and serious. She strode across the drive with brisk steps, her hand outstretched.

"Welcome, Fatma Hanim Efendi. We are honored to have you here. When I received your note I thought it most appropriate that our first Turkish student should be accompanied by her grandmother." The woman spoke Turkish with a strange accent. It took Halide a moment to realize that the speaker was none other than Dr. Mary Mills Patrick, the director of the school.

Chapter Five

When they first moved to Scutari, Halide had loved to play among the trees in the apple orchard. A century older than the mansion, the orchard had once belonged to the guardians of Karaca Ahmet Cemetery. The local people believed that spirits still inhabited the gnarled trunks and that on moonless nights they emerged from the musty prisons to reclaim their land from the living. After sundown the women of the harem refused to set foot there, and even in the daylight they were wary of standing too close to certain trees for fear of angering the peris. Apples were gathered only after they had fallen to the ground.

Three weeks after her first day at school, Halide was waiting for Salih Zeki in their usual place in the orchard beside the old wall. She had persuaded her father that the atmosphere amidst the old trees was more conducive to study. The truth was that she wanted to be alone with Salih Zeki, far from the prying eyes of the harem women.

She tilted her chair up against the wall and let her head fall into the ivy. Mathematics was not her favorite subject. Its obstinate precision exasperated her, and she had yet to appreciate any beauty in its logic. But she remained determined. She had to prove to herself, and to Salih Zeki, that she was as intelligent as the young men he had taught in Paris. She sat upright as the gate clicked and, pushing her hair out of her face, pretended to be absorbed in her math book. In a matter of seconds he would be beside her. She kept her head down, relishing the moment of his arrival.

"What's this then, French furniture? How accommodating." Salih Zeki had his back to the sun and she could see the silhouette of his wide-brimmed hat and of the dark coat thrown over his shoulders.

"The gardener's boy moved everything from the men's quarters," Halide said playfully. "This here is a pampered scholar."

He tossed his coat across the table and shifted his chair close to her side. "Did you finish the assignment?"

"I did it on Friday night when I got back to the harem. Granny was very annoyed."

"Why?" He ran his eye over the page, unable to find a single error.

"She wanted me to go with her to the mosque, but I had to finish this so I refused."

Salih Zeki hesitated before replying. "Next time it might be better to go with her and to do your homework afterward."

"By the time prayers have finished I'm too tired to think of working."

"Your grandmother takes her faith seriously. You should respect that."

"I know," Halide said impatiently, "but I don't want to fail. All the other girls are ahead of me." The last thing she wanted was a lecture from her tutor.

"You're coming along, don't worry," he said. "You will catch up in no time."

Salih Zeki reached into his pocket and pulled out a sheet of paper, which he placed in front of her. "I've brought a test for you this morning. It's a summary of everything we've covered so far."

Halide bent over the page, and while she pored over the questions he lit a cigarette. How pleasant it was, he reflected, to sit in this quiet spot with the clear sky overhead and nothing but the songs of birds to disturb them. Halide was the perfect student, intelligent, receptive, and pliant, and he was being paid handsomely. What more could a man ask for? In Paris he had become accustomed to working with women, but they were confident, talkative women, outgoing to the point of being overwhelming. He had never adjusted to that aspect of French life.

Halide surprised him by announcing that she was done with the test before he had finished his cigarette. He stubbed it out with his foot and went over her answers.

"Twenty out of twenty. Excellent work, Halide."

"Will I be as good as your students in Paris?"

"Oh, better," he said without thinking.

"Dr. Patrick says women can be the equal of men."

"Dr. Patrick is an extraordinary person, and I would say yes, she is the equal of any man." Not wishing to upset Halide, Salih Zeki chose his words carefully. Mary Mills Patrick had, in his opinion, exceptional credentials. In addition to a degree in classics, she was the first woman to have earned a master's in psychology from the University of Heidelberg. He found her habit of looking men straight in the eye rather disconcerting. He had observed this mannerism in many of the Americans he had encountered; in a woman he felt it was almost obscene.

"I think she is wonderful. Whenever I'm with her, which isn't very often, I want to say something to please her."

"You must please all your teachers," he murmured.

"Why? Some of them are rather stupid." Halide glared at him, then blushed. "I'm sorry, I forgot myself."

"You did indeed, but you're probably right." Without thinking, Salih Zeki laid his hand on her arm. The feel of her skin excited him and he pulled away, determined that such a foolish lapse should not occur again.

⚘

IT WAS DUSK before their lesson drew to a close. In the west, the sky had faded from blue to purple. The air had cooled, and Halide shivered in her thin dress. Salih Zeki watched her eyes darken and wondered what was troubling her.

"What's the matter?" he asked at last.

"I was thinking about my sister. I hope she's all right."

"Is there any reason she shouldn't be?"

"I don't know."

Technically speaking, this was true. Halide seen her sister only once in the four weeks since school had started, when, at Mahmoure's request, they had met at the French Tea Salon on the Grande Rue de Pera. They had been chaperoned by Teyze, who, much to Halide's amazement, had taken an immediate and inexplicable dislike to the place. It had been a listless occasion. Despite Halide's best efforts, Mahmoure had been distracted and had hardly touched her tea. When it came time to leave she was reluctant to return home and hung about by the door, pretending she had mislaid her gloves.

"We must go inside, before you catch a chill," Salih Zeki said, interrupting her thoughts. He retrieved his greatcoat and tossed it around her shoulders. It was heavy and dragged on the ground as she walked. Hampered by the weight but unwilling to offend him, Halide compromised by clutching the bottom of the coat with one arm while carrying her books with the other.

When they reached the crest of the hill the mansion lay before them, lights blazing on the lower floors. From a distance they heard voices raised in dispute, and as they drew closer the cries turned into sobs. Concerned, Halide ran ahead.

"Wait for me," Salih Zeki said with deliberate calm. "If something is wrong I must be with you."

She complied without hesitating; it seemed perfectly natural to do as he asked.

Not another word passed between them until they had arrived at the rear door of the harem. Inside, the sound of crying continued unabated. Salih Zeki hesitated before following Halide into the house. The lights in the corridor burned low; the furnishings were nothing more than dark forms enclosed by an amber mist. Halfway along the passage they came face-to-face with Arzu, who was hurrying toward them waving her hands.

"There you are, Halide!" she said. "We've been looking everywhere for you."

"I was in the orchard with Zeki Bey. It's Sunday, tutoring day."

"I told the girls to look there first. They're so superstitious, it's ridiculous." Arzu shrugged her shoulders.

"What's going on?" Suddenly the crying crescendoed and Arzu turned and hurried off in the direction from which she had come.

"Follow me, child. Oh, your poor grandmother!" she muttered. Salih Zeki and Halide exchanged glances. He was on the point of excusing himself when she put out her hand and touched his arm. "Don't go," she said. "I think my father will be in need of a friend."

When they reached the main hall they found Granny sitting on the stairs hunched over her walking stick. The smile she gave them was filled with relief and sorrow.

"Salih Zeki Bey at your service, madam." He clicked his heels and bowed formally.

"Salih Zeki, of course, I remember you now. You are a friend of Edib's, a scholar of some sort."

"I am thus honored, madam," he said with a smile.

Across the hall one of the doors to the salons stood slightly ajar and the sound of childish laughter came from the other side. Arzu beckoned to Salih Zeki and Halide to follow her.

"Come in," she said. "Your nieces and nephew arrived unexpectedly before evening prayers." She tried to sound casual, but her heart wasn't in it.

"And Mahmoure, is she with them?"

"Your father will explain."

"Perhaps I should go," ventured Salih Zeki. Any excess of emotion alarmed him.

"I would rather you stayed," Halide said quietly.

"In that case I cannot refuse."

"Is that your voice I hear, Zeki Bey? Come in, we are in need of your wisdom." Edib appeared at the door. He kissed his daughter on both cheeks and then extended his hand to Salih Zeki.

Mahmoure's children sat cross-legged on the floor in the small salon, their hands folded in their laps. As soon as he saw Halide, Ali Shamil, who was little more than a year old, let out a shriek. His nurse bounced him up and down on her lap until, stunned by her gyrations, he quieted down. Halide's attention was diverted from this spectacle by the sight of Mahmoure's mother-in-law, who sat in a corner with her head bowed and her eyes closed. She clutched a rosary of prayer beads, weaving them through her fingers with deft precision.

"Why is Nurdan Hanim here?" Halide demanded of her father. "Don't spare me, I'm not afraid to know the worst."

Edib stared past his daughter as if struck by a sudden and unwelcome thought. He leaned forward and whispered. "Mahmoure has left her husband. Ahmet is in the men's quarters; he is too upset to see anyone. His mother brought him here and she is demanding a divorce."

Edib reached into his coat and pulled out an envelope, which he handed to his daughter. The note was addressed to Ahmet; it was brief and to the point. Although Mahmoure expressed some sadness at leaving her children, there was not a hint of regret in her tone. Halide looked up; through the half-open door she could see her sister's children. How could she do such a thing? Keeping a tight hold on the letter, Halide thought back to that day in the cemetery. There had been something desperate in the way she had clung to Riza. She had known then that Mahmoure would not stay put for long.

Chapter Six

The grounds of the American Girls College were tended by local Turks who avoided any contact with the unveiled girls. Trees were pruned, the flower beds weeded, and the paths swept when classes were in session, but one corner of the grounds had been left conspicuously untouched: a wild patch, beyond the kitchen, with two enormous fig trees. Protected from the wind and basking in the heat of reflected sunlight, the trees flourished and their branches swept to the ground. Like all Turks, the gardeners treated the fig trees with circumspect regard, for they were known to shelter spirits. They didn't prune or cut back the encroaching undergrowth, and somehow a groundless fear of snakes lurking in the uncut grass kept the students away. Only Halide was not afraid. She found a refuge in the dark cavelike space under the old fig trees.

Halide was training herself to think in English. This had been Salih Zeki's idea. If she was to succeed, she would have to think like her peers and become fluent in English. He advised her to keep a journal in the leather-bound book he had given her. The discipline of recording every thought and action in English might ease her transition. The diary form was Western in origin; it would train her to think of herself as an individual with emotions and thoughts deserving of attention.

"Even after three months I still feel out of place," she wrote. "The other girls are friendly, but I am a curiosity. At first I thought it was because I was a Muslim girl in a Christian school, but gradually I'm starting to realize that many of these girls don't think that way, especially the ones who have come from America."

Someone called her name, a soft voice of indeterminate origin. She looked up for a moment and, seeing no one, returned to the diary. "Halide," the voice persisted. Surprised, she dropped her pen. No one else knew about this spot.

"Halide, Halide . . ." The voice trailed off into a whisper. A breeze rippled the heavy leaves, drowning the call in a rattle of movement. A second voice began, trilling and melancholy. The first voice called her name again, and the voices crisscrossed back and forth on the breeze. Then, as suddenly as it had come, the wind subsided and the voices stopped. Halide stood up and brushed away the twigs clinging to her skirt. Since school had started the spirits had been quiet. Why were they back now? Halide closed her diary and put her pen into her book bag. Perhaps sitting in the shade of a fig tree was not such a good idea after all. She scolded herself at once for having such a foolish thought: this was the American school; there were no peris here.

Halide started back along the path toward the main building. At the gate she almost collided with one of the senior girls, who greeted her with a look of relief.

"Halide, we've been looking for you everywhere!"

"Were you calling me?"

"No, you must have heard one of the others. Dr. Patrick asked the senior monitors to find you."

"Dr. Patrick? Why?"

"Your father's here," the girl said, taking her by the hand.

⚜

"THERE YOU ARE, my dear." Stating the obvious, Edib rose to greet her. He had been sitting in one of the deep armchairs in Dr. Patrick's study, wondering if he would find his daughter much changed. A month had elapsed since she had left the harem to begin the fall semester—too little time, he concluded, to see if his expectations would be fulfilled.

"Has something happened?" she asked with concern. Why else would he be here in the middle of the school week?

"We've had news of Mahmoure," he said. Halide leapt up with excitement to embrace him. He cupped her face in his hands.

"Is she safe?"

"In a manner of speaking." On close inspection Edib decided there was a slight improvement in his daughter's appearance. She seemed alert and was less awkward in her movements.

"Where is she, Father? Please tell me," Halide urged.

Edib pulled a crumpled sheet of paper from his coat and handed it to his daughter. The note was short and to the point. *"Riza and I have reached Antalya. We are with Ali Shamil. May God preserve you and keep you all in good health. Mahmoure."*

"So she did it," Halide sighed wistfully. "She went and found him." From the day of Mahmoure's abrupt departure, the image of the three children, separated from their mother, had never been far from her mind. Yet she sympathized with her sister.

"Sit down, child." Edib patted the seat of the chair next to his. "There is more to this story."

"You look tired. Is there something the matter?"

"My friend Ali Shamil Pasha is dead. He died two weeks after Mahmoure arrived in Antalya, but news of his passing only just reached me."

From the time of their first meeting in Mecca, before Halide was born, Edib's love for Selima had always bound him to this unpredictable man. Of course he had known about Selima's first marriage, but it had taken time for him to realize that Ali Shamil would always occupy a special place in her heart. The love she retained for her first husband hung like a specter over their marriage, which was otherwise close and happy. She was the one woman he felt he had truly loved. Teyze was beautiful, he had been attracted to her at first, but there was within her a desperate void he could not fill.

"I'm so sorry," Halide whispered. Her father was obviously saddened, and she did not know what else to say to comfort him.

"I feel so empty. I can't imagine life without him there."

Years had passed since that night in Yenikapi, but Halide could remember Mahmoure's father as clearly as if it had been yesterday. There was something in his spirited kindness that had touched her heart.

"He was a proud, courageous man. I think the humiliation of exile was more than he could bear."

"I am confused, Father," Halide murmured. "How is Riza connected with Mahmoure's father?"

"For the past seven years, since Riza left the city, he has been living in Antalya under the protection of Ali Shamil."

"But why? You told us he went into the cavalry." Halide rose and walked around her father's chair and across the room to the fireplace, where she leaned against the mantel and waited for him to tell her more.

"There was no commission, no cavalry unit in Bursa, nothing. I was forced to lie to everyone to protect Riza, and myself."

Halide felt the ground shifting under her feet. "Why?"

"By chance I learned that Riza was about to be arrested. In those days my offices were on the same floor as the palace branch of the secret police. A list of suspected dissidents in the military academy was delivered to my office by mistake. Riza's name was on it. I burned the list at once, which gave me a few days' grace. Then I summoned Riza to the men's quarters, and together we engineered his escape."

"What did he say?"

"He confessed he was actively connected to the Paris branch of the Young Turks. This changed everything. He had to get away at once, and the only man I could trust was the man who owed me his life, Ali Shamil. I sent word to Antalya and he agreed to hide Riza from the authorities on condition that Riza give up his quest to marry Mahmoure."

"Now it all makes sense," Halide said, thinking back to the conversation she had overheard that night when Mahmoure had returned to her father.

"By some act of providence that list was not duplicated, and my story about the commission was believed at the palace." Edib leaned back in his chair and stretched his legs out in front of him. "It was hard for me to maintain the deceit; I hate lying. To make matters worse, I was deeply saddened by his opposition to the system I have devoted my life to."

"You loved Riza," Halide said gently. "I think you showed great courage."

Edib walked over to the window, blinking away tears to conceal his emotion. Outside, a group of girls were sitting on the lawn laughing. He was moved by their gaiety. This was the life he wanted for his daughter. He would not let her suffer the fate of Mahmoure.

"I wish Mahmoure could have come here too," he said as much to himself as to Halide. "But she showed no interest in learning. Marriage seemed the only answer. I didn't know what else to do." He threw his arms out in a gesture of helplessness.

"Granny always says we cannot fight fate."

"And you believe that?"

"I don't know. I guess Mahmoure is fighting it with all her strength." The letter was still clutched in her hand. With slow, deliberate movements, she tore it into small pieces. Bit by bit she dropped them into the fireplace and pushed them into the unlit coals with the tip of a poker.

Chapter Seven

In early November the first cold weather enveloped the city. Icy winds whirled in from the Russian steppes, scattering the last autumn leaves and churning the waters of the Bosphorus. Under

the dark gray sky the city looked suddenly somber and a permanent gloom draped the streets of the old city. Wrapped in a light
cloak, Teyze hurried ahead of her companions. She felt light-
hearted, released from her exile in Scutari, and her eyes darted
over the merchandise. Despite her long absence from the book
market she had not lost her ability to discriminate. Her instinct for
a bargain never failed her.

Salih Zeki was disconcerted by the speed with which Teyze
moved through the market. He had been charged by Edib Bey to
take care of his wife and daughter, but Teyze was making the task
difficult. Salih Zeki preferred to linger over every stand, perusing
the goods with careful attention. If need be he would gladly engage the proprietor in conversation about the relative value of
Persian court documents and Egyptian medical texts. Salih Zeki
loved to talk. He relished every opportunity to engage an expert in
discussion of his field. Never pretending to know too much, he
was an attentive listener. Listening was a skill, he told Halide; to
listen was to learn.

Halide, for her part, was upset by Teyze's refusal to walk with
them. It was late morning by the time they arrived in the old city,
and the Sahaflar Carsisi, the book market, was thronged. Several times Halide found herself pushed against her tutor. She
pulled away quickly and he walked on, apparently oblivious.
Teyze did not like Salih Zeki. She thought him repulsive but
was careful to disguise her feelings for fear of offending Edib. If
she guessed at Halide's growing attraction to her tutor, she said
nothing.

They had been walking for some time when Teyze finally
stopped outside a stall in the main square. The owner was an old
acquaintance who had sold her many books in the days before her
marriage. As soon as he saw her, he began to declaim her long ab-

sence. Glasses of tea were called for, and there was much bowing as Teyze made her way into the cramped stall. Halide followed, but Salih Zeki, after making sure they were safe, chose to continue on alone. He relished the thought of a few solitary moments among books and manuscripts.

Teyze held her glass in her gloved hand and maneuvered it around her veil to her mouth. She was wearing a brown velvet cloak fastened at the neck with a silk cord imported from Paris. On her feet were delicate leather boots fitted close to her ankles. Surrounded on all sides by dusty shelves piled high with books and fading velvet divans, she made an arresting figure.

"I have missed you, madam. You were one of my favorite customers," the bookseller said in a high-pitched voice. He could not have been more than forty but he knelt with difficulty as he placed a stool under her feet. He was a portly man with downward-slanting eyes that gave him the appearance of being pained.

"Alas, life takes unexpected turns," Teyze said with a forced smile.

"I'm relieved to see you again. These days so many of my customers disappear without a word." The man looked up meaningfully but said nothing more.

"I've been living in Scutari for several years, but I might as well be in Konya. I've no idea what's going on these days in literary circles."

"Times are hard, spies are everywhere. I must be careful, Fikriye Hanim Efendi; I know you'll understand." The bookseller tugged at his ear and made a sign.

"I do, I do." Teyze nodded. Why, Halide wondered, was he addressing Teyze by her maiden name? Didn't he know she was married?

"There is a new novel you might like, *Zehra*, by Nazim Nazibade. His style is reminiscent of Zola. The poor soul died

recently—such a loss, such a loss . . ." He wrung his hands the-
atrically. "Let me fetch you a copy from the back room."

With a pang of regret for the old days when she came regularly
to the market, Teyze watched the bookseller disappear through a
curtained doorway.

"Why isn't it out here if it's so good?" whispered Halide, fidgeting with her veil.

"Zola has been banned," Teyze whispered. "To emulate his
style means risking the wrath of the censors. Abdullah has to be
careful or his business will be closed down."

"What's so terrible about—" Halide broke off, interrupted by
the appearance of a plump, well-dressed woman in the front of the
store. When she saw them the woman drew back, obviously surprised to find the room occupied. In one swift glance Teyze took in
her fur-trimmed cloak, matching hat, and fine kid gloves. From
her light step she judged her to be young.

"Is Abdullah here? I have an appointment." The woman had
a low voice that was almost drowned out by the hubbub of
passersby.

"He's in the back, he won't be long," Halide replied. Teyze
started to sip her tea, affecting slow disdain.

"Would you like to sit down?" Halide said, starting to get to her
feet.

"No, please stay where you are. I've only come to collect an
order for my husband. The coachman is waiting." With an awkward movement she gestured toward the street.

"Do you buy a lot of books here?" Halide said, anxious to alleviate the uncomfortable silence.

"No, I don't read very much." The woman brought her hand to
her throat and fingered her beads. Just then the curtain was pushed
aside and Abdullah returned carrying a pile of books, which he set
in front of Teyze. On seeing the newcomer he bowed.

"Forgive me, madam, I didn't know you were here."

"I've come to collect my husband's order." She stumbled over her words, as if making the request flustered her.

"What is the name on the order, madam?"

"Edib Pasha of Yildiz."

Halide felt as if she had been dealt a hard blow to her chest. Out of the corner of her eye she saw Teyze stiffen. Moving slowly, Teyze leaned forward and put the tea glass on the floor. Her hands were shaking, and the glass swayed on its small saucer. Noticing nothing out of the ordinary, the woman bade them farewell and turned toward the street. Abdullah hurried after her, calling for the boy to carry the books.

THE PALACE of Yildiz was a collection of pavilions and kiosks, each no more than two or three stories high, set among lush gardens and enclosed by a high wall of stone and flint. Edib's offices were on the second floor of the Buyuk Mabeyn, an art nouveau kiosk between the Sultan's quarters and the offices of the minor bureaucrats. It was approached through a rococo arch protected by the Sultan's personal bodyguards. To Salih Zeki's consternation, they were stopped twice, but Teyze brushed aside their questions with an authoritative wave and hurried on. At the door of Edib's office a liveried eunuch barred their way. He was dark and rotund. When he moved, his body undulated as if devoid of bones.

"Whom shall I say is calling on my esteemed master?" He used a vernacular peculiar to the closed world of the palace.

"I am Edib Hanim. I must see my husband at once." Teyze rapped her fan on the wall. With a cursory bow the eunuch ushered them into an empty room.

Halide took in the details of her father's office as if contemplating the features of a rival. The truth was that, compared with their home in Scutari, it was disappointing. The office was lit by harsh electric lamps and cluttered with gilded furniture grouped against the wall like young girls sitting out a dance. A marble bust filled a corner near the window and heavy curtains cut out the daylight. The air was infused with the smell of cigarettes. The eunuch turned to Halide and beckoned her to follow him. Once they were seated he leaned against the doorpost and sullenly examined the back of his hand.

"Tell your master we wish to see him at once." Salih Zeki glowered. He wanted nothing more than to rid himself of the sight of this insolent creature. Goaded by the sound of a male voice, the eunuch hurried away.

"I still don't think this is wise," Salih Zeki murmured as soon as the door closed.

"It's not your life that is in question," Teyze said sharply.

"Then talk to him alone. Consider Halide's feelings—"

"I'm staying here until my father puts Teyze's fears to rest. There must be another family with the same name in our old neighborhood."

The sudden appearance of Edib cut the conversation short. He had been working since dawn and looked haggard. Salih Zeki rose to greet him.

"What brings you here? Has something happened?" Edib asked, blinking rapidly like a man coming from a dark cave into the light.

"An urgent matter has arisen. We must talk," Teyze said with still composure, her eyes fixed on his expression.

"Can't it wait?" he said irritably. "I return to Scutari at dawn. There is a crisis afoot—"

Teyze dismissed his protest with a wave of her hand. "Tomorrow will be too late. My happiness depends on your answer."

Astonished, Edib made a move to sit down, then thought better of it. Teyze began to pace up and down the room.

"This morning, at the book market, Halide and I were visiting Abdullah the bookseller when a strange woman happened to enter." There was no point in wasting time, she thought; she saw no use in a more circuitous approach.

"This woman was collecting an order for an Edib Pasha of Yildiz. She claimed to be his wife."

Edib paled, taken by surprise.

"Now you can assure us that it is all a mistake," Halide interjected. Like a man who has been ambushed on a road he knew to be dangerous, Edib looked pleadingly at his attackers and shook his head.

"Don't tell me . . ." Teyze put her hand over her mouth and turned away. Edib held out his arm, half afraid she might faint, but she drew back from him. Halide sat numb with horror.

"Under the law—" He spoke in a strangled voice.

"Damn the law! I thought we loved each other. If you needed someone else, why didn't you tell me?" Teyze choked on her tears. Edib remained silent, conscious that his daughter was watching him.

"*Why?* Answer me!" Her fists clenched at her side, Teyze's face contorted into an enraged mask.

"My marriage is recent. I meant to tell you, but the secret police uncovered a plot to kill the Sultan. The would-be assassins came dangerously close, and I was compelled to remain here."

"What a meager excuse."

"I'm sorry, truly sorry you had to hear it this way."

"You were my life, my soul. What is to become of me now?" Teyze asked, struggling to maintain her composure.

"Nothing will change. You are my first and senior wife with a fine home in Scutari, where I will come as often as time permits. I value and esteem you as before."

"And what about the heart of it?"

"The heart of it?" Edib looked puzzled.

Halide closed her eyes. A gaping chasm threatened to engulf her, just as it had when her mother had died. Only this time no reassuring voices came to placate her. She knew at that moment that her life would never be the same again.

"I think it's time for us to leave," Salih Zeki said, stepping forward. "The hour is late and the ferries do not run after the last call to prayer." He did not like the way Halide had slumped in her seat. "Come, Halide. Say good night to your father." He extended his arm, and Halide took it without a word.

"I will dispatch a messenger at once," Edib rallied. "A carriage will be waiting for you on the quay at Scutari." There was work to be done, arrangements to be made: he was in his element once more.

HAVING FOUND a seat in the first-class cabin, Halide huddled in a corner and pressed her face against the window. Outside, a light rain was falling. The waters were choppy, and soon the swaying of the boat lulled her into a semisleep. While she rested, Salih Zeki went over the events of the day. He was relieved that Teyze had decided to remain at the palace with Edib. He had no desire to share Halide's company with a hysterical woman who, in his opinion, should have accepted her husband's second marriage with calm acquiescence.

It was, for him, disturbing to learn of yet another plot to kill the Sultan. The CUP had been smashed and the opposition was weak, and he suspected that the would-be assassins were nationalists, probably Armenians or Albanians, for they were the most aggressive. Salih Zeki had no sympathy for terrorists who, with their reckless disregard for life, had proven they were willing to sacrifice even their own people in their struggle for independence.

If the Sultan were to die now, who would replace him? Another scion of the house of Osman? An army officer under the thrall of the Germans? Or a government minister lacking imagination and intellect? The choice was bleak. In his opinion, intellectuals were the only people capable of saving the Ottoman Empire from extinction, but after Abdulhamid had lured the Young Turks back to the city the intellectual opposition had been dispersed and demoralized; they were certainly not ready to assume power.

Since returning to Constantinople, Salih Zeki's conscience had been troubling him because he too had succumbed to the promises of Abdulhamid, a man he had worked hard to overthrow. In one way he had been fortunate: the promise of a high-salaried teaching post at the naval academy had been fulfilled. His former colleagues who had resisted the blandishments of Jelaleddin Pasha and remained in Paris were angry and disappointed by his perceived betrayal. He wanted to prove to them that he still sought the overthrow of the present regime. Here in the city he had heard of disparate cells of opposition slowly rebuilding after the catastrophic summer of '96. If only he could find out who they were and join their ranks again! Salih Zeki sighed. In these turbulent times politics could not be avoided, but in his heart he longed for the peace and tranquillity that nurtured his work.

Salih Zeki stretched his legs and turned his attention to Halide, who had fallen asleep. Poor child—what a shocking day she had just endured. Although he sympathized with Edib, Salih Zeki did not understand why he had concealed this second marriage from his daughter and wife. It disturbed him to see Halide get hurt. He was, he realized, somewhat captivated by her naive charm. Perhaps, he thought, watching her sweet face, it would be better if he were to find a reason to end their association. The last thing he could afford to do was to fall in love with this child.

Halide woke with a start and stared around at the empty cabin. For a moment she could not remember where she was. The sight of Salih Zeki reassured her.

"You must be hungry," he said gently.

"I'm cold," she whispered. Hours had passed since she had last eaten, and she longed for the taste of something sweet.

Just then a boy no more than ten years old came into the cabin carrying a tray laden with tea and candied fruit. His hair was plastered to his skull, and rain dripped over his forehead. The cold night air gushed in after him through the open door.

"Two sage teas, young man, with plenty of honey," Salih Zeki called out.

"I have no money," whispered Halide.

"Don't be silly, I have enough." Salih Zeki reached into his coat.

"No, you should not pay for me—"

"Why not?" He shot her a look of such intensity it caught her off guard.

"I don't know," she whispered, relieved that her bewildered expression was hidden by her veil.

"Keep the change," he said, handing some coins to the boy, who smiled in gratitude and went away whistling.

Halide lifted her veil as she brought the cup to her mouth. "This is good," she said, warming her hands with the hot tea.

"The perfect antidote for shock," Salih Zeki said, watching her lips part over the edge of the cup.

"Am I in shock?"

"It's not every day one discovers a new stepmother."

"I hadn't thought of it that way." As she savored the taste of the sweetened tea, memories of childhood and forbidden sweets came back to her. In those days she had had absolute faith in her father's judgment. She realized, sadly, that she would never be so certain again.

"You're trembling." Salih Zeki's voice softened as he leaned toward her.

"I'm cold." Halide's fingers tightened around the cup.

"Here, let me give you my coat."

"No, keep it, please. The tea will warm me up."

By now they had reached the middle of the Bosphorus, where the currents were strongest, and the boat began to rock from side to side. Reaching out to steady herself, Halide accidentally put her hand on Salih Zeki's leg. Horrified, she pulled away.

"I'm sorry, I didn't mean to—"

"Think nothing of it. The straits are unusually turbulent tonight."

"I was afraid I was going to fall."

"Perhaps I ought to sit beside you. That way you can lean against me for support. Your father would never forgive me if you were to be injured while in my care."

"If you say so," she stammered.

With a single stride he changed seats and slid his arm along the back of the bench to steady himself. Numb with confusion, Halide held tight to her cup and watched the steam rise and warm the tip of her nose.

Chapter Eight

Teyze pressed her face against the carriage window. Outside it was pitch-black; the moon was hidden behind a bank of cloud. Suddenly she regretted leaving Edib's offices so hurriedly. They had talked together for a long time after Halide and Salih Zeki had left. The more he had tried to make her understand, the more agonizing his presence had become, until she couldn't stand it anymore. He had urged her to remain until morning, but she had been too distraught to listen. When she'd walked to the door she had kept her eyes lowered, conscious that he was watching her every move. How she'd longed for him to say something to prevent her from leaving! But he'd remained silent and let her go.

Teyze heard a splash followed by a mild curse as the groom descended into a pool of water. His boots squelched in the mud as he walked around to her door. The driver called out that they must not dally, the hour was late and the horses were restless. "We can't get any closer to the quay," the groom said apologetically. "With your permission I can lift you onto dry ground." Teyze nodded quietly and pulled her cloak around her.

The first touch of icy air made her shiver. The groom scooped her up in his arms and carried her like a child. She closed her eyes and, without meaning to, savored the warmth of his body. He hesitated before setting her down on the dry stone, as if reluctant to leave her alone like this so late at night. Then the driver goaded the horses into a trot and, bounding across the mud, the groom leapt into his seat and gave her a parting wave.

Teyze turned toward the ferry station, a squat chalet-style building painted white and gray. A lamp burned above the doorway and the interior was lit by gaslight. From behind a small ticket window an elderly man surveyed the new arrival. What was an unescorted woman doing out alone at this hour? And such an elegant figure, in European clothes and delicate boots, useless against the elements.

"How long before the next boat leaves?" Teyze inquired, tapping the glass.

"There's no other ferry tonight, ma'am. The last one left soon after the watchman made his rounds."

"No ferry? That can't be. Is there a private boat I can hire?"

"Another storm is approaching, ma'am. It's not safe on the water. The currents are very strong."

"But . . ." Teyze looked behind her, as if expecting the carriage to reappear, but there was only blackness.

"First ferry comes at dawn. By then the bad weather will have passed, God willing."

"What am I to do? Where can I go?"

"You must shelter in here, ma'am. It's dry and safe. I'll rest outside."

The ticket man emerged from the office. He was unusually tall, with hunched shoulders and a slightly lopsided walk.

"You are very kind." Teyze cast her eyes downward from habit, although he could not see her face beneath the veil.

"It's nothing, ma'am. If you don't mind me saying so, a lady like yourself should not be wandering around alone in the dead of night." He held the door open and bowed as she entered.

Teyze collapsed onto the narrow bench, put her head back against the wall, and closed her eyes. Her body ached with a fatigue so extreme it pierced her bones. Outside she heard the rumble of distant thunder. The door flew open, hurled back by a blast of wind, but she was too weak to move. A strong arm reached in and closed it without a sound, and before she knew it she had dropped off to sleep.

Teyze slept fitfully for an hour or two and was woken by a loud clap of thunder. She stumbled to the window and looked out. A storm lashed the shore. Lightning crackled over the churning waters and a bolt of lightning illuminated the vessels moored downstream near the palace. Alone with her misery, Teyze felt numb.

Earlier that evening, rushing away from Edib, she had prayed for a swift end to her misery. In her imagination she saw herself plunging into the Bosphorus from the deck of the ferry. No one would notice in the dark: a splash, the noise drowned out by the sounds of the engine, her spirit free at last. She assured herself that her absence would not be noticed for days. Halide would be back at college, and Granny's mind was fogged by age. It would be assumed that she had stayed with Edib, until her body washed up on the shore. Seized with regret and guilt, Edib would be called upon to identify her remains, his new marriage forever tainted by her death.

Teyze's dark thoughts were interrupted by the patter of rain against the window. She narrowed her eyes and peered through the glass, hoping for a glimpse of home.

Above the roar of the wind Teyze could hear the sound of water lapping against stone. She unlatched the door and walked out into the night. The old man was asleep under the eaves, his face turned to the wall. The wind whipped her skirts and lashed her veil across her face until it smothered her. She wrenched it off and tossed it into the air so that it flapped away like a wounded bird, landing in the Bosphorus with a faint splash. As she crept forward over the slippery stones, her eyes became accustomed to the dark. Suddenly she stopped: the vast expanse of water spread out before her. She stood paralyzed by her old terror for what seemed like an eternity.

"Madam, madam, stop!" She felt her arms pinned to her sides as a pair of strong hands grasped her around the waist. She could feel a man's breath coming against her neck in short gasps as he dragged her back across the cobblestones.

"Forgive me, madam, but one more step and you'd have been in them waters." The ticketmaster dropped her at the open doorway and then clutched his hands over his face. He turned away violently and started to sob. Stunned, Teyze watched him without moving.

"What is it?" she ventured, struggling to keep her voice from breaking. With his back to her, he motioned as if to push her away.

"Cover your head, ma'am, I beg of you." Teyze put her hand on her wet hair. Water ran in droplets down her forehead and trickled to the tip of her nose. "I'm a pious man, and I ain't never seen a woman unveiled outside my family."

"Forgive me," she whispered softly. "I don't know what came over me." To her amazement, tears of gratitude blurred her vision.

"The peris are about on nights like this. They play tricks on the mind. Stay inside, and I'll make sure they keep away."

Kicking the door shut, he shambled off into the night. After a short while he returned with a scarlet rope tied with garlic bulbs, which he attached to the doorpost. Then he lay down across the threshold and fell asleep. Teyze was kept awake by his loud rhythmic snoring until fatigue overcame her and she fell into a fitful sleep.

AT DAWN Teyze was awakened by the chorus of gulls swooping over the quay. Her body ached and her damp clothes had chilled her to the bone, yet her first feeling on awakening was relief. Beyond the window the sky was clear; a bright sun had begun to dry the cobbled quay. Farther downstream she saw fishermen casting their nets into the waves. Sailors swabbed the decks of square-rigged trading vessels; even the crews of the German warships moored close to the palace were busy on deck.

At the edge of the dock Teyze noticed the ticketmaster standing astride a capstan, his arms crossed over his chest. He was staring at the Asian coast. Panicked, Teyze seized her cloak and pulled it around her so that she was covered from head to toe. Tugging at the hood until it reached below her chin, she moved toward the door.

"Ferry's on its way," the man said with a smile. She peered through the fabric of her hood and saw that far in the distance a small craft chugged in their direction.

"Want some coffee, ma'am? It'll warm you up."

"Why yes, thank you." She leaned against the building for support. The crisp air lifted her spirits.

"I'll fetch you something to cover your face," he said. "You'll never make the ferry trip like that."

The cloth he brought was rough and smelled of fish, but it served its purpose. Suddenly a wave of horror convulsed her. If it had not been for the intervention of this man, her body would be rotting under the waves at this very moment. "I am most grateful to you," she said awkwardly, turning to him. She wanted to say more, but the barriers of correct behavior rose up to stop her.

"It's my duty to give shelter to a stranger," he said. "We are all creatures of God."

"Your generosity must not go unrewarded." Teyze fumbled in her purse. He had witnessed her act of desperation and shared her secret, a secret she would never tell another living soul.

"This fine morning is all the reward I could hope for, ma'am." He turned abruptly away from her and hurried off.

Beyond the ticketmaster's hut, the skeletal trees of Yildiz glistened in the morning sun. Teyze felt weak. Her life with Edib was over, and she would never return to this part of the city. It was impossible for her to imagine what the future might hold. Just then the ticketmaster returned with her coffee. Teyze held the cup to her nostrils and savored its sharp fragrance.

GRANNY BROKE the wax seal stamped with Edib's initials and slit open the envelope with an ivory knife. She was sitting in her usual place in the bay window at the back of the harem. On clear mornings such as this she could see the Karaca Ahmet Cemetery sprawled across the hills, and the cluster of cypresses where the dervish graves were to be found. Ali Bey Pasha's grave was on the other side of the trees, overlooking the Scutari harbor. Granny regretted missing her daily visit to her husband, but Teyze's condition was too serious to leave in the hands of slaves and serving girls.

Three days had passed since Teyze had come back to Sultan Tepe, and at first she had done nothing but lie on her divan and stare listlessly at the ceiling, refusing all food and drink. The slaves took her to the bathhouse and bathed her in hot water mixed with rose petals, then rubbed her down with healing oils and wrapped her in woolen shawls. Granny coaxed her into eating a little sherbet, and gradually her anguish stilled but the pain in her heart refused to go away.

"So he has written to me at last," Granny announced.

"What does he say?" Teyze glanced up, not knowing whether to be alarmed or relieved. She was lying on the divan under a mound of blankets and shawls.

"He apologizes for the untimely manner in which I learned of this union," Granny replied guardedly. "Events at the palace prevented him from telling me earlier." It was going to take great tact to balance the concern and affection she felt for Teyze with the need to maintain a relationship with Halide's father. She understood why Edib had remarried. Men needed sons, and Teyze had passed the age of childbearing.

"Does he say anything about me?"

"Somehow he learned that you had passed the night on the quay, and he wants to dispatch a court doctor to attend to you in case you have caught a chill."

"It's love that ails me, not the weather," Teyze said bitterly. "What doctor can cure a broken heart?"

"Time mends all pain. You will see: this too will pass." Perhaps I am being hard on her, Granny thought to herself. Heartache cannot always be so easily mended. It is adjusted to and tolerated, but after profound loss life is never the same again.

"Just getting from hour to hour is agony," Teyze said despondently and slumped back under her blankets.

If only Teyze had borne a child of her own, Granny said to herself, this transition would have been much easier. Women aren't like men. They are mothers above all; their children are the center of their lives.

"What else does he say?" Exasperated by the old lady's silence, Teyze spoke more sharply.

"Give me a chance, my eyesight isn't as good as it was." Granny held the letter up to the light and slowly read over the next paragraph. He had written to her in a simple script, so that she could read the letter without assistance. At first the import of what he wrote did not sink in; she read the letter again to make sure she had understood him correctly. This time the shock caused her pincenez to fall off her nose.

"His new bride is the daughter of Arzu's niece."

"I don't believe it! How insulting. To be abandoned is one thing, but for an ordinary woman, a member of the servant class?" Reeling with shock, Teyze closed her eyes and tried to recall what her rival looked like. She had been well dressed but, come to think of it, there was something coarse in the way she had addressed the bookseller.

"Oh Lord, now I am related by marriage to my own house-keeper!" Granny continued to stare at the letter in horror.

"How did their paths ever cross?"

"I have no idea, but his lack of respect for my feelings is incomprehensible."

"Edib never cared for social status," Teyze said quietly. "He thought it led to the decay of our system."

Granny wasn't listening. She sat back and read on, shaking her head and making hissing sounds between her teeth. "He wants to divide Sultan Tepe into separate apartments large enough to accommodate both of you equally."

"Is he trying to kill me?" gasped Teyze.

"He will have to understand that I can never receive his new wife into this house," Granny said with crisp caution. "It would mean acknowledging her as equal to my daughter." She folded the letter and tucked it inside her shawl. "I must write to him at once."

From the start Fatma Hanim had harbored doubts about his marriage to Teyze. Edib had wanted nothing more than a mother for Halide, this much was clear. No doubt he had pretended to himself he needed a companion, a woman to comfort him in his darker moments, but Edib was essentially a solitary man. He had loved Selima helplessly, like a schoolboy with a crush. Granny had never confused Edib's strong sense of duty with the capacity to experience enduring love. She felt sorry for Teyze, who was beset by romantic illusions and longed for more. With Edib she was doomed to disappointment.

"Do you suppose Arzu knows?" Teyze asked weakly, breaking the silence.

"Oh no, she'll be appalled when I tell her."

"Maybe she can throw some light on the mystery of their meeting."

"Does it matter? The deed is done. One must live with the future, not the past." Granny turned and gazed out the window. A light mist had formed over the stream beyond the stables. It rose and fell as if moved by the wind, yet the branches of the trees were quite still. So they are here with me, Granny thought, gazing out over the land. They have gathered to protect us. Or do they intend to cause more trouble? The mist swelled and shivered like a faint breath on a chill morning, and she felt secure in her knowledge that the spirits were present.

Chapter Nine

The house at Yildiz was smaller than Halide had remembered. Every window was hung with heavy damask. The front door, painted a startling shade of crimson, was flanked by a pair of manicured bay trees that Granny would have judged in bad taste. Halide hesitated before mounting the steps and ringing the doorbell. Standing alone in the narrow vestibule, she regretted having come all the way from Scutari in the middle of the school week for no other reason than to meet her father's new wife. A maid answered the door and, without a word of greeting, ushered her into a small room.

When she was a child, the house had been light and airy like the mansion at Beshiktash, furnished in simple Ottoman style with white curtains and velvet-covered divans. Now the place was crowded with furniture. The air smelled musty, and heavy curtains cut out the light. Before Halide could take in all the changes, the door burst open and her father came in, still wearing his coat.

"Forgive me, Halide. I was detained at the palace."

"I've only been waiting a few minutes," she said, standing up awkwardly to greet him.

"I wanted to be here in person to greet you." He removed his gloves and tossed them on a side table. When he embraced her, Halide smelled the sour smoky aroma of the palace still clinging to his clothes.

"You look tired," she said.

"I've had an awful week. The Sultan is still deeply disturbed by the attempted bombing of the council of ministers by terrorists from the eastern provinces. I haven't slept for days."

"Was anyone killed?"

"Alas, yes. And revenge for these deaths will only lead to more bloodshed."

"Can't the government do anything to stop it?"

"They're powerless to intervene. These days we are ruled from Yildiz Palace, and now that the Sultan fears for his life I don't know what will happen."

Edib had never revealed his concerns to his daughter before; his work had always been something he kept to himself. Halide was silent, afraid that anything she would say might break the spell.

"Greece, Albania, the Arabs," he continued, "everywhere we turn there is violence and revolution. Where will it end? Where will it end?" There were dark circles around his eyes and his face looked haggard. Moved by pity, Halide was determined to be on her best behavior and to get through the meeting without any awkward moments.

Tea was waiting for them in a large room overlooking the garden. Here more changes had been effected—bright silk had replaced the old velvet, and the curtains were so fringed and flounced they could have been discarded ball gowns. Next to the French doors was a table spread with lace and European china. At its center a three-tiered cake stand overflowed with pastries.

"What do you think?" Edib asked, his mood lifting at the sight of the pastries.

"It's quite different from the way it used to be," Halide said cautiously.

"Mamounia likes things to look pretty. It's not really my taste, but if she is happy . . ." Edib wanted his daughter to feel that she belonged here. He even planned to surprise her with a room of her own. His new wife would not object; it was not like her to do so. Edib took the pot and started to pour the tea. Halide looked around for a servant, but there was none to be seen.

"Mamounia prefers to be informal," Edib said, registering her confusion. "She'll be down in a minute. She's nervous about meeting you."

"But why? I'm not a scary person, am I?"

"She is a simple girl. I have boasted of your brilliance, and naturally she feels intimidated." He stopped pouring and smiled at his daughter.

"I'm nervous about meeting her too," Halide said, casting her eyes down.

"There's nothing to fear." Edib reached over to hold his daughter's hand and squeezed it a little too tightly. "She means well. You'll like her, I think."

"But she knows that I'm close to Teyze." Halide looked up at her father as if searching for an answer to a question she didn't dare ask.

"Mamounia accepts the situation," Edib said, pulling back and tending once more to the tea. "She has always known about the Scutari household."

"Then she knew who we were that day at the book market?"

"No, she found out later. Try one of these éclairs," Edib said, eager to change the subject. "I told Mamounia how much you liked them, so she went all the way to Pera to get some for you."

"I'm not hungry."

"You must eat something after such a long journey."

Halide heard a rustle behind her. The first impression she had as she turned to see who had come into the room was that she was faced with the phalanx of an enemy army. It took her a moment to recognize the woman from the book market, for the three newcomers all looked alike. They had the same wide mouth and brilliant cheeks; under their lace caps their fair hair was arranged in identical ringlets. Conscious of her own dark looks, Halide blushed. The women took in her reaction, like eagles eyeing their prey, then looked at one another. Then the youngest and prettiest disengaged herself and advanced toward Halide.

"Welcome, my dear Halide. I have heard so much about you from your father." As they embraced, Halide felt the woman's body tremble.

"These are my sisters, Nighiar and Meltem. They are staying with me for a while." The two women nodded and circled the tea table, murmuring appreciatively at the display of cakes. They were plump, with round arms and wide hips.

"Doesn't she run this house beautifully?" said Meltem.

"The decor is so pretty. We all dreamed of living in a house like this." They cooed back and forth across the tea table.

"I do exactly as Edib tells me," Mamounia confided with a giggle. "I want him to be comfortable."

"He is a lucky man. I always say you spoil him, Mamounia!"

"Oh my, these cakes are delicious. The French know how to do things."

"I prefer European things, don't you, Meltem?"

"Mamounia tells me you live in Scutari. I haven't been there since I was a child, it's so far away."

Halide responded as best she could but found it more comfortable to keep a distance from the cooing sisters. They were unlike any women she had ever met before, and she did not know what to say to them. Edib mistook her silence for shyness and smiled to himself contentedly. As far as he was concerned, everything was going according to plan.

Chapter Ten

Granny decided to replace the faded lampshades in the hallway outside her suite with beaded lanterns fashioned from colored glass. She loved shiny trinkets that shimmered like a rainbow when the light hit them. When her husband was alive he had feted her with gold jewelry, which she'd polished and shined herself and stored in a leather trunk. Ah, Ali Pasha had been a generous man, given to bursts of extravagance that contrasted with his unworldly ways. How she missed him! Still thinking about her late husband, she almost collided with Halide, who was home for the weekend.

"Why, child, there you are. I was wondering what had become of you."

"I've been in my room studying. I have to make up for the day I missed when I went to Yildiz."

"You haven't told me anything about the visit," Granny said sweetly.

"There's nothing to tell. I was only there a couple of hours. Father brought me back to school before sundown."

"How are they managing in that little house?" This was as close

as she could come to being circumspect. Halide's reticence was almost more than she could stand.

"They seemed comfortable. A little crowded, perhaps—she has
her sisters staying with her."

"So I hear," Granny said with a mischievous smile. "The cook
tells me they don't like to be apart. I wonder if your father realized
that before he married."

Halide shrugged. From the moment she had arrived home, the
women of the harem had plied her with questions. News traveled
fast, and she was amazed at how much they already knew about the
new Edib Hanim. Ten years before, the cook had lived across the
street from Mamounia's family in Haskoy, a village on the banks of
the Golden Horn. Even as children, she said, the sisters were
known for their blond good looks, giving rise to rumors about
their natural origins. The gardener's wife had briefly attended
Koran schools with Meltem and reported that their mother didn't
want her daughters associating with the neighborhood children.
There was general agreement that the sisters had inflated ideas of
their own importance. Arzu had little to say beyond the fact that
she was estranged from her family and outraged by this affront to
social order.

"I'm looking for one of my books, the New Testament," Halide
said, hoping to change the subject. "It's disappeared."

"How should I know where it is?" Granny snapped impatiently.

"This is the third one that's vanished. It happens every time I
come home."

"Really?" Granny said with exaggerated emphasis. "How odd."

"I distinctly remember it was in my room this morning." Halide
had a feeling that her grandmother knew more than she was letting on.

"What are they teaching you in that school, Halide, that you
need to take Bibles with you wherever you go?"

"Among other things we are learning about Buddhism and Christianity."

"Blasphemies!" Granny exclaimed in horror. "Allah is the one God."

"That's not the point, Granny," Halide said gently, anxious to avoid a misunderstanding. "My professors are not trying to convert me; they are just teaching us the history and philosophy of the great world religions."

"Come, child, there are no other religions. Ours is the true faith and everything else is a blasphemy. You should close your ears to their teaching." The old lady had heard long ago that Buddhists worshiped idols during the time of Jahiliyya, the dark era that preceded the coming of Mohammed.

"I'll be in serious trouble if I don't find that book," Halide sighed. "It came from the Boston Mission in America, and can't be replaced."

"I'll take a look around," Granny said. "Who knows, perhaps the peris are playing tricks on us again."

Shaking her head, the old woman started toward the stairs. America, she said to herself. Before Halide went to this college she had barely heard mention of the place. She herself had no idea where it was or what they did there. What do they want from us, she wondered. Why are they sending their holy word such a long distance for our children to read? But she didn't want to cause trouble for her granddaughter, so there was nothing to do except go to the *selamlik* library and retrieve those infidel volumes from beneath the cushion where she had concealed them.

SALIH ZEKI and Edib Pasha were deep in conversation, oblivious to the interest they aroused in this part of Scutari, where the homes were humble and street dogs mingled freely with the laborers.

Edib, who had come from a meeting with the grand vizier, wore a tight coat buttoned to the neck, straight-legged trousers, and a fez decorated with a gold cord. Salih Zeki's suit, bought in Paris several years before, was threadbare at the elbows. A wide red scarf was wrapped around his neck, and his felt hat was pulled down low to his ears. Earlier that morning, the two men had boarded one of the Imperial caïques and crossed the straits from the quay near Yildiz Park to Scutari. When they'd landed they'd dismissed their carriage and started out for the mansion on foot. Edib had said he felt more at ease talking in the open. He suspected he was being watched by the intelligence service, and he thought the men's quarters in Scutari had been infiltrated by an informer. The Sultan had forbidden his subjects from attending foreign schools, although many court officials chose to ignore the prohibition. Edib was certain that Abdulhamid knew he had enrolled his daughter at the American school. His decision had been a source of rumors and gossip for months—it was one thing to teach a son European ways and learning, but a daughter? What good could possibly come of that? Edib had chosen to ignore the rumors, but a matter of this importance could not pass without investigation.

"I wouldn't be surprised if your personal valet was the culprit. One does not know who to trust these days," Salih Zeki said.

"It's better to trust no one."

"What a dismal condition for existence."

"There are so many informers and they generate so much paperwork, the intelligence service will soon need new offices," Edib said with a wry smile.

"I hear our worthy ruler stays up late into the night reading every word."

"My Lord Sultan works hard on behalf of his people. He cares for them like his own children."

"If he is so caring, why was he so quick to abolish the constitution?" Salih Zeki asked heatedly.

"Too much freedom is not always a good thing," Edib said. "We must move slowly and cautiously along the path of progress."

"Oh come now, Edib, you don't mean a word of what you say! We are moving backward, not forward. The government ministers are powerless, the Sublime Porte is a sham, and every decision emanates from the Sultan."

Edib flushed and looked down, hoping no one had heard this. The street was deserted, but the sound of their voices ricocheted off the cobblestones. "Measure your words carefully, my friend," he said under his breath. "One never knows who's listening."

"I am appalled by the power of the Sultan," Salih Zeki said, lowering his voice. "He thinks he is Suleiman the Magnificent. How can we Ottomans become part of Europe when we are ruled by a despot?"

"I beg of you, my friend, be careful, if only for my sake. I have many enemies at court, especially among the ulema."

"What's their problem with you? I thought you had them on your side."

"They don't approve of my educating Halide."

"Hah, that's tantamount to a revolution!" Salih Zeki said ironically. "What dangers can a young girl wield with a pen?"

"We have a duty to ourselves to make the most of what we are. I'd do the same thing all over again if I were to have other children," Edib said, his cheeks flushing.

Salih Zeki gave his friend a sidelong glance, wondering if he was trying to tell him something. Since that day at the palace when Teyze had caused such a scene, Edib had never so much as mentioned his new wife. Poor Edib: his marriage had been harshly criticized. Enlightened friends were scornful, for polygamy was perceived as an outdated institution. It was unbecoming for a liberal, educated man to marry again. At home, Fatma Hanim Efendi and Teyze had refused to accept the second wife on any terms, despite her legal status. Not a single person, not even his daughter, had made any attempt to understand the logic of his behavior. To Salih Zeki it was obvious. Besides, the ideal of monogamy was irrational; it gave rise to hypocrisy and deceit. He had seen proof of that in Paris.

They strode on without speaking, each lost in his own thoughts. At the top of the hill the road forked left, snaking between tightly packed houses until it gave way to the outer wall of the Mirihma Mosque. Looking over his shoulder, Salih Zeki saw the minarets rising above the jumbled rooftops. Edib turned down a narrow alley leading to a flight of steep steps. The smell of singed meat drifted from a nearby garden, and the sound of laughter issued from behind a door. At the bottom of the steps they came across a sallow man in baggy trousers holding a brass jug. Balanced on a flat stone beside him was a bucket of burning charcoal.

"A *sahlep* seller!" exclaimed Salih Zeki. "I haven't tasted *sahlep* since I was a boy. How much for two cups?"

The man held up six fingers. Salih Zeki nodded, and the vendor unhooked a pair of cups hanging from the rim of the bucket and passed them to him. He poured the warm liquid without spilling a drop. The vendor had that pinched expression of poverty Salih Zeki had come to recognize since returning from Paris. Moved by pity tinged with contempt, he handed him a large bill and told the man to keep the change.

"This is welcome on a cold December morning." Edib curled his hands around the warm cup.

"My grandmother used to make me *sahlep* every day during the long winters of my childhood."

"Where did you grow up?" Edib had never heard his friend mention his childhood before.

"In Kadikoy."

"That's not far from here! But surely that's an Ottoman Greek district?"

"We lived in a Turkish neighborhood near the harbor, and always got along with our Greek neighbors. I suspect I have a few drops of Greek blood somewhere in my veins."

"I was born in Salonika," Edib said after a pause. "I never knew my parents. They might have been Greek or Armenian." Sometimes he wondered if his liberal views were inherited from ancestors he never knew.

"Even if they were, would it change anything? You were raised to be an Ottoman Turk."

"And that is the condition of my soul." Edib drifted off, lost in thought. Salih Zeki was tempted to ask what he meant by this but thought better of it, and they lapsed into silence.

Salih Zeki took a deep breath of salty air and was filled with a sense of well-being. It was good to be back where he belonged, with the sweet taste of *sahlep* lingering in his mouth. Despite living in Paris for many years, he was and always would be Turkish in his heart.

"Where is your family now?" Edib asked at length.

"They're dead. I've been alone for many years."

"Solitude is not good for a man. You need a wife to look after you, run your household, and bring you comfort. I speak from experience."

Salih Zeki did not respond at first. Mistaking his silence for anger, Edib began to apologize, but his friend cut him short. "Your proposition has a great deal to recommend it," he said, "but unfortunately wives and families are expensive. That is why I need to talk to you."

Edib drained his cup and returned it to the vendor. He did not want to admit that his own finances were in a sorry state. If Salih

Zeki needed money, there was little he could do to help; he could not afford to pay more.

"I want you to be the first to hear my good news," Salih Zeki said grandly. "I've been offered the directorship of the observatory."

The newly built observatory was perched on the highest hill in Pera, just behind the Grande Rue. The directorship had been offered to Salih Zeki at the behest of the Sultan himself, who was anxious to keep a man of his intellectual stature within the Ottoman system and not lose him to a rival European institution. Zeki Bey's knowledge of advanced mathematics was crucial to the astronomical research being conducted at the observatory, and in addition his name would add prestige to their work. The position would entail some travel to Europe, but the terms of his contract were so generous the Sultan was confident Zeki Bey would not be tempted by rival offers from European universities.

"Congratulations!" Edib put his hand out and clasped his companion by the shoulder. "I'm overjoyed, and the honor is well deserved."

"From now on, my time will be taken up with preparing for my new post. My Sunday tutoring visits will have to be curtailed."

"I understand, don't give the matter another thought. Dr. Patrick tells me Halide is doing well at school."

"She has become very attached to me," Salih Zeki cautioned.

"That's normal! You are a famous scholar worthy of her respect."

"I'm somewhat concerned that this sudden termination of our association may have a negative affect on her."

"I think Halide will be delighted to hear of your good fortune," Edib said, dismissing his concern with a wave of his hand.

"I would prefer to tell her in my own way," Salih Zeki insisted. "I will write her a letter this afternoon."

Halide had become deeply attached to him; he could see it in the quiet affection with which she greeted him. His lack of money and the difference in their status were, he knew, obstacles to any further relationship. Although this new promotion would tilt the balance in his favor, he doubted Halide could be happy with a man like him, a man twice her age, from another class and upbringing; a man who carried complicated baggage from the past.

THE LETTER was given to Halide as she was filing into the dining hall for tea. It had been delivered to the secretary's office that morning, but Dr. Patrick did not allow anything to interfere with the school day, and it lay on a stack of mail until lessons were over. Halide recognized the handwriting at once: Salih Zeki formed his letters in the same precise manner in which he calculated math problems, with none of the flourishes of her own script. Clutching the envelope, she excused herself and made her way into the garden, where she could be alone.

A cluster of late-blooming chrysanthemums lay across the path, drooping under the weight of their petals. As Halide knelt down to rescue the dying flowers, the letter slipped from her hand. She wiped the envelope with her sleeve and inspected it closely. Why was he writing to her in the middle of the week? Was he giving her extra homework, or canceling this Sunday's lesson? That was it, she reasoned. He was probably caught up by an emergency in Paris or Salonika. Unable to contain her curiosity any further, she tore open the envelope.

Dearest Halide, she read. *Forgive me for intruding on your school day. I have just returned home after a congenial meeting with your father . . .* Her eye rushed over the next few lines. Stay calm, she told herself. . . . *these appointments are effective immediately so, with your father's permission, we have agreed to terminate your lessons at*

*once. Your father has promised to keep me informed of your prog-
ress . . .* The page swam in front of her eyes, and Halide felt suddenly faint. She threw her coat down on the grass and flung herself
on top of it. With ritual precision, she balanced the chrysanthemums on her chest and slowly read the last lines of his letter out
loud.

*. . . I know you will be a success. Remember to adhere to the princi-
ples of reason, and do not allow your heart to get the better of you.
Your friend, Salih Zeki.*

What did he mean by that? Had he guessed that she was drawn
to him? How embarrassing! He must think her a foolish lovesick
girl, not a scholar worthy of his admiration. Suddenly Halide
wished she had never met this man. She wished she could forget
about him and find someone nearer her own age, from a good
family, so that Granny would be satisfied. How many times had
she prayed for someone like her father, handsome, learned, with
fine manners and a balanced view of the world?

She lay staring at the sky until darkness fell and the first stars appeared. The more she thought over his words, the deeper her pain
became, until tears flowed down her cheeks and filled her eyes and
she could no longer see the stars.

Chapter Eleven

Halide did not see Salih Zeki again after that letter. She settled
back into her course work with a fierce determination to
succeed. She continued to keep her diary, but she was more
guarded with her emotions. Now her work, not Salih Zeki, became
the focus of her concerns. As the months passed, her command of

English rapidly improved, and by spring she had become one of the most promising students in her class.

Halide's thoughts often turned to Mahmoure. She wondered what had become of her sister after Ali Shamil's death. Was she still with Riza? Were they happy? In her heart Halide believed it was not right to leave behind three small children. She felt sorry for Ahmet, whom she saw once at their home in Suleimaniye.

As winter gave way to spring Halide returned less often to Sultan Tepe and began to grow apart from Teyze. She went home now only once or twice a month, and when she did she found herself spending more time with Granny. She knew that the old lady was anxious about the preservation of her faith, and made an extra effort to go to the mosque whenever she was home.

ONE WEEKEND in late April, Teyze set off as usual with Granny and Arzu to visit the tomb of Ali Pasha. It was almost noon by the time the three women reached the dervish enclosure deep in the heart of the Karaca Ahmet Cemetery. Heirs to the tradition of Haci Bektash, Jalaloddin Rumi, and the other dervish saints around whom the great brotherhoods had coalesced lay side by side, surrounded by a ring of dark cypresses. The Sufis based their lives on an unquestioning trust in God. Poets, visionaries, some said madmen, they rejected orthodox Islam in favor of a more personal relationship with God. Their rejection of the orthodox was so strong that some Sufis even refused to observe the holy holidays or pray in a conventional mosque. These rebellious sentiments permeated every level of Turkish society, from the steppe lands in the east to the cosmopolitan environs of Constantinople, and the great Sufi brotherhoods held a powerful position in the Ottoman world.

The women stepped over ivy, honeysuckle vines, and wild roses, scaring away the cats playing on the half-cleared mounds.

"Don't the dervishes have any respect for their dead?" Granny grumbled, waving her stick over the tangled undergrowth.

"I heard the gardener from the lodge stopped coming before the summer. It's too dangerous for him to be associated with a heretical sect in these uncertain times." Arzu was still panting after the uphill climb.

Granny hacked one of the vines with the tip of her walking stick. "If I weren't so old, I'd do the task myself."

"Stop, you'll hurt yourself," Teyze said, drawing alongside Granny and reaching for her arm. She thought the wildness better suited the resting place of the dead. What did they care for fresh roses or crowns of anemones?

"I can't stand by and watch these graves fall to pieces," Granny said with resolve. "We must return here with one of our own gardeners."

"An excellent idea, ma'am. May I suggest we bring tulip bulbs and plant them in time for next spring?" Arzu dropped her heavy basket and paused to catch her breath. She took out an embroidered cloth and shook it violently before laying it on a flat piece of ground between the tombs. "I'll set the food here, out of the wind."

"We're close to the resting place of Mustafa Efendi. He was a friend of my father's, a man who liked his food and was wise when it came to matters of the heart." The old lady nodded knowingly at Teyze.

"You must stop wasting your prayers on me," Teyze retorted with a weak smile. "I have accepted my fate. Besides, I thought we were here to pray for Halide."

"We are," Granny said. "We have to guard her soul with every resource available. That Dr. Patrick impressed me as a powerful woman."

"Halide says her teachers are well educated and happy to live alone without husbands. Perhaps there is something we can learn from them, after all."

"Oh come now, Teyze, don't talk nonsense." Granny dismissed the bitterness in Teyze's voice, confident that time would soften the raw edges of her pain.

A twig cracked in the trees behind them, startling Teyze.

"Mercy, what is that?" cried Arzu.

"Just a bird," Granny said.

"I can see someone walking on the other side of the cypresses."

"Is it a spirit?" By now Granny's curiosity was piqued.

"No," Teyze laughed, "our apparition appears to be flesh and blood."

The intruder showed no surprise at finding himself the object of their startled attention. Keeping a respectful distance, he bowed and withdrew to an area of high grass between the trees and the tombs. He was taller than average, with a refined, intelligent face. His beard, thick and carefully combed, reached almost to his throat. His long hair was drawn back and tied at the nape of his neck, and his rather large hands were knotted over the end of his stick.

"Forgive me for intruding on you." He addressed them in a deep voice with a slight accent.

"On the contrary, it is we who have intruded on you." Granny scrutinized his dark blue cloak and staff and decided he must be a dervish, though not from the area.

"My name is Suleiman Efendi," he said, as if in answer to her stare. "I came here to pray at the tombs of my Bektashi brothers."

"My late husband belonged to the same order," Granny said. "Ali Pasha of Beshiktash. He is buried in another section of this cemetery. But where have you come from? Your accent tells me you are not from around here."

"I've recently arrived from the Balkan provinces of Albania

and found refuge at the dervish lodge near Scutari." His manner was circumspect, as if he were accustomed to treating even the most harmless remarks with caution. He remained solemn as he spoke, but there was an air of calm about him that was reassuring.

"Albania," said Granny with a frown. "Albania, why is that name so familiar?"

"There are many Bektashi in that part of the world."

"My late husband had a connection there, or was it his brother?" Granny shook her head. "Alas, my memory is not what it was."

"What brings you to the city?" Teyze decided it was time to intervene. The stranger radiated a kind of quiet energy, and she was immediately drawn to him.

"These are difficult times," the man said, tightening his grip on his stick. "There have been uprisings in Albania, and reprisals have been swift. We have friends here in the capital," he added enigmatically.

"Things are not much better here," Teyze whispered. For centuries the Bektashi had advised the Sultan's bodyguards on matters of religion. Fifty years earlier, when the guards revolted, the Bektashi were slaughtered in the streets and mention of their name was banned. These lessons of history were not lost on Abdulhamid, who kept members of the order under close scrutiny.

"Did you pass through Adrianople on your journey?" Granny asked.

"I stayed there for a while."

"Did you encounter the great Fuad Pasha, my husband's cousin? He was an important man in that part of the world."

Arzu, who was setting out the food, paused to remind her that the old Pasha had died three winters before.

"Ah," sighed Granny, "I forgot. At my age it becomes hard to distinguish between the living and the dead."

"Your sensibility is a blessing," he said and smiled.

Teyze noticed that lines on either side of his mouth rose in a deep curve when he spoke and his eyes moved from side to side, as if taking in every detail.

"Please honor us with your company," Granny said, gesturing toward the dishes of pilaf, chicken in walnut sauce, and grape leaves. "We were just about to eat."

The dervish eyed the food with enthusiasm. "The honor is mine," he said. "I haven't eaten today—we're woefully short of food."

"Surely the people give you alms? Dervishes have always been welcome at my door, although I regret to say most are not as genteel as you."

"You are most generous," he said and did not elaborate.

The stranger sat down on the edge of a tomb, taking care to separate himself from the women. Teyze later learned that his pride had been wounded at being mistaken for one of the wild-eyed holy men who wandered from town to town decked out in animal skins. In the Albanian provinces he had led his sect through dangerous encounters with the Ottoman authorities. He was a man of fearless determination.

There was a great deal that Teyze would find out in the months to come, for the chance meeting in the dervish cemetery would prove to be a turning point in her life.

Part Four

Chapter One

The prize-giving ceremony was to be held at the college in early December. The night of the ceremony was bitterly cold; Halide was forced to wait in the vestibule of the main building, where she had an unobstructed view of the door. Behind her the lobby filled with visitors. A cloud of cigar smoke swirled around the bright chandeliers and the strains of the carol singers were almost drowned by the hum of voices. A gong rang, announcing dinner, and conversation subsided as the crowd surged toward the dining room. A lone chorister sang "Silent Night."

Halide hurried outside and scanned the driveway, which was jammed with carriages. She twisted her hands nervously. Her father had promised to arrive early and said he would come with Teyze and Granny. She hoped nothing had gone wrong with this fragile plan. When news of her prize was first announced, Edib had wanted to bring Mamounia to the ceremony, but Halide had been adamantly against it. Mamounia's presence would have made it impossible for Granny and Teyze to attend, and would have embarrassed her in front of her friends. She was proud of her father's liberal views, and deeply moved by the risks he had taken to send her to the American school, but it was hard for her to understand how he justified to himself being married to two women.

More than a year had elapsed since his third marriage, and during that time the schism between the Yildiz and Sultan Tepe households had grown deeper. Edib rarely came to the Scutari mansion anymore, so that during vacations Halide was compelled to visit him at his home in Yildiz. She had nothing in common with Mamounia; conversation was forced, and the lack of sympathy between them made it difficult for Halide to relax in the room her father had so lovingly prepared for her. The situation was no better at Sultan Tepe, where Granny and Teyze watched her every move, searching for signs of conversion. Teyze's concerns waned as her involvement with the dervishes increased, but Granny remained vigilant.

Halide found refuge from the escalating tensions of her home life in the school library, where she became absorbed in her work. She was seized by the same excitement she had known as a child when she'd first learned to read. Toward the end of the fall term of her second year her name was added to the dean's list, and one of her stories won a governor's award. "You must be very clever to win an award for writing English in a school full of Americans," Granny had observed when Halide had told her the good news.

"They're not all American, Granny," she'd laughed. "We've got Armenian, Bulgarian, and Jewish girls, even some Greeks."

"Greeks, eh? Well, never mind, it's still a great honor."

"Salih Zeki told me to keep a journal, and writing in it has been good practice. I've been doing it for over a year now . . ." Her voice had trailed off: it was useless to explain to her grandmother that writing in the journal had become an obsession; recording her dreams and desires seemed to rid her of troublesome demons.

"Halide, *Halide*, is that you?" Her father's voice jolted her back to the present, and she turned to see him pushing his way through the crowd. "I didn't recognize you. What are you doing in a veil?"

"With so many strangers around, I didn't feel comfortable being bareheaded."

"But all the other girls . . ." He tried to hide his disappointment. "I mean, you're the only one. Don't you feel conspicuous?" There's nothing I can do about it now, Edib said to himself, but later I must ask her why, after more than a year at the American school, she insists on clinging to this regressive symbol of modesty.

"Did you have trouble getting here?" Halide asked, stung by his criticism.

"We were delayed waiting for Teyze. She was delivering food to the poor with the dervishes."

"I gather she's very busy these days. Granny told me the harem women call her the second Saint Rabia."

"Was there another one?" Edib said. He had meant this to be a joke, but Halide took his remark seriously.

"Haven't you heard of Rabia of Basra, the first Sufi saint? She lived in the Syrian province about a thousand years ago."

"I seem to recall having heard something about her." Teyze's sudden and complete espousal of charity work annoyed him. It was a laudable undertaking, yet he found the idea of his wife ministering to the poor in the company of unkempt dervishes demeaning.

"I'm doing a piece about her for the school magazine," Halide continued.

"Isn't there something more up-to-date you could write about?"

"Dr. Patrick was very interested to learn that there were women saints amongst the Sufis."

The evening had not begun well. Edib seemed tense, almost distracted. He took Halide's arm and steered her across the hall, casting an admiring glance out of the corner of his eye as they passed a group of women in low-cut dresses. Some students, easily recognizable in their serge dresses and crisp collars, backed away as he walked by.

"Where are we going?" Halide asked.

"Your grandmother and Teyze are waiting in the carriage around the back. They were afraid to come to the front door because of the crowds."

"Too many Christians, you mean?"

"Exactly." He smiled.

Halide glanced up at the clock on the wall. "I have to go," she said. "In five minutes all the prizewinners are supposed to assemble near the stage."

"Let's meet after the ceremony in the upstairs dining room. Wait, Halide." He caught her by the hand and pulled her toward him so that his face was almost level with hers. "I want you to know that I am very proud of you. I only wish your mother could share this occasion with us."

"Oh, she is here," Halide said, looking at her father through the folds of her veil. He grasped her shoulders, ready to protest, but the steadiness of her gaze silenced him.

❧

THE CEREMONY was held in the assembly hall, once the reception area of the old men's quarters. When the girls college had taken over the mansion, the dividing walls had been demolished and the salons combined to form a single space large enough to hold more than two hundred people. On this occasion it was filled to overflowing. The crowd stood two deep along the walls, applauding and smiling as the prizewinners passed to the front of the room. Professors and school governors sat crowded together on a small platform where a Christmas tree sagged under the weight of its ornaments. Dr. Patrick stepped forward and held her hand up for silence. The lights dimmed. The prizewinners nudged one another in anticipation.

When her name was announced, Halide stood up and stared around her with a rush of pride. Applause thundered in her ears. As she brushed past, the previous prizewinner hissed at her to hurry.

Halide mounted the platform, her heart pounding with excitement, scarcely heeding Dr. Patrick or her congratulatory murmurs. A book was pressed into her hands and she curtsied, mumbling her thanks. Returning to her seat she glanced at the back of the hall—a side door had opened, bringing an arc of light flooding in from the outside. A man entered the room, his back to the stage. He turned and walked quickly in the direction of the lobby.

Halide sat for a moment, wondering if she was seeing things. If it was Salih Zeki, what was he doing here? And why hadn't he told her he was coming? She looked again, but the door had closed and the back of the hall was covered once more in semidarkness.

Bending low to avoid being noticed by the line of dignitaries, she crept past the other girls and into the aisle. Under cover of a burst of applause, she pushed open a side door and found herself in the empty hall. Salih Zeki was nowhere to be seen. Nervous and excited, still carrying the prize under her arm, she raced toward the garden.

"STOP, ZEKI BEY, stop!" she cried, but her voice was drowned out by the sounds of the night. In the gray moonlight she could see the outline of a figure walking along the drive, his head lowered. She ran after him, calling his name as loudly as she dared, fearful of alerting the gardeners, who were doubling that night as security guards.

The man stopped and swiveled around sharply. Seeing him

hesitate, she started to run faster. The wind whipped her veil into her eyes and she tore it off so that she could see the way ahead. She had no difficulty catching up with him: under the guidance of Dr. Patrick, in whose Puritan heart flourished the conviction that a healthy body bred a healthy mind, she had grown strong.

"Halide, my God, what are you doing out here?"

"When I left the stage I caught sight of you at the back of the room . . ." she stammered.

"I had to leave early. I am expected in Galata—my carriage is waiting at the end of the drive." He gestured in the direction of the gate but made no move to leave.

"Must you go so soon? Father's here and Granny and Teyze. They'll be so sorry to have missed you."

"You know me—I dislike crowds," he said softly. "Once I had seen you receive your prize there was no need for me to stay."

"You came all this way just to see me?"

"I wouldn't have missed it for anything," he said with a smile.

"But how did you know?"

"Your father told me." He felt suddenly weak and confused: he had not expected to meet her face-to-face.

"It's all thanks to you!" Halide said excitedly. "If you hadn't encouraged me to write a diary, I never would have mastered English composition."

"The prize is your own accomplishment, Halide. I take no credit for it."

The silence that followed was broken by the sound of the wind blowing through the trees. Salih Zeki shifted from one foot to the other, wondering what to say. Halide's confidence began to evaporate, and she immediately regretted her impulsive behavior. What was she doing out here alone in the dark with the head of the observatory, an important man in the academic community, while she was nothing more than a schoolgirl? She began to tremble, whether from cold or fear she could not tell.

"You're shivering," he said. "Here, take this." He unfastened the buttons of his coat and draped it over her shoulders. It hung so loosely on her small frame she had to tie the sleeves together to keep it from slipping off.

"You always wore this coat, even when the weather was warm," she said through chattering teeth.

"I bought it in Paris. I have become very attached to it, like an old friend." A ferry horn echoed across the canopy of night.

"Please go if you have to catch the boat. Don't let me keep you," she said, desperate for him to stay.

"I can leave later."

"They come every hour. Of course, you know that." Her heart was pounding so loudly she felt certain he could hear it.

"Perhaps we should sit down." He glanced over his shoulder. The moon was almost full, and he could see down the road winding back toward the school. There was no one around.

"I think there's a glade back here under the plane trees." Halide leapt over a shallow ditch, trailing his coat in the long grass. She had no difficulty finding the patch of ground, half remembered from the summer. Once or twice they collided in their quest, drawing apart the moment their arms touched. She let his coat slip from her shoulders and laid it flat on the ground between the roots of a large oak tree.

"That's better. At least we're out of the wind." He sat so close to her his breath brushed her face.

"Did you enjoy the ceremony?" Halide stared at her feet, trying to think of something interesting to say.

"I was astonished by the change in you, Halide. You've grown up in the last year."

"Granny says I'm old enough to marry!" She tried to make a joke of it but regretted it at once.

"There will be many young men eager to marry you when the time comes," he said stiffly.

"I'm not getting married yet," she said impetuously. "I have too much to do. I'd like to go to Paris, the Sorbonne . . ."

The sight of her young face so close to his was more than Salih Zeki could stand. Without thinking, he leaned over and kissed her, silencing her chatter with his tongue. He was stunned by the urgency of her response. Their bodies intertwined, and he felt himself spinning into a dark hole. "This is insanity!" he whispered, pulling away.

She clutched his neck and tried to pull him close, but he held back, tensing his shoulders.

"We must, my God." He took a deep breath to calm himself and pushed himself up onto his knees, fearful at any moment they could be caught in the lights of a passing carriage.

"Wait, Salih Zeki, there is something I must tell you." She was trembling now from the force of her emotion.

"Don't say something you'll regret," he said sharply. "It's time to go back inside."

"But I don't understand!" she cried.

"If it's any consolation," he said, looking off into the distance, "you should know that your feelings are returned. But you are a schoolgirl, and I am a man who is old enough to be your father."

"So what? I don't care!"

"I must go. Your family will be wondering where you are." With that he helped her to her feet. They walked together in silence back to firm ground, and he waited while she made her way alone along the drive toward the school. How could it be, he wondered, that the order he had worked so hard to attain had been shaken by this slip of a girl? He was cross with himself, yet inwardly, he was overjoyed.

※

"ONE WOULD never know we are but a stone's throw from Sultan Tepe," Granny mused, staring around the college's dining room. The ceremony had ended and the families had dispersed; Teyze and Granny were waiting to rendezvous with Halide and her father.

"Everyone here is more elegant than I had expected. I wish I'd worn one of my evening dresses," Teyze murmured uncomfortably, aware of the curiosity they had aroused among the other parents. Though she had chosen to wear a light silk scarf that barely covered her face, they were the only veiled women in the crowd.

"You look beautiful. That shade of green complements your eyes."

"This is an afternoon dress, it's not appropriate. From the way the invitation was worded, I thought it was an informal occasion."

"I didn't think you cared about these trifles anymore."

"It's Halide I'm thinking of, not myself," Teyze said quickly. "I don't want to embarrass her."

Granny pretended to take her at her word. There was still a trace of the fashionable grande dame in Teyze, despite her recent espousal of Suleiman Efendi and his teaching. Six months before, she had taken the dervish as her master, and under his tutelage she was pursuing the path to perfect wisdom. Granny was horrified: in her opinion, a person had to be either insane or truly devout to undertake such a difficult journey.

"I hope Edib finds her. He has been gone more than half an hour."

"Why didn't you go with him? He would have been delighted. It's obvious he still cares for you."

"I had the opposite impression. He raced outside as if he couldn't wait to escape." Teyze fanned herself to cover her confusion.

"He's too embarrassed to admit his mistake. Now the novelty has worn off and he's left with the reality of being estranged from his family and friends, and married to a bore with social ambitions beyond her station. I almost feel sorry for him."

"Well, in any event it's too late. I have another life now."

"Doing what, being a benefactor to the dervishes? They're no substitute for a husband. You're too beautiful to sacrifice yourself to good deeds."

"If I didn't support them they would be destitute and the poor people of Scutari would go hungry. They need me, which is more than can be said for Edib."

The old lady pursed her mouth in disapproval. "Don't forget that you are still his wife."

"There are times when I wish he would seek a divorce."

"Divorce is such a drastic step." Granny tried to recall the circumstances surrounding the only divorce that had ever occurred in the family, apart from Selima, who was too young to count. A distant cousin lost custody of her daughter to an unpleasant husband and much suffering followed. The daughter came to a sad end, and everyone put it down to the unnatural ending of the marriage.

"Halide is almost seventeen, and capable of understanding that we are better off being free of each other."

"Seventeen?" echoed Granny. "I forget how the years pass. It's time I brought up the subject of her marriage with Edib."

"Shouldn't you ask Halide first?"

"What does she know of these things?"

"Halide is being raised to think for herself and might not appreciate plans for her future being made without her." Teyze was amazed that the old lady could think of marriage at a time like this.

At the sight of Edib, striding across the room with Halide at his side, Granny's expression brightened.

"I found Halide waiting outside, at the top of the steps," Edib said as he joined them.

"In this weather?" Granny exclaimed disapprovingly.

Edib shrugged with the air of a man for whom the behavior of young women remained a mystery.

"I'm sorry to have kept you waiting," Halide said, rushing to kiss her grandmother's hand.

"Now that you're here, perhaps we can call the carriage." The old lady levered herself upright with her stick and poked the back of the chair. "I still get a backache from sitting for too long in these things."

They were about to leave when a tall girl with pale blue eyes came up to Halide. "Did you catch up with your father?" she asked in English. "I saw you running after him."

"My father? He's here." Halide lifted her veil and the girl followed her gaze toward Edib, who was helping Teyze with her cloak.

"I mean the man in the greatcoat, the one with the beard. I went outside because I felt faint and I saw you both in the drive."

"That was my uncle," Halide said, gathering her wits. "He had to leave early, and I wanted to thank him for coming."

So these are her friends now, Granny mused, watching the conversation through her veil. Do they all resemble this pale loop of a girl, too tall and too angular for beauty, who will certainly have trouble finding a husband unless her family is very wealthy? Goodness, what is Halide doing, removing her veil in public, and looking at her father in such a strange way? Her face is strained, almost frightened. She must be feeling the uneasiness in the air tonight. As soon as we drove through the gates I sensed it. The spirits are restless; they have been disturbed by this intrusion of foreigners onto their land.

THE GIRLS were filled with excitement. Addresses were exchanged and plans were made to see one another at parties and dances over the vacation. Halide took no part in these discussions. She knew that once she returned to the harem, the door to the Christian world would slam behind her. Any invitation to the home of an infidel friend, a place where women were unveiled and the sexes mixed freely, was certain to invoke a polite refusal from her grandmother. Attending dances was out of the question. Only a chaperoned visit to the Pera tea rooms remained a possibility. Halide consoled herself by devising elaborate plans to see Salih Zeki without arousing her grandmother's suspicions.

In the week between the prize-giving ceremony and the start of Christmas break, Halide had thought about him all the time. Try as she might, she could not help herself. Her feelings disturbed her because they interfered with her class work and concentration. Dr. Patrick placed a high premium on a woman's education and impressed on Halide the responsibility inherent in being the first Turkish girl at the school. Dr. Patrick made worldly achievement seem so simple, but Halide was not sure she possessed the same cool competence and disregard for the norms of society. In Salih Zeki she had found the model for everything she wished to be: a respected scholar, an enlightened thinker, and an excellent teacher. His intellect awed her. He was the only man she knew who was capable of guiding her, although she was forced to admit she did not know many men outside the family.

By the time the last day of term arrived, the girls' trunks were lined up in front of the main building awaiting collection. They had been carried from the dormitories by a local Turkish youth hired for the week to help with the extra work. From snatches of conversation she overheard between the servants, Halide gathered that he was a student at the newly opened high school in Scutari. He thought himself a cut above the other servants, because unlike them, he was literate.

Early on the afternoon of her departure Halide made her way into the hall, dressed in her traveling cloak and boots. She was looking forward to going home. A noise in the corner startled her. She saw the Turkish boy leaning against one of the pillars, his attention absorbed by a paper. As soon as she drew near he gave her an angry glance and hurried away, dropping his newspaper in his haste. Upset by the stern expression of his face, Halide retrieved the journal and called after him, but he did not hear her.

It had been months since she had seen a Turkish newspaper, and her eyes wandered over the headlines. There was news of unrest in the old city and a report of a riot in Galata involving some Italian seamen. She was bemused by the amount of space devoted to social activities. There were detailed accounts of a party at the French embassy, a dance at Madame Dumoile's mansion, and a diplomatic reception at the home of the German ambassador. At the foot of the back page a small headline announced the departure of the head of the observatory. Had she been in a hurry, she might have overlooked it. It was reported that Salih Zeki Bey, director of the Imperial Observatory, had left for Paris on the midnight train from Sirkeci Station. The reason for this unexpected departure was "personal," and the director hoped to return by the end of the month. In his absence, Halik Efendi would assume his responsibilities, and the annual examinations would proceed on schedule.

Chapter Two

S now had fallen during the night, and a crisp layer covered the ground around the mansion. Teyze lifted a corner of the shade and looked outside. The darkness was tinged with gray, a sign of the approaching dawn.

"As soon as it's light we can leave," she remarked to Halide, who was seated on the divan sipping a glass of tea. The two of them had decided to take their morning meal together in one of the rooms near the kitchen. Despite the cold, the room was warm, thanks to the recent installation of a German stove built to the same specifications as the ones in Yildiz Palace.

"I think Granny should stay home," Halide said. "I don't like to think of her sitting outside in the cold."

"Nothing deters her. She never misses a day at the cemetery. I'll give her my extra coat, and she can put it over her knees."

Halide couldn't help noticing that Teyze's dress was fraying at the edges, but she had gone to great lengths to look beautiful. Her face was powdered, her eyes ringed with kohl, her lips stained red in contrast to her pale skin.

"I'm so pleased you're coming with me, Halide. We need the extra help. Now that winter is here the situation with the refugees is desperate. If Suleiman Efendi had not organized a group of his followers to feed them, they would starve."

"I'm eager to meet this *efendi* of yours. You've talked so much about him."

"He is an extraordinary man, you will sense that at once. You must treat him with reverence. Although I sponsor their work, don't forget he is also my Sufi master."

"I thought women weren't allowed to become Sufis," Halide said skeptically. As far as she knew, with the exception of early saints like Rabia and Zulaykha, women were excluded from the ranks of the enlightened.

"The Bektashi are different. Their order has always accepted women."

"Of course, I forgot." Halide took a sliver of white cheese from the platter. "Grandfather told me when I was a child."

"Women rarely follow the path. Most have too many responsibilities—husbands, children, a home. But I am different," she added wistfully.

"I thought finding a master was a long process." Halide hoped to revive Teyze's spirits by engaging her further on her favorite subject.

"I was fortunate to find my master without having to search."

"Why Suleiman, why not one of the other teachers?"

Teyze, who had been pinning her hair up with tortoiseshell pins, paused, her hands still resting on her head. "From our first meeting in the cemetery I felt connected to him. Then, through my work with the poor, I came to know and trust him. Trust is an essential element between master and novice." Halide noticed that when she talked about the dervish, Teyze's face took on a strange expression. "In time I will have to surrender everything—my will, my worldly concerns. So you see, the choice of master is pivotal to my well-being, my very existence."

Halide frowned. She did not like Teyze's choice of words. They suggested a repudiation of the world she was only just beginning to experience.

"In time I will have to give up my comfortable life at the harem, but I don't mind. Things that used to matter now seem unimportant, like buying European clothes, and reading the latest French novel."

"Where will you live?"

"I haven't thought about it. I'm only a novice, and the first thing I have to do is help the poor for at least three years, until Suleiman thinks I am ready to move on."

"I hope you're not doing this because of Father."

Teyze's hands dropped to her sides and her cheeks flushed.

"Wouldn't it be better to stay here at Sultan Tepe and work for the poor?" Halide persisted.

"I cannot be dissuaded, Halide," Teyze said with a smile. "Believe me, your grandmother has tried."

"I want to understand," Halide said softly.

Teyze glanced out the window. "It's getting light; it will soon be time for us to leave." The thought of seeing her master again excited her. He had come into her life when her temper was low and her will to live was almost extinguished. God had brought him to Scutari for a purpose, he had told her. They were meant to meet.

Wrapped in layers of cloaks and sheepskins, the three women huddled in the carriage. Despite the bitter weather, Fatma Hanim Efendi had refused to miss her daily visit to her husband's tomb. By the time they reached the market, the streets were thronged with people. Teyze and Halide dismounted, leaving the old lady to continue on to Karaca Ahmet alone. They linked arms to stay warm and crossed the street pressed close together.

Teyze stopped by a stall lit from overhead by a line of small oil lamps that swung to and fro in the breeze. She poked the vegetables, sniffed the fruit, and disputed the quality of every item on display. Then she began to bargain in a loud voice Halide had never heard before. Soon a crowd gathered around them. When the price was agreed upon and a delivery date assured, Teyze drew a leather purse from under her cloak and, note by note, counted out the money in full view of the spectators. Unbeknownst to

Halide, this happened every week. Word of Teyze's philanthropy had spread.

The drizzle turned to rain and they hurried on in the direction of the covered bazaar. The air inside the bazaar was infused with the smell of spices from Yemen, dried fruit and dates from Syria, and apricots from central Anatolia. Not far from the entrance, Halide noticed two men leaning against a spice stall, sipping coffee. They wore peaked caps and were clean-shaven, which made them stand out from the crowd. When Teyze passed they turned to watch her until she was almost out of sight, taking no notice of Halide, who followed several steps behind.

The aisles converged in the center of the market in an open area where tables and small wooden chairs were crowded around a fountain. Teyze stopped and trailed her fingers in the cascading water. "I almost lost you back there," Halide said, wondering why Teyze's hand was shaking.

"One more stop." Teyze shook the water off her fingers and wiped them on her cloak.

"Teyze, did you see those two men by the entrance?"

"I can't talk now, I have to see Rengin before she closes."

"But I thought . . ."

"Tell me later." Teyze threaded her way between the crowded tables and disappeared into a modest stall fronted by barrels of dried fruit, olives, and loose tea. Overhead the sign read RENGIN HANIM, COMESTIBLES.

A woman of about thirty emerged from a door at the rear. She wore pantaloons under a loose tunic, and heavy clogs. Like most workingwomen, she did not wear a veil, but her hair was covered with a cotton scarf. The woman cleared a space in the front section of her stall and asked them to sit down. A boy brought them hot apple tea in glass cups, and while the two women went over Teyze's list item by item, Halide stared around her, taking in the familiar sights of the market. She felt she had been away for a long time.

❦

WHEN THEY were finally finished, Halide and Teyze left the bazaar and followed a little-used goat path that wound its way over the hills above Scutari. Teyze refused an offer of a lift on the delivery cart and insisted on going by foot, even though the rain had reduced much of the track to a mass of mud and stone. They climbed steadily, pushing against the wind until they reached the crest of the hill. Here the path dipped toward the valley, where the roofs of the dervish lodge were half hidden among the treetops. Teyze stopped, pushed back her veil, and inclined her face to the sky.

"I don't think we should wait around out here where it's so exposed," said Halide nervously. The sense of unease she had felt all morning refused to go away.

"The walk tired me out," Teyze said. "I'm not as strong as I used to be."

"We should have ridden on the oxcart."

"The dervish lodge is being watched. It's wiser for me to go in through the back way."

"Watched, why? I thought only refugees were housed there."

"And some followers of Suleiman who traveled with him."

"Who are they?"

"Faithful Muslims, brother dervishes from Albania—no one to be afraid of."

The wind caught the hem of Halide's cloak and blew it against a thornbush. As she bent over to extricate herself, she glanced back along the path and noticed a man walking in their direction. He was about a hundred yards away, but when he saw her he stopped, and she had a chance to look at his face. She unhooked her cloak and turned back to Teyze.

"Did you know there was a man behind us?"

Teyze caught her breath. "Are you sure?"

"See for yourself, he's about halfway up the hill."

"We'll have to go at once!" Teyze pulled her veil back down and started off down the trail, and Halide had no choice but to run after her.

"Wait for me! He's probably just a goatherd or a villager."

"Don't waste your breath talking, we have to get to the road."

"I thought you were tired," Halide said reproachfully.

"Not anymore. Now stop asking questions."

The open land gave way to woods and the path merged with a stream. Soon their boots and clothes were splattered with mud. Halide looked back and saw the stranger running down the hill. He was gaining on them fast.

The trees grew more dense, and they found themselves in a part of the wood where the ground was carpeted with dead leaves. At last they lost sight of their pursuer and walked on with a sense of relief, believing the danger had past. Gradually the path leveled off and widened into a dirt road. Just as Teyze thought she could not go another step without resting, an oxcart laden with firewood lumbered out of a gap in the trees. She broke into a run, waving her hands and calling out for the driver to stop.

"PUT IT OVER there, next to the dried beans." Teyze pointed to the wall. She tried to sound composed, but the sight of the stranger had unnerved her and her voice was weak. Bent almost double under the weight of the sack, the man shuffled across the barn and dropped his load by the wall.

"That's the last one, ma'am." He turned his weatherworn face toward her and bowed.

"Five sacks of turnips, three of cabbages, seven carrots . . ." According to her calculations, the shipment was complete.

"Fifteen bags in all, ma'am. That was heavy work." Shifting from one foot to the other, he waited for Teyze to dismiss him.

"We've finished unloading. Tell the men to move the carts and bring them into the drive." Halide was amazed. At home in the harem Teyze was almost apologetic when she addressed the servants.

"As you wish, ma'am." The man hurried out of the barn, passing a sturdy woman in loose trousers and clogs. The sleeves of her tunic were rolled to her elbow, and there was flour all over her hands.

Teyze turned to Halide. "Come, child, it's time to bake bread. There's a lot to be done before sundown."

"But I've never made bread in my life," Halide protested.

"It's time you learned. After all that work with your brain, simple labor will do you good."

"What will I do? I'll only be in the way."

"Nonsense, we'll have you sifting the flour."

"What about my dress?"

"We'll cover you in an apron. Now hurry, we have many mouths to feed."

Halide had never seen Teyze like this before: authoritative, practical, very much in command. At the far end of the yard a dervish in leather jerkin and clogs was chopping wood and piling the hewn logs next to the kitchen door. He bowed as Teyze passed by. Halide realized that this community was the household Teyze had never had. Even after her marriage she had always been a guest in the place she called home. Here she was the chief *hanim*, respected and needed by everyone.

"Teyze Hanim, I've been looking for you." The speaker was

taller than the other men and, despite the cold weather, dressed only in a thin cotton robe.

"Suleiman Efendi, what are you doing in the kitchen?"

Halide started at the name. The man who stood before them was younger than she had expected, his eyes filled with such intensity she had to look away. His entire being gave the impression of suppressed power. Halide understood at once why Teyze had fallen under his spell.

"There were two men at the gate asking for you by name," he said. "I sent them away, but you must go inside. It would be dangerous for you to be seen from the road. People such as this do not give up easily."

Teyze complied without a word. Suleiman Efendi's warning struck her as ominous: her master wasn't given to exaggeration. In the kitchen the smell of fresh bread assured her that her work was well under way. Soon they would ride into town, the carts laden with meals for the destitute of Scutari and the refugees from the Balkans who crowded the streets for want of a home.

Chapter Three

On the twenty-seventh of December a carriage was dispatched from Yildiz and Halide was driven, unescorted, as far as the inner gates of the palace, where Edib was waiting. He had sent for his daughter because he had important news to tell her. Timing was important, and he thought it better to wait until they were alone. He had been prepared to take a leisurely stroll through the palace grounds, but Halide sped up the hill ahead of him, pausing impatiently while he hurried to keep up.

Since her last visit there had been a great deal of construction. The palace complex had been transformed with the addition of new workshops and kiosks designed to look like Swiss chalets. A dozen guards stood at attention before the main gate, their rifles drawn close to their sides. A two-story building, shuttered and silent, ran the length of the first courtyard. They walked on toward the chalet kiosk. Halide stared at the sloping roofs and gingerbread woodwork. It was impossible to imagine the leader of the Islamic world living here, like a character in a Swiss fairy tale. Yildiz had none of the dignified beauty of Topkapi, the abandoned palace above the Marmara Sea waiting for the tides of history to restore it once more to its faded glory.

"Halide, stop dawdling. There is much I have to show you." This was said with an edge of irritation. It had not escaped Halide's attention that her father was more tense than usual.

"I only wanted to see where the Sultan lived."

"It isn't wise to linger too long outside his residence."

"Why, will the guards mistake me for a spy?"

"Security is not a joking matter, Halide."

"Where is the kaiser's palace? One of my friends told me it was right next door to the Sultan's."

"Nonsense. Kaiser Wilhelm's residence is an extension of the Sultan's quarters. He was an important visitor, we could not have housed him anywhere else." Edib gave an uneasy laugh.

Leaving the immense chalet and the scarlet-turbaned guards behind them, they turned onto a shaded walk that ran beside the stables. A few yards farther on they stopped to watch four white horses walking around a yard led by their grooms.

"These stallions were recently imported from the Hejaz, the holy land of Mecca. They are for the Sultan's personal use."

"What magnificent animals! Look how they hold their heads, like proud gazi warriors," she murmured.

"They are treated like princes. The Sultan built a new stable for them, no expenses spared. It is said that only the Arab grooms know how to handle them."

To Edib these horses were disturbingly untamed. His first thought was to protect his daughter, but when he took her arm to walk away she shook him off, protesting that she had never seen such beautiful creatures. It was then Edib realized that the changes he had seen in her were not only superficial.

When they reached the garden adjacent to Edib's office, a man approached them from the other end of the footpath. As they crossed paths the stranger stepped back and exchanged a polite greeting with Edib. Halide turned and stared after him.

"Is something wrong, Halide? You've become very quiet." Edib reflected that girls of her age were subject to mood swings. He would have to adjust to this change too.

"Who was that man we passed?"

"An associate of Fehim Pasha's. Why do you ask?" he said suspiciously.

"I'm almost certain he followed me and Teyze last week when we went to the dervish monastery."

"No no, that can't be. You must have mistaken him for someone else." Edib did his best to hide his concern.

Of all the spies, secret policemen, and informers in Istanbul, Fehim Pasha was the most infamous. He was a grandson of the Sultan's wet nurse and therefore an honorary cousin of Abdulhamid. Plump and cold-eyed, he ran the palace arm of the secret police and was known to take pleasure in personally torturing his prisoners and extorting terrible bribes from would-be victims.

"I remember his face. I first saw him outside the covered bazaar and again when we were walking over the hill to the monastery. Teyze refused to take a carriage; she was afraid of something."

"Slowly, slowly," Edib said, reaching out to steady his daughter. "Start from the beginning and tell me everything."

"It was Saturday, and I'd offered to help Teyze. I knew the dervishes could use an extra hand . . ." In a halting voice, Halide went over the details of their outing.

"Suleiman Efendi," Edib said at last. "I had heard a rumor that he was in the city, but I certainly didn't connect him with Teyze." He took a cigarette from a case lying on a nearby table and pressed it against a glowing ember in the brazier beside him.

"Who is he, Father? Teyze tells me he is a great teacher and she has taken him as her master."

Edib exhaled slowly and watched the smoke rise in the air. "If that's the case, she may have aroused the suspicion of the authorities."

"Why?"

"Suleiman Efendi is an Albanian nationalist."

"What's a nationalist, Papa?"

"It's hard to explain in Turkish, because we don't use the same political terminology as the Europeans. We don't even have a word for nationalism, but it is the curse of our time."

"Salih Zeki Bey has told me a little about it. Is something wrong, Father? You've gone very pale."

"Once he's set his sights on an adversary, Fehim Pasha doesn't tend to lose much time. We should get back to Scutari as soon as possible. I'm sorry to ruin your visit; we'll do it again another time."

"What about the surprise?" Halide asked.

Edib stared at his daughter obliquely, as if he had no idea what she was talking about. Then his brow cleared. "Of course, it slipped my mind completely. Oh, it's good news, my dear, wonderful news. You have a sister—she was born two days ago. Her name is Nighiar."

❦

BY THE TIME Edib and Halide reached Scutari the shadows had grown long over the quay and the waterfront was almost deserted. On the ferry they had discussed the baby. Halide had plied her father with polite questions about her weight and the color of her eyes, all the while wondering if he loved her less now that he had another daughter. For his part, Edib was impressed by his daughter's calm acceptance of the news. He had dreaded the prospect of an emotional scene and was pleased to see how much she had matured. He applauded himself for removing her from the harem, where the closed atmosphere gave rise to hysteria and superstition.

At the bottom of the hill leading up to Sultan Tepe their carriage lurched to one side, throwing them both to the floor. Their driver cursed and pulled over to the side of the road and came around to apologize, his face twitching with anger. Another driver had come toward them at a dangerous speed in the middle of the road, he told them, leaving no room to pass. Edib assured him they were unharmed and they continued their journey, shaken but relieved, while the driver muttered aloud about strangers on the road.

The moment they turned into the drive, Halide knew something was wrong: the gates had been left half open and the gatekeeper's kiosk was deserted. As they approached the house, she saw a knot of people standing on the steps in front of the door. In their midst was her grandmother, leaning against Arzu with her face in her hands. Her head was covered in a lace nightcap and her hair flew out in unruly clumps, as if she had been aroused from sleep. When they caught sight of Edib and Halide, the group broke apart and the old lady hobbled over with tears in her eyes.

"What has happened?" Edib asked sharply.

"Two strangers came just moments ago and took Teyze away.

They drove off at a great speed," Arzu said, hurriedly reaching out for her elderly mistress to prevent her from falling.

"That was the driver that nearly knocked us over!" Halide exclaimed. "Let's go after them. They can't get far on that road—it only leads to the quay."

Edib made a move toward the carriage, then stopped in his tracks.

"We're wasting time, let's go!" Halide clutched hold of her father's sleeve and tried to drag him across the drive. One by one, he gently pried her fingers free.

"It's best to take care of these things through the proper channels," he said slowly, returning now toward the step.

"You work for the Sultan!" she cried out. "They wouldn't dare disobey you."

"Come, Halide. We'll go into the *selamlik* and discuss this in a calm manner. Arzu, please take Fatma Hanim Efendi inside and give her some sweet tea. This has been a dreadful shock."

ONCE THEY WERE alone in the privacy of the empty salon, Edib appealed to his daughter in a gentle voice. "Trust me, Halide, I know what I'm doing. The men who took Teyze are only following orders, and nothing would have been gained by my going after them. I will appeal to the grand vizier in person and try to regain her freedom. I can't make any promises. Quite unwittingly, Teyze has made some dangerous associations."

"How is Suleiman Efendi dangerous?"

"Forget his name, his face, everything," Edib said with passion. "The safety of our family depends on it."

"Will he be arrested as well?"

"I don't know, but as soon as I learn something I will get word to you. In the meantime you must return to school and put these events out of your mind. The most important thing is for you to complete your education with honors."

"Promise me, Father, that you are not in danger." Halide clutched his arm and held so tightly that her fingers dug into his sleeve.

"Of course not," Edib laughed. For more than a year he had been watched day and night by agents of Fehim Pasha. The surveillance was so thorough, they had to know beyond a shadow of a doubt that he was loyal to the Sultan. Now he was grateful for their scrutiny.

Chapter Four

When Halide returned to school she kept the news of Teyze's arrest to herself. Maintaining secrecy took its toll: she was disturbed by tormented dreams and often lay awake watching the moon rise through the half-open window. During the day she was tired and found it difficult to concentrate on her schoolwork. Teyze's whereabouts remained a mystery. With this uncertainty hanging over her, Halide withdrew, carefully recording her fears in the abbreviated Turkish she had taken to using in her journal. It wasn't long before her grades fell and her teachers began to wonder what had happened. When a summons came at last from Dr. Patrick, she was almost relieved.

The white walls of the waiting room were hung with portraits of severe Bostonians, board members and benefactors from the American Mission. A full-length mirror framed in wood was mounted on the wall across from the windows, and this object held an unremitting fascination for Halide. In the harem, mirrors were displayed with their glass turned to the wall, in accordance with the holy law. Only Teyze had a jewel-encrusted hand mirror, which she allowed herself to use when the moon was waning and the peris were less inclined to be lured by the glittering glass. In her father's house there were Venetian wall mirrors made of smoked glass, but they were hung high on the wall, and their reflections were diffuse. When Halide had first caught sight of herself in the full-length mirror at the American school, she'd had to force herself to turn away.

While she was waiting for Dr. Patrick, curiosity got the better of her and Halide walked over to study her face with a critical eye. She was supposed to look like her mother, but Selima had been a beauty and she thought herself ordinary. Nine years had passed since her mother's death, and Halide retained nothing more than a vague impression of translucent skin and hollow eyes grown dark with illness. Her own features were small and even, framed in frizzy hair that refused to conform to fashion. In the set of her mouth she saw a marked resemblance to her father that pleased her. "All being is a shadow, an illusion, a reflection cast on a mirror," she murmured, quoting Molla Jami. The lips of the other girl moved, but the Sufi's words went unheard.

"Come in, Halide. I hope you haven't been waiting long." Dr. Patrick emerged from her study and gave Halide a kindly smile.

"No, no, I just arrived." Halide turned abruptly to face her and the outline of her palm remained imprinted on the glass.

Dr. Patrick took Halide's arm and guided her into the study. For twenty-five years the girls college had been the focus of Dr. Patrick's professional life. She had been there from its inception, an eager participant in the experiment to bring women's education to the Near East. Although it was open to all girls, regardless of origin, they had never had a Turkish student before. Dr. Patrick was determined to do everything in her power to help Halide succeed.

"Sit down, make yourself comfortable. Would you like tea?" She motioned toward one of the overstuffed armchairs arranged around her desk.

"No thank you." Halide was too nervous to think of food.

"Are you eating well? You seem to be losing weight. We have a Turkish cook, so the diet shouldn't be too dissimilar to what you have been accustomed to."

"The meals are delicious," Halide said, looking down at her hands and wondering why Dr. Patrick was talking about her diet. She had assumed this meeting was about her falling grades.

"I want you to feel completely at home here," Dr. Patrick said pointedly.

Halide murmured that she did. This was true: the scholarly atmosphere of the school and the freedom to run at will in the grounds made her unusually happy.

"When I first came to the East I was twenty-one, not much older than you are. Until then I had spent my entire life in Iowa." Dr. Patrick removed her glasses and leaned back in her chair. "I was an adventurous girl, and my father understood this. With his encouragement I left my home and family and went to Erzurum, to help the beleaguered Christian community."

"Erzurum," murmured Halide. "That's in the East, a long way away."

"The journey took three months. Father came with me as far as Chicago; then I traveled alone to London, Vienna, and Constantinople. The most dangerous part of the trip was at the end, when I crossed the mountains behind Trabzon." Dr. Patrick paused.

"I'm telling you this, Halide, because I want you to know that I understand your situation."

"But I'm not adventurous; I've never been outside of Constantinople."

"You're one of the first Turkish women to reach beyond the harem and attend a Western school. You are setting an example for others to follow."

Halide started to relax. "My father helped me," she said. "I would not be here without him."

"We were lucky, you and I. Others are not so fortunate. I remember the first time I saw women in seclusion. I was on a steamship sailing from Constantinople to Trabzon. There were many prominent Turks on board, but the women were all confined to their cabins. They never came on deck to take the air or mix with their fellow passengers. It was only when we docked that I had a glimpse of veiled figures being shepherded into closed carriages. The thought of those wasted lives made me very sad."

Halide crossed her hands in her lap and wondered what Dr. Patrick would think about the convoluted circumstances of life in the harem at Sultan Tepe. She also wondered what this had to do with her poor academic performance.

"But I didn't call you in to tell you my life story," Dr. Patrick said with a smile. She scanned the top of her desk and drew out a sheet of vellum from beneath a glass paperweight. "Yesterday evening I received this letter from your father."

"Is it bad news?" Halide interjected with alarm.

"Not exactly. He didn't go into details, he simply asked me to tell you that the Sultan has commuted your stepmother's sentence. In lieu of deportation she will be confined to the harem of Ciragan Palace. I trust this means more to you than it does to me." She looked at Halide over the top of her glasses.

"Father told you about Teyze's problems?" Halide was amazed

to hear that he had revealed anything about the family to a stranger.

"No, he says nothing," Dr. Patrick replied.

Stunned, Halide sat motionless, not knowing whether to weep with relief or sadness. "I don't know what Teyze did wrong, that's the strange thing," she murmured. "No one, not even my father, seems sure. It had something to do with a dervish called Suleiman Efendi."

Where Ottoman politics were concerned, Dr. Patrick had learned to remain circumspect. For the first part of Abdulhamid's reign, the governments of Europe had regarded him with wary approval. To all appearances he was instituting political reforms and modernizing the Ottoman state. After the attacks on the Armenians, everything changed. Appalled by the anarchy and bloodshed, the diplomatic community protested vigorously, but the palace ignored their complaints. The Americans, who had previously distanced themselves from the colonial policies of Europe and remained neutral toward the Sultan, were angered by the bloodshed. As a sign of protest they had refused to fly the American flag and decorate the embassy on the anniversary of the Sultan's accession.

"How was your stepmother connected to the dervishes?"

"She worked with them."

"What did she do?" Dr. Patrick tried to conceal her amazement. "I didn't think women of her class could associate with men to whom they were not related."

"Teyze sponsored their work with the poor. It's not uncommon for wealthy women to do that, especially the Bektashi, who have women in their order. Teyze was like a mother to me. Since her arrest I've been very worried."

Dr. Patrick glanced over the letter again. She had understood that Edib Pasha and his wife lived in Yildiz, while Halide remained in Scutari with her late mother's family. This was the first she had heard of another wife. She rose and walked over to the window. There was so much about this complex society she did not understand.

"You are in my care now, Halide, and your well-being is important to me. You have a great future ahead of you. Your knowledge of Ottoman, Arabic, and Persian, combined with the education you are receiving here, will allow you to play an important role in your society." Halide listened attentively but said nothing.

"So I am going to make a suggestion that may startle you," Dr. Patrick continued, turning around abruptly to face her. "I think you should write all this down. You have an unusual facility for expressing yourself in English. Perhaps you should make Teyze's misfortune into a story."

"What sort of a story?" Halide asked doubtfully.

"Her life, as you understand it. We can never know the truth of another person's life, so the story will have to be your own." Dr. Patrick hoped that writing would help Halide come to terms with the arrest of her stepmother and remove the weight that was interfering with her studies.

"Where would I begin?"

"Begin at the beginning, when Teyze arrived at your home."

"But she was at Yildiz Palace before that," Halide said, starting to warm to the idea. "I didn't know her then."

"Use your imagination. Invent her life as you think she might have led it."

"Do you want me to hand some in to you every week?"

"No, I want you to do this for yourself." Dr. Patrick wanted to give her girls the inner strength and confidence to make the most of the life that lay ahead of them.

A bell rang in the corridor, signaling the start of morning break.

"You must excuse me, Halide, I have a class to teach." Dr. Patrick rose and extended her hand. "You have my permission to use the senior library. It will be quieter there." She gave Halide a pat on the back and turned to leave the room.

DURING THE eighteen months she had spent at the American school Halide had made few friends. She felt intimidated by the boisterous confidence of her schoolmates, and preferred the company of younger girls in the preparatory department. Between classes she joined in their childish games with an enthusiasm that amazed her. She discovered a simpler self whose development had been smothered by the death of her mother and the strain of her father's marriage to Mamounia. With the exception of Mahmoure, she had never had a companion of her own age. She remembered her sister with love and awe, and as the years passed it became less painful for her to look back on their time together. The thought that they might never see each other again was something she dared not consider.

Intellectually, Halide was far ahead of her peers. Her classical Ottoman education, combined with her private tutoring, gave her an advantage in every subject except mathematics. As a result she found herself placed in advanced classes with girls who were two or three years older. Compared with her, these students were relatively sophisticated. They had traveled to Europe and America, socialized with men and among strangers.

Aznive Bougasian was one of the few girls in the upper school Halide felt comfortable with. Aznive's parents were Armenian rug merchants from Kayseri, a prosperous city in the heart of Anatolia. She spoke English with a heavy accent the other girls mocked. She was plump and awkward, with a mane of unruly dark hair she kept tied in a heavy braid. Her pinafore was always creased, and the collar of her white shirt was a mess, yet there was something about her that appealed to Halide. They were outsiders, drawn together by their difference. When Halide left Dr. Patrick's office, Aznive was waiting for her.

"I heard she'd asked for you. Is everything all right?" Aznive used the quaint old-fashioned Turkish of the interior.

"There was a message from my father," Halide said quickly.

"He is well?"

"He wants me to go and see him."

"But your last visit was not so long ago."

"That's true." Halide had deliberately avoided telling Aznive about tea at her father's house. She ran the risk of unwittingly revealing details of his third marriage and preferred to keep it to herself.

A bell sounded and Aznive caught her arm. "If we don't hurry we will be late for Miss Fensham's class."

"I've forgotten my Bible," Halide said, irritated by her own carelessness. The prospect of comparative religion class made her heart sink. Miss Fensham's teaching style was intense but limited in its scope. There was no doubt in her mind that Protestant Christianity was the premier faith. She taught the precepts of Catholicism and the other great world religions as if they were pale imitations of the one true austere word of God.

"You can share mine."

"Miss Fensham will think I did it on purpose."

"Now, why would she think that? People often share books."

"I feel she's always watching me."

Aznive gave her an enigmatic smile. "I am Orthodox; don't think that sits well with her Protestant soul."

"Perhaps we should both convert to Buddhism," Halide said with a laugh. They linked arms and walked on down the long hallway lined with watercolor paintings of the Rockies and the Arizona plains. Students hurried to and fro clutching their books.

Halide and Aznive moved as one to the side, the hems of their skirts sweeping against the white wainscot. Subdued voices mingled all around them with the clang of the final bell.

Thinking back over their conversation, Halide was struck by Dr. Patrick's advice. After months of recording her dreams, thoughts, and fears in her diary, writing in English had become second nature. But she wasn't certain Teyze's story was the one she wanted to write. Close as they were, she had never understood what had made Teyze decide to follow the path of the Sufis. But there were other more pressing concerns weighing on her. Since she had been at school, the voices had faded and she had not dreamed about her mother for months. She wondered if her gift was ebbing away, and this left her feeling ambivalent. On the one hand, she was relieved to be left with the clarity of mind needed for her intense intellectual work. Yet she was saddened by the loss of the connection to the past.

Chapter Five

"Don't say anything about the dervishes, or Mustafa Efendi, not one word. Talk about generalities, the bad winter, what you're doing at school. No, wait, perhaps it's better not to talk about that either, since the Sultan still doesn't approve. Just ask her how she is, tell her you miss her." Edib spoke in a low voice so that the guard, standing some distance away, would not hear them.

"I have to give her a message from Granny," Halide said.

"Try to keep it brief; they'll listen to every word."

Edib and Halide were waiting in a vast gilded chamber lit by a succession of chandeliers. Pink cherubs and plump blue clouds danced across the ceiling, and the walls were covered with neo-rococo paneling. Except for the console tables in between the French doors, there was no furniture of any sort, so they were forced to stand. At the far end of the room a pair of double doors decorated with swirling peacocks stood ajar, and through the crack came the strains of a piano.

"I believe that's a waltz; it must be one of the princesses. They play very well, don't you think?" said Edib.

"Are we near the harem?"

"It's just beyond those doors."

"Is that where she lives? I imagined she was detained in a solitary room."

"She is living in Prince Murad's household. He and his entire family have been detained here at Ciragan for years."

Traditionally Ottoman princes had been strangled to avoid conflicting claims of inheritance to the Caliphate, but in recent years this practice had been abandoned. Privately, Edib felt that this slaughter of innocents cast a long shadow across the Ottoman dynasty. Though Murad had been spared, his incarceration was akin to slow death.

"So poor Teyze has come full circle. She is a palace lady once more."

"She is lucky to have escaped deportation and certain death on those treacherous boats. She never should have allied herself so closely with an enemy of the Sultan."

After Teyze's arrest, Edib's worst fears had been confirmed. Suleiman Efendi was a leader of the Albanian nationalist movement. His privileged position as an Ottoman and a Bektashi had allowed him to make his way to Constantinople without raising the suspicions of the provincial police. No one was sure why he had come. Edib suspected that he needed to raise funds and make contact with other Albanians living in the capital. There were a number of editors and writers, members of the intellectual community, who were Albanian by birth. Their sympathies lay with the nationalist movement, and they worked quietly to promote their cause.

"But Teyze hated palace life. The women are locked up like animals, never allowed beyond the harem gates. Apparently they used to beg visitors to describe the streets of Pera, even Beshiktash, so they could imagine the world outside and save themselves from going mad."

"Teyze was always prone to exaggeration," Edib said, wishing Halide would keep her voice down.

Just then the doors swung open. Caught off guard, Edib turned to see who was coming. A group of veiled women in European dress swayed across the floor behind the guardian of the harem, an imposing black eunuch dressed in a frock coat and corded fez. In his right hand he carried a scroll, which he unfurled with a flourish. Disregarding the usual formalities, he began reading aloud the limitations of their visit. Edib stood at attention, as was customary with court protocol.

After the free and easy atmosphere of school, Halide felt the tension press like an invisible hand against every inch of her body. While the eunuch droned on she noticed, half hidden among the flurry of women, a slender figure veiled in light organdy. It was Teyze. Less than a month had passed since they had visited the market together and she had watched Teyze organize the distribution of food with the assurance of a commander overseeing her troops. The change in her was startling.

The eunuch and his entourage walked back across the room, and Halide's gaze followed them until they had almost reached the doors of the harem. Teyze remained behind. They found themselves alone, watched over by a lone guard posted at the far end of the room.

"What are *you* doing here?" Teyze exclaimed, looking at Edib.

"The Sultan granted me a single visit. Didn't they warn you I was coming?" Edib was taken aback by her animosity. He had hoped for some small sign of appreciation.

"No one tells me anything. I am isolated with a brood of unhappy, restless women."

"I'm sorry to hear you say that. It's comfortable here. The palaces are equipped with every modern convenience, even electricity." To cover his feelings, Edib fell into the habit of being formal.

"You know better than to be deceived by appearances, Edib Pasha. On the surface, everything is normal: we are well dressed and well mannered, we have books, even the use of a piano, but all of this false finery means nothing to me." She stopped and pushed her veil back over her head, revealing a face that Halide thought thinner but every bit as beautiful as before. "Why am I telling you all this? You don't know what I'm talking about. You have never wanted to understand." Teyze deliberately avoided acknowledging Halide, who was doing her best to remain invisible.

"I'm sorry, Teyze, I did everything in my power to help you. If the Sultan hadn't heard my petition you would have been deported."

"Deportation would have been preferable to life in this gilded cage. At least I would have been free to wander where I choose and to take my own chances."

"I didn't want to see you sent away," Edib said simply.

"Surely my disappearance would be convenient for you now."

"What do you mean?"

"Divorce me. I don't know why you hang on."

"Since your arrest there has been pressure from the grand mufti, but I won't give in. You are my wife, and your demise is my responsibility. I cannot abandon you." He had a sudden longing to reach out and stroke her cheek with the back of his hand, but he stopped himself, afraid his touch might hurt her more.

"Why didn't you think about that before?"

"Because I was a fool."

"Get out of my sight! This is too much to bear." Teyze swung around and put her hand up to her mouth.

Stung by her outburst, Edib walked over to the window and laid his forehead against the glass. He would never forgive himself for leaving Sultan Tepe and allowing Teyze to fall under the spell of a man like Suleiman Efendi. Women made judgments with their hearts, not their heads. If the law had allowed him control over her dowry, the dervishes would not have benefited so liberally. But alas, freedom had proven to be her downfall. Even now, Edib could not allow himself to concede that his remarriage had devastated her. She had always seemed so remote, a beautiful anomaly whose motives and desires he had never understood. Their marriage had, in his opinion, been successful in its own way.

"He wants to help you," Halide said quietly to Teyze, looking after her father with pity.

Teyze ignored her remark and seized her by the shoulders. "God heard my prayers!" she said. "I have been begging Him for one last chance to see you. You look healthy and radiant. It is His will that you are going to survive all these troubles." She began talking feverishly in French, so that Edib would not understand.

"Not a day passes when I don't think about you. Listen, Halide, learn from my life and from Mahmoure. Be careful in your choice of husband, and never give yourself completely to a man. You will have all the chances I never had—be strong, Halide, learn to trust yourself and to believe in what you feel is right."

After this outburst she settled down to polite conversation. "How is your dear grandmother?"

Halide was baffled by Teyze's abrupt change of mood. "She told me to tell you your dowry monies are safe. The harem was searched, but she concealed the box under a divan and feigned sleep. Even the police did not dare to disturb an old lady."

Teyze gave sigh of relief. "That money is yours, I have no use for it in here. It will provide you with an ample dowry."

"But I'm not getting married!" Halide protested.

"You will one day."

"By then you'll be free and in need of the money yourself."

"No one ever leaves this place, Halide. Murad and his family have been here for more than twenty years."

"Why? What did you do?"

"I don't know." There had been no formal charges placed against her, no trial, nothing. "My accusers claim Suleiman Efendi is an enemy of the Sultan."

"Father says he is a nationalist."

"To me he is a teacher. He never once spoke of politics."

"After your arrest the dervishes told Granny that Suleiman Efendi had disappeared." Before Halide could say another word, Teyze clapped her hand over her mouth and signaled for her to be careful.

"I would give anything to know where he's gone," she whispered. "If it's the last thing I do on this earth I must get word to him. Promise me you'll help me." She looked up nervously and saw the doors of the harem open slowly. The eunuch emerged and, seeing the two of them huddled together, his expression soured. Overcome by desperation, Teyze caught hold of Halide and pulled her close so that her mouth was next to Halide's ear.

"Find my master, help me," she whispered. "Tell him I'll continue along the path; there are books here I can study. I will love him until the day I die."

"Where do I . . ." Halide stopped; the eunuch was barely three feet away. He had slid across the polished boards so fast that his feet hardly seemed to touch the ground. Behind him came the harem women, smelling of patchouli and jasmine. They clustered around and pulled at Teyze until she was forced to release her hold and fell to the floor, screaming for help in the whirl of movement. Halide was elbowed aside and almost lost her balance. Somewhere in the background, behind the sound of sobbing, she heard her father's voice denouncing the eunuch for his lack of civility. Through her tears she saw the women half carrying, half dragging Teyze through the doors and slamming them with such force the painted peacocks shook.

SITTING IN the senior library, Halide went over the facts in her mind. She shuffled the truths and arranged them piece by piece, so that they balanced like *locum* on the great brass scales at Haci Bekir's sweetshop. Here was the Sultan, God's representative on earth. Her father, grandparents, and their grandparents before them were an integral part of the Imperial order. Here were the guardians of Eyoub and beneath them the chief coffeemakers, sweets makers, and rabbit dancers. It had always been this way, forever.

When she was a child, Halide had taken for granted the existence of the Imperial Palace, and the great army that wore red turbans and bright uniforms and marched in the procession before the gates of Yildiz. The Sultan had been and always would be the temporal guardian of Allah's will, the ruler of an Islamic domain that stretched beyond the gates of Mecca, from the gulf of Arabia to the Caspian Sea. At the American school she had learned that the earth had boundaries and dimensions, that her beloved Constantinople had an outline, a place on the map between the Anatolian peninsula and Rumelia. Knowledge was defined through facts, and facts were arranged to create order. The shifting nature of recorded history became apparent as she tried to organize the truth of her own life into a story.

Where had her father come from? He was vague about his past, save that he was born in the port city of Salonika. He was a person apparently without a family and possessing few friends until her mother had come into his life. Then there was Teyze. For more than half her life Teyze had loved her like a mother, tended her, cared for her, yet she came from the north, near the Black Sea, and had long since forgotten her family. Those people she thought of as ancestors had trained her for marriage as a gardener cultivates his prize roses. Mahmoure—ah, just the echo of her name sent Halide into despair! Mahmoure, who had followed her heart and vanished from their lives, was the child of a mother she had hardly known. The only solid figure in this shifting prism of her family was her grandmother.

Halide stared out the library window. She wondered if she could bring this disparate material together in her own language. She wanted a heroine who would transcend the limitations of the harem without losing the quality of her soul. If she could only grasp the perceptions of the poets and mold them to her own ends, she would have the story she wanted. A portrait of herself as she would like to be, a woman of both worlds, the old and the new.

A small brown bird settled on the sill and attacked a pile of crumbs. Close by, the sound of a pen scratching across paper brought her attention back to the present. A senior girl, a golden-haired American named Jennifer, looked up from her work and smiled. Halide bowed her head and resumed her writing. Jennifer was the kind of girl she found intimidating. To avoid attracting unnecessary attention, Halide pretended to be analyzing the work of Ibn Khaldun, and surrounded herself with his books. She was going to begin her novel, of this she was determined. Whose story she would tell, however, she hadn't yet decided.

Part Five

Chapter One

Edib had aged, Zeki Bey thought to himself. It was deplorable that such a conscientious man should have to suffer for his beliefs. Two years had passed since Teyze's arrest, and in that time Edib had been denied promotion, despite his ability. To compound the insult, the Sultan had relegated him to the position of third secretary and brought in a virtual illiterate from the Arabian peninsula to replace him. This new trend of favoring Arabs over more qualified men troubled Salih Zeki. He felt it was a sign of desperation on the part of the Sultan, and a threatened man was a dangerous man. He paused to adjust his glasses, then fell back into step beside his friend. They were strolling through Hagia Sophia Square in the direction of the mosque where Edib, under orders from the grand vizier, was to make an inspection of recent renovation.

"I don't understand why they sent me," Edib said impatiently. "I know nothing about architecture. I told the grand vizier we are bankrupt and cannot afford to go on refurbishing mosques with gold veneers and marble."

"They're testing your loyalty," Zeki Bey answered. "Be patient, don't let it upset you."

Edib ignored his friend and continued with his train of thought. "We're in debt to the Europeans. I haven't been paid for months, nor have the other bureaucrats. It infuriates me to see money spent so imprudently. If we don't curb our spending, we will soon be facing economic disaster."

"The Sultan doesn't see things that way. These expenditures are part of an overall plan to strengthen his power. As long as the Islamic institutions remain visibly strong, the people have hope."

"One day we'll run out of money and the treasury will not be able to pay the army, then the trouble will start . . ." Edib coughed dryly and glanced around him nervously. "Anyway, it is a pleasant change to be away from Yildiz. I'm glad you could come along at the last minute."

"I never miss a chance to visit Hagia Sophia," Zeki Bey said, surprised by this outburst from his generally circumspect friend. "The design of the dome is a miracle of geometry."

They passed under a stone archway and made their way along a graveled path to the outer doors of the mosque, where a cluster of men with long beards and flowing robes were gathered on the steps. When Zeki Bey and Edib arrived they moved to one side reproachfully, as if the newcomers were cursed with the plague. Zeki Bey acknowledged them with a bow. Edib advised his friend to keep walking.

"They don't like the way we're dressed," he said under his breath. "Anything remotely European is anathema to them."

"Good God, I didn't know such attitudes still existed."

"Change is frightening; there is a backlash to our reform movement. Fortunately, fifty years of progress cannot easily be revoked."

"You are an admirable optimist, Edib." Either that or a fool, he thought. Progress will only be possible once the constitution is restored and this despot removed forever. It must be hard for men like Edib, deeply entwined with the system, to imagine a world where the sons of Osman are no more.

They walked on in silence, lost in thought until they entered the cavernous darkness of the mosque. In a corner a group of workers were chiseling slabs of red and black marble. Edib excused himself and went over to talk to the head mason, a burly man in a leather apron.

Salih Zeki was content to be left alone. The lightness of the soaring dome filled him with awe. It appeared to float in space, impervious to the gloom below. Hagia Sophia was, in his opinion, the most beautiful building in the city. It never ceased to amaze him that twelve centuries ago Italian engineers had had the mathematical expertise to design a dome of such dimensions. Their knowledge was no doubt inherited from the Romans, masters of monumental architecture. It gave Salih Zeki a measure of comfort to reflect that the great mosque, once a cathedral, had outlasted its Byzantine creators and would, no doubt, survive the demise of the Ottomans.

Suddenly Edib was at his side again. "The man I need to speak to isn't here," he said with clear frustration. "This was all a waste of time."

"Not at all—this visit has been most enjoyable. I'm delighted you asked me to join you."

"I have to confess, Zeki Bey, I did not invite you here simply for the pleasure of your company," Edib said slowly, choosing his words with care. "Although I am always happy to see you, I have a problem to discuss, a matter of some urgency."

Edib took his friend's arm, and together they strolled into the immense hall separating the entrance from the dome of the mosque. The musty smell of damp stone mixed with the odor of burning oil. Through a crack between the tall bronze doors, thin rays of light cut across the dusty air. Robed figures, some turbaned, hurried by with their heads bowed. Salih Zeki felt he had stepped back in time to the era of Suleiman the Magnificent. "Urgency?" he echoed, raising his eyebrows.

"It concerns my daughter."

"Ah, Halide," he said wistfully.

"She graduates in two months."

"Time passes too quickly at our age."

"Halide will be the first Turkish student to graduate from the American Girls College, and she is one of their finest scholars. My esteemed mother-in-law, heedless of this achievement, insists on finding her a husband."

Salih Zeki frowned. "I hope the candidates are worthy of her."

"They are pleasant young men from good families, but intellectually they are not her equal. Marriage to any one of them would be a disaster."

"I'm afraid I cannot think of anyone who might make a good match. My students come from modest backgrounds."

Edib allowed himself a smile. "You don't understand, Zeki Bey. Halide needs an intellectual, a teacher, a reform-minded man who is not rooted in the past. Someone who respects her abilities and for whom she has high regard."

"What are you suggesting?" His heart began to race.

"I am proposing you marry my daughter."

Salih Zeki's mind raced fitfully. He could feel his body shaking and chastised himself for his weakness. "I am honored by your suggestion," he said at last, trying to collect his thoughts. "She is an exceptional young woman. But I am not certain I have the means to provide for her in the way she would expect."

"Halide is provided for. Teyze, from whom I am now divorced, has made her dowry over to her. It's an unusual arrangement, but it protects her money from being seized by the treasury." Edib spoke with great agitation. He turned now to face his friend. "I trust you will understand that this is very confidential."

"Of course," Salih Zeki murmured. What a stroke of good fortune—one might almost believe in fate! He had dreamed of possessing this girl. She was everything he desired, yet his background and lack of personal funds had prevented him from daring . . .

"So you are in agreement?" Edib said eagerly.

"I would be overjoyed." Salih Zeki's voice had grown louder, and he was hushed by an Imam standing close by.

"There is just one condition," Edib whispered, keeping a wary eye on the cleric. "You must give up your associations in Paris."

Salih Zeki felt the color drain from his face. "How do you know about that?"

"There are informers everywhere, even in France."

"Among the Turkish exiles?"

"Please don't ask; my information is confidential."

"What have you been told?"

"After what has happened with Teyze, I cannot risk Halide's future by announcing her betrothal to a documented opponent of the Sultan."

"You mean my alliance with the Young Turks?" Salih Zeki said, trying to conceal his relief. "I give you my word that is over. Don't forget, it was the Sultan himself who invited me and many of my colleagues back to Constantinople."

They started toward the door arm in arm, arguing over the Sultan's reforms. As they stepped into the bright daylight, Zeki Bey suddenly stopped. "Wait, my friend: you haven't told me what Halide thinks of all this."

"Halide cares for you. She says nothing to me, but I am not blind. She will be overjoyed when I tell her."

"And Fatma Hanim Efendi, what will she think?"

"She'll come around," said Edib with a smile.

Zeki Bey strolled back toward the main gate with a new lightness in his step. At last the zenith of his ambition was within sight. He would have time and the means to write his masterwork while enveloped in the comfort of family life, so long denied to him. This image of domesticity was so vivid, so sharp a desire that the world he had left behind in Paris melted into the perimeters of his mind like a bad dream.

❦

EDIB SURVEYED the room with the eye of a connoisseur. Everything was exactly as he remembered it. Nothing had changed: white shades trimmed with lace covered the windows, and the familiar smell of lavender came from the pillows and shawls covering the divans. Even his mother-in-law appeared to be untouched by the passage of time. Moving with the unhurried pace that had always marked life at Sultan Tepe, Arzu transferred a cup of coffee onto a silver tray and offered it to him with a deferential nod.

"This is a welcome surprise," said the old lady sitting in her usual seat by the window. "We have not seen you here since Ramazan."

Edib knew this was a rebuke. "Your hospitality always makes me feel at home," he said with a polite bow.

"I assume you have come in response to my letter." Granny was in no mood for courtesy this afternoon.

"It arrived on my desk last week," he said carefully.

"Thanks to Teyze's generosity, our options have increased, and I wanted you to be the first to know how many suitable candidates I have found. No *görücü* could have done better—don't you agree, Arzu?"

"They are a worthy group, ma'am," the housekeeper said, nodding in acquiescence.

"Ragib Bey, the grandson of my childhood friend Shayeste Hanim, is related on his mother's side to the Sultan."

"Remember there's a history of epilepsy in that branch of the family, ma'am," Arzu countered.

"The house of Osman always was a little eccentric," Granny chuckled.

"It's an impressive list, Fatma Hanim; I marvel at your industry. It is just that I too have been giving this matter some serious thought." Edib tiptoed over the intricacies of harem conduct, more complex and delicate even than the boundaries of court protocol.

"If you have a young man in mind, I would be pleased to add his name to the list."

"I have received a proposal from someone who will, I am quite certain, be agreeable to Halide. A man I would be delighted and honored to have as my son-in-law."

Granny looked at him with surprise. "You sound as if your mind is made up."

"I would not dream of making such an important decision for Halide without your consent."

"Don't keep me in suspense," Granny said testily. "Who is this would-be suitor?"

"Salih Zeki Bey."

"Zeki Bey," echoed Granny, feeling faint. "But he's old enough to be her father!"

"He is barely forty, in the prime of life. I have known him for many years, and he has promised me he will take great care of her."

The old lady stared at her son-in-law in horror. Who was Zeki Bey? Beyond his reputed brilliance and excellent manners, she knew nothing about him. She shook her head. From the beginning she had sensed that this business of educating Halide would lead to disaster.

"My choice obviously disturbs you," Edib said with concern. He had not expected an immediate embrace of his scheme, but Zeki Bey was not as implausible as all that; he was, after all, a distinguished scholar and a man of importance in the intellectual community.

"Where does he come from? Where was he born?" Granny asked, fanning her face with her hand.

Edib answered as best he could but, as with all his friendships, he realized there were gaps in his knowledge. He had never pressed to uncover a great deal about Zeki Bey's past. He felt uncomfortable asking personal questions and preferred in general to remain on neutral territory.

"Have you spoken to Halide?" Granny said at length.

"Not yet, I wanted to see you first. When her exams are over I will tell her the good news."

Fatma Hanim was not consulted again with regard to Halide's betrothal. She knew that Edib had made up his mind, so she decided, in the interests of harmony, to keep her concerns to herself. Salih Zeki was too old and there was something unstable in his core. He was not a faithful Muslim; in fact he showed no interest in religion and this worried her. Granny doubted that Salih Zeki had the capacity to help anyone except himself. In the meantime, she would pay attention to her dreams and advise her granddaughter accordingly.

EDIB DELAYED telling Halide until he was certain that Fatma Hanim had accepted his decision. He waited until she came to his house in Yildiz, then took her aside late in the evening when his wife and baby daughter were asleep. Halide was overjoyed but did her best to conceal her feelings in case he guessed at the depth of her attachment to her tutor. Yet the thought of marrying such a distinguished man made her nervous. Could she live up to his expectations? Was she clever enough? It was only afterward that she wondered how Salih Zeki might feel.

Chapter Two

Granny lifted her hand up to the windowpane and narrowed her eyes until they were almost closed, but all she could see was a blurred impression of trees bent double under the force of the wind. She sighed loudly. This storm sweeping in from the south was going to upset all their plans. September was usually bright and clear, and she had gone to great lengths to select the date. Peyker had consulted both the spirits and the almanac, and the Imam had deemed the autumn an auspicious time for fruitful unions.

Behind her, Granny heard the servants moving furniture and setting up tables to accommodate the plates of pilaf, roast lamb, and stuffed mussels, and the mountains of sugared fruit that had been stored in the basement since Bairam. More than three hundred people were expected. Everyone in the neighborhood, from the chief fireman to the undersecretary of finance, from the Imam to the grocer, had been invited, along with their families. Anticipation was high: Halide Hanim's wedding was the big event of the year.

The past two weeks had been hectic. Relatives had arrived from as far away as Van in eastern Anatolia; many of them planned to remain in Scutari for the duration of the autumn. Somehow the great house had accommodated them. The *selamlik* was full, and extra girls had been hired from the town to help serve the overflow in the harem. Arzu complained that she hadn't seen such a crowd since Ali Pasha's funeral. Baking and cooking for so many people, in addition to preparing the wedding feast, was taxing her nerves.

Granny picked up a silver teaspoon and turned it over absentmindedly. Ferry boats coming from the European side were sure to be delayed, and Arzu might be gone for the entire morning. She walked around in small circles. The serving girls working nearby put her behavior down to nervous tension. It was a pity, they whispered, that the weather had changed so abruptly on Halide's great day. Overcome with impatience, Granny crossed to the main door and opened it a crack. The wind swept in, sending dead leaves scurrying across the polished floor. She was about to slam the door shut when she saw a barouche turning into the drive from the Scutari road. They had arrived at last.

"Forgive me, ma'am, I had to wait for hours at the quay. Most of the boats coming from the other side were canceled." Arzu hurried across the hall toward her mistress, brushing the last drops of rain from her dress.

"Did you recognize Hatice's nephew?" Granny asked, scanning her face anxiously.

"I did, ma'am. He wasn't hard to find in that dark blue robe and turban. He is removing his wet garments and promises to present himself in a few minutes."

This news made Granny apprehensive. Now that Osman Efendi was in her house, her plan was turning into a reality.

"I've never gone against the laws of the Sultan," Granny said with concern.

"It's God's will, ma'am. You're not doing anything wrong."

The old lady contemplated this remark. It was a subject to which she had given a great deal of thought lately. "He heard my prayers, Arzu," she said. "He guided Hatice Hanim and her nephew to the dervish cemetery so we might meet."

"There are no coincidences in life, ma'am." Arzu had never doubted that mankind was controlled by forces beyond its control.

"The Imam told me that most government laws are man-made and do not come from God. So we are not breaking the holy law."

"I hope you didn't say anything to him about Osman Efendi." Arzu turned a wary eye on her mistress, who was frequently inclined to say the first thing that came into her head.

"No, I was very careful and talked only about Halide's wedding. It was the Imam who brought up the subject of the law. He has some very strong opinions."

"It must be our secret, ma'am, the three of us."

"If anyone asks you what he's doing here, tell them he is a wedding guest."

"I will, ma'am." Arzu paused to gaze around the paneled hall. Everything was in order. Her life been devoted to the maintenance of this order, and she was proud of her loyalty to Fatma Hanim Efendi and her family.

A slender man with a weather-beaten face and cropped hair suddenly appeared at the top of the main staircase. He hesitated, as if uncertain whether or not to descend. Catching sight of Granny, the newcomer came rushing downstairs with the nervous agility of a mountain goat, rousing the curiosity of the servants working nearby. Granny led him into one of the back rooms overlooking the stable yard and closed the door. Arzu remained in the hall, overseeing the preparations for the wedding.

BY EARLY EVENING, the celebration was well under way. The air was filled with cigarette smoke and the sound of laughter drifted up the stairs to the second floor, disturbing some of the elderly visitors who had retired to bed early. Most of the guests had gravitated toward the grand salon, where they gathered around the bride and groom. For the benefit of those at the far end of the room, Halide and Zeki Bey stood in front of the great bay window on a low platform covered with prayer rugs from the harem. Edib was wedged between them, his arms draped around their necks.

"Has he forgotten who he is?" Granny complained to Arzu, who was sitting beside her in the window seat. "My late husband always comported himself with dignity. He believed it was the mark of a true Ottoman."

"Ali Pasha came from the old school. There are few of his caliber left these days, ma'am."

"I fear that applies to all of us." The old lady shifted in her seat and tilted her head until she caught sight of Halide, her eyes fixed adoringly on her husband. The basis for this union was a mystery to her. Why would a young woman of eighteen be drawn to someone twice her age, and such a strange-looking man at that? She herself had been lucky: her parents had had the good sense to marry her off to the most handsome suitor in the city, a man who happened, not incidentally, to be her first cousin. How excited she was when she first saw him! Feelings of compatibility, and happiness, came later.

Guests clustered around the platform where the bride and groom were standing. Halide clutched her husband's hand so tightly her knuckles turned white. Despite the bad weather and the whispers of the harem women, her wedding day was everything she had hoped for. Surrounded by family and neighbors, she felt secure and loved, even beautiful.

If only Teyze and Mahmoure were here to share her wedding day. Gazing across the rain-drenched garden toward the old city, Halide wondered where they were at that moment. Would she ever see them again? Would she be able to thank Teyze for giving her this new life with the man she loved?

Flushed with happiness, Edib stepped forward to speak. "This is a proud moment for me, as I watch my beloved daughter become the bride of one our leading scholars. As most of you know, three months ago she was a mere schoolgirl, graduating with distinction from the American school, the first Turkish student in history to achieve this honor." There was a burst of applause, but Edib held his hand up for quiet. "I know that Halide will be a standard-bearer for women of the future. She will light the way toward unity and understanding between the great world empires."

"Father, you're exaggerating again," Halide whispered as she flushed crimson.

This comment caused some laughter among the guests standing nearby, but Edib was unfazed. Giving her an affectionate nudge, he continued. "Without a modern education system combining the best of the Ottoman with the best of the European, our great tradition will not survive. We must hold firm in our pursuit of democratic ideals."

Granny was stunned. This was a wedding, not a political gathering, and besides, sentiments such as these were dangerous. She looked around to see if others were as shocked as she was. Her guests appeared unfazed. Either they hadn't heard him or they must not have understood the implications of his comments. To her dismay, Halide and Zeki Bey were nodding with approval, and when her father paused to take a breath, Halide leaned forward and kissed him.

The old lady's attention was diverted by the sight of Osman Bey coming toward her from a side door. The storm had passed, and it was time for him to leave. The journey south would take at least five days, depending on the weather. He repeated his assurance that their secret was safe.

Osman, who thrived on the open plains and rocky terrain of Anatolia, was pleased to be on his way again. After receiving Granny's blessing, he slipped out the side door and into the yard, where the fastest horse at Sultan Tepe was waiting for him.

Chapter Three

The newlyweds moved into an apartment beneath the observatory on the Grande Rue de Pera, where Salih Zeki's post entitled them to live free of charge. The building had been constructed five years before, in the European style common to most of the buildings in the area. Compared with Sultan Tepe, Halide's new home was modest. Its three interconnecting salons overlooked the main street, and a warren of smaller rooms rambled the length of the building. There were neither men's quarters nor a harem, and it was a shock for Halide to find herself sharing a home without the boundaries she took for granted.

Halide chose for herself a small room at the back under the roof, with dormer windows and a sloping ceiling. Here she kept her books and papers, her journal, and the manuscript of her novel, which, after two years of work, was almost finished. Salih Zeki's study was on the main floor.

After a brief honeymoon in the Princes Islands, Salih Zeki had returned to his study and buried himself in his work. At the time of their marriage he was compiling what was to be his masterwork, *The Turkish Mathematical Encyclopedia,* and had quit his teaching post in order to devote himself full-time to his writing. He worked for as much as twenty hours a day, and Halide was given the task of translating texts for him from English into Turkish. Doing translations gave her great satisfaction. No matter how prosaic the subject, unraveling the pattern of expression and transferring it from English into Turkish was akin, she found, to solving a complex geometry problem. She loved to discover the human element, the voice of the individual writer with all its nuances of mood and experience. Unfortunately, with the additional demands of running a house and managing servants, she was left with little time for her own work. Salih Zeki was an exacting scholar, and it took all her energy to keep up with his needs.

"Have you finished the piece I gave you? My publisher wants this section by tomorrow morning." The door between Salih Zeki's study and the research room was open. His eye rested on the back of her neck as she sat bent over the table. Several months had passed since their wedding, yet his desire for her was, if anything, stronger than before.

"It was done ages ago, but the segment seemed incomplete. I'm doing the next chapter in case you have need of it."

"Oh, my dear, what would I do without you?" Salih Zeki looked at her with unconcealed admiration.

"He's an interesting writer; his use of language is unusual. I'm not sure I've captured the gist of his style."

"It's only the facts I want, dear love."

"But it's impossible to ignore the forms of expression without losing something."

Halide turned toward her husband, and he marveled once more at her transformation. She radiated passion. He was afraid that every man who came into contact with her would sense it.

"Let's stop for a while," he said. "I'll ring for the servant and she can bring us café au lait and croissants."

"But it's lunchtime. The cook has made some sort of French soup."

"I need coffee." He drew up behind her, rested his hands on her shoulders, and closed his eyes. She smelled scrubbed and fresh. It was almost more than he could stand to be so close to her; and without thinking, he dug his fingers into her skin.

"You're hurting me." She put her hand over his and held it.

He bent over and kissed her neck at the point between her collar and her upswept hair, where her skin was exposed. Moving with deliberate purpose, he closed the door to his study and locked it. She knew what was about to happen: she had known it from the moment he had looked at her. They lay down on the sofa at the back of the room and made love, his need for her so urgent they did not even undress. When they were finished she moved close to his side and listened to the rhythm of his heartbeat.

"What are you thinking?" he whispered. It made him apprehensive when she was silent like this.

"When I was growing up I never imagined anyone could be happy being in love. The harem women sang such plaintive songs about loss and betrayal—love seemed like a necessary burden that had to be endured."

"We Turks are naturally melancholy."

"What makes you say such a thing?"

"Perhaps it's my mood today." He was feeling despondent. There was something he had to tell her, and the prospect weighed on him. A letter had arrived that morning warning him that further delays might be catastrophic. Summoning all his courage, he took a deep breath and turned to her.

"Halide, I have to go away for a while, to Paris."

"How exciting! When do we leave?"

"It breaks my heart to say this, but I can't take you." He ran his fingers across her cheek.

"But I'd love to go to Paris and see the Seine, and Versailles. Besides, it's the perfect opportunity for me to practice my French!"

The thought of her mixing with his French friends filled him with distaste. "An unexpected emergency has arisen," he said. "I have to go at once."

"You promised we would never be parted for a day," Halide pleaded.

"Don't remind me," he said, rather too sternly.

"I don't understand." Her eyes narrowed. This was the first time he had broken his word. She wasn't hurt so much as concerned.

"When I was in Paris I associated with a group of young Ottomans who opposed the Sultan," he said hastily. "After I was appointed head of the observatory, I cut all ties with them and told them that henceforth I would be more effective propagating European ideas through my work here in Constantinople. They need me now, and it would be far too conspicuous if you were to accompany me. Please don't ask why. It's better if you are not involved."

"Are you in danger?"

"No, I'm not in any danger. That life is all behind me now; nothing matters to me anymore except you and our life together."

There was so much love in the look he gave her that her anguish gave way to guilt. "And your work?"

"*Our* work—I couldn't do it without you. No one has your skill, not even the graduates of the translation school." He stroked her hair and pulled her into him so tightly she had to push him back.

"When will you leave?" she whispered, caressing his face with the tips of her fingers.

"Not for a few days." He leaned his head against her breast, feeling light as air. This happiness buoyed him as if he were suspended by a slender cord above the cares and concerns that had hitherto marred his existence.

THE DAY BEFORE he was due to leave, Zeki Bey returned from the old city carrying a small package under his arm. He set it on the table in the hall, along with his gloves and fez, and called for Halide. At the sound of his voice she came running out of the office and immediately caught sight of the parcel. Had he remembered his promise to buy her cakes from the Pera tea rooms? Soon after they were married, he had asked her to stop walking in the Grande Rue. It was, he said, improper for a young Turkish woman to wander unescorted in the European district, where she was certain to attract the wrong kind of attention. Halide did not protest; she preferred the back streets to the bustle of the main thoroughfare. The only thing she missed was the chance to admire the window of the tea room, with its ever-changing display of pastries.

"How did your meeting go?" she asked.

"Damat Ilsahn Efendi is as crazy as ever," he laughed.

"Crazy? What do you mean?"

"The man is fearless. No sooner have the authorities closed down one of his newspapers than he opens up another under a new name. He doesn't give a damn what they think. He prints the truth about the government when no one else dares, yet somehow he avoids prosecution." Parcel in hand he strode into the small salon, which served as a repository for the overflow of books from his office.

"Why did he want to see you?" Halide asked, following close behind him.

"We're old friends. He asked me to contribute some articles to his latest journal. I didn't have the heart to refuse him. He's one of the few people I genuinely admire."

"So you agreed?"

"I said I'd let him know after I had talked it over with you."

"With me? What have I got to do with it?" Salih Zeki had never sought her advice on matters outside the home, so his announcement surprised her.

"If I accept, you will have to write them. He wants the first one by next week. I can't possibly write anything in time as I'm leaving for Paris tomorrow."

"I've never written an article for publication," Halide protested.

Salih Zeki turned to his wife with a broad smile. "It's no different from writing an academic essay. You are a much better writer than I am; your use of language is freer and far more concise."

"What will I say?"

"This may give you some ideas," he said. He picked up the parcel and began to rip the paper off in strips, revealing a second layer underneath. Frowning with annoyance, he pulled off the stiff card piece by piece.

"Why, it's a magazine!" she exclaimed as the last wrapping fell away, somewhat disappointed not to find her favorite pastries.

"This is no ordinary publication, my dear. I've brought you the latest copy of the *Mechveret*."

"What's that?"

"It's the voice of the Ottoman exiles in Paris. Needless to say, it's banned over here. Ilsahn has it sent to the foreign post office in Galata under a plain cover." He handed her the magazine. These mail centers were an unusual feature of life in the Ottoman world. Subject to the same rights as embassies and foreign consulates, they were free from the scrutiny of the authorities and were being used increasingly often by dissidents living abroad to keep in contact with their colleagues.

Halide's curiosity was piqued, and she began to flick through the flimsy pages. All the articles were in French, written by men she had never heard of. She skimmed over a poem by someone called Ahmet Riza. It wasn't very good. "These are long pieces— it would take me weeks to write something like this. Besides, I'm a storyteller. I don't know the first thing about politics."

"Damat is eager to publish new fiction, as long as it's provocative."

"But even a short story takes time."

"I hate to refuse him; he's a man of rare courage." Not for the first time, Salih Zeki regretted the necessity of going to Paris.

"Will he wait until you get back?"

"The first edition must be published by the end of the month. I know," he said at last, stabbing his finger in the air as if addressing his students. "Why don't you send him one or two chapters of your book?"

"It's about women," she said awkwardly.

"A controversial subject these days." He caught hold of her hand and kissed it gently. "Please, my dear, do it for me. Damat is desperate for material."

"If you really want me to."

"Just be sure to avoid words like 'constitution' and 'democracy'; you can get these ideas across with more subtle insinuations."

Halide gave him a rueful smile. "My main character is struggling to escape from her polygamous husband—she hasn't got time to think about politics."

"Is that what your book is about?" Salih Zeki looked at her in what she thought was a peculiar way, half angry, half amused.

"You've only read the second part. She marries again for love and becomes a Koran chanter *after* she has escaped from the marriage her family arranged."

"Marries again, that's new."

"I drew on the experiences of Mahmoure and Teyze," Halide said softly. "They live in my imagination, and it brings them closer to me."

"I'm not sure it's advisable to take too much from real life." Salih Zeki tugged at his beard in a gesture she knew was a clear sign of irritation.

"Is something wrong?" she asked, wondering what had upset him. She touched him on the shoulder, causing him to start.

"The chapters I read led me to believe that your protagonist, what was her name . . ."

"Rabia."

"Rabia, that's it. An odd choice; it's not even a Turkish name." He frowned, displeased by the religious reference.

"It's symbolic."

"I thought Rabia was unmarried and devoted herself to educational reform."

Halide took a deep breath and decided, just this once, not to explain anything. All her longings and unformed hopes for the future were reflected in the destiny of Rabia, who retained a connection to the old world yet achieved a measure of independence because she was paid to chant the words of the Prophet. Although Halide had not initially intended for the story to take such a turn, Rabia's remarriage was a consequence of her independence.

"I'll go and get the manuscript; then you can select the chapters you want me to send. This way there will be no misunderstandings."

"I'll pen a letter to Damat Bey at once. The girl can take it to his office in the morning."

As she hurried out of the room, the smell of cooked pilaf wafted through the half-open door, and the agreeable clatter of cooking pans reminded him that lunch was almost ready.

Chapter Four

Before he left for Paris, Salih Zeki wrote to Granny asking her to stay in the apartment with Halide. She refused. It was unthinkable for women of her class and generation to live without the privacy of a harem. She did not say this, of course; instead she sent him a polite handwritten note outlining the difficulties of reorganizing her household and moving so far away from the tomb of her late husband. But accompanied by Arzu, Granny traveled from Scutari to Pera at least twice a week while Salih Zeki was away. There were no set times for her visits, and if she happened to arrive when Halide was working, she was content to sit in the main salon and look out over the rooftops, toward the hills of old Stamboul.

She did not much like Pera, whose wide streets and glittering stores seemed to her encased in a brittle shell. Not long ago the public gardens at Taksim had been the site of a Christian burial ground, uncultivated land full of wildflowers bounded by ancient cypresses. When she was no more than five or six years old her mother's Armenian maid had taken her there to visit the grave of a sister who had died of typhoid. She retained a distinct memory of a stone cross looming dark against the sky and of Varvara kneeling in prayer. Now Taksim Park was filled with unveiled women promenading to the accompaniment of brass bands and the cries of vendors hawking water ices. Her city was vanishing.

"Poor Varvara, she was a devout woman," Granny said out loud. "She wore a metal cross around her neck. It swung from side to side as we hurried among the graves, looking for what I do not know."

"That was long ago," said Halide, who had heard this story many times before. "There is almost nothing left now of that time."

"You startled me, child. I thought you were in your study. Where is Arzu?"

"She's gone to the market; we were out of white cheese."

"That's very adventurous of her." Granny gave Halide a sharp look. "Are you feeling unwell? You look very pale."

"I must have eaten something disagreeable. I have been feeling ill all morning."

"What you need is some fresh air and quiet. It isn't healthy for a Turkish woman to live in a place like this."

"Oh, Granny, please don't start that again! I'm happy here. This is Zeki Bey's home—he loves the European quarter."

"You need a place in the country," the old lady sniffed. "What will you do when the heat of the summer sets in?"

"I hadn't thought about it. I'm sure we'll manage." Halide crossed the room and knelt beside her grandmother.

"It's fortunate that I still worry about you. I prayed for guidance and, as always, with patience and faith, a suitable home was found."

"What do you mean?" Halide asked, trying not to appear too keen.

"Recently I was offered the lease of a mansion belonging to my second cousin Hatice Hanim. It looks exactly like our old home in Beshiktash." Confident that she had captured Halide's interest, the old lady paused and glanced out the window. It was unnatural to live like this, she thought, suspended above ground, without the sanctuary of a garden and trees.

"Where is it?"

"On the island of Antigone. The ferry stops there on the way to Buyuk Ada. Hatice and her brothers are too old to make the journey from the city, so they decided to let it on a long-term basis. I told them I would find out if you were interested."

"But how will we ever pay for it? Salih Zeki's salary barely covers our expenses."

"You must use Teyze's dowry."

"Oh, I could never touch her money. What will she do when she is released?"

The old lady sighed, knowing in her heart they would never see the palace lady again. "Teyze would wish it for you," she said gently. "Don't forget how happy she was at Beshiktash."

"Well, it does sound tempting. There are times when I yearn for peace. Although I'm very happy here," she added hastily.

"I will make arrangements for us to go Antigone and see for ourselves what condition the place is in. I haven't been there for years. If it's not falling to pieces I will negotiate terms with Hatice's brother."

THREE DAYS later Halide found herself in the blue-and-gold lounge of the Princes Islands ferry, along with Arzu and her grandmother, who was enlivened by the prospect of an outing to one of the old haunts of her youth. At the port in Antigone they hired a closed carriage. Soon the town was behind them, and they climbed up a steep hill through a pinewoods. The horse moved slowly and the older women fell asleep, lulled by the sway of the carriage. Halide was too excited to rest. Even before they reached the house she imagined living in the solitary pinewoods with Salih Zeki, away from the demands of the observatory and the friends who dropped by at odd hours and monopolized his company. Here they would be alone together, and she imagined that this would put his mind at ease.

An ivy-covered wall loomed into view, punctuated by a delicate wrought-iron gate. Close by the gate Halide saw a young man sitting cross-legged on the ground. He wore a peaked cap and a woolen scarf wrapped around his face. At a glance Halide took him to be Christian. He ran to unfasten the lock and hailed the driver as they rode through.

A massive rhododendron hedge gave way to an overgrown garden crowded with bushes and withered weeds. Directly ahead of them was a three-story mansion whose facade was covered by a skeletal wisteria vine. A line of windows ran the length of the second floor; their painted shutters were a faded green. The balustrades supporting the porch were entwined with ivy and the remnants of wild roses, whose brown petals littered the unswept steps. Despite the overall impression of neglect, an unseen hand had polished the doorknobs and cleaned the windows of the lower floor.

As soon as she saw the house, Halide knew this was the place where she would raise her children. The carriage stopped and Granny woke with a start, clapping her hands with joy.

"Oh, it's just as I remember it! A little overgrown perhaps, but nothing the gardeners can't fix. What do you think, Halide?"

"I love it." Fearing that her response was inadequate, she added, "It's Beshiktash all over again."

"When I was a young woman I used to spend the summers here with Hatice's family. They were some of the happiest times of my life." Supporting herself with her hand, Granny edged toward the door and, refusing Halide's help, lowered herself onto the drive. She stood for a moment, staring about in some confusion.

"Really, this is too bad. I was assured that the young men who look after the place would be here to show us around. Where are they?"

"A Christian youth let us in. I could send the coachman to find him," Halide offered.

"I can't wait around all day for servants." With a shrug of impatience, the old lady mounted the steps to the verandah, pushed the door open with her stick, and disappeared inside. Arzu and Halide looked at each other, then hurried after her.

They found themselves in a dark room with high ceilings. The curtains were drawn and the lamps extinguished. Halide could just make out the silhouette of a double staircase with carved balustrades and a small landing surmounted by a stained-glass window.

"I'm going to open the curtains. Stay where you are, Granny, I don't want you falling." The floorboards creaked as Halide walked across the floor. She tugged at a cord and a swath of light cut across the furnishings, which were improbably rough-hewn and covered with kilims.

"Well, it's changed a bit since my day!" Granny exclaimed.

"I heard that Osman Bey, one of their nephews, was living here until a few days ago. This furniture must be his," said Arzu.

Granny tapped a divan with the tip of her stick. "We don't have time to stand about; the last ferry leaves at sundown, which is early at this time of year. I want to check the floors and walls down here for damp. Arzu, you take the kitchen, and Halide can do the upstairs."

Halide wandered from room to room like a ghost returning to the scene of its mortal life. Light drizzled into the empty halls and corridors through dusty glass. At any moment she felt she might come across her mother or glimpse her grandfather taking the air on one of the paths through the pinewoods. It wasn't that the houses were exactly alike—Beshiktash had been larger, grander in design and scale—but the feeling was the same. She reached the end of the landing and discovered that the last door was stuck. She pushed against it with her shoulder until it flew open, almost tossing her to the floor.

The room in which she found herself was in complete disorder, cushions stacked against the wall and overflowing ashtrays scattered on the carpet, along with empty tobacco tins and rolling papers. There were books and papers strewn everywhere. She bent over and picked up a copy of Voltaire's *Candide*. There was no inscription, nothing to indicate to whom it belonged or why it was there. The air smelled of stale smoke. Stifling a sneeze, Halide went to open the window. It was locked. Frustrated, she pressed her face against the glass. The window afforded her a broad view across the pinewoods, down to the sea. On the horizon the minarets of Istanbul were enveloped in a haze.

She saw a movement out of the corner of her eye and instinctively drew back into the shadows. The youth she had seen by the gate was kneeling in the narrow space between the hedge and the wall. Every so often he scraped at the dirt with his fingertips. Halide strained forward. Did the books belong to him? Without a second thought she ran out of the room, along the darkened corridor, and down the stairs. She escaped through a side door off the pantry that led her into a walled yard, but by the time she reached the hedge, the boy was gone.

TWO DAYS later Halide trudged down the flight of narrow steps connecting the Grande Rue to the center of Galata. It was cold and the sky was overcast. She had wrapped herself in a cloak and covered her head with a shawl. Usually one of the maids went to collect the mail at the end of the afternoon, but more than three weeks had passed since Salih Zeki's departure, and she could not bear to wait around all day. True to his word, he had written to her every day, but his letters came in batches of four or five, often with a gap of several days in between. Lately mysterious pen marks had appeared on the envelopes. Once they looked as though they had been ripped open and hastily resealed, with no attempt made to hide the damage. Before leaving he had warned her that the mail coming from Europe, particularly Vienna and Paris, was often examined by the authorities, but she had dismissed the idea as laughable. Now she was afraid.

It wasn't often she ventured out alone, particularly into this part of Galata, which was inhabited by Italians and Armenians. She was conscious of being the only Muslim on the street, but there were few people about at this hour and the passersby took no notice of the veiled figure in the dark cloak. She stopped on the corner beside the ironmongers. Up ahead she could see the post office, a nondescript red-brick building next to a Greek Orthodox church.

The post office was deserted except for a priest and a young woman carrying a crying child. At the counter she gave the clerk Salih Zeki's name; she had to repeat it twice before he understood her. With an apologetic smile the young man handed her a form with instructions listed in Greek, Armenian, French, and Ottoman, and asked her to sign.

There was only one piece of mail, a slim beige envelope addressed to Edib Bey, with a return box number in the old city. Why was someone writing to her father at their box number, she wondered. Didn't they know he had been elevated to Pasha? She tucked it into a pocket of her cloak and hurried away, blinking hard to avoid giving way to tears of disappointment.

Passing through the outer door, Halide collided with a clean-shaven man who touched his cap and murmured an apology in Turkish. After proffering an embarrassed response, she ran outside. A light rain had started to fall.

Halide pulled her shawl up close and made her way back along the street. She was about halfway up the hill when the rain descended in earnest. Water gushed down the open drains and poured over the steps in a swollen stream. She ducked into the nearest doorway to wait until the downpour had passed.

A sound of footsteps echoed in the street. She peered around the archway and saw the same man she had bumped into at the post office splashing up the stairs two at a time. His coat flapped out behind him and water dripped from the rim of his cap. He stopped just a few feet away from her, taking heavy gulps of air. His face was red, and his pale eyes were fixed ahead. When he had recovered, he dashed on up the stone steps and into the Grande Rue, where he hesitated before heading off in the direction of Taksim. Halide remained concealed in the doorway, curiously relieved that he had not seen her.

When she arrived home she put the letter on the hall table, along with Salih Zeki's mail, where it lay waiting for his return. Two days later a telegram came announcing his expected arrival at Sirkechi Station on the night train from Salonika.

Chapter Five

"This letter is for you, dear one. I am not Edib Bey." Salih Zeki waved a sheet of paper in the air and strode into the study, where Halide was in the process of translating a manuscript he had brought back from Paris.

These days, Salih Zeki was content to work at home. As he was director of the observatory, his work was, in the main, administrative, and while he was compiling his encyclopedia, an assistant took care of most of the paperwork. He went in daily to help his staff analyze new data from other astronomers and mathematicians based as far away as Berlin and Vienna, but he was quick to hurry home.

"For me? But it's addressed to my father." In the excitement of his homecoming, Halide had forgotten the fruitless outing to the post office just three days before. "Is it good news?"

"Excellent." Salih Zeki's eyes shone.

"Then you read it to me—it will make the tidings doubly special."

"It would be my pleasure," he replied with a playful bow. He pulled out a chair and sat down facing her, legs spread wide, one elbow resting on his knee. Holding the letter close to his eyes, he began to read in a slow and sonorous voice.

Honored Sir,

    I am in receipt of the documents you sent me. Your work reads with a clarity and an honesty I've never before encountered in our mother tongue. The story immediately engaged me, and I am eager to know what becomes of Rabia. If you are agreeable, it would be an honor to publish your entire book in a serialized form in my new journal, *Haykiris*. I hope this suggestion meets with your approval. If so, perhaps we might meet in the near future to discuss financial arrangements. Please thank my esteemed friend Salih Zeki Bey for referring you to me.

Yours etc.,
Damat Ilsahn Bey.

Halide's hand dropped. Her pen, loosened from her grip, rolled to the floor with a clatter. She looked at her husband with amazement.

"High praise indeed," Salih Zeki said. "Damat is a discerning editor, and he is rarely this enthusiastic."

"I can hardly believe it!"

"You have, as he said, an unusual style."

"Do you think I should agree?"

"Of course, you silly goose. I'll respond on your behalf."

"I finished the last chapter while you were in Paris. The manuscript is in my room, so he can see it as soon as he wishes."

"We'll send it first thing in the morning." Salih Zeki pressed his hands together and propped his chin on his fingertips. "On second thought, I think it would be more advisable for me to take it there myself. Then I can negotiate with him in person and make sure the financial terms are favorable."

"Please tell him that I wish to be known by my married name."

He puckered his brow. "I don't think that's wise."

"But I'm Halide Hanim, wife of Salih Zeki Bey," she protested. She was proud of being married; it propelled her into the adult world, where a wife was a person of consequence.

"I must tell you that I signed the letter Edib Bey because I was afraid that if Damat realized that the manuscript came from a woman, he might not give it the same serious consideration."

"What do you mean?" She was astonished by this admission.

"Unfortunately, most women are uneducated and incapable of making a meaningful contribution in the intellectual arena."

"You must say something to him, convince him that we women are just as able." She struggled to keep her irritation under control.

"Facts are facts: you are an exception, and Damat Bey is unaware of this. The most important thing is to get your manuscript published in any way we can." He drew her close and kissed her forehead.

"I don't like to deceive people," Halide said with a frown.

"Neither do I, and as soon as circumstances permit, I will reveal the truth. But in the meantime we are compelled to do what we must."

"I was going to say it's a pity other so-called liberals don't share my father's views, but then he has behaved so thoughtlessly toward Teyze I'm not sure what he thinks of women after all."

Sensing that they were venturing into dangerous territory, Salih Zeki glanced down at the translation she had left lying on the table. "You've been working hard," he said. "Why don't we take time off and celebrate your triumph. We will go to the Pera Tea Rooms tomorrow afternoon."

HALIDE WORE his favorite dress, the one made of pale blue velvet with the scalloped hem and lace collar that fastened in a prim bow at the dip between her collar bones. Now that her father no longer ordered her dresses they were made by a seamstress in Kadikoy, a Greek woman who owned a Singer sewing machine sent by a cousin in America. Salih Zeki had bought her a bottle of cologne from Paris, and to please him she dabbed some behind her ears and in the curve of her wrists. With her hair scraped back into a tight knot and the lightest of veils covering her face, Halide left the apartment feeling somehow different. In the Grande Rue she walked beside him, like a modern wife, holding his arm.

Since their wedding they had rarely gone out together. Salih Zeki did not enjoy socializing, or so he said. He preferred to stay at home, savoring the novel comfort of domesticity. He wasn't used to the company of women, but for her sake he had engaged a couple of local girls to clean, an Armenian cook, and a laundress. He did not want her energy wasted on the minutiae of household tasks.

He moved at a brisk pace, pausing to exchange a word of greeting with the store owners who doffed their hats as he and Halide passed. It seemed that everyone knew him. Even the *simit* seller standing on the corner near the flower market waved from across the street. Halide gripped her husband's arm and hurried to keep pace. When they passed Paquin, the official dressmaker of the Imperial harem, she cast a longing look at the window, where a concoction of black-and-cream satin was prominently displayed, but she dared not ask him to stop. Farther along the street a feeling of nausea rose in her throat and she coughed, covering her mouth with her free hand. A dull pain started behind her eyes. She had been feeling this way for weeks, but today of all days it was particularly bad. She feared she had inherited her mother's sickness and had written to her grandmother asking if they might consult Peyker. Salih Zeki would never approve of consulting a seer, so she'd resigned herself to secrecy.

By the time they reached the Pera Tea Rooms, Halide was out of breath. Salih Zeki removed his fez but advised her to keep her face covered. His severity surprised her, for she'd had no intention of revealing herself to a room full of strangers. The maître d'hôtel swept forward and greeted him by name.

"Have you met him before?" she whispered as soon as they were seated at one of the better tables near the window.

"His brother is the Sultan's chief of police."

"You're joking—I thought he was French!" she exclaimed, stealing a backward glance at the elegant figure in tails and bow tie.

"He was a student at the Academy of Translators; now he puts his talent to other uses. Everyone knows, of course—everyone of any importance, that is."

"He's a spy, you mean?"

"No, my dear, nothing that dramatic. An observer, shall we say."

"Has he been here long?" she asked innocently.

"Years and years, since before I went to Paris. I once brought him a pair of cuff links from a jeweler on the Champs-Élysées, and he's been grateful to me ever since."

Their tea arrived on a silver tray borne by a waiter in white tie and tails, and Halide's thoughts slipped back to her first excursion to the tea room with Riza and Mahmoure. She didn't want to spoil the occasion.

"Indian or Chinese, ma'am?" The waiter was beside her, teapot in hand.

"Chinese, thank you."

"Sir?"

Salih Zeki nodded almost imperceptibly. He slipped his arm behind Halide and sighed as the waiter leaned forward to pour the tea. "As I recall, the éclairs are exceptional," he said.

"They were always my favorite." Halide stuck her fork into the chocolate icing, and cream oozed over her plate. Her stomach lurched uncomfortably. She eased the fork under her veil and took a mouthful, but the taste of the cream made her feel ill. Suddenly she began to cough fitfully.

"Are you okay? Can I get you something?"

"No, I'll be fine."

"Here, drink some water."

"I can't," she gasped. She put her hand over her mouth, feeling at any moment she might choke.

"Halide, you've gone white. What is the matter?"

"I'll be all right." Halide did not want to spoil their outing.

He leaned over and took her hand; it felt damp and clammy. "You are obviously unwell, my dear," he said, mindful of the history of illness on her mother's side. "Perhaps we should see my doctor; his office is only a few streets away."

"I don't want to leave—this is such a treat."

"We can come another time, when you feel better."

"You promise?"

He gave her a look of concern and impatience. For no good reason she thought of the thrush's nest she had found in the laurel bushes during their last summer at Beshiktash.

"You'll enjoy his company. For a German he is unusually cultivated."

"Who is?"

"My physician, of course. What's the matter with you, my dear? You're very preoccupied today."

"I'd forgotten." She bit her lip and unwittingly cut into the skin.

"Dr. von Schlesser will have you back to your usual self in no time."

Halide closed her eyes and tried to remember where she had heard that name before. The room swam in front of her when she stood up, and she clung to her husband to steady herself. Outside Salih Zeki searched for a cab. It was early evening and the drivers were busy as the last shoppers made their way home. From far away Halide heard the cries of the muezzin rising and falling at discordant intervals.

A MANSERVANT ushered them into the waiting room and informed them in resonant German that the doctor was out and due back at six o'clock. Halide sank onto a sofa beneath a portrait of the kaiser in full army dress, his hands clasped over the hilt of a sword. Salih Zeki browsed through one of the medical journals on the table. Every now and then he glanced over at the marble clock on the mantel. Halide was glad he had insisted on seeing a doctor.

Just before six they heard the front door slam. After a brief exchange with his manservant the doctor came into the waiting room, still carrying his bag. He extended his hand to Salih Zeki and shook it warmly. When Halide was introduced, he greeted her with the distant courtesy he reserved for all his women patients. His eyes were now webbed with wrinkles and his bushy sideburns had turned gray, but Halide recognized Dr. von Schlesser at once: this was the man who had tried to keep her from her dying mother.

Advancing years had done nothing to soften his manner. Once they were settled in his study, the doctor addressed Salih Zeki in German and asked him to describe her symptoms. When Halide tried to answer herself, he ignored her. At times like this women were known to be hysterical, he murmured, oblivious to her command of the language. She retreated into angry silence, wondering what he meant. Gradually their conversation drifted away from the subject of her health and they fell into a discussion about the growing German-Ottoman friendship. Salih Zeki admired the Germans: they were great scholars and reliable allies; their military strength balanced the might of their old adversaries, the Russians. But German money had helped finance the building of the Berlin-to-Baghdad railway, and Salih Zeki expressed concern about the Turkish debt to the Deutsche Bank, a debt von Schlesser dismissed with a wave of the hand. Then, almost as an aside, the doctor let slip that it was likely Halide was pregnant.

Salih Zeki started. He searched for an appropriate phrase, but nothing came to him. Halide lowered her eyes. Now their intimacy had been revealed by this cold-eyed stranger, and she felt a strong urge to run away. Pregnant! She'd never suspected it, not for a moment.

Chapter Six

Esteemed Sir,

My husband left a copy of *Haykiris* lying on our dining room table; quite by chance it was open to your story, and I read it. When they came to visit I read it to my sister-in-law and my friend—in secret, of course. Now we are waiting for the next edition to appear so we can find out what will happen to Rabia. Speaking personally, I think she must leave her husband. I only wish I had done the same thing at her age. It's not worth wasting a life being unhappy. She has no children, no ties of kinship to keep her bound for eternity to a violent, selfish man. Rabia must throw herself on the mercy of her parents and beg them to take her back. My sister-in-law disagrees; she believes it's a woman's lot to suffer. This is also the opinion of my friend.

You write with a poet's skill and a woman's soul. I want to know how you, a man, can know so well the secret longings of women's hearts. Are you close to your mother? Did she tell you her troubles? Sons are a woman's greatest blessing. When you finish reading my letter burn it, please. I don't want my husband to know I've written to a stranger. I've never done such a thing before.

Halide's eye flashed over the signature, which was hurried and indistinct, as if the writer was afraid of revealing herself. She placed the letter facedown on the pile beside her and folded her arms on the tabletop. Once she was done she would put it in the fire, along with the other correspondence that contained a plea for anonymity. Their secrets were safe with her. She admired these women's courage. Many had expressed outright fear of their husbands, describing lonely lives of servitude and violence more terrifying than anything she had imagined in her fiction. They spoke of feeling powerless and unhappy, too afraid to offer resistance for fear of being divorced or deprived of their children. Others envied Rabia's access to education, and expressed a longing for the same advantage. Her favorite letter came from a seventy-year-old woman who thanked "dear wise Edib Bey" for revealing new possibilities for women's lives and giving her hope for her great-granddaughter's future. There was criticism, of course. An Imam from Yesilkoy accused her of being an instrument of the devil, and a "faithful believer" warned her to change her views before it was too late.

Her story touched naked pain, but despite their pathos, the letters afforded Halide a measure of satisfaction. Finally she was doing something to help others. By drawing on the human element deep within herself and expressing it in a modern form unfettered by tradition, Halide knew she had found her way.

When Salih Zeki entered the apartment through the back stairs from the observatory, Halide was so engrossed with her mail she did not hear him until he appeared in the doorway.

"Did you see Damat Bey?" She looked up at him hopefully.

"We had a meeting this morning, and he is overwhelmed by the response to your work. He predicts that sales of *Haykiris* will double."

"Not on account of my story, surely?"

"Nothing like it has ever been published before, Halide. You write like a man, yet your characters are seen from a woman's point of view."

"It's the only perspective I know."

"A well-known publisher has shown interest in buying the manuscript. Damat and I were outlining the terms we shall demand." He pulled out a chair and sat down beside her. His expression changed as his eye fell on the letters.

"What on earth is all this?"

"My readers have written to me saying how much they like my work."

He frowned. "Don't let flattery distract you, my dear."

"They tell me about their lives." She picked up the pile of letters and compressed it between her palms. The paper felt light as air.

"Did you finish translating Burke's essay on geometry?"

"It's on your desk," she murmured, only half listening. There were times in the past when she had glimpsed hardship and desperation in the eyes of the male refugees who lingered around the mosques, but the faces of the women were hidden beneath their veils. In the future she would look more carefully for signs of their suffering.

Salih Zeki made a move to get up and then changed his mind. "You don't seem very excited by my news. Your book is going to be a success, Halide. Before you know it you'll be renowned throughout Constantinople."

"It won't make a difference to me; my readers think I'm a man."

"If you must know, I confessed to Damat that the writer Edib Bey was none other than my wife." He had not meant to tell her so quickly. He had planned to save it for the evening, as a prelude to love. Lately she had been withdrawn, almost cold, a change of emotion he ascribed to the pregnancy.

"Was he surprised?" she said evenly.

"Not exactly. He knew you were highly educated, and he'd put two and two together. But"—the back of his throat felt sticky, and he coughed—"for the sake of continuity he thinks it better to maintain the nom de plume until the entire book has been published."

"I'm pleased you told him. Now we're not deceiving your friend."

"Damat admitted he would not have read the manuscript had he known it came from a woman. I was right, you see."

Halide nodded. Zeki Bey could always be trusted to know what was best, she reflected, even in the unpleasant matter of Dr. von Schlesser. Her husband had persuaded her that he was the finest and most knowledgeable physician in the city and that she had a moral obligation to their unborn child to give herself the best care available. With the tips of her fingers Halide spread the letters out across the table. Her brow furrowed as she stared at them. Salih Zeki reached forward and smoothed the creases with the palm of his hand. It disturbed him to see her troubled.

THE LETTERS kept arriving, two, three, sometimes four a day until the end of the month, when the second installment of her novel was published. Then the deluge began. By the time April came around, she had received more than three hundred letters, many of them anonymous. Halide filed a few in a box under the bed, but most were burned. She fed the flames herself, watching until the last shreds of paper were consumed. The laments and fears of her readers crept into her imagination. She often found herself waking in the night, with the overwhelming sense that something was wrong. What it was exactly she could not recall. The source of her unrest lay just beyond her grasp, on the perimeters of her dreamworld.

Acting on her behalf, Salih Zeki signed a contract with a publisher who specialized in new Turkish fiction, and plans were made to issue her book toward the end of the year, around the time her child was due. Money was exchanged and deposited in Zeki Bey's account at the Ottoman Bank. Between them, they agreed to invest it for their unborn child.

The sales of *Haykiris* soared. This was a mixed blessing for Damat Ilsahn because it brought him, once more, to the attention of the authorities.

As her pregnancy continued Halide remained detached from her success; as far as she was concerned, once the book was conceived it disappeared from view. She never went to the journal's offices on the outskirts of Fatih; she did not meet her publisher. She stayed in the apartment studying and translating, and waiting for the next warm spell, when they could return to Antigone.

Mahmoure and Teyze were constantly in her thoughts. She wished she could send a copy of the manuscript to Teyze but feared it would only cause more trouble. Even letters were forbidden, so she could not tell her the joyful news of her pregnancy. On a clear day Halide could see Ciragan Palace from the deck of the ferry as she crossed the straights to Sultan Tepe. It was such a strange feeling to know that Teyze was there, yet so inaccessible she might have been in Damascus.

Since her pregnancy was diagnosed Halide longed to share the experience with her sister. This child she was carrying was related to Mahmoure, and the sense of being bound by these ties made Mahmoure's absence almost unbearable.

Chapter Seven

A t first Salih Zeki had resisted the idea of renting another home. The island was too far away, he argued, and a mansion was an unnecessary extravagance. If Halide needed a house, what was wrong with a smaller one on the banks of the Bosphorus? In an even voice she told him not to fret about the rent; it would be paid from Teyze's legacy, and her grandmother would furnish and maintain the house with the same scrupulous attention she gave to the harem at Scutari. It would be a home befitting his status as director of the observatory. Salih Zeki eventually gave in and even allowed his wife a preliminary visit, provided she was accompanied by Granny and Arzu, whom he referred to rather grandly as "the chief housekeeper."

The first thing Halide saw when she entered the house on Antigone was the copy of *Haykiris* lying on a brass table in the hall. "I wish those boys wouldn't leave their things lying around," Granny said irritably. "There's enough to be cleaned without adding to the work."

"Are they still taking care of the house?" Halide asked, slipping the journal into her traveling bag. Granny knew nothing about the novel, and it was better that way. Halide wasn't sure she'd approve of Damat Ilsahn and his politics.

"They are indeed. From the look of things, they're doing a good job." She pushed open a door with the tip of her walking stick and examined the room with a critical eye. "I told Hatice's brother to let them know we were coming."

"Maybe they forgot," Halide offered.

"Oh, they'll be here," Granny said. "Their livelihood depends on it." The old lady settled into a window seat and surveyed the room. The rough-hewn fixtures had been replaced by simple Ottoman furnishings, and Arzu's white cotton curtains fluttered in the breeze.

"I can hear someone upstairs. I'll let them know we've arrived." Halide started toward the door, but her grandmother called her back. Granny's hearing wasn't what it used to be; she had asked Halide to help her through the upcoming interview. She was going to tell the boys what was expected of them now that the family would be in residence for the summer.

The footfalls drew closer and the door swung open. Arzu started and drew herself up straight.

Time had not dealt kindly with Riza. His face was drawn and lined, and the hair at his temples had turned gray. Confronted by Granny and Halide he tensed; his first impulse was to turn and run. Then he snapped to attention and bowed in a gesture that bespoke the young officer he had once been. Halide's heart raced so fast she thought it would burst. She scrambled to her feet, dashed across the room, and flung her arms around his neck.

"So we are discovered," he whispered, clasping Halide in an awkward embrace. Mahmoure, who was standing several steps behind him, ran across the hall toward the main door. "Come back," he called after her over Halide's shoulder. "We're safe."

Eyes darting like a cornered animal, Mahmoure crept back to the salon. She was wearing the suede jerkin and trousers that had once belonged to her father. Her hair was gathered in a knot under a boy's cap, and stray hairs fell over the collar of her shirt. Halide released her hold on Riza and grabbed Mahmoure before she could run away again. The sisters held each other in a tight embrace, tears running down their cheeks.

"I can't believe it," Halide gasped. "It's the answer to all my prayers."

"I missed you, I missed you all," Mahmoure sobbed.

"Ach, Mahmoure Hanim, what do you think you look like in those clothes?" Granny shook her head.

Arzu slipped out of the shadows and went around to the kitchen to make coffee. This was a family affair; she took pride in knowing when to be discreet.

"How long have you been here?" Halide cupped her sister's face in her hands and covered it with kisses.

"Since the beginning of April." Mahmoure drew back suddenly, aware of Halide's protruding belly. "My God, look at you—you're pregnant!"

"Almost five months," Halide said, holding tightly to her sister's arm.

"It seems like yesterday we were children playing in the garden at Beshiktash." Mahmoure, who rarely gave a thought to the past, suddenly wanted to weep for time lost.

"That was long ago," Halide said, closing her eyes. "If you only knew how I've prayed for this moment."

Mahmoure wiped away her sister's tears with the back of her hand. "I was never one for prayers," she said with a smile. "But if you prayed, somebody heard."

"The God of your ancestors," said Granny sharply. "That is who heard Halide's prayers and mine."

Mahmoure turned and clasped the old lady's hand.

"If you had paid more attention to your faith, my child," Granny said with a sigh, "your fate might have been an easier one than the path your heart has chosen."

"I had no other choice." Mahmoure glanced up and smiled at Riza, who had drawn back and was watching the three women through half-closed eyes. Color had returned to his cheeks, and in the bright daylight Halide thought he looked almost handsome. Just then Arzu reappeared carrying a samovar.

❀

"I'VE BEEN MARRIED almost two years," Halide said, carefully sipping her hot tea. "My husband and I have an apartment on the Grande Rue, just up the street from the tea rooms."

"Oh, I'd give anything to taste one of those cakes again!" Mahmoure closed her eyes and tried to recall the taste of cream and chocolate mixed with the sharp aroma of Indian tea.

"Her husband is a renowned scholar and director of the observatory," Granny said with a touch of pride.

"He was my math tutor and a friend of Father's. His name is Salih Zeki."

"Where have I heard that name before?" Mahmoure gave Riza a querying look. "Didn't someone called Salih Zeki Bey send you books from Paris? It was years ago, when we were still at Beshiktash."

"You must be thinking of someone else," Riza replied. "I don't know a Salih Zeki."

"Maybe." Of course there was that other matter, she remembered vaguely, some kind of scandal about a woman. Riza was right; it couldn't be the same man.

"My husband lived in Paris for years," Halide interjected.

"I think I have the names confused," Mahmoure said, leaning her head against Riza's shoulder and bringing the conversation to an end.

You did it for me, I know. Selima's voice echoed in Granny's mind. *Now my children are together again; the circle is complete. Beautiful girls, aren't they, Mother?* the voice went on. *So different, yet each reflecting something, like two halves of a whole.*

"Are you all right?" Halide shook her grandmother's arm. The old lady was so still Halide was afraid she'd stopped breathing.

Granny sat up with a start. "I must have dozed off."

"Your eyes glazed over—it gave me a scare."

"It's nothing, dear, just old age."

"What an extraordinary twist of fate that of all the houses in the city, you should have chosen to rent this one," Mahmoure exclaimed.

"One might almost think it was arranged," Riza said, giving her a wry smile.

"As a matter of fact, it was." There was a silence; the three of them waited for Granny to say more. Then Halide laughed, thinking that her grandmother was making a joke.

"Your escape, this sanctuary, our reunion, everything was arranged by me and the spirit of Ali Pasha."

"But I was kidding!" Riza said, draining his cup.

"Your grandfather sent me a man I could trust, my cousin Hatice's nephew Osman, a Bektashi."

"Osman was your go-between?" Halide was incredulous.

"I'm not sure what you mean by that," Granny said primly. "Without Osman none of this would have been possible. He agreed to help, at great risk to his own safety."

"But how did you know where to find us?" Mahmoure asked.

"We were in touch with your father until the day he died. You don't think I would have let you go so easily?" Granny said, a mischievous smile on her lips. Much to her surprise, she had enjoyed instigating the conspiracy; it had added excitement to her quiet routine.

"But he never said a word to me!" Mahmoure sat back on her heels and looked at her grandmother with bewildered amazement.

"If it was known, our lives would have been imperiled. No, Ali Shamil would never have betrayed us. Even the messengers did not know who the correspondents were. They made contact with

Arzu at the vegetable market. The secret police would never suspect an old woman . . ."

"That still doesn't explain how you two were persuaded to return." Halide, still reeling from the shock of seeing her sister, couldn't quite assimilate what Granny was saying.

"We led a quiet life in Antalya, farming, running the house. After Ali Shamil died I didn't want to stay, but we had nowhere to go," Mahmoure explained. "Riza was still wanted by the authorities, so we were fugitives. Although my father's family would have protected us forever." Life in Antalya had been comfortable but confined. Riza and Mahmoure had fared well in the warm climate and fresh sea air, but as the years passed they'd found themselves longing for city life.

"I felt I didn't belong, and I missed being involved in politics," Riza added.

"When Osman Bey befriended us and offered us the chance to come north, it seemed too good to be true."

"At first I refused, suspecting a trap." They exchanged glances, as if the memory of their disagreement was still painful. "Then Mahmoure had her dreams and I was persuaded."

"Night after night Ali Shamil came back to me in the company of Osman Bey."

"You see," Granny said, rapping her fist on the coffee tray. "When you listen to your dreams, everything turns out well."

Never in a million years would Halide have thought her grandmother was capable of such a scheme. People could be such a mystery! No matter how close one was, it was impossible to know another person completely.

"You saved our lives," whispered Mahmoure. "Thank you."

"Nonsense," snapped the old lady. "It was my duty to keep this family together. Abandoning your children was unforgivable, but you will pay the price and, who knows, one day you may be united again, God willing. As for you, Riza, I don't understand the charges against you, but having seen the injustice done to Teyze, I don't trust the ethics of your accusers."

"What happened to Teyze?" Mahmoure and Riza asked in unison.

"I'm tired—Halide can explain. It's time for me to go and rest." The voices in her head had been quieted at last. They had started again only recently: first Ali Bey, then Selima. Did this mean the time was drawing closer? Not yet; she had to care for Halide's unborn child. The ways of the ancestors had to be passed on.

HALIDE COULD not wait to tell her husband about the emotional reunion in Antigone. When she did, Zeki Bey recognized Riza's name but could not recall where or when their paths had crossed. He listened with interest, but her naïveté troubled him. In a society saturated with spies and informants, harboring fugitives was a risky undertaking, and as long as Mahmoure and Riza were living at Antigone their presence threatened the entire family. The story of Granny's deceptively artless defiance confirmed his impression that the old lady had unlimited reserves of strength beneath her slightly batty ways. Above all, he was interested to learn about the growing opposition among officer cadets. This was news to him. The army was the basis of the Sultan's power, and if the future leaders of the armed forces were discontented, the Sultan was in a more precarious position than he had realized.

When Salih Zeki had taught at the naval academy, his official standing had forced him to keep his association with the Young Turks a secret. He had not heard of any dissent among the students, but that didn't necessarily mean anything. He made up his mind to find out more from Riza as soon as the opportunity presented itself.

Chapter Eight

Along the Bosphorus the gardens and hillsides swelled with yellow-green foliage. Catkins drooped over the sweet waters, and the chilly air of winter gave way to warm breezes sweeping off the sea. As the days grew longer, the city took on a festive aspect; by evening the streets and parks were thronged with people released from their winter hibernation. Ignoring the doctor's orders to take a daily walk, Halide remained in the apartment, working to complete her translations before the baby was born. Every morning, after a breakfast of white cheese and toast, she retired to her second-floor room, sat cross-legged on the divan beside the window, and spread her books around her. To keep the air circulating, she threw open the window.

Each day she recorded the progress of her pregnancy in her journal, then she made notes about the new characters swirling around in her head. The seed of another book had taken root, about a Muslim girl born at the dawn of the new century who later marries a Christian musician and gives birth to the leader of a country where the religions coexist in peace. Religion was, after all, at the heart of the tensions with Europe. Halide believed there had to be a way to combine the best of both cultures and religions. She was afraid to say anything about this to Salih Zeki, who disapproved of her continuing devotion to her faith. Lately their relationship had changed, and she felt at times as if she were pounding helplessly from the far side of a glass wall. By day he was courteous and distant, guarded yet attentive; at night he turned away, as if afraid of her swelling body.

Unbeknownst to Halide, Dr. von Schlesser had warned Salih Zeki that pregnancy was likely to induce mental instability in a woman of her background. Years before, he had attended her mother, and he knew for a fact there was a history of sickness and hysteria in the family. Halide's unusual intelligence rendered her physically vulnerable. It was one of life's ironies, he declared, that only peasants and common people who lacked mental acuity were equipped to undergo childbirth unscathed. Salih Zeki had taken his warning to heart. He talked the matter over with Edib, and between them they'd agreed that one of them would be present in the apartment at all times. Edib would alter his schedule to accommodate this new demand.

❦

"FATHER, YOU'RE so kind; I'll tell the cook to make us herb omelettes for lunch." The three of them were sitting in her study. Edib, who had arrived after breakfast, had brought fresh eggs from a farm near Yildiz.

"I doubt I can get back in time; my meeting with the first dragoman at the German consulate is scheduled for noon." Edib drummed his fingers nervously; Halide thought he looked strained.

"Send my best regards to Ambassador von Bieberstein if you see him," Salih Zeki said with a formal flourish. "I have told him many times how much I admire his people; they are our only true allies."

"I agree," Edib said, nodding thoughtfully. "Only Germans seem genuinely interested in an alliance. The motives of the other powers are suspect."

Halide listened as they discussed the advantages of an increased German presence in the city. If only they would go downstairs, she thought, doodling on her notepad. I love them dearly, but this is my time to work, and I have seven pages to complete before the day is over.

"You'll catch a chill from that breeze," said Salih Zeki, who seemed suddenly to remember she was there. He slid across the divan and reached for the catch of the open window. On the corner a hurdy-gurdy man played to an audience of old men.

"I'll be damned," Salih Zeki exclaimed. The tips of his ears turned crimson, a sure sign of anger. Halide put down her pad and moved to his side, stroking the back of his neck to calm him.

"What is it?" she murmured.

"That's no ordinary street musician. He's watching this building." He clenched his fists and frowned at Edib Pasha. "How dare they," he cursed under his breath.

Outside, the music stopped and the old men drifted away. The musician removed his fez and mopped his brow with a checkered cloth. It was then that Halide saw clearly his clean-shaven features, and realized it was none other than the man from the post office. She was about to say something when she remembered she was not supposed to have ventured out alone.

"Are you certain?" Edib rose and stood behind them, craning his neck to see over their heads. Salih Zeki took another look. As he bent over the sill, Halide noticed for the first time that his hair was beginning to thin at the crown.

"He's staring right up at this window. I've a good mind to wave at him."

"Don't be rash," said Edib, taking hold of his shoulders.

"What do they want with us?" Halide asked.

"Our association with Damat Bey must have come to their attention."

Edib Pasha, accustomed to being spied on, gave a weary shrug. "Everyone is suspect these days, especially journalists."

"The interior minister gave me his personal assurance that I would not be troubled," Salih Zeki said, barely suppressing his anger. "It was one of the conditions of my return."

"But that was several years ago," Edib cautioned. "Things have changed."

"The Sultan is not a fool. He knows that men like me are invaluable to him. Why, just the other day the grand vizier wrote to me, on behalf of Sultan Abdulhamid, offering extra monies to bring researchers from Paris to help with work on my encyclopedia. The palace thinks my project will enhance the intellectual image of the regime."

"Really?" said Edib, clearly impressed.

Halide listened in silence. Why hadn't he told her about the palace's offer? When her father rose to leave, Salih Zeki took her arm to help her off the divan, but she shook him off and made her own way down the stairs.

❧

"I DON'T UNDERSTAND," Halide said much later, after her father had gone and they had eaten the eggs, washed down with goat's milk and honey. They were sitting together in the small salon, reading by the light of a single oil lamp.

"Mmmm," he murmured, not lifting his eyes from his book.

"Why didn't you tell me about the researchers from Paris?"

"The matter is not yet settled; I didn't want to raise your hopes needlessly."

"I didn't know the Sultan was aware of your work."

"*Our* work, my dear, yours and mine. I think we are both of interest to the authorities."

"Don't exaggerate," she said with a blush.

Salih Zeki put down his book and contemplated his wife over the top of his reading glasses. "First you graduated from the American school, then you married me, a distinguished intellectual and a known associate of the opposition. Now you have published an incendiary book with Damat Bey. Oh no, my dear, you can be sure he is keeping an eye on everything we do."

"It can't be . . ." she stuttered feeling suddenly fearful. "I stay at home, I lead a quiet life. I'm not a threat to the Sultan."

"You have been trained to think for yourself," Salih Zeki replied, "and you are conversant in the languages of the so-called infidels. A dangerous combination."

"But I don't know anything about politics!"

"These days everything is political—every thought you entertain, every sentence you write, every book you read."

"I'm not sure I understand."

"The Sultan gives the appearance of making reforms, but after he abolished the constitution he made sure all power was his and his alone," Salih Zeki said in a calm voice. "This suppression and censorship has gotten worse over the last twenty-five years. Enough is enough!"

"But if the Sultan was deposed, who would lead us?"

"A government defined by a constitution."

"Like they have in America?"

"Ah, we can only dream of such a society. Let's start with restoring our own constitution and go from there."

"So that's what you and Damat Ilsahn are working toward."

Salih Zeki returned to his book. "Don't trouble your sweet head with all this; it will make you ill."

Chapter Nine

During the last week of May the family moved to Antigone. Granny went first with Arzu to get the great house in order. They had to hire a private boat to accommodate the quantities of furnishings, pots, porcelain, candles, rugs, and leather-bound blanket trunks filled with clothes and shawls, as well as a summer's supply of rose-water *locum* from Haci Bekir. Riza met them at the quay with an oxcart. The fisherman looked on with bemused astonishment as Arzu directed the unloading while Granny, in tiers of mauve lace, waited in the shade of a plane tree, eating a water ice. In a break with tradition, she had ordered the maids and cooks from the Scutari harem to remain at home. There was a chance that one of them might recognize Mahmoure, or stir up rumors about Edib's protégé. For cleaning and cooking they would make do with women from the nearby village.

Salih Zeki traveled with Halide, who was relieved to be leaving Pera, although she said nothing of this to her husband. Throughout the voyage she sat on the deck, her face turned toward the Princes Islands. At first Antigone was nothing more than a speck on the horizon, but as the ferry drew closer and the buildings of the town became differentiated from the dark pinewoods, she clutched her husband's hand with excitement. Her touch moved him, and he lifted his attention from his book and watched while the ferry slowed and rounded the point to the harbor. He had never been to the islands before. They were home to the Ottoman elite and the religious minorities who made their money from trade.

The afternoon was warm and sunny. Buds swelled on the

rhododendron bushes, and the roses were starting to bloom. Their scent filled the air as Halide and Salih Zeki pulled into the circular drive in front of the house. Everyone was waiting for them on the verandah. Riza came down the steps ahead of the women and bowed to Salih Zeki. He was pleased to have another man around, especially one who was sympathetic to the cause.

"I've heard a lot about you," Salih Zeki said to Riza once they were alone on the verandah. Halide was inside resting, and the older women had retired to their rooms. Only Mahmoure remained downstairs, flitting between the house and the garden like a restless moth.

"Our paths have crossed before, indirectly," Riza said. Zeki Bey turned abruptly and gave Riza a quizzical glance. "I am Riza Efendi, formerly care of the Pera post office." Passing between the hall and the main door, Mahmoure stopped to listen.

"But of course, I should have put two and two together. What a pleasure to meet you at last." Salih Zeki inclined his head and tried to remember Riza's connection to the Paris group.

"I was your go-between. Your people in Paris would send their journals and pamphlets to me and I would take everything back to the academy."

"Wasn't it dangerous to use your own name?"

"In those days the opposition in the military schools wasn't organized, and the authorities didn't take any notice of us." Riza watched Salih Zeki carefully as he spoke. What a strange-looking man, he thought to himself. I wonder what Halide sees in him.

"The rapid growth of the CUP took us by surprise. We underestimated the strength of the student movement."

"By then I was in Antalya and had no idea what was going on."

"I wondered why you disappeared so suddenly," Salih Zeki Bey said, pacing the room with long strides. It had all happened so long ago that he had trouble recalling the sequence of events.

"We were betrayed by an informer. I was lucky. Edib Pasha warned me in advance and I escaped, but I could do nothing to help my colleagues."

"I do remember hearing something about it. Ferid Bey must have mentioned it. He was a friend of yours, wasn't he?" Salih Zeki probed with care. He had a feeling that Riza knew more than he let on.

"I met him only twice."

"That's all?"

"I never trusted him. He saw me once in the Pera Tea Rooms— I was there with Mahmoure and Halide, who couldn't have been more than seven or eight at the time. He came blustering in to greet me. Looking back, I have often thought the encounter was no accident; soon after that my name was known to the secret police."

"You think Ferid set you up?"

Riza spoke slowly. "I think he was a double agent."

"You may be right." Zeki Bey began to relax. It was evident that Riza had been in exile for many years. Salih Zeki had come to feel that reform had to be effected from within the establishment to avoid bloodshed and social turmoil. He felt he was of greater use in a position of power in Constantinople than he had ever been teaching mathematics in Paris. "There were so many like Ferid, playing both sides," he mused, turning back to Riza. "I wonder what became of them all?"

"I heard Ferid was arrested and exiled to Libya."

"Poor devil," Salih Zeki said with a rueful smile. "I wonder if he survived the boat trip."

Riza shrugged and Salih Zeki waited to see what he would say next; the young man was evidently in a garrulous mood.

"The Sultan may think he's got rid of us," Riza said with passion, "but he is wrong. He still has enemies in every corner of the Empire. He's old and tired; he can't keep up the fight forever."

Salih Zeki gave Riza a wry smile. "I was always puzzled by Abdulhamid's policy of exiling the opposition. He couldn't bring himself to kill them, so he sent them away. As a result, his political opponents are alive and well in every city from Cairo to Geneva."

"It is almost funny looked at that way."

"It's absurd!" Salih Zeki exclaimed, letting down his guard.

"One of my former colleagues from Harbiye is teaching at the medical school, and another is an administrator at the staff college. They tell me their students are still vehemently opposed to the Sultan."

"You meet openly with these people?! Supposing you're recognized?" Salih Zeki was alarmed: such risky behavior endangered the entire family.

"We go together, disguised as brothers. I've even been to some of the meetings."

Mahmoure crossed the verandah to join them. She slipped her arms around Riza's shoulders and leaned her chin on his shoulder.

"How very unorthodox," Salih Zeki said stiffly.

"Didn't Halide tell you?" Mahmoure asked with excitement. "This was how I escaped undetected, dressed as a man."

"We have never discussed your flight."

"Riza and I share everything, especially the risks." She gave her lover a knowing smile.

"Don't worry, Zeki Bey, I would never do anything to endanger Fatma Hanim Efendi and her family. At the first hint of trouble we will leave." Riza looked at Mahmoure, who nodded in agreement.

"Where could you flee?"

"Damascus, Salonika—anywhere there are sympathizers to our cause."

The heat of the afternoon was intense, and Salih Zeki put his hand to his throat to loosen the knot of his tie. Then, excusing himself, he rose to take his leave.

"Now, why did you pretend to me you didn't know him?" Mahmoure whispered as soon as Salih Zeki was out of sight.

"I never pay any attention to gossip," Riza said, kissing her forehead.

"But—"

"No buts. He's family now, and we have an obligation to Halide and her unborn child." He took Mahmoure's hand and led her into the garden, where the primroses had wilted for want of water.

Resting above them, in a small room on the second floor, Halide drifted between waking and sleeping.

"Aren't you hot in here?" Salih Zeki strode across the room and pushed open the shutters.

"I was asleep," Halide mumbled drowsily.

"I hope our talk didn't disturb you."

"No, no . . . I was fine." Through the lingering haze of sleep she watched his silhouette move from the window and draw close beside her.

"I've just found out Riza was once one of my couriers. Quite a coincidence, really."

"Mahmoure said she remembered your name, but Riza insisted she was wrong. What were you doing in Paris?"

"You should be more careful when you speak of the past," Salih Zeki said sharply.

"The three of us were just talking among ourselves," Halide said defensively.

"You never know who's listening." He brushed the hair out of her eyes, leaned over, and kissed her lids gently, the way he used to when they were first married.

"I was having such a vivid dream," she said with a yawn. "My mother was here, sitting exactly where you are now. She wore a white robe I remember from when I was a child."

"Quiet down, my love. Your imagination is getting the better of you." He pressed close to her side and slid his hand over her breast.

"Don't be so hard on my imagination," she said. "It is the crux of who I am."

"Surely the crux of who you are must be, at least in part, that of a wife, my wife." He propped himself on his elbows and studied her profile. His scrutiny flustered her, and she turned away. "Our life together must be the basis for everything else." Before she had time to respond, his lips caressed her ear. He eased her back on the divan and began to make love to her, gently at first, then with a passion he thought he had lost.

"I was afraid you didn't love me anymore," she murmured when they were finished and lying side by side. Warm air blew in through the window and filled the room with the scent of the pines.

"What gave you such a foolish idea?" he asked.

"You've been distant."

"My work is not going well," he said. "I am missing some crucial data, and I'm afraid I left it in Paris."

"Why didn't you tell me?"

"In your condition, I didn't want to trouble you." Salih Zeki closed his eyes and sighed. The drowsy heat overtook him, and with his arms entwined around his wife in a firm grasp he fell into a dreamless sleep.

Chapter Ten

Life in the house on Antigone took on a rhythm determined by the call to prayer and the rising and setting of the sun. The slow pace ground on Salih Zeki's nerves, and before long he found an excuse to return to the city. His assistants arrived from Paris in late June and proved to be ill-equipped for life in Turkey. Research had fallen behind schedule, and the paperwork had mounted. Alarmed, his second in command at the observatory sent word to the island begging him to return. Salih Zeki did not relish telling Halide about his impending departure. To his surprise, she seemed not to mind, a reaction he ascribed to her condition and the excitement of being with her sister again.

Mahmoure and Halide made daily excursions to the beach, taking the back path through the pinewoods while Granny and Arzu rode in the oxcart, along with the hampers of food and blankets. Usually Riza drove them, but on the days when he disappeared into the city his place was taken by the gardener's son.

Every evening after dinner Halide worked on her translations, writing by the light of a single candle. When the house was quiet, her mind became clear. All the while the new life grew inside her, pushing against her abdomen and shifting the folds of her dress. She worked on, competing against the constraint of time.

The summer passed without mishap, without incident. As one day melted into the next, Halide made plans to have the child on Antigone at the end of September, two weeks before Dr. von Schlesser had told her the baby was due. Convinced she could induce the birth by force of will, Halide shared her plans with her family. Immediately Granny got in touch with the local midwife and Arzu brought the ribbons, blankets, pillows, and poultices out of storage, along with the baby clothes preserved from one generation to the next between layers of Bursa silk. It was agreed that Halide should not consult Salih Zeki, for even the slightest allusion to the possibility of a traditional birth sent him into a rage. He was, Halide noticed, unusually edgy, and each time he left for the city she experienced a sense of relief tempered with regret for the way things had once been.

As her time drew close Halide prayed for her water to break before her husband would take her home to Pera. Granny made the long excursion to Rumeli Hisari on her behalf to pray at Selima's grave. It was no good appealing to the dervish saints, she explained to Arzu; they might not understand. Even Mahmoure made a half-hearted attempt to pray for an early delivery. She accompanied Halide to prayers at the dank, dark mosque, although she was far from certain of being heard. Then, just as the last leaves fell from the plane trees and the wild rose hips withered on the bushes, it looked as if their prayers had been answered. A series of violent pains shook Halide's body. Riza rode into town to fetch the midwife, a sharp-featured woman with a brisk manner who was married to the island blacksmith. It proved to be a false alarm, but the time was close, she warned, a matter of days. Halide was ordered to stay in bed. It was then that Granny made the decision to send for Zeki Bey and Edib. They were both on the ferry, crossing from the mainland, when Halide's baby girl took her first breath. The birthing bed was hung with red ribbons, and prayers were offered at the mosque for the well-being of mother and child.

HALIDE WOKE in the middle of the night, disturbed by the screech of an owl. She stood by the window of her room. Below her, the garden was silent. A ribbon of moonlight rippled across the surface of the waves, and in the distance on the horizon, between the night sky and the sea, she could see the thin black outline of the city. Soon they would return to the bustling streets of Pera, but things would be different now. Holding the tiny bundle in her arms, enveloped in that sweet smell of baby skin and milk, she had understood what it meant to love, truly love. No one could have told her that such feelings were possible.

Halide wondered if Salih Zeki felt the same. Since the birth they had not been alone, and she tried to suppress the suspicion that he was avoiding her. The physical aspects of pregnancy had made him uncomfortable. She had heard him say as much to Dr. von Schlesser several months before, while she lay on the table in the examining room in the company of a German nurse. Von Schlesser's response had been drowned out by a passing trolley car, and the next thing she knew the men were discussing news of the latest maneuvers in the Balkans and the nurse was covering her legs with a green cloth in readiness for her examination. She tried to remember how close she and Salih Zeki had once been, but the time before the birth of their daughter was like a distant view seen from the wrong end of a telescope.

A wisp of cloud slid across the moon. A woman emerged from behind the rhododendrons and walked slowly up the drive toward the house. Her gown was high-necked and boned at the waist and a small train swept the ground in her wake but left no mark on the gravel drive. Halide pressed her face against the glass, trying to see who was wandering in the garden at this late hour, but the woman's features were hidden by her veil. As she drew closer, Halide remembered the dress. It was the one Teyze had worn on the day of her marriage to her father; she had brought it out from time to time after the wedding.

Halide's heart was pounding. Could it be, had news of her

child's birth reached Ciragan? Her hand fumbled with the lock on the window. By the time she had it open, the woman had passed beneath her room and was approaching the verandah steps.

"Teyze, is that you?" Tears came to her eyes as she called Teyze's name out loud again. Her call was greeted by a stark silence. "Stay where you are, I'll come down and unlock the door." She didn't dare raise her voice, for fear of disturbing the nurse and baby asleep in the next room.

The woman mounted the steps without making a sound. As she turned toward the verandah, Halide saw her profile outlined by the light of the moon. It was Teyze—there was no doubt in her mind—but how strange that she did not turn around. Halide headed for the door, neglecting in her haste to bring a candle. The hall was dark, and she almost tripped over the carpet on the landing. Step by step she made her way downstairs, holding tight to the banister.

The front door was locked from the inside, and in the pitch black it took her several minutes to get it open. Her body shook at the thought of seeing her beloved friend again. How many years was it since they had last met—three, four? Not long after her visit with her father, the Sultan had banned anyone from entering or leaving Ciragan Palace. So much had happened since then! The door creaked open and the grinding of hinges echoed through the house. Halide panicked, certain the noise would waken Arzu, who slept downstairs near the kitchen.

"Teyze, where are you?" She tiptoed onto the verandah.

"You've nothing to fear," she whispered. "It's me, Halide." She walked barefoot over to the steps and scanned the drive and the rose garden beyond. But of Teyze there was no sign.

"What are you doing, child! You'll catch your death in this cold air."

Startled, Halide whirled around. Her grandmother was standing in the doorway, holding an oil lamp in one hand and supporting herself against the door with the other.

"Granny, you won't believe it! Teyze's come to visit. I saw her not five minutes ago, but I can't think what's become of her."

The old lady hung the lamp on a hook by the door. In the subdued yellow light, Halide saw that her eyes were filled with tears.

"Granny, what is it?"

"Here, child, take this. Keep yourself warm." She hobbled to Halide's side with the aid of her stick and tossed her shawl around Halide's shoulders. They gazed into the empty garden in silence.

"I thought I saw Teyze." Halide started to shiver and drew the shawl tight.

"Where, dear? Where did you see her?"

"In the garden, wearing her wedding dress. But now that I come to think of it, that dress was given away years ago."

"Teyze is dead, my dear. We got word from Ciragan after you had gone to bed. Your husband thought it better not to wake you."

They stayed up until dawn talking about Teyze's life, reliving the days at Beshiktash before the death of Ali Pasha had changed things forever. The most mundane details of her everyday existence were conjured in a rush of reminiscence. Granny recalled teasing her about the box of beauty spots imported from Paris, and with a twinge of regret Halide remembered the night of the fire. It was then it all began, Teyze once confessed to her, the business with her father. How many times she had wished privately that they had never married! All of their lives might have been so different.

"She was so devout; being separated from Suleiman Efendi was a disaster from which she never recovered," Granny said, dabbing at the corners of her eyes with her handkerchief.

"But none of this would have happened if Father hadn't married again," Halide said defiantly.

"You mustn't blame him—he wanted more children. It was obvious to all of us, even poor Teyze. She was searching long before that happened. It was fate: your father was meant to marry that woman so that Teyze could be freed."

"I'm not so sure . . ." Halide shook her head. Teyze had loved her father; she had seen it in every gesture. The devotion to Suleiman Efendi had come out of hopelessness and humiliation.

"Teyze was intended for a higher purpose in this life," Granny continued wistfully. "She ventured where few women have dared. She was destined to search for the elusive truth of the masters. Suleiman was a wise master, a good man. I don't believe he was mixed up in a conspiracy, but wherever the truth lies, it can't help Teyze now."

Halide stared off into the garden. Everything looked the same as before: the driveway was undisturbed, and there were no footprints in the grass to mark the passage of their spectral visitor. For a moment she wondered if her vision of Teyze had been nothing more than a vivid dream, but she quickly rejected this notion. She had been wide awake and had seen her beloved friend for the last time.

Why had she had this sudden and unexpected visitation? Had the exhausting process of giving birth left her vulnerable, or were Teyze's death and the birth of her daughter linked in some way? One thing was certain: Teyze was still with them; Halide felt her warm presence all around.

"Didn't you have any warning signs, Granny? You were close to Teyze. Surely you would have known something awful was about to happen."

"At my age death is no longer a tragedy. If Teyze was tired of life, her passing might have been a blessing for her."

"Are you implying that she killed herself?"

"Absolutely not!" Granny said vehemently. "Teyze would never do such a thing; it is forbidden. The messenger from Ciragan simply said she had had a short illness. We will never know what really happened."

"She didn't look well when I last saw her, but that was years ago." Halide tried to recall the look on Teyze's face as the eunuch pulled them apart that day at Ciragan.

"This Sultan is a monster," Granny said suddenly, interrupting Halide's thoughts. "He is responsible for this tragedy." The old lady stroked her stomach, which was rumbling quietly, the way it always did these days in the morning. "Never in my life have I been interested in politics, Halide, but nowadays I think something has gone terribly wrong."

Granny lapsed into silence. To her annoyance, the voices started up again, babbling indistinctly and claiming her attention. Were they going to disturb her morning with their insistent chatter, or would they quiet down once the muezzin had called her to prayer? She would pray for Edib; he was certain to feel guilt about Teyze. She would also pray for Salih Zeki. The more she saw of him, the less she understood this man. He had behaved strangely when the messenger had come, insisting to the point of rudeness that Halide be left to sleep. Behind her, Granny heard footsteps, a clink of china, and the labored breathing of Arzu. She turned to see her housekeeper bustling in from the kitchen, carrying a coffee warmer and two cups.

Chapter Eleven

A constant rumble of trolley cars mixed with the cries of vendors and the howling of street dogs kept Halide awake as she lay on the divan by the open window, letting the wind cool her body. Two months after giving birth, she was still tired. Now another day was almost over, and it had taken every ounce of her energy to climb the stairs to her study under the eaves. She stared out across the Golden Horn toward Eyoub cemetery, where the cypresses were shrouded in a light fog. Her eyelids drooped, and when she closed her eyes her mind raced with thoughts of tasks left undone.

Dusk was gathering and the first lights flickered on in the street. The city appeared as it always did at this hour, bathed in a glow of purple receding into gold. Halide let her mind wander unguarded. She saw herself once more as a child, sitting with Teyze in the great bay window above the Bosphorus, waiting for the day to draw to a close. She could almost smell the delicate jasmine oil Teyze always wore on her wrists and in the crook of her neck. Granny was right: the dead are always with us, she reflected. Long after she was gone, when her face would be but a memory to baby Fikriye sleeping in the arms of her Greek nurse, the sun would continue to rise and set over the dark hills of Constantinople. Thoughts of her child brought her back to the present.

Halide shivered and turned back to the room, scolding herself for being fragile. She must begin to work again before her mind became dulled by inactivity. And yet it was so hard for her to think of anything but the baby! Even the notes for her new novel remained untouched. She picked up a book of poetry and leafed through it, but the words swam in front of her eyes.

She heard a noise on the landing and her grandmother came in, panting from the exertion of climbing the stairs. She eyed Halide, then limped over to the divan. "Soon it's time for prayers," she gasped, sinking down beside her. "I thought I'd come up here with you. I don't like to pray in front of the nurse."

"We'll pray together. I've been negligent lately."

"When I gave birth to your mother I was ill for weeks. I couldn't feed her, so they brought in a milk nurse. I felt my soul had been sucked out of me. Now as I get older it's the outer shell that's disappearing, in a manner of speaking." She chuckled, patting the folds of her stomach.

"I never knew you were ill in childbirth."

"Oh yes, and your poor mother. She was never the same." She turned away and tapped the windowpane with her finger. "It's restless out there. I don't like the look of that mist. Before long all the city will be enveloped."

"If only the spring would come. I want to return to Antigone, and take the baby away from this noise and dirt."

"Will Salih Zeki mind losing you?"

"He'll be relieved." Halide could not hide the sadness in her voice. "We are behind schedule, and now that the apartment is full of nurses and baby things he finds it hard to concentrate."

Granny had always suspected that living without the privacy of a harem would lead to difficulties. What did men know of babies, especially a cerebral creature like Zeki Bey? Heaven preserve us from men like him, she thought. She didn't know how Halide put up with him.

"I can't wait to go to Antigone and see Mahmoure again," Halide said. "We have so much time to make up."

"I'm sure she misses you and the baby. It must be lonely out there in the winter."

Halide leaned against the pillows. Her back ached again. "Now that I'm a mother I don't understand how Mahmoure could have left her children. Do you think she has any regrets?"

"Your sister is not one to reflect on the past. What's done is done, and she moves on. You must remember, Mahmoure never had a mother. I think she suffered from the loss." Granny said slowly, "Ali Pasha and I never should have allowed Ali Shamil to take her. But the law was on his side."

"Her father adored her . . ."

"He certainly did, but Ali Shamil's love was a powerful burden for a young girl to bear."

"What do you mean?"

"He loved those close to him with an intense and possessive passion. Ali Shamil had energy and charm to spare. Sometimes I think he was the only man Mahmoure ever truly loved."

"How can you say that?" Halide cried out. "She loves Riza—look what she did for him, and it's clear when they're together."

"No woman could resist being adored the way Riza adores her. He is a good-looking man who offered her an adventurous life. Domesticity cannot contain a restless soul like hers."

Halide looked at her grandmother with amazement. The old lady moved her head closer and whispered conspiratorially. "Furthermore, Mahmoure and Riza are bound by a common purpose." She paused and glanced behind her, as if to make sure no one was listening. "They want to get rid of Abdulhamid."

"How do you know all this?" Halide exclaimed.

"I'm not blind," Granny said with a contented smile. "At least not yet."

THE WOMAN had been watching them for quite some time. At first Halide had paid no attention, since their party had been attracting admiring glances all afternoon on account of the baby. They were picnicking on a grassy bank by the Sweet Waters of Europe. It was unusually warm for December, and the unexpected sun had brought crowds of women and children out into the parks. Some lounged on blankets under the drooping branches of the willow trees; other, more daring spirits paddled boats up and down the placid blue streams.

Not one of them had a baby as beautiful as little Fikriye, Granny noted with pride. The picnic had been her idea. She had hired a caïque large enough to hold seven people and filled it with baskets of food and drink, warm shawls, and cushions, so that they might pass the afternoon together as a family, the way they used to in the old days.

After they had moved from Beshiktash, Granny had lost the habit of planning family excursions. With her daughter and husband gone, there seemed no point. But the birth of her great-granddaughter had reawakened memories of those long summer afternoons with Selima before the illness took hold. In those days Ali Pasha had a personal boatman, a handsome Christian whose charms created havoc in the harem, and frequently Ali Pasha came with them. He took great pleasure in the company of his women, and preferred nothing more than whiling away the hours in an open caïque listening to the songs of the waterbirds.

"Why is that woman staring at us?" asked Peyker the seer, who was spending the month at Sultan Tepe. Granny adjusted her head covering and observed the strangers through her lorgnette.

"Wherever we go these days people look at us because of the baby," Halide replied with evident pride.

"Babies are like tiny human magnets," Granny retorted.

Halide shaded her eyes from the glare of the sun and studied the party of unveiled women, obviously foreign, who were sitting out beyond the willow grove. "Perhaps we know them," she said. "Maybe one of them is a girl I went to school with."

"How would they recognize you under that veil, Halide?"

"I didn't think of that," Halide sighed. "How surprised they would be if they knew I was a mother."

"Why? It's perfectly natural," Granny said, pulling the corner of the shawl away from the baby's face. "What else are they planning to do with themselves?"

"I suppose they're going to work. Some were planning to travel. But I'm not sure what my friends are doing—I've lost touch with them."

Oh dear, she sounds so sad, Granny said to herself. The poor child claims to be content, wrapped up in her writing like a solitary Sufi, but a woman needs the company of her own sex. It's not natural to live alone in an apartment with a husband and baby. Look how happy she was on Antigone with all of us around her!

"They're talking about us," Peyker said, taking another sip of mint tea. "I can tell by the way they keep looking over here."

"I don't think I've ever seen foreigners here before," Arzu chimed in. "They usually prefer to go to the gardens at Taksim."

"One of them is getting up. My goodness, is she coming over here?" Granny adjusted her lorgnette and watched as a woman detached herself from the group and walked rapidly across the grass toward them, taking long, confident strides.

"Will we be offering her tea, ma'am?" asked Arzu, retrieving a clean cup from the basket at the base of the willow, thereby stirring the Greek nurse, who was slumped against the tree trunk, half asleep.

"Absolutely not," Granny said firmly.

The stranger stopped a few feet away and introduced herself in French. "Please forgive the intrusion," she said to no one in particular. Her manner was apologetic, almost servile.

"I'm the only one here who speaks French," Halide said, feeling flustered. "But there's no need to apologize."

"My friends and I thought we recognized your carriage." The woman looked past her at the oxcart stationed beside the road.

"The carriage is rented," Halide said quickly. "We've come from the Asian side, and we hired the driver in Eyoub." For some reason, she was reluctant to tell the woman where she came from.

"So you're not the family of Umit Bey?"

"No, I don't know anyone by that name."

The woman hesitated, as if waiting for her to say more. "I am Isabelle Chadelet—does the name mean anything to you?"

Halide shook her head.

"Then I have made a mistake, I apologize." The woman clasped her hands and leaned forward into a bow. "I won't trouble you any longer." She glanced at the baby, then turned and made her way back across the grass. Halide watched her until she reached her friends.

"What did she want?" Granny said sharply, studying the stranger through her veil. Unlike the few Frenchwomen Halide had encountered, this woman was neither elegant nor beautiful. She had an intelligent face, free of makeup and other artifice, and seemed unconcerned about her appearance. Her auburn hair was gathered carelessly under a straw boater.

"She mistook us for someone else." Halide turned to her grandmother and relayed the conversation, just as she used to in her days at the American Girls College.

"It's a good thing you can talk their language," Granny said, pleased to have the intrusion behind her. "There might have been no end of confusion."

Chapter Twelve

Two weeks later, Halide hired a carriage to take her to Eminonu, on the other side of the Galata Bridge. The quay was not crowded at that time of the morning, so she was able to see clear across the cobbled street to the mooring where the Princes Islands ferry was about to dock. She remained in the hired carriage along with the Greek day nurse, who was holding Fikriye. The baby was asleep. Halide leaned over and lifted her child's hand with her forefinger and stared at the tiny nails, pink and shiny like perfect seed pearls.

Halide saw Mahmoure at once, in her checkered suit, her fez set jauntily at the back of her head, swinging her arms as if she hadn't a care in the world. She watched through the window while Mahmoure strolled across the quay. A casual observer would have seen nothing unusual about this carefree young man on a day's outing to the city.

"Good morning, Halide Hanim," Mahmoure said as she flung open the carriage door with a flourish.

"Welcome! Your ferry was on time for once," Halide said, sliding along the banquette to make room for her sister.

"Who's this?" Mahmoure asked, casting a wary eye at the Greek nurse.

"Don't worry, she's from the islands. She doesn't speak a word of Turkish." Out of habit Halide leaned forward to embrace her sister, but she stopped herself just in time.

"What's the point of hiring someone who can't speak the language?"

"It was Granny's idea. We have to be careful because of you and Riza."

"Granny's amazing, she's planned everything down to the last detail," chuckled Mahmoure. "Still, it was a risk bringing her along."

"I had no choice—I can't go out alone."

Mahmoure stretched her legs out in front of her and whistled under her breath. "Just this once you need not have told anybody."

"I don't feel comfortable going out by myself. Besides, if Salih Zeki found out, he would be very angry." Relations between them were still cool. Salih Zeki rarely came home for dinner, and he complained that the baby was taking up too much of her time. Halide told herself it was better this way; had they lived in a traditional home, she would have been confined to the harem, for men rarely spent time with their women during the first months of a child's life.

The carriage swung into the main road connecting Tophane with the Galata Bridge. Halide braced herself against the back of her seat as they lumbered on. "I instructed the coachman to stop at Suleimaniye Mosque," she said. "I want to leave Fikriye and her nurse in the mosque, where they'll be safe. I hope you know what you're doing!"

"I need to see them again," Mahmoure said. Halide said nothing, content to leave it at that.

When she had run away, Mahmoure's passion for Riza and the overwhelming desire to see her father had prevailed over everything else. But the birth of Fikriye had aroused in her unexpected feelings of curiosity and longing. More than three years had passed since she had last seen her children, and she ached with the desire to know what had happened to them. The decision to leave them had not been easy, though it had taken her a long time to admit this to herself. Lying on his deathbed, Ali Shamil had told her to go home and take care of his grandchildren; the boy was his namesake, he said, and heir to the Bedirkhan name. This was something Mahmoure had never considered. In her eyes, the children had always been Ahmet's, and any feelings she might have had for them had been submerged by resentment and anger. She had felt imprisoned by motherhood. Since her father's death she had come to see things in a new light. Much as she loved Riza, they were rootless, while the tie to her children would bind her to them for the rest of her life.

Mahmoure felt her chest tighten as the minarets of Suleimaniye loomed into view. She drew an embossed case from her pocket and lit a cigarette to steady her nerves. The sidewalk was thronged with young men in white robes and skullcaps. They were students from the *medresse* run by her former father-in-law, fledgling Imams and members of the ulema.

"We'll stop up here, by the gate to the women's garden." Halide touched her arm and nodded at the outer wall.

"Thank you. It won't take long, I promise."

Already Halide half regretted coming along. But ever since they were girls Mahmoure had had this ability to persuade her into dangerous situations. Supposing the children were not at home. Worse, what if someone recognized Mahmoure? The entire family would run the risk of arrest.

"It's five minutes to the house from here," said Mahmoure. "We'll wait at that curve where the street widens, and as soon as I've seen them we'll leave."

"I hope your mother-in-law hasn't altered her routine."

"Somehow I doubt it. These prayers are the main event of her week. She always took the children herself and sat with them in the front row. It had to be the front row—she'd make a huge fuss if it was taken. I used to go, but then I stopped, which caused me no end of grief."

The driver reined to a halt a little way beyond Mahmoure's old house. Halide watched her sister with tenderness as she leapt out of the carriage and paced up and down in the dusty street. She didn't have to wait long before two small figures, veiled from head to toe in black, came out of the house and stood motionless on the verandah.

"Why are they veiled?" Halide whispered, leaning out of the carriage. "Nezihe is only nine, and Emine must be seven."

"What has she done to them!" Mahmoure turned away from the two stark and silent figures and lit another cigarette. This was going to be harder than she had anticipated.

"Maybe we should go." Halide sensed that her sister was upset. But it was too late: the house door banged open and a sturdy boy no more than four years old dashed into the street. His dark curls and mischievous expression identified him at once.

It's my son! Mahmoure thought, her heart pounding. She'd have known him anywhere. Stubbing out her cigarette with her heel, Mahmoure was suddenly overcome by an unexpected desire to touch him.

"Come back here, Ali Shamil! You'll be the death of me!" From inside the house, a woman's voice called after him.

"Father said I could stay home," the boy shouted back defiantly.

"That's a lie! You'll fry in hell for saying such a thing."

"It's them, all right, but where is your mother-in-law?" Halide leaned out the carriage as far as she dared. She didn't relish the thought of encountering the Imam's wife.

"He looks just like my father," Mahmoure said in a flat voice. Then, before Halide could stop her, she started off down the street. The girls saw her first and turned away; well-brought-up Muslim girls did not stare at strange men. Only the little boy bared his teeth in a mischievous grin and, keeping one eye on the stranger, began tossing stones into a nearby garden.

"Stop that at once! Oh, my goodness. Look at your clothes, with dust all over them. What will your grandmother say?" A woman appeared in the doorway and shook her finger admonishingly at Ali Shamil. It was Mahmoure's former kitchen maid; Halide remembered her from their Saturday visits many years before. The boy laughed and stuck out his tongue.

Mahmoure had almost reached her son when Halide noticed, to her horror, that they were the only people on street. Everyone else had left for the mosque. The boy picked up a stone and lobbed it along the ground. It bounced off Mahmoure's ankle and came to a rest in the gutter. She cried out in pain.

"You naughty boy, apologize to the gentleman at once!" The maid marched down the steps and the small veiled figures craned forward. In a low voice, Mahmoure assured them that no harm had been done. Mahmoure looked at the boy longingly, then turned toward her daughters, who shrank against the wall of the house. She reached out her hand, then hesitated, uncertain what to do next. Watching from the safety of the carriage, Halide tensed. Finally, Mahmoure turned on her heel and limped away. The boy tossed one last stone after their carriage and, with a shrug of resignation, went up the steps.

"WHAT A LITTLE devil! Did you see the way he threw that stone at me?" Mahmoure said with obvious pride.

"Granny told me the last time they went to visit them little Ali Shamil pulled at Arzu's skirt so hard she almost fell over."

"We know what side of the family that behavior comes from," Mahmoure said with a weak smile.

"You look a little pale. Are you all right?"

Mahmoure pressed her face against the window to take a last look at her old street. "The boy was the image of my father. I didn't expect that."

"I'm sorry you didn't get to see the girls. Nezihe looks a lot like you, but the little one has your spirit."

"I didn't know you still saw them. Why didn't you tell me?"

"I never knew what to say. Granny and I visited Suleimaniye a couple of times before I had the baby, but your mother-in-law doesn't like it and didn't encourage us to come back."

"Did the children ask about me?"

Halide looked down at the floor and shook her head.

"I shouldn't expect them to. They were so young when I left." Mahmoure reached into her pocket and brought out the cigarette case. Halide noticed that her hand was shaking. "My father wanted me to go back to them. I couldn't, of course, I'd have been arrested at once. But I'll never forget how upset he was. I didn't mean to bring him grief on his deathbed."

Halide reached forward and grasped her sister's arm. "Don't feel sorry for me, Halide," Mahmoure said. "I would have died a thousand deaths being stuck in Suleimaniye with Ahmet and three children. Of course it's hard for me to see them again—they're my kids."

"You were in an impossible situation," Halide said warmly. "I can't imagine what I would have done in your place."

"When I left I knew it wouldn't be easy. For months afterward, whenever I saw a child my heart ached, but gradually the pain eased."

"And now?"

"I'll live with what I've done."

"I can't imagine being married to a man I didn't love."

"It wasn't just Ahmet, it was the whole situation: the house, the in-laws, the feeling of being stuck without hope of escape."

As they approached the great mosque, Halide heard the voice of the Imam calling the faithful to prayer. *You cannot hide,* he chanted, *you cannot hide, we know where you are.* The outer walls of the graveyard rose up beside them and the press of worshipers brought the carriage to a halt. Mahmoure wished suddenly that she could be far away from this accursed city, safe in a place where she and Riza had no memories tugging at them and no ties.

"I'd forgotten what day it was," Halide moaned. "We'll never get near the garden in this crowd."

Once they left the vicinity of the mosque, the crowds disappeared and the horses picked up speed. They passed the charred remains of a recent fire and through the smoke Halide saw the outline of a ruined aqueduct rising above the crowded roofs. "We must be out of Suleimaniye," she said, rapping the side of the carriage with her fist.

Mahmoure squinted. "I think we've reached the outskirts of Fatih."

"Sultan Mahmud Caddesi, Molla Hikmet Sokagi," Halide said, reading the street signs out loud. "I wonder who these men were."

"Religious tyrants, most likely." Mahmoure had paid no attention to religious matters, until she had married the son of an Imam. Now Riza's secular views had rubbed off on her, coloring the anger she still felt toward her in-laws.

"I don't know this area at all," Halide said, ignoring her sister's remarks.

"Neither do I."

"Why, that sign says Mevlevi Sokagi! That's where my publisher lives." Halide pressed her face against the window. The wooden houses stood close together, separated by a narrow alley. Slates were missing from the roofs, and peeling paint scarred the door frames.

"Which one is his house?" asked Mahmoure.

"I don't know. All the mail goes to a post office box, but Salih Zeki comes here to visit him sometimes."

"Let's drive up and take a look."

"No," Halide said uncomfortably. "Let's leave it at that. I've got to get back for Fikriye."

"I'll tell the driver to turn around at the top," Mahmoure persisted, brightening at the prospect of an adventure.

Halide relented, moved in part by her curiosity to see the home of this stranger who had played such a pivotal role in her life. A woman emerged from a three-story house down the street, freshly painted, unlike its neighbors, in an alarming shade of blue. Her clothes were unusual for this part of town; she wore a checkered cotton dress of European design. Startled by the sound of hooves, the woman turned and Halide found herself looking at the gay, somewhat chaotic Frenchwoman who had introduced herself in the park. She shrank back against her seat, thankful for the anonymity afforded by her veil.

Chapter Thirteen

The baby woke early the next morning. Halide slipped out of bed and carried her to the nursery so as not to disturb Salih Zeki, who had come home late the night before. She had made them both coffee, and they'd sat up talking until well past midnight. It had been weeks since he had shared his concerns with her. Not long after Fikriye's birth he'd moved his office to the naval academy, where he had resumed his part-time teaching post. The pressure of both writing and teaching was starting to take its toll; nothing was getting done properly, he'd said, and he was falling behind schedule. To make matters worse, the research assistants who had arrived from France proved to be of little use. They didn't speak a word of Turkish and couldn't attend to the simplest errand. Halide had listened sympathetically, in a haze of sleep. She was not a mathematician, and there was little she could do to help him at this stage. Besides, between caring for the baby and attending to her own writing, she had little time for anything else.

Salih Zeki held her hand and felt close to her again for the first time in many weeks. He apologized for his distant behavior. Never having had much to do with babies, he was, he confessed, a little afraid of his daughter's helplessness. Once the book was finished, he would try to be a more attentive father. Halide hadn't mentioned the trip to the old city with Mahmoure; she knew he would not approve. This was the second time she had withheld something from him, and she'd found it easier than she had expected.

Halide had lain in bed awake long after Salih Zeki had fallen into a fitful sleep, wondering what it was he had been trying to tell her. The memory of their conversation was still with her when she awoke the following morning. Cradling her daughter against her breast, she thought she heard his voice calling.

"Halide, where are you?"

She looked up, protecting Fikriye's head with her hand. It wasn't her imagination playing tricks—her husband had stumbled into the nursery, still wearing his nightshirt and slippers, his eyes red for want of sleep. The sight of him looking so disheveled amused her, but she stopped herself from making any comment.

"Sssh, I'm feeding her," she whispered, drawing the baby close.

"I'm sorry, I didn't mean to disturb you."

"She'll be done in a few minutes."

"I'll get coffee and wait in the salon." He turned, hesitated, and looked back over his shoulder. "There's something I have to tell you," he said. "Will you join me as soon as you can."

"What's wrong?" Halide asked, but by the time she looked up he had turned back abruptly and was gone.

Halide heard the kitchen door slam and wondered why he was suddenly so restless. She finished feeding the child and put her down to sleep, then went to join her husband in the salon.

"She's sleeping." She smiled at Salih Zeki awkwardly. It felt strange to be sitting in their formal salon wearing nightclothes and drinking coffee from the kitchen china.

"Ah, to be a baby!" Salih Zeki sighed. "Held in your arms all day without a care in the world."

"I'm sorry to have kept you waiting. Feeding Fikriye took a little longer than I expected."

"I suppose it's hard to gauge these things," he said, running his hand through his hair. She was so composed these days it unnerved him. Her face looked drawn, and she had lost that rosy glow he had once found so appealing. She was a woman now, and like almost every other woman he had known, she was beginning to be weighed down by domesticity. He had dreamed about having a family, but now that it was upon him he was starting to have second thoughts. He didn't like feeling this way and scolded himself for being so foolish, but the nagging discontent would not go.

"I'm tired." She rubbed her eyes with her fists. "What was it you wanted to talk about?"

"If I'm out late tonight I'll sleep in here," he said.

"No, don't do that. It doesn't matter if you wake me."

"I must do something about my schedule."

"Perhaps you should give up teaching. It takes up a lot of time and interferes with the work on your book."

"What would we live on, now that there are more mouths to feed?" He immediately regretted his choice of words. He sounded like a common shopkeeper.

"We have Teyze's legacy," Halide reminded him, startled by his bitterness.

"She meant it to go to you, not me. You know I can't accept it."

"The money is ours to share," Halide said quietly. "All I'm asking is for you to let me pay our bills with it."

"It's out of the question! I cannot be seen to be supported by my wife."

"Is that what you wanted to talk about, money?"

"No, no, there's something else." He turned his head away and went over the things he planned to say. He must stay calm, he told himself. This was not going to be easy for either of them.

"As I told you last night, I am concerned." He began fidgeting with the lapels of his dressing gown. "My book is far behind schedule."

"I wish I could help, truly I do. I thought the move would make things easier. I hated to see you go, but the apartment is too small for all of us now that our baby is here."

"It's better this way. I can use the library and exchange ideas with my colleagues."

"What is it? You look upset."

He wheeled around to face her. "I sometimes wonder if you understand how much this book means to me. I've been working on it for seven years, since I lived in Paris. Just the other day I received a letter from my former sponsor, Henri Chadelet, a wealthy engineer. He reminded me I'd planned to have it completed by now."

"You've never mentioned him before," Halide said. "Who is he?"

"There's a lot I haven't told you about the past." They heard the baby crying from the far end of the apartment. Halide made a move to get up, but he caught her by the wrist.

"No, stay and hear me out. The nurse will take care of her."

"She may still be hungry," Halide said, pulling away.

"What I have to say is of the utmost importance." He let go of her arm, and she remained frozen in front of him.

"Very well." She rubbed her skin with the tips of her fingers. Through the walls, the crying continued.

"Where was I?"

"Your sponsor."

"Oh yes, yes." He pressed the tips of his fingers together. "Perhaps I should start from the beginning. It will clarify things, help you understand. Ten years ago, when I fled to Paris, my colleagues and I thought we had left forever. The Sultan was erasing fifty years of progress, and life here for intellectuals had become intolerable. France, by comparison, was like a dream. We were free to write and publish what we wished. I found a job teaching at the Sorbonne, and it was there that I came to the attention of an industrialist, Monsieur Henri Chadelet. I was processing mathematical formulas that were of great help to the engineers in his employ. To cut a long story short, he offered to sponsor me. Without his generosity, I never would have been able to continue my research."

Halide listened closely. She had never heard him talk in such an open way about his past.

"I never dreamed the Sultan would one day offer me immunity if I returned. He is attempting, in his own way, to modernize the Ottoman state. The work I was doing in France was sorely needed here, and my name added prestige to the roster of Ottoman intellectuals he sought to assemble in the capital."

"That's why you were so angry when you saw the hurdy-gurdy man," she exclaimed. "We were being watched, and that went against the terms of the deal you made with the Sultan."

"Exactly. The very next day I sent a message to the chief of police. The man was removed, and neither you nor I will be bothered again."

"I wondered what became of him."

Zeki Bey shrugged. "I'd forgotten about it, it's not important. What matters to me now is finishing the encyclopedia. Monsieur Chadelet intends to travel here to see the progress of my work. He has a personal interest in it, you understand?"

Halide nodded. Zeki Bey took a deep breath. He was coming to the most difficult part, and when he looked into her wide eyes, his courage almost failed him.

"I met Henri through his daughter, a brilliant but socially unconventional woman who was one of my students. Later she assisted me with my research. Her father wanted her to succeed in the field. He made her employment a condition of the sponsorship. As a woman, she had found it impossible to get a job in academia."

"I didn't know things were that bad in France," Halide said.

"When the research assistants turned out to be inadequate, I sent for Mademoiselle Chadelet. She arrived two days ago and is staying at the French embassy. However, we are not in Paris, and for me to be seen working with a European woman is out of the question. I stand to forfeit my job, the observatory, everything I have worked for, unless . . ."

"Unless what?" Halide said, feeling the blood drain from her face.

"Unless I marry her. I am, you see, allowed by law to have a second wife."

"Marry her?" she gasped. The room swam in front of her, and she fell back as if she had been dealt a blow.

"She has agreed to convert to Islam," he added. He steeled himself, determined to stay calm. But nothing happened. To his astonishment, Halide remained in her seat, folded her hands in her lap, and regarded him steadily without saying a word.

At first Salih Zeki tried to reason with her, begged her to help him with his terrible dilemma, but she refused to respond. Rising slowly, Halide left the salon and locked herself in her room. She felt as if a cloud had descended and smothered her once happy life. Even the sight of her child, their child, provoked an outburst of sobbing. The nurse gathered the baby up and lulled her in the comfort of the nursery, and Halide took to her bed, where she stayed for several days.

Salih Zeki sent for the doctor, who came at once. He attributed her symptoms to depression, a common consequence of childbirth, and prescribed a regime of rest and fresh air. He instructed Zeki Bey to keep the baby out of sight until the "mood has passed." He left some medication beside the bed, but Halide threw it away.

Toward evening the following day, Salih Zeki made another attempt to talk to her. She had unlocked the door and asked the maid to bring some soup, so he took this as a sign that she was calming down.

"Can't we discuss this like rational people?" He sat on the edge of the divan and tried to take her hand, but she snatched it away. "Mademoiselle Chadelet is the only person who is familiar with the research I did in Paris. Without her help I will be in serious difficulty; you must try to see this from my point of view."

"Do you love her?" she said at length. Her voice came out in a whisper.

"I esteem her. She is an excellent scholar."

"And what about me and our child?"

"You are my family."

"But do you still care for me?"

He hung his head and looked at the floor. The truth was, he did not know what he felt anymore. Now that she was a mother her innocence had been defiled. What was worse, childbirth had impaired her intellect. She was no longer the agile scholar eagerly hanging on his every word. He raised his eyes and looked at her face, which was red and swollen from crying.

"It doesn't matter anyway," she said, reading in his expression nothing more than pity.

"Of course it matters. You and the baby are all I have. It's just that my work is important, it's who I am."

"What kind of person is this Mademoiselle Chadelet? If she is willing to leave her country and sacrifice her faith, she must care deeply for you."

"Oh, that's nonsense. Isabelle doesn't have your obsession with religion; she is a freethinker, an atheist."

"Isabelle? Did you say her name was *Isabelle*?" Her voice rose in horror.

"What of it?"

"And she arrived in Istanbul two days ago."

"That is correct."

"You are lying! She's been here for at least two weeks." How many other lies were there, she wondered, remembering the slim figure in the park in her straw hat.

"You're hysterical. Let me send for the maid; she'll get you some sweet tea."

"No wonder she was curious," she mumbled. "How did she know I was her rival?"

"What are you talking about, my dear?" He started toward her, but she put out her hand to stop him.

"Don't come near me," she said firmly, just loud enough so he could hear. "You must never come near me again."

"Come now, Halide, be sensible. This woman is just a colleague. Marriage will regularize our association. Besides, her father is coming here."

Halide covered her ears and bent her head away from him, unwilling to listen to another word. If only he would go away and leave her alone, she thought, instead of staying like a spectator at a blood sport. Alone in peace, she could think clearly.

FOR THE NEXT three days Halide remained in her room weeping. She refused anything but soup; solid food stuck in her throat. When Salih Zeki tried again to talk to her, she sent him away. Her mind was made up. The moment she had discovered the lie, her faith in him had been shattered. Until that moment she had trusted him completely. He was her ideal; she had adored him. She still loved him, but now things were different. There was no choice: they must separate and eventually be divorced, although without his consent divorce would be impossible. She told herself she was a mother and it would be unthinkable to raise her daughter in a home in which there were two wives sharing the favors of her father. Hour after hour she sat by the window, watching the clouds drift above the rooftops, and wondering what the future held for her.

Salih Zeki would not change his mind. She was certain he would marry this woman and that together they would complete his encyclopedia of mathematics, which mattered more to him than anything else. Looking back, she realized how foolishly naive she had been to marry a scholar, a man who lived in his mind and found it uncomfortable to be contained by the conventions of marriage and children. She had been swept along in a childish fantasy of being the mother she had so briefly enjoyed, of having a strong, loving husband to support her in pursuit of her dreams. Being married was what she was supposed to do. She closed her eyes and laid her head on the cool pillow.

She heard a low thud, and then the sound of breathing as someone stopped on the landing. It wasn't Salih Zeki or one of the maids, and at this time of day the baby was asleep. The door handle turned. She raised her head and said nothing. The handle turned again, this time more violently; then a familiar voice called out: "Open the door, Halide! I need to talk to you." It was her father. Within a minute she had admitted him, and he was seated in the embroidered chair across from her.

"What's all this about a separation?" He gave her a pleading look, as if to say, Tell me this is nothing more than a misunderstanding.

"Father." She sat down opposite him and put her hands on his arms. It was obvious he was going to try to dissuade her.

"Tell me why."

"He wants to take a second wife, a Frenchwoman he knew in Paris."

"So he told me, but is that so intolerable? He doesn't feel for her as he does for you. You are Turkish, an Ottoman, one of his own people. This woman is a foreigner."

"Don't, dear Father, don't—it's hopeless. I know what I want; I'm not a child anymore." She was intent on staying calm. If she broke down, she knew he would stroke her hair just as he had when she was a young girl.

"Think of the family, your baby. Is she to grow up fatherless?"

"All my life I've been an obedient girl, deferring to you, and then to Salih Zeki. I never disobeyed you, I never said no. I did exactly what you wished and without question. I succeeded in my studies, won prizes at school. Why, I've even written a book and it was published under a pseudonym because I was a woman. But just this once . . ." She was on the verge of tears and took a deep breath to stop herself.

"I think I understand," he said quickly.

"I can't share him, and now I no longer trust his word. What is left?"

"Perhaps if I spoke to him, would you reconsider?"

"No, never." She withdrew her hands and intertwined her fingers in her lap. Tilting her head, Halide could see the graveyard at Eyoub through the window. Poor Teyze, not a day went by when she didn't think of her.

"Perhaps it's rest you need," Edib urged. "You've been through a lot in the past few months."

"Nothing will change my mind, Father. I'm thinking clearly for the first time in my life." She did not want to tell him that Teyze's death had made her more determined not to share her fate.

"I thought Teyze would make you a good mother," he said after a long silence. "I never should have married her in the first place. It wasn't fair."

"How did you know?" she gasped.

"As soon as Salih Zeki told me what was going on I blamed myself. If I had not married again . . . What's the use of going over the past?" he said impatiently. "The damage is done; I must live with the consequences."

"I have a responsibility to my daughter. She must not grow up seeing her mother demeaned. Everything I have achieved would be undermined." She looked up, seeing him, for the first time, not as a father but as a man.

"Not a day goes by when I don't think about Teyze and what I might have done differently," he whispered. "Not a day."

"You behaved very badly," Halide said, shaking her head.

"Can you ever forgive me?" he asked, startled by her calm severity.

"I hope you learned that despite what the law might say, women have feelings, very deep feelings that can be easily shattered." Edib nodded but said nothing. "You have another daughter now, who I hope will benefit from your wisdom."

"Yes, my little Nighiar. She's not like you, of course." He came over and kissed her on the forehead. "No one's like you."

"Will you send her to the American school?" she asked.

"Of course," he said. "She must have the best."

It didn't make sense, Halide thought, and it never would. Why couldn't he treat his wives with the same respect? Without warning, the pain of the past few days suddenly swept over her like a wave. "Help me, Father," she whispered, "I'm dying inside."

"Anything, Halide." He came over and held her in his arms. "I'll do anything."

"Take us away from here. Take the baby, and her nurse and me. We'll go to Sultan Tepe, and Granny will look after us."

Chapter Fourteen

An early-morning mist hung over the cemetery, veiling the cypress trees and gravestones and covering the ground with a silver dew. Ferns and bushes bent under the weight of the dew, and the grass lay flat across the tombs. Behind the mist, the rising sun hung in the sky like a crimson ball. Two women, veiled in black, made their way along the slippery path across the crest of the hill toward the dervish enclosure. Dampness clung to their clothes and seeped through their leather boots, but they walked on undeterred. They moved slowly, pausing now and then to read an inscription or push an overhanging branch out of the way. Gradually the sun moved higher and the outer edge of the mist began to melt away.

These days it was Halide who accompanied her grandmother to Karaca Ahmet, now that Arzu's arthritis was causing her pain.

"I never thought I'd get here today," sighed Granny, wiping a fallen tombstone with a kerchief. "The damp always makes my bones ache."

"It's unusually foggy," Halide observed. Clouds obscured the tops of the cypresses and cut off the view of the Bosphorus.

"It's always like this in January."

"I'd forgotten what month it was. Time passes too quickly." An overwhelming sadness caught hold of her; already the anniversary of her marriage had long passed. At moments like this she thought she would sooner die from the suffocating pain than spend the rest of her life grieving. "I hope I'm doing the right thing," she said, more to herself than her grandmother.

"You must pray for guidance," Granny murmured. The old lady had never taken to Salih Zeki. He wasn't a man suited to marriage, she'd known that from the start. Then there was that disturbing rumor that Mahmoure had unwittingly confirmed, something about a mistress in Paris, a Frenchwoman. Apparently his moral lapse had created friction with his Young Turk associates.

"Sometimes I wonder if I'll ever forget him, if someday this pain will be nothing more than a distant memory."

"You're young, Halide. Time will heal your hurt, trust me. In general I disapprove of divorce, but in this case perhaps it's for the best."

"Suppose he refuses? Legally the decision is his, not mine."

"Your father will talk to him."

"I'm not sure Father understands. He is still trying to persuade me to return."

"My dear, your poor father is caught between one world and another. He doesn't know if he's an Ottoman Turk or a would-be Englishman. This is a woman's dilemma: follow the directions of your heart and be thankful that God has preserved your faith. When I think of the buffeting winds that have swirled around you, filling your head with infidel ideas, it is a miracle your soul has remained intact."

"I've told you not to worry, Granny; my faith has never been shaken," Halide said quietly.

She turned and looked to the west, where the clouds had cleared and a watery sun lit up the European shore. Already the boulevards of Pera would be bustling with tradesmen, and in the backstreets of Kumkapi, Galata, and Suleimaniye the markets would have been thronged since dawn. Perhaps she would return there one day, when the pain had subsided, and Fikriye was old enough to be left with her nurse. She had a responsibility to her correspondents, who even now were buying fish at the market, shaking dust from their rugs, and preparing their homes for the coming of Ramazan.

When she'd returned to Sultan Tepe, Halide was saddened but not surprised to learn that Riza and Mahmoure had left Antigone and were said to be living in Salonika. According to her father, a cadre of rebel officers in the Third Army Corps were stationed on the outskirts of the city; some of them had been colleagues of Riza's at Harbiye. Halide calculated that their departure came a matter of days after the ill-fated visit to Suleimaniye. No one saw them leave. With the help of a local fisherman they had slipped away under cover of darkness, taking nothing more than a small bag. On Granny's instructions Arzu had traveled from the mainland to examine the belongings they had left behind; she burned their papers and concealed their clothes in a trunk in the attic.

"Halide, I'm curious," Granny ventured. "I read your book, Arzu bought it for me, and I was wondering if—"

"You read my book!" Halide cried with a start. "Why didn't you tell me?"

"What with your return to Sultan Tepe, and the excitement of baby Fikriye being here, it slipped my mind," Granny said demurely.

"What did you think? Did you like it?"

"I've never read anything quite like it before," she began cautiously. "It was very believable."

"I was afraid you might be offended because I tried to be open about Rabia's feelings."

"I was a little shocked at first, but when I got used to it I found myself wanting to read more."

"So it worked," Halide said eagerly. "I mean, you wanted to know what happened next."

"I certainly did." The old lady nodded. "By the way, she was right to leave her first husband."

"You wouldn't believe the number of women who wrote and told me she should have stayed because it was her duty to her family."

"I remember seeing the piles of letters in your office; it was amazing how many strangers had written to you." Granny stopped; climbing the last steep bank leading into the dervish enclosure always left her out of breath.

"I had no idea my story would touch a nerve with so many women, and a few men too. It's consoling to think there are some out there who sympathize with the lot of women."

"Family life is not what it was. People no longer live with their relatives, they're alone—" Granny was about to say "like you and Salih Zeki," but thought better of it. "Your story must have given these lonely souls some hope that they were not forgotten."

"In one way or another, I think it helped them. They seem to feel less isolated knowing that they are not alone in their suffering."

The old lady leaned against a tree and regarded her granddaughter with admiration. "You cannot ask for more," she said. Halide's book had impressed her more than she'd thought it would. She had been helped, of course, by the spirits of her ances-

tors, for no twenty-year-old could have had access to such wisdom.

They had reached her grandfather's grave. Close by there was
an outcrop of rock where Granny sat down and mopped her brow
with the corner of her shawl. "But I wondered," she began, still
feeling breathless, "if you were thinking about your mother when
you made Rabia into a Koran chanter?"

Halide tried to recall the origin of her ideas. The book had been
written before her daughter was born, and that time now seemed
long ago. In those days she hadn't thought about readers, and the
idea of being published had never entered her head. She had
wanted to write about Teyze and Mahmoure, but in the end their
stories became woven into her own. Rabia came to represent a personal ideal, that of an independent woman, married to a man she
loved and living a life circumscribed by her faith. "Maybe," Halide
replied at length, "the image of the girl singing in the mosque is
still vivid."

"Rabia is living the life your mother wished for but never
achieved." Granny put her hand to her mouth to stop herself
breaking with emotion. "There was a time, after the divorce from
Ali Shamil, when your mother thought about taking up Koran
chanting again. She was desperately lonely, Mahmoure was living
with her father, and I know she missed both of them." The two
women exchanged knowing looks; Granny had never before spoken to Halide about this time in Selima's life. "Her days were
empty, and the voices of the spirits were silent. By chanting the
words of the Prophet your mother felt she could use her gift to
touch the souls of those who heard her. I remember her telling me
that when she was singing she felt most in touch with the world beyond ours."

Halide ran her hand over her grandfather's tombstone; it was icy cold. Fine shreds of moss caught on her fingers "When I was writing I sometimes felt as if my ideas were coming to me from dreams I had long ago forgotten," Halide replied at length. "Perhaps my mother helped me—her prescence has never left me. Even now, although she is long dead, I know she is close by."

"Do you hear her voice still?"

"No, her voice has been silent for several years."

"I suspected as much." The old lady watched their shadows flicker across the graves, like puppets in a shadow play. "I never dreamed things would turn out like this," she said with a smile.

"I'm not sure I understand."

"Your gift, my child. I have waited years to see how it would manifest. It has come, in our family, in such strange and unexpected forms. Your great-grandmother was a seer like Peyker, and your great-aunt became a wandering dervish! The men in our family were mortified. Your mother chanted the Koran until she remarried, and now here you are using your gift through the weaving of tales."

Halide stared at the European shore. The mists had cleared, and she saw the Galata Tower outlined against the slate-gray skies. As a child, talk of the gift had alarmed her. She had not wanted to see the spirits, and her mother's voice had never conveyed any message of enlightenment. It was learning that had changed her life, the wisdom of both East and West. It had lifted her beyond the tradition of her forebears yet kept her rooted in the land she loved. For this she had to thank her father; whatever his shortcomings, she would always be grateful to him. "I am planning my next book," she said, "about a woman scientist who works for an enlightened Sultan."

"Be careful, child. Politics are dangerous."

"After seeing the way Teyze was treated, and watching father scorned for his beliefs, I am not afraid of the authorities. We have to live and work for what is right."

"Whatever you do, you have my blessing, and the blessing of your grandfather."

"I'll begin by writing regularily for Damat Ilsahn's new journal. I should get you a copy, so you know what I'm doing." The old lady shook her head. "Leave me to my prayers and the realm of the spirits. The world I knew is dissolving, I feel it everywhere. I am afraid to look beyond Scutari anymore."

EPILOGUE

The Young Turk revolution was one of the oddest political events in history. When it finally occurred, in July 1908, Sultan Abdulhamid was not deposed, but he was forced to recall the parliament and surrender most of his power. Starting in 1906 a series of minor uprisings had shaken the Ottoman Empire, the most serious of which were in eastern Anatolia. These revolts were financial, not ideological, in origin; neither the army nor the bureaucracy had been paid in months. Soldiers and civil servants quit their jobs in droves. As the momentum increased, corrupt officials and governors were deposed, and discontent spread. Young Turks exiled to Anatolia fanned the mutinies with their revolutionary propaganda. By 1908 the ferment had moved from Anatolia and Syria to Constantinople itself.

The fall of the Sultan began in Salonika, with an uprising by the Third Army Corps. The Sultan sent Nazim Bey to investigate the problem; he was subsequently shot and wounded. Alarmed, the palace dispatched a commission of inquiry. Troublemakers were rooted out and sent to Constantinople. One of these, Enver Bey, disappeared into the hills rather than report to the capital. From here on violence against agents of the Sultan escalated until Abdulhamid, fearing for his life, announced the restoration of the 1876 constitution. The Ottoman Empire exploded with joy.

In 1909 the Yildiz Palace complex was dismantled and Sultan

Abdulhamid was forced to abdicate in favor of his brother Reshad, a Mevlevi dervish. Power was concentrated in the hands of the Young Turk leadership, a triumverate headed by Enver Bey. From 1908 to 1918 the population of the Empire was decimated by four major wars, culminating in the tragedy of World War I. The Ottomans, having sided with the Germans, were destroyed. With the defeat came the end of *konak* life as depicted in this story. The Ottoman elite were dispersed, and later civil war broke out between the nationalists, supporters of Mustafa Kemal (later known as Atatürk, the father of Turkey), and the armies of the Sultan's government, who were backed by the European powers. Eventually the nationalists prevailed, and the secular government effectively abolished the Ottoman culture, changing the written alphabet to Latin and turning the Turkish people to the West both politically and culturally.

EVENTUALLY, after many years, Salih Zeki agreed to a divorce and Halide Edib married Dr. Adnan Adivar, an associate of Mustafa Kemal's. She went on to become the sole female member of Kemal's nationalist government in exile, a convinced admirer of Woodrow Wilson's fourteen points. She wrote twenty-five novels, two plays, and numerous articles, short stories, and translations. Later she taught English literature at Istanbul University. She died in 1964. In Turkey she is a revered national figure.

Fatma Hanim died before the First World War. Arzu remained in Istanbul with Halide's child, who was sent to America when Halide fled to Angora in 1919, at the age of thirty-seven, to join the nationalists. Arzu died of old age in the 1920s.

Edib Pasha, a longtime supporter of the Committee for Union and Progress, retired from public life after the Young Turk revolution and lived quietly with his third wife and their three daughters, all of whom were educated at the American school.

Salih Zeki Bey completed his mathematical encyclopedia. He later went mad and was confined to an asylum, where he died prematurely in 1921, during the occupation of Istanbul.

Mahmoure and Riza joined the Young Turk revolutionaries in Salonika and became an integral part of the revolution. They married but had no children. It is not known how Mahmoure became involved in the Kurdish revolt of 1925 in southeast Anatolia, an uprising that led to draconian restrictions. Riza remained in Salonika, and the separation eventually destroyed their marriage. No one knows what became of Mahmoure.

The American Girls College was later merged with the boys school, Robert College. To this day it is considered one of the finest schools in Turkey.

Glossary

abla	older sister
Bairam	three-day feast at the end of Ramazan
caïque	light rowing boat used on the Bosphorus
efendi	gentleman, title given to literate people
gazi	one who fights on behalf of Islam, war veteran
görücü	matchmaker
grand mufti	head of the *ulema* (see below), religious leader
Hajj	annual pilgrimage to Mecca
hanim	term of respect for a woman, wife, lady, mistress of a household
Imam	religious leader
Janissaries	elite force of Imperial soldiers
konak	wooden mansion set in its own grounds
locum	gelatinous sweet, usually flavored with rosewater, sometimes called Turkish delight
mahalle	neighborhood, quarter, district
medresse	religious school, usually attached to a mosque
Pasha	title denoting high rank
Ramazan	month-long religious festival of fasting; ninth month in the Muslim year
sahlep	hot, sweet drink made of milk and the powdered root of wild orchid
selamlik	men's quarters

Sublime Porte	Bab-I Aali: literally, colonnaded gate below which the Sultan's throne was placed during receptions; later became a synonym for the Ottoman government
Sufi	form of Islamic practice, a personal search for mystical ectasy and union with God
tekke	dervish lodge
ulema	theologians, religious scholars

Acknowledgments

I am deeply grateful to my agent, Edward Hibbert, for being steadfast and supportive, and to my editor, Joy de Menil, whose intelligence, insight, and attention to detail have given me an invaluable lesson about the art of editing. I want to thank Professor Sukru Hanioglu, who encouraged my interest in the life and work of Halide Edib, and whose comments on my manuscript were extremely helpful. To Professors Talat Halman and the late Charles Issawi I owe thanks for helping me to appreciate the culture of the Ottoman world.

A special thanks to my daughter, Charlotte Rudge, and to Jane Kramer, Marcia Welles, Bob Towbin, and Patricia Bosworth, for taking the time to read and comment on the manuscript. Finally I want to thank my son, Joe Rudge, for his good-humored support, and Katy Kazan, Judy Morris, and Nick Kazan, for always being there.

About the Author

FRANCES KAZAN is the author of the novel *Good Night, Little Sister,* has an M.A. in Turkish studies, and is a regular contributor to *Cornucopia.* She is married to the director Elia Kazan and lives in New York.

About the Type

This book is set in Fournier, a typeface named for Pierre Simon Fournier, the youngest son of a French printing family. He started out engraving woodblocks and large capitals, then moved on to fonts of type. In 1736 he began his own foundry and made several important contributions in the field of type design; he is said to have cut 147 alphabets of his own creation. Fournier is probably best remembered as the designer of St. Augustine Ordinaire, a face that served as the model for Monotype's Fournier, which was released in 1925.